where the river runs wild

ALEXANDRA AYRES

First Edition: November 2025

Published by Northern Creek Press LLC

979-8-9919800-2-9 (Paperback - Ingram)
979-8-2684623-5-7 (Paperback - KDP)
979-8-9919800-3-6 (Ebook)

Cover Design by Mel D. Designs
Editing by Simply Write
Proofreading by English Proper Editing Services

For the wild ones. This one's for you.
And if you're just here for another hot Scotsman, don't worry.
I've got you.

BREE

I t always starts like this.

Not with yelling, slammed doors, or cruel words. Though, they always come later, after the tension winds tight enough to strangle the air right out of the room.

It starts with silence that settles in my bones and curls cold fingers around the back of my neck. The kind that makes me careful. Makes me small.

I was just in Scotland for a week with my best friend, Juliette, pretending life was all castles and cobblestone. Only the magic evaporated somewhere over the Atlantic and now I'm back in Kentucky. I've been home less than an hour, and yet I still smell the sea salt, my cheeks hurt from laughing too hard with Juliette and her boyfriend, Knox, and I'm feeling that good kind of tiredness that only comes from feeling free.

I spent a week breathing. *Really* breathing.

Now I'm back in a house that makes me feel like I'm holding my breath.

Dillon's pacing our living room again in the same worn path between the couch and the window. He runs both hands through his hair, fingers tugging hard at the strands like maybe, if he pulls hard enough, the thoughts crowding his head will scatter and offer him peace.

I want to reach out and pull him into me the way I used to. Run my fingers over the muscles in his shoulders and kiss the space between his brows, hoping my touch will bring him back.

I should've let it go. I should've smiled, nodded, swallowed whatever stupid thing I'd said to tip him over the edge this time. I don't even remember what it was, but it was something harmless and ordinary. It's never because of some earth-shattering betrayal, like you'd expect. It's always the little things, like the way I leave my coffee mug on the counter instead of putting it in the dishwasher. Or commenting about his mom's birthday party. Or, god forbid, questioning our future together.

I draw in a shallow breath. "Dillon," I say, my voice barely more than a whisper. "Please talk to me. Whatever it is, we can work through it."

His pacing stops. For one hopeful moment, I think I've reached him.

"Work through it?" He laughs, but there's no humor in it. Just that hollow sound I've come to dread. "There's nothing to talk about."

I reach for his arm anyway, fingers grazing his sleeve. "Please, Dillon. Just sit down with me for a minute—"

It happens so fast. His arm slices through the air, the back of his hand catching a vase and sending it skidding off the mantle. The crash comes a beat later, the vase exploding against the wall.

I flinch, my arms covering my face instinctively. When I lower them, he's frozen, his hand hanging midair. His brow furrows, as if even he doesn't recognize what he's done. He never apologizes in moments like this, though. He just stares at the destruction.

My eyes drop to the scattered pieces, tracing the jagged curve of blue and white ceramic against the wood, and something in my stomach twists hard enough to hurt. The vase had been a housewarming gift from my mom when Dillon and I moved into this place, and I thought we were building a life together.

Now it's nothing but another mess I'll sweep up.

"Dillon…" I say softly, but he doesn't acknowledge me. Not even a twitch in his shoulders, no sign that he's heard me at all.

I never wanted him to become a police officer. Not because I didn't believe in him but because his soul, his *heart*, was too pure. I loved how deeply he felt. How fiercely he believed in people, in second chances, in goodness even when it wasn't easy to find. I used to think his heart was the safest place in the world, but now that feels like a lifetime ago.

One terrible night on the job two years ago stole him from me. He had been the first on the scene during a high-speed chase that ended in a car wreck that involved a family with a child no older than five. He couldn't save them. He tried, but by the time he got there, it was too late. The trauma of that night followed him home. He didn't speak about it, but I could see the way his eyes seemed permanently shadowed by something terrible. After that, he shut down.

The man who used to hold my hand like I was his whole world vanished in an instant, leaving a hardened, distant stranger in his place.

I've tried to hold him together with nothing but shaky hands and good intentions. To be soft when the world turned him hard. To believe, with every stubborn beat of my heart, that love could be enough if I just stayed patient enough, quiet enough, *careful* enough.

The trouble is, on nights like tonight when the alcohol takes hold, there's no reasoning with him. No hope of finding the man I used to know beneath the layers of anger and pain that envelop him.

He's never laid a hand on me, but it's been close. And close is a funny thing because it worms itself under your skin. It makes you flinch before there's a reason to. It keeps you up at night, staring at the ceiling, wondering how long until it'll turn into something else entirely.

No one else knows what he's going through, and he's made it painfully clear I can't tell anyone. So for the last two years, I've become a master of disguise. Smiling when it hurts, being bubbly when my insides are crumbling, playing the part of *normal* Bree when nothing feels normal at all. Keeping up the act is exhausting, like wearing a mask that gets heavier with every passing day and every aching hour. But how do I leave him? How do I walk away when he's drowning? He needs me. I'm the only thing tethering him to this world. Even if loving him feels more and more like letting myself sink right alongside him, I can't walk away.

"Clean this shit up, Bree." His voice cuts through the air like a blade that doesn't care where it lands. "I better not step on a goddamn piece of it."

The words don't sting anymore. The empty threats have become so familiar and woven into the fabric of our days that they're just another part of our routine.

I draw in a breath that barely makes it past the tightness in my lungs, the thud of my heartbeat loud enough to drown out everything else. I don't risk a glance in his direction as I cross the room to pull out the broom and dustpan from their spot by the garage door.

This version of me always feels like a script. My quiet movements. The illusion of control I desperately cling to. It's a dance I've practiced so many times that keeping my tone low, my hands steady, is like muscle memory now. *Don't show fear. Don't spark more fury.*

"I'll get it. Just sit down, okay? Don't walk over here, please. Neither of us needs to get hurt."

He mutters something under his breath, but I don't ask him to repeat it. Instead, I focus on the shards of the vase, carefully sweeping them into the dustpan. The pieces glitter under the light, deceptively pretty. I wish it were just the vase that was broken.

I will my tears to stay hidden. Crying only makes things worse.

My mind drifts to my parents. They're still so happy and so in love after all these years, and I used to think Dillon and I were on the same path. For a while, we were. Our first eight years together weren't a lie or a dream. They were real, and they were ours.

Even so, love's not supposed to feel like hanging on by your fingernails.

Somewhere along the way, between long shifts and periods of silence, between the weight of what he saw at work and what he carried home, we stopped being on the same side of the fight. I used to tell myself it was the job that changed him, and that if he could resign, if he could just choose me over the darkness, maybe we'd find our way back.

But he never did, and I think, deep down, I stopped waiting for him to want to.

I know he's angry, that there's a pain inside him so deep and tangled that I'll never fully understand.

I've loved him through every rough patch, every bad night, every fight that left me feeling like I was clawing my way out of quicksand with every breath I took. I've been patient and held on tighter than I ever thought I could, pretending that my strength could be enough for both of us.

5

Still, as the last of the fragments scrape into the dustpan, the weight of it all settles hard in my chest. Heavier than grief. Heavier than anger.

Maybe I've known for a while now that one day I'd hit the limit of what I could carry. No matter how tightly I hold on, love was never meant to be an endurance sport.

I'm so tired of putting energy toward something that keeps breaking me in return.

I can't do this anymore. I can't keep pretending that this is normal. My hands tremble, but I force myself to stand tall as I turn to face him.

"I can't do this anymore, Dillon."

He looks over at me, his eyes bloodshot and unfocused. "What are you talking about?"

"This," I say, motioning weakly around the room. "I can't keep waiting for the next time you're going to explode or break something else."

"You're not leaving me."

I take a breath. "I'm not saying goodbye forever," I tell him, my tone gentler now. "I think I'll stay with my parents for a while. Just until we figure out what's next."

He lets out a bitter laugh. "Figure out what's next? What does that even mean, Bree? You're bailing."

"I'm not bailing," I say, my voice cracking just a little. "I'm stepping back. You need space. I need clarity. This," I gesture around us, "isn't working. But that doesn't mean I've stopped caring."

He shakes his head, pacing again. "You walk out that door, don't bother coming back. I swear to god, Bree—"

"I don't think you mean that." I keep my tone calm, measured. "And I'm not going to fight with you. I'll come by tomorrow to get a few more of my things while you're at work. We'll talk another time. When things aren't so...tense."

"I'm not giving up," I add quietly as a reminder. "I'm just giving us a chance to breathe."

I don't wait for his response. If I do, I might lose my nerve entirely. I whistle for Nugget, our German shepherd who's been cowering in the corner, watching us with worried eyes. He pads over to me, tail tucked between his legs. "Come on, buddy," I murmur, running a hand over his velvety fur. "We're going for a ride."

I grab his leash from the hook by the door and clip it to his collar. He follows me obediently, glancing back at Dillon with a whine.

"You're not taking my dog," Dillon snarls, taking a step toward us.

"He's *our* dog. I'm not leaving him here like this. And this doesn't have to be permanent, Dillon. I'll be back, okay?"

His jaw clenches, but he doesn't argue. I think he knows Nugget will be better off with me for the time being.

I open the door, the late summer air wrapping around me. Nugget hesitates on the threshold, ears twitching, then trots out beside me like he's known all along this was coming.

I don't look back, and it's not because I don't care. God, I care *too* much. If I see his face, I might lose the little bit of resolve I've scraped together.

"This isn't forever," I say, more to myself than him.

The door clicks shut behind me, and for the first time in a long time, I breathe. Not easily. Not fully. But just enough to take the next step.

one

BREE

I'm almost twenty-eight and I've been holed up at my parents for the past three months. Not exactly the glowing picture of adult independence I imagined in my twenties.

The pale yellow walls of my childhood bedroom haven't changed since high school, and neither has the slight squeak in the floorboard by the closet. I'm standing in the middle of it all, stuffing the last of my things into my suitcase and zipping it shut with a little more force than necessary. I turn to double-check that my dress is still hanging neatly in its garment bag. That dress is more than just fabric and stitching. It's my golden ticket, my armor, the one thing that'll make it look like I have my life together, even when everything else makes it feel like it's coming apart at the seams.

It's coming on the plane with me, no question. If I'm the reason Juliette's surprise engagement is anything less than perfect, I'll never forgive myself.

I refuse to show up looking like a walking disaster. I've watched her work so hard for this, fighting through her own messes, and this is her time. I'm going to make sure she gets it, even if I have to fake it through the whole damn thing.

My best friend. My beautiful, lucky, best friend managed to find herself a hot-as-sin Scottish guy who not only wants to wife her up but is also flying me out for the occasion. Knox, future fiancé extraordinaire, booked my flight just so I could be there and witness her moment of happiness. Who even does that? A guy who knows how to treat a lady, that's who. Talk about hitting the jackpot.

I'll be attending this party as single and solo as they come... Well, sort of.

I still stop by every now and then to check on Dillon. I know this version of him isn't the real him. And not all of his days are bad...just most.

I've had months to sit with all the silence and space. Somewhere in the ache of missing him, everything started to come into focus.

Technically, we're still together. I walked out when he was already crumbling. Breaking up felt like twisting the knife. I couldn't do that to him when he was already drowning.

So I held on. Just barely. Clinging to this fragile thread of hope that maybe he'd find his footing again. That he'd reach for me. Fight for us. That the man I fell in love with would resurface, even if it was just in pieces.

He didn't. He hasn't.

Eventually, I picked up the phone and called his parents. Not because I was angry or to punish him, but because someone needed to know. Someone had to see what I couldn't fix anymore.

It wasn't cruelty. It was the kind of mercy that shatters you when you realize love isn't always enough to save someone.

What I haven't said to anyone, not to Jules, not even to myself is that he didn't just break the house. He broke *me*. His words, the way he's chipped away at me over the past couple of years, have left marks that I can't scrub off. I used to be the girl who made everyone laugh, who believed in people, in love, in the idea that things could get better.

Now? I don't recognize the reflection staring back at me most days because I'm wearing a disguise, and everyone buys it because they want to, but deep down, I know it doesn't fit anymore. The smile, the lighthearted laugh, the way I breeze through conversations as if everything is perfectly fine... It's all a performance. And I hate that he's the reason why, because in trying to save him, I've lost sight of myself. We were supposed to be partners, tackling life side by side, but instead, I've spent so much time picking up the broken pieces of him that I forgot to protect my own. For all the love I've poured into him, all that's left is this facade.

The truth I've been avoiding is creeping in louder and louder these days. We haven't really been together in months, not in any way that counts. And if I'm being honest with myself —it's about damn time I start—I need to go into this trip with a clear head without being weighed down by what-ifs and half-hearted maybes.

So I'm stopping by his place on my way to the airport because it feels like the right thing to do. It's time to look him in the eye and finally tell him I'm not coming back.

The trip's going to be a blur anyway. I'm driving myself to the airport because it barely qualifies as a getaway. I'm spending three days in Scotland, just long enough to watch my best friend say yes to forever, then I'll be back on a plane, racing to make my shift in Lexington. Why? Because not a single soul at the hospital was willing to pick up even one shift so I could take an extra day off. *Thanks for nothing, guys.*

"Hey, sweetheart," my dad says from the bedroom doorway. "Want me to get those to the car for you?"

When I first moved back in, I told myself it would be temporary. I wasn't sure if I'd need my own place or if I'd be going back to Dillon. I wanted to leave my options open, and now I know I'll be needing my own place because I can't go back there.

"Yes, please. Just don't touch that dress with your greasy, buttery whatever fingers."

Dad freezes, his eyes flickering to the dress hanging carefully in its garment bag, then back to me. He's still in his Saturday uniform of cargo shorts, a faded tee from some forgotten 5K, and socks with sandals, because apparently that's a hill he's willing to die on.

His hands shoot up in surrender. "Got it, suitcase only," he chuckles, grabbing my bag off the bed. "Are you sure you don't want me to drive you?"

I know why he's asking, and it has nothing to do with the actual act of sitting behind the wheel. My dad's been trying to find every excuse under the sun to stop me from going over to see Dillon.

"I'll be fine." I force a smile that doesn't quite reach my eyes and busy myself with tugging the zipper a little higher on my suitcase, like maybe if I look preoccupied enough, he won't notice the crack in my voice.

"My return flight is coming in late," I add. "I don't want you guys driving all the way out there."

I catch that look in his eyes, the one that says *you know damn well that wasn't why I was asking.* Except, I'm a grown woman and I know what I'm doing. I can handle this.

He doesn't argue, though. He just gives me a shake of his head before turning and walking out of the room.

I grab the dress carefully, cradling it like it's fragile and follow him down the stairs and out to the car. Nugget comes bounding toward me, tail wagging so hard it's almost a blur. I crouch down to meet him, scratching behind his ears and ruffling his fur as he wriggles in pure happiness.

"I'm going to miss you so much, my big boy." My heart aches with a little twist of guilt for leaving him behind. "Be good for your grandparents."

Dad rolls his eyes, but I can see the smile tugging at the corners of his mouth. He might pretend to be annoyed by Nugget's endless affection, but I know deep down, he secretly loves his furry grandchild.

"Bree! Are you heading out already?" Mom calls from the front door. She's wearing her usual reading glasses, short blonde hair tucked neatly behind her ears. "Hold on, let me grab the card for Juliette."

I turn back around, stepping back onto the porch as she hurries inside. A minute later, she's back, holding out a congratulations card in an envelope, the words *For Juliette and Knox* scrawled across the front in her perfect handwriting.

"I guess I'll keep that for myself if she says no."

She swats my arm with a quick laugh, her eyes narrowing. "Oh, stop. Are you going straight to the airport?"

"Mm, no. I'm going to stop by Dillon's on the way."

Her smile falters, replaced by the same worry I've seen etched on her face for months. It's a look I know well, one that I've seen mirrored in my dad's eyes, too. My disaster of a relationship isn't just my problem anymore. It's spilling over into the lives of the people I love, and I hate that. But the truth is, somewhere, deep down, Dillon's still the wonderful, sensitive man we all knew and loved. It's that very tenderness, that same heart, that led him into this mess in the first place.

"My sweet girl... Be careful, okay?"

I nod, trying to assure her everything's going to be fine, even though I'm not entirely sure myself. I give her a quick hug and say my goodbyes, knowing full well I'm rushing. I'm hoping to keep it quick because, honestly, I can't afford to be late for this flight. I'm already cutting it close. Landing mere hours before the party is risky enough.

I climb into the car and head out. The drive is short, and before I know it, I'm pulling into the driveway of what used to be *our* place. Now, it's just his. The porch light I used to leave on for him now flickers without meaning, and the flowerbeds we planted together are half wild and forgotten.

I step out of the car, my feet heavier with every step I take toward the front door. I knock gently, my knuckles tapping against the wood. Gone are the days when I could simply walk inside without hesitation. Now, I'm an outsider, waiting for permission to enter.

From the other side of the door, I hear his stumbling footsteps, and my heart sinks. I knew, realistically, that he'd probably already be drinking. Still, a part of me had clung to the hope that maybe this time would be different. That maybe, since his shift hadn't ended that long ago, he wouldn't have had time to spiral.

The door swings open, and there he is, that familiar mess of brown hair even more unkempt than usual. His hazel eyes, once so full of light, are dull and unfocused. There's stubble on his jaw he used to be too proud to let grow, and he leans on the doorframe like it's the only thing holding him up. "What are you doing here?"

I try, and fail, not to flinch. It's not what he says, it's how he says it. Like I'm an intrusion rather than the woman who once knew every corner of his heart.

"Hello to you, too," I reply with a forced smile. "Can I come in for a minute? I'm on my way to the airport but wanted to check in with you."

His words are slurred. "I don't need a babysitter, Bree.

Besides, I don't know why you're showing up here acting like you care when you packed your shit and left."

This is going exactly how I feared. *Great.*

I step inside anyway, the door closing behind me with a click that seems louder than it is. The air is thick with the sour tang of old beer and neglect as I follow Dillon to the couch, my heart sinking farther with every step.

"Oh, Dillon..."

The living room is a disaster. Empty bottles are scattered across every surface, the remnants of nights spent hiding from memories. This place used to be filled with so much laughter and love. It's hard to remember now, with the mess and ruin surrounding me. It's just a shell of what it once was, much like the man slumped before me, as if he's not really here at all.

"I'm not here to babysit you," I say gently, lowering myself into the armchair across from him. "I just came to see how you're doing."

He snorts. "I don't need your pity, and I don't need you playing hero."

I wince at his words, sharp despite their slurred delivery. "Dillon, we both know that isn't what this is. I love you, always, but watching you destroy yourself is tearing me apart. I can't keep pretending like it's not happening...and standing by while you throw everything away."

"Then don't watch," he mutters, his voice low and bitter. "Just go. That's what you're good at, isn't it? Leaving when things get tough?"

His accusation hits me like a slap, and for a second, I'm stunned. The irony is almost laughable. I want to shout, to throw every sacrifice, every sleepless night, every damn time I chose to stay right back in his face. Instead, I swallow it down, forcing myself to keep calm and hold the pieces together for just a little longer.

"That's not fair. I've been here, trying to help you for months. *Years.* But you have to want to help yourself, too."

His face twists with sudden rage. "Help me? You call walking out helping me? If you really wanted to help, you'd have stayed."

My heart feels too big for my chest, pounding like it's trying to escape, like maybe it wants to take me away from this house and this man I used to love so fiercely I would've cracked myself in half just to keep him whole.

I push myself up from the chair. "I've made my decision." The words are stones in my throat, but they need to be said. "I think it's time we let go. I can't keep holding on like this, and I think you know that, too." I pause, looking down and finding it hard to meet his eyes. "I need to move on, and I think you do, too."

For a moment, there's nothing but silence. Then everything happens at once.

He lunges forward, his hand seizing my wrist in a jarring grip that sends a lightning-bolt ache shooting up to my elbow. He's *never* touched me like this before.

His eyes are wild, pupils blown wide. I don't think he even sees me. "So that's it? You're just done for good?"

"Dillon," I say, careful to keep my voice gentle and even. "You're hurting me."

For a second, there's a flash of the old Dillon in his eyes, the one who used to hold my hand like it was something delicate.

I twist my arm as he loosens his grip. The sudden release sends me backward, and I stumble, hip catching the edge of the table with a crack of bone on wood. I hit the floor, and for a heartbeat, I can't speak. Can't think. I just stare up at him in stunned silence.

His expression morphs, the anger draining out of him. "Bree..." he whispers, horrified. "I-I didn't mean—"

I push myself upright, wincing at the jolt in my leg and the throbbing in my wrist. "Dillon..." I whisper, not sure who I'm talking to anymore. The man I loved has to be in there somewhere, but right now, I can't afford to look for him.

He steps toward me, hand half lifted like he's going to help me up. Something inside me jerks hard. My breath sticks in my throat, and I flinch before I even know I'm doing it.

"Don't." My voice breaks, barely more than a breath. "Please...don't."

His hand drops. He turns away like the sight of me hurts and sinks back onto the couch. "Bree, I'm sorry. I didn't mean to..."

"I know," I say. And I do. That's what makes this situation so dangerous.

I stand on legs that don't want to hold me, every inch of me screaming to get out of the room. He doesn't follow. Doesn't stop me. Doesn't beg. And I don't look back. Not when I reach the door. Not when I close it behind me with a quiet click that feels too gentle for what just happened.

It's only in the car, behind the wheel with my hands trembling against the leather, that the first tear slips free. Just one. I wipe it away and force myself to sit up straighter. I've got a plane to catch.

I'll fall apart later.

BREE

I'm probably repressing a lot of stuff, and sure, this isn't the healthiest coping strategy, but right now, it's not about me. Jules doesn't know I'm here yet, and she has no clue what I've been going through. I'm not about to trauma dump on her. Not today. I've spent so long keeping it in that the silence feels safer than the truth. Like if I say it out loud, it becomes real. And real means someone might see just how messy it's gotten, and I don't want to be someone else's burden.

Knox was supposed to pick me up from the airport, but I don't see him anywhere, and now I'm wondering if I should call him. But what if he's with Jules? Great, now I'm second-guessing everything.

Just as I'm about to dial Juliette's aunt, my phone already halfway to my ear, a truck pulls up to the curb in front of me. I freeze, eyes widening in surprise. Well, I'll be damned. It's Callan, Knox's brother.

My first meeting with Callan a few months ago was a shot of adrenaline straight to my veins. We spoke for all of five minutes, and I knew right away I'd met my competitive match.

He strolled into the room with the kind of confidence that flirted with recklessness. He had these blue eyes that were alive with mischief, dark sandy-blond hair tousled just enough to suggest he'd either come from a wild adventure or was about to start one. He was tall with broad shoulders, effortlessly handsome, and had a grin that made you think he knows a little more about life than the rest of us.

"So, you're the infamous brother I've heard so much about," I teased, but my heart was already picking up speed.

He grinned back, that knowing smile of his spreading wider as he leaned in slightly, clearly ready for the battle of wits he could already sense coming. "And you must be the troublemaker I was warned about."

"Guilty as charged."

His gaze was locked on me, but the moment he leaned in closer, a small, treacherous part of me couldn't help but notice how close he was. His scent, a mix of leather and spice, lingered in the air, dangerously close.

"I'm curious. What kind of trouble are you really into?" he asked, his voice low, like he was savoring the question.

I smirked, willing myself to stay in control. "Oh, you know, just the usual daring escapades and maybe a little light vandalism."

His laugh rumbled through me, deep and warm, like the sound itself was a touch too intimate. I had to fight to keep my focus.

I took a step back, forcing myself to remember who I was. Who I had to be. I had to remind myself of the boundaries that existed in the game we were playing. Remember who he was, too.

I was helping Dillon. That was my focus. He was my priority. All the rest was...noise. For just a minute, I didn't have to be *the person everyone relied on, the one who always had to be strong, the one who never got to let her guard down.*

It felt like a luxury I hadn't realized I'd been missing until now. And damn it, it was so easy to fall into. And that was the problem, wasn't it? It was too easy.

I quickly shoved the thought away. This wasn't about me, not really. It couldn't be. So why did it feel so good to just forget that for a second?

He rolls down his window, and the sound of his voice pulls me out of my thoughts like a snapping of fingers. "Hey, Sunshine! Get in the truck!"

Sunshine? What the—?

I shoot him a questioning look, my eyebrow arched in disbelief. "Sunshine? Seriously?"

He leans back against the seat, a smug smile plastered on his stupid, handsome face. "What can I say? It suits you. You brighten my world."

That damn Scottish accent rolls off his tongue like honey with a hint of trouble. He could say anything, absolute nonsense, and I'd probably still take it as a compliment. And worse? I'd let him get away with it. Every single time.

"Flattery, huh? What's next, calling me Princess?"

"If that's what you're into," he replies with a wink. I try to shake off the provocative comment, but damn, it does something to me.

"But I think Sunshine fits better," he continues, not missing a beat as he gets out of the truck. He's wearing a gray henley and a pair of dark denim jeans. His hair's a tousled mess, like he ran a hand through it on his way out the door and didn't bother to fix it. He strides around to grab my bag, hoisting it easily and tossing it into the backseat. "You're less likely to throw a fit over losing a shoe at midnight."

I lay the dress gently on top of my bag. "Ah, turns out you

don't know me as well as you think you do. I'll throw a fit *and* the other shoe."

That damned deep laugh vibrates through me, leaving a trail of goosebumps in its wake. "I missed ya, lass. You're a fun one."

He opens the door for me, and I slide in, my hand quickly pulling the sleeve of my shirt down over the bruise Dillon left. I don't want him to see it because I'm worried he'll care, and if he cares, that opens a door I don't know how to walk through.

I glance over at Callan as he slides into the driver's seat. "So, how'd you end up with the short end of the stick? I thought Knox was supposed to pick me up."

He presses a hand to his chest with a dramatic gasp. "Am I not good enough for you?"

I roll my eyes but can't hold back a small laugh. "Oh, please. Just answer the question."

He flashes me another grin that could melt ice. "Knoxie Boy slept in. Seems my future sister-in-law has a bit of a wild side."

"Oh, I love that for her. I'll be sure to tell her you're the one spreading the word."

He chuckles, a mischievous gleam in his eye. "Aye, go right ahead. I'll deny it all and blame it on you. Just try me."

The conversation flows so easily with him, like we've known each other for years instead of just a few brief encounters. It's clear Callan knows how to put just about anyone at ease. He's the type of guy who can light up a room without even trying. There's this fearless energy about him that says he'd dive headfirst into anything just because someone dared him to. I find myself wanting a little of that confidence.

I'm staring, lost in thought, and he catches it immediately. He raises an eyebrow, that familiar smirk tugging at the corner of his mouth. "What? Already lost for words?"

I roll my eyes, pulling at my sleeves again as heat creeps up my cheeks. "Hardly. Just trying to figure out how I'm going to survive while trapped in a vehicle with you."

His eyes follow my hand movements, and I immediately stop. I'm trying to hide the bruise, not draw attention to it. The moment his gaze meets mine again, his brows furrow slightly and concern flickers across his face.

"If you say so, lass," he replies, his tone softening for a brief second. "Buckle up. It's going to be a wild ride."

Before I can respond, he shifts the truck into drive, slams on the gas, and we rocket forward with an almost alarming speed. My heart leaps into my throat, and for a split second, everything in my body screams to brace for impact.

"Good god, Callan! Are you trying to kill me already?" The words slip out before I can stop them, but it doesn't matter. I can't even hear myself over the ringing in my ears.

He immediately eases off the gas, and the truck slows down, the roar of the engine fading. For a moment, there's nothing but the pounding of my heart, loud enough to drown out the world.

"I didn't mean to scare you," he says, his tone shifting in an instant. "I'm sorry."

His usual playfulness is gone, replaced with worry. His eyes flick over to me for a fraction of a second, then back to the road, his grip on the wheel tightening just a little. It's like he's trying to read me.

"I'm just messing around," he adds, quieter this time. "I wouldn't put you in any real danger. You're way too precious for that."

The words should be comforting, but I've learned to respond to danger in ways that no one can fix with a smile or a joke. I *need* to feel safe. Right now, all I feel is the tightness in my chest.

CALLAN

I don't know Bree well enough to say something's off, but, uh...yeah, something's definitely off. She's lost somewhere in her head, twisting the edge of her sleeve. And those eyes of hers? Normally, they're steady. You could dive into those bright blue pools and just float, no problem. But right now? They're all over the place, darting around like she's trapped in some maze and can't find her way out.

I clear my throat, drumming my fingers on the wheel. "You good?"

She blinks like she didn't hear me the first time, then gives this little shrug that's way too casual to be real. "Peachy."

"Right. And I'm a nun."

That earns me a snort, but I don't let it drop. "Seriously. You sure you're good?"

She shoots me an unamused look, but there's a flicker of panic behind it, gone so fast I almost think I imagined it.

"I'm fine, Callan," she says.

And then, like the flip of a switch, she's back at it, firing off some witty comment like nothing ever happened. Maybe she's just weird. I can deal with weird. Weird is fun.

I like Bree. She's got that kind of humor that always keeps me on the edge of a laugh, and she's just as reckless as I am. We'd be a damn disaster waiting to happen, but the kind that'd be exhilarating as hell. Too bad she's off-limits. Her boyfriend's a lucky bastard.

"So, how's Jamie?" she asks. "That's who you were seeing last time I was here, right?"

"Aye, that was her. Didn't go anywhere, though. I was just a rebound. Too feral for her taste."

Her comforting, easy laugh bursts out, filling up the whole cab. It's one of those laughs that makes the air lighter, like it's not just noise but sunlight. I wasn't kidding when I called her Sunshine. She really is like that.

"Feral," she laughs, shaking her head. "That's the most accurate description of you I've ever heard."

I chuckle, a little too loudly, and quickly change the subject. "And how's your guy? I thought he might've come with you."

The silence that stretches out after my question makes a knot twist in my stomach. Maybe I shouldn't have asked. I should've kept it light like we always do. Then again, it's me. I'm always running my mouth without thinking.

And there she goes again, fiddling with the edge of her sleeve like it's the only thing keeping her from falling apart. It's like watching someone try to hold themselves together. I can't help but feel like I'm seeing something I shouldn't.

"He, uh, couldn't get time off."

"Ah, that stinks." I offer a sympathetic shrug.

She shakes her head, a small smile pulling at her lips. "It's okay. It'll be nice to spend some time away, just me and Jules."

The way her voice falters a little makes my stomach

tighten. I can be a bit pushy sometimes, but something is telling me not to. Instead, I clear my throat. "Aye, but just so you know, 'good' doesn't exactly scream 'living your best life,' you know?"

Another hint of a smile tugs at her lips, and I exhale a quiet sigh of relief. That's better. I don't do well with sad shit.

"Maybe I'm just after a sliver of peace for a change."

"A sliver of peace?" I hum thoughtfully. "I can respect that."

She shoots me a look, eyebrow arched and lips twitching like she's holding back a full-blown grin. "Something tells me that you and peace don't exactly get along."

KNOX AND JULIETTE's engagement party is already in full swing by the time the sun begins its slow descent, and of course, the party's a hit. How could it not be? My big brother finally found his person. It's like she's been a part of the family for years, no question.

I catch a glimpse of them across the courtyard. Knox pulls her in, his hand finding her waist with that instinctive kind of tenderness, like there's no version of reality where he's not holding onto her. She leans into him without thinking, laughing at something he murmurs just for her.

I've never been the settling-down type. I've laughed off commitment like it's some outdated concept I was never meant to fit into. But watching them together? I might not be ready to throw in the towel just yet, but...maybe I'm starting to see the appeal. Bree looks stunning tonight. So beautiful it makes me forget how to breathe. Her blonde hair frames her face like it's been touched by the gods, and that floor-length dress hugs her curves with the kind of devotion that makes it hard to believe it ever belonged to anyone else. I'd be a damn fool not to notice.

She's standing off to the side, gaze distant, completely lost in whatever's going on in her head. Her fingers absently twist the bracelets on her wrist, and it's clear she's not exactly part of the festivities right now. That's not gonna fly.

I spot Rose, Juliette's aunt, across the courtyard and jog over, feeling that familiar mischievous spark. She's been working at the distillery with me and Knox for years, so she's family now, too.

"Hey! Rose!" I call out, my voice cutting through the chatter. She turns, her face lighting up with that signature wide smile of hers.

"What's up?"

"I know Bree's staying with you while she's here. You mind if I snatch her for a bit? Looks like Knox and Jules are about to head out. I'll drop her by your place later."

"Sure thing." She nods. "I'll leave the door unlocked for her."

I lean in and kiss her cheek. "You're the best. Drive safe, aye?" I give her a quick wave before turning to make my way over to Bree, who's still standing off to the side, her thoughts a million miles away.

"I didn't know they let angels walk around without an escort."

Her eyes brighten instantly, a spark of amusement flickering there, and she lets out that laugh that always gets to me. "At least I left my halo at home," she teases. "Didn't want to make the rest of you feel bad."

I offer a playful bow. "Well, guardian troublemaker at your service. You're coming with me, Sunshine."

Her eyes skim over me, quick, almost shy, but they don't miss much. It's a subtle sweep from my shoulders to my shoes, a scant pause like she's trying not to make it obvious she's looking...or maybe she's hoping I don't notice. But I do.

She tilts her head, that mix of curiosity and challenge dancing in her eyes as she meets my gaze. "And where do you think you're taking me?"

I give her my most mischievous grin, leaning in just a little and lowering my voice. "It's a surprise. Hope you can hold onto that dress of yours."

My comment lands exactly how I had hoped, judging by the confusion in her eyes and the sudden flush creeping up her cheeks. A little victory, that. I quickly grab her hand and give it a gentle tug. "Jules and Knox just left, so we're free to go. Ready for an adventure, Sunshine?"

I try my best to ignore how perfectly her hand fits in mine as we step into the cool night air. Not sure what's going on there, but the way our fingers lock together makes my heart do funny things. I'm not about to overthink it.

She stops dead in her tracks when she spots my bike, her eyes widening. "You're not serious. You want me to get on that? In this?"

"Aye, I do. Here, put this on." I slip off my leather jacket and drape it over her shoulders. "This will keep you warmer and safer."

Her eyes narrow with suspicion. "But what about you?"

Her concern is cute. "I'm all good, lass. A little chilly weather never bothered me."

She eyes the bike like it just insulted her mum, her brow furrowed and lips pursed in a playful pout. It's honestly a little hysterical, watching her stand there with her hands on her hips looking like she's squaring up for a fight. At the same time, beneath that fierce expression, there's a flash of hesitation.

It's like she wants to accept the challenge, but she's still sizing it up. The fire in her eyes says she's close to choosing.

BREE

I glance at the bike, at him, then back at the bike. My palms are already clammy, and I'm pretty sure I just forgot how my legs are supposed to work. I wipe my hands down the sides of my dress like that'll magically make me braver.

"Ever been on a bike before?" Callan asks.

I shake my head, a small, jerky motion I try to disguise with a shrug. "Nope."

His eyes are gentle now, like he's seeing right through the bravado I'm barely holding together. He's charming, I'll give him that. Even as he stands here, all rugged good looks, scruffy edges, and magnetic energy. I try to steady my breath, but it's pointless. When he drapes the jacket over my shoulders, the warmth of it and *him* sinks into me, the familiar scent of leather and spice wrapping around me like a hug I didn't know I needed.

And then he grabs a glossy black helmet, holding it out toward me. "Here you go. Safety first."

I take it, but my fingers fumble over the smooth surface like I've never held a helmet before. A few years ago, I wouldn't have blinked at this. Adrenaline and throwing myself headfirst into the unknown used to be my language. But now there's this spark of hesitation.

Before I can figure out how to work the straps, he steps closer, his hands brushing against mine as he gently takes the helmet.

"Let me," he murmurs as he adjusts it for me. His fingers graze beneath my chin as he fastens the clasp, and it sends a shiver straight through me. Nerves, not fear, but still enough to leave me unsteady.

Then he flips the visor down with a smirk that's pure mischief. It's cocky and irresistible. "Lookin' good, Sunshine."

I watch as he swings his leg over the bike and settles into the seat. He glances over his shoulder and pats the space behind him. "You coming?"

I hesitate for a beat, the cool evening air catching the hem of my dress as it flutters around my ankles. My fingers toy with the fabric at my sides as I eye the bike, less like a machine now and more like a dare I'm not sure I can take back once I say yes.

I step closer, gathering the length of my dress in one hand and awkwardly hiking it just enough to swing a leg over without flashing the whole street. It's far from graceful. I wobble slightly, one hand catching on his shoulder for balance, but I settle behind him, tucking myself in close, the heat of his body seeping into me even through the layers of clothing.

"Hold on tight," he says before the engine growls to life.

I slip my arms around his waist, fingers interlocking over his abdomen. He tenses for a moment, muscles flexing beneath my touch, before relaxing back into me.

"You ready for this?" he calls out, his voice rising above the engine's rumble.

A grin spreads across my face before I can stop it. It's impossible not to match his energy. "As ready as I'll ever be!"

He reaches to pull my hands a bit tighter, pulling me closer against his back, and it's impossible not to notice how firmly he's built.

Knox's little brother, who? There's nothing little about this man.

His hands move to the handlebars as he revs the engine. The vibrations pulse through me, igniting every nerve like a live wire as I grip him a little harder. The intoxicating scent of something rich and slightly sweet, something entirely *him* surrounds me.

He guns the accelerator, and we peel out of the parking lot. The sudden burst of speed makes my breath catch in my throat, panic flaring immediately.

I don't breathe at first. My heart's in my throat, my stomach somewhere near my knees, and for one awful second, all I can think is *what the hell am I doing?*

Then Callan shifts slightly, one hand dropping from the handlebar to brush over mine where it clings to his waist. It's quick, maybe even unconscious, but the message is there. *I've got you.*

That small gesture settles me. The thrum of the engine is still loud in my ears, but his steadiness cuts through the chaos. I let out the breath I've been holding, pressing in closer, letting the heat of his body subdue the fear still prickling at the edges of my consciousness.

My thighs hug his, my instincts kicking in as I give myself over to the motion. The speed no longer feels like a threat. It's a release.

The world around us melts into a blur of motion and color, and somewhere inside it, I find the calm. The roar of the engine drowns out the noise in my head. The ache. The doubt. The fear. Time folds in on itself, and then gradually, he eases off the throttle.

We roll to a stop and Callan kills the engine at a stunning lookout point. Neither of us makes a move to dismount. The warmth of his body is too comforting to give up just yet.

The lake below stretches out like a mirror of inky blackness, perfectly still beneath the midnight sky. The distant mountain peaks are bathed in a silvery glow, their edges tempered by the moonlight. Autumn wraps itself around the landscape, the crisp air carrying a faint bite that doesn't stand a chance against Callan's warmth.

"Where are we?" I whisper as I pull the helmet off. It feels almost wrong to speak louder.

"That's Loch Tummel we're looking at," he replies, his accent sliding over the words with that dangerous charm. "And Schiehallion over there." He gestures toward the distant hills.

The contrast of the wild rush of the ride fading into this serene quiet hits me like whiplash. My heart is still racing, but now it's not just from the adrenaline.

"It's beautiful." I don't even think about it. I just lean forward and rest my chin on his shoulder like it's second nature, and the second I do it, I freeze. What am I doing?

He goes still beneath me, just long enough for me to start pulling back, heart stuttering with the urge to apologize. Then the tension melts from his shoulders as he leans into the contact.

"Aye, it is," he says quietly. "Thought you might appreciate it. A little bit of that peace you were looking for."

I do appreciate it. More than I can explain. Before I can respond, his hand comes to rest on the outside of my thigh, offering a reassuring squeeze. It's meant to comfort, but instead, a sharp twinge of pain shoots through me. My breath hitches, and I wince slightly before I can stop myself. That's the leg that took most of the impact yesterday, and the bruise beneath my dress reminds me with every movement that it still hurts like hell.

He notices my reaction and assumes I'm cold. "Sorry, I forgot it's kind of chilly out here. Let's get you to Rose's."

I nod, choosing not to correct him. It's easier to let him think it's the cold, not the pain, that's bothering me. I shift slightly, trying to adjust my position and reach around him, but as I do, the sleeve of his jacket catches, pulling it up just enough to expose my wrist. He reaches back at the same time to pull my hands tighter around his waist—his touch stills when his eyes land on my arm. "What the hell is this?"

The blood drains from my face. I'd done such a good job convincing myself that if I could keep it out of sight, I could pretend everything was fine. But now, Callan's eyes are locked on the dark purple bruises wrapped around my wrist like some twisted bracelet. Ugly, splotchy shadows in the unmistakable shape of fingers cover my skin.

He jerks his head to look at me over his shoulder, his expression frozen somewhere between shock and disbelief. His eyes flare with hurt, confusion...fury.

It's hard to keep up the charade with him looking at me like that. We're supposed to be lighthearted. Carefree and joking around. I want to go back to that.

Yet, it's the outrage in his eyes that sticks, and I know it's not aimed at me. I *know* that. And when he suddenly swings his leg off the bike and turns to face me, I flinch.

He stops short, and I see the moment he notices. The fire in his eyes fades, giving way to a tenderness that knocks the air from my lungs.

His jaw tenses, and he drags a hand through his hair like he's trying to get ahold of himself. When he speaks, his voice is lower, gentler. "I would never hurt you."

He says it like a vow, not a defense mechanism. Then, quieter, "I'm sorry if I scared you."

I shake my head as I force down the knot rising in my throat. "No, you didn't," I whisper. "I'm sorry. I just..." The words scatter before they reach my tongue, too tangled to make sense of.

He takes a careful step closer, his eyes glancing to my wrist. "Can I see?"

I hesitate, my instinct to guard it flaring hot, but his gaze pulls the fight right out of me. I nod once, extending my arm and letting him gently take my hand in his. His touch is featherlight as he pushes the sleeve up, revealing the full extent of the bruising.

His breath catches, his jaw clenches, but his touch remains gentle as his thumb brushes over my skin. "Please tell me who did this."

My heart hammers against my ribs as I scramble for words, desperately searching for something that won't betray the truth or shatter the fragile wall I've built to protect myself.

"Bree. Talk to me. What happened?"

The sound of my name almost makes me flinch again. He's serious now. I don't think he's ever called me anything but some playful nickname. Sunshine, troublemaker, lass. He's not playing now. And once you let someone see the cracks, they'll either expect you to fall apart or try to fix you. Neither sounds like relief.

"It's not what you think." Wow, that came out sounding way less convincing than I intended.

"I think someone grabbed you. Hard. And if I was a betting man, I'd say it wasn't a female."

I close my eyes, trying to control my breathing, but it's no use. The cool night air is suffocating, pressing in on me from every direction.

"It was just a misunderstanding. I handled it."

His eyes drill into mine with a fire that's part frustration, part concern. "Handled what, exactly? Because from where I'm sitting, it looks like someone hurt you."

This is it. The moment I've been dreading. The moment I admit the thing I never thought I'd have to say out loud. "It was Dillon...but just once. It was an accident, and no one else knows about it."

The words are like acid coming up my throat. I hate that I said his name and made it real by letting someone else carry even an ounce of it.

I should've kept it locked down and thrown away the key. I know how to survive in silence... It's safe there, even if it is lonely.

I don't want pity—I just want to handle it quietly. Despite it all, Callan's not looking at me like I'm weak. He's looking at me like I matter, and somehow...that's worse.

His entire body goes rigid, but his touch on my wrist remains gentle. "Please tell me you notified the authorities."

I shake my head, my voice coming out quiet. "Callan, he's a cop. I don't want to ruin his career. He's going through some things, and I left him. It's not going to happen again. I'm also a grown woman, by the way," I snap, trying to regain some control. "I know how to handle myself."

My frustration falls flat, crushed by his unwavering concern. His eyes darken, the fury morphing into something even more protective. "I don't care who he is, Bree. It's not your job to protect his career. Grown woman or not."

The tears that have been threatening to spill for two days press against my eyelids, ready to make their grand entrance. I try to blink them away, but they're relentless. I can't stop them. "We have a lot of history. It's complicated."

I'm not sure if he even realizes it, but his thumb is still

tracing slow, soothing circles on my wrist. He's grounding me, offering steadiness in the chaos. His words are laced with that raw, protective fire, and it makes everything inside me tremble.

"There's nothing complicated about it. He hurt you, plain and simple. He's lucky he's thousands of miles away, or else I'd be tracking the bastard down and showing him what it's like to be on the receiving end."

The anger in his eyes slices through the comfort he's trying to offer, like a knife cutting through butter. Only the butter's me.

"Where else did he hurt you?"

I swallow hard, the lump in my throat as heavy as a stone. How much do I even say? Will it really change anything? What does it matter? The mess is already made, and the pieces are scattered all over the place.

His voice drops, firmer now. "Bree. Where else did he hurt you?"

And just like that, my resolve breaks. The tears I've been holding back fall one after another. I didn't realize how much I needed to let this out, how much I needed someone to know. It's both terrifying and a relief at the same time.

"My leg," I say as I try to catch my breath between sobs. "I-I fell. After he grabbed me."

He shuts his eyes as he takes a slow, steadying breath. His nostrils flare as if he's trying to hold back some wave of anger. When he opens his eyes again, his voice comes out calmer. "Show me."

I carefully lift the hem of my dress over my thigh, trying to keep some semblance of modesty. He kneels beside me, his eyes drawn to my leg like a magnet. The sharp intake of his breath cuts through the air.

"Christ," he mutters under his breath. "Bree, that looks terrible."

The sympathy in his eyes crashes over everything I've tried to hold back. He's too kind. Too *real*.

His gaze lifts to mine. "How bad does that hurt?"

"A lot, actually," I admit. "Only when I touch it, though. It's fine otherwise."

He gently pulls the skirt of my dress back down over my thigh before he stands. When he speaks, his voice is soft but firm. "What he did was inexcusable, no matter the circumstances. I won't say anything to anyone if you don't want me to but don't do this alone. You can talk to me, aye?"

I nod because the lump in my throat is too tight for anything else. His kindness hits me harder than I expected, and I feel a rush of emotions I wasn't prepared for. I've never let myself lean on anyone, and I didn't think it would be Callan when I did. But this side of him... It's stirring something inside me that I'm not ready to face, let alone admit.

"Thank you," I finally manage to whisper.

He reaches out, his hand hovering for a moment like he's asking permission, before gently wiping away the tear that escaped down my cheek. "You don't have to thank me, Sunshine," he says. "That's what friends are for, right?"

Friends. Right. It's just...now I'm getting all sentimental, and this is veering way too close to Hallmark movie territory for my liking. I need flirty Callan back. The one who makes me roll my eyes and laugh, not this sweet, gentle version that's messing with my head. Time to reel it back in before my heart gets any more confused.

"Friends, huh? So, I can count on you to bring me ice cream at three in the morning if I ask?"

He smirks, that mischievous glint sparking back to life in his eyes. "I'll bring the ice cream...but only if you promise not to cry over rom-coms again."

A laugh bubbles up as I recall the time Jules got wasted in

Edinburgh and Knox had to babysit her while Callan got tasked with bringing me back to my hotel room. We ended up hanging out for a while, and there were indeed rom-coms and tears involved.

"Deal. But you're really going to judge me for having emotions?"

"Never." He grins. "Your emotions are safe with me, Sunshine."

WHEN HE DROPS me back at Rose's, I thank him for the ride, my fingers brushing against his as I hand his helmet and jacket back to him.

He says it again. "You can talk to me, Bree."

I nod, but I don't *want* to talk about it.

His gaze settles on me, open in a way that leaves no room for doubt. "I won't tell anyone."

I leave it at that. It's easier to walk away than let him see how much I want to believe him.

CALLAN

I need to drag my arse out of bed and get ready for work. Knox won't be showing up to the distillery. At least, he better not.

I'm lying in bed, staring at the ceiling as I think about last night. I hate that my first reaction was anger. Not at her. Never at her. Still, the fact that she's been dealing with an abusive boyfriend alone? Yeah, that flips a switch in me. It was like some primal, protective instinct kicked in.

I'm worried because I know myself. I can be a lot without meaning to. I push too hard when I'm just trying to help. I don't want to do that to her. What I *do* want is to take even a fraction of the weight off her shoulders.

Before finding out, having her on the back of my bike was something I never imagined happening. I relished the way the vibrations of the engine thrummed through her body, her arms locked tight around my waist while her thighs were snug against mine...

Christ. Nope. Not going there.

It's not like that for her. Not after everything she's been

38

through. She just got out of an abusive relationship, for god's sake. The last thing she needs is me being a selfish asshole, letting my brain short-circuit over the way her body fits against mine. Or how good she smells. Or how her hand felt in mine. Or how I've wanted to kiss the hell out of her from the moment I met her months ago.

Christ. I shove the thoughts aside and get out of bed. After getting ready and throwing on jeans and a T-shirt, I grab my leather jacket. I'll take the bike to work today. The cooler temps don't bother me, especially not when I'm chasing that sharp kind of freedom only the road can offer. There's something about the engine's low growl and the wind ripping past that strips everything else away.

God knows I could use that today.

The crisp air bites as I head outside to the detached garage, that flicker of anticipation sparking to life. As soon as I swing the door open, the familiar scent of oil and leather hits me.

I grab my helmet off the hook, slide it on, and throw my leg over the bike. I twist the key and the engine rumbles to life, powerful and loud. Just the way I like it.

I take the scenic route, veering onto the winding road that hugs the riverbank. The water's restless today, its surface rippling with an energy that matches the unsteady rhythm of my pulse.

Rivers have always had this odd way of settling me, though. Maybe because I see a bit of myself in them. The way they move, relentless and unyielding, carving their path no matter how many twists, turns, or obstacles try to get in the way. There's a kind of defiance in it. A refusal to be anything but what they are.

I get that.

I have enough time to swing by the café and check in on my sister, Lucy. Ever since she took over for Mum, she's been running the place like a pro. Still, I can't help but worry. She's got this habit of putting everyone else first, working herself into the ground to make sure everything's perfect.

The bell above the door jingles as I step inside, and Lucy's face lights up with that impossibly sweet smile of hers. It's the kind that could thaw even the iciest bastard.

It doesn't last, though. Her eyes scan over me, and just like that, the warmth vanishes. Her smile falters, replaced by a deadpan stare.

"You rode that death trap over here?" she says flatly. "Great. Now I can't even send you off with a coffee to go!"

I chuckle, shoving my hands deep in my pockets. "Sorry, sis. It was a death trap kind of morning."

She rolls her eyes, but it takes all of two seconds for her to switch into little-sister mode, leaning on the counter with that cheeky, all-knowing smile. "Come on, don't hold back. You know I'll get it out of you eventually. What happened last night?"

I shake my head, exhaling through my nose. "Aye, fine. I took Bree out after the party."

Her eyes shine with that same curiosity I've seen from her my entire life. "Uh huh, and?"

"And...nothing," I shrug. "She needed cheering up, and I think I managed that."

The teasing fades, and she studies me with that unnerving little sister intuition she's had since we were kids. "Something's wrong," she says, her voice softer now. "What happened?"

I sigh, dragging a hand through my hair. "Bree's been having a really...rough time. I won't say more than that. It's her story to tell. She hasn't even told Jules. I really think she needs someone to talk to, Lou. And that someone isn't me."

The truth stings the second it's out.

I'm not soft enough. Not careful enough for what she's

dealing with. Last night, all I wanted was to take her away, keep her close, and make damn sure the bastard who hurt her never got the chance again.

And then I saw it. The fear in her eyes when my anger slipped through. I'm not the guy who yells, who clenches his fists like he's one wrong word away from swinging. But I was right there. Teetering.

And it'll probably happen again, because the thought of someone hurting her, touching her, *scaring* her... It twists something inside of me, and suddenly, all the calm I've worked for evaporates.

She nods, sympathy etched into every line of her face. "Poor thing. How long is she staying?"

"Not long. I'm taking her back to the airport tomorrow afternoon."

Lucy gives a thoughtful hum. "I'll reach out to her, all right? We talk sometimes. I'll make sure she's okay."

That stubborn look crosses her face. The one that says the decision's already made, and there's no point in arguing.

I chuckle, shaking my head. "You don't have to do that, Lou."

"I know," she says, quieter this time. "But someone needs to look out for her, too. She deserves to know someone cares, don't you think?"

There hasn't been a single day in my life I haven't been grateful for my little sister's big heart. "You're the best, you know that?"

Her grin is back in an instant. Smug little thing. "I know. Now go on, get out of here."

"Aye, I'm going. Promise me you'll take a break soon, yeah?"

She waves me off. "I'll think about it."

I glance back as I head for the door. She's already deep in

conversation with another customer, that same bright smile glued to her face, like the world couldn't possibly throw anything her way that would make her flinch.

I make a mental note to swing by later and make sure she actually takes that break, even if I have to drag her out of here myself.

BREE

"Girl, let me see that rock again."
We're sprawled out on the couch at Juliette and Knox's place, and I can't resist the urge to get a closer look. She holds out her left hand, and I lean in. The vintage ring on her finger? It's straight-up magical.

"Damn, he's good," I murmur, tracing the air around it with my finger like I can feel the sparkle. It's mesmerizing, the way the light hits it just right.

I ignore the tiny ache that presses in. It's definitely not jealousy, I swear. Just a small, innocent wish that maybe, one day, I'll have my own version of this fairytale.

"This thing looks like it was plucked right out of a dream."

Her eyes light up, that dreamy glow taking over her face, and a little rosy blush tints her cheeks. "I know, right? It's perfect."

"Perfect?" I snort, leaning back into the couch. "Girl, it's a masterpiece. Now, talk wedding to me. When are we doing this thing? Where? Oh! And the most important part—what color am I wearing?"

She bites her lip, her gaze going all starry-eyed. "I really don't want to wait very long," she says, practically floating in her own little world. "I'd love to get married in the spring."

"Well, we'll make it happen. There's no way Knox would tell you no anyway." I shoot her a knowing smirk. I mean, let's be real. The guy's whipped in the best way possible.

"That's so true." Then her smile softens, and she shifts gears. "Oh, hey. I feel so bad that I didn't get to talk to you much last night. I was a bit overwhelmed. How's Dillon?"

Just like that, I'm yanked back to reality. There's a familiar twinge in my chest, like my heart hiccupped. Without thinking, I tug at the hem of my sleeve, trying to hide the fact that it's a touch harder to smile than usual.

My mind scrambles for something palatable that won't open the floodgates. I could lie. I've done it before, smiled and said "we're great" so many times it's almost muscle memory. But the thought of saying that now makes my stomach twist.

I don't owe anyone the whole truth, but I owe *myself* just a sliver of honesty.

"He's okay. We're...taking some time apart right now."

There. That's a half-truth I can stomach. Not the full wreckage, not the bruises beneath the fabric, but enough to breathe through.

Her eyes widen, her brows shooting up in surprise like I've just told her I'm running away to join the circus. "Bree, what? When did this happen? Oh my god, are you okay?"

I hate the panic in her voice.

Juliette's always seen Dillon and me as a power couple. And she would've been right, two years ago. The look in her eyes tells me she's bracing for devastation, and I just can't fake it anymore. I'm not devastated. I'm...scared? Maybe. Relieved? Yeah, that one's way closer to the truth.

I take a deep breath, trying to keep the mood light. Because, honestly, if I don't, I might just crack. And if I start crying, I'll never stop. "We just...grew apart. Ten years is a long time, and people change, you know? We were kids when we started dating. I think we just realized we're not the same people we were back then."

It's the cleanest explanation I've got but even saying it out loud doesn't make it any less heavy. And it's believable, right?

Judging by the look on Juliette's face? Nope. Not really. She's not buying it.

"I won't push you because I know that doesn't do any good," she says, her eyes holding a quiet understanding I'm not sure I deserve. "Whenever you're ready to talk, I'll be here. Always."

I nod, grateful for the offer, but the burden is already sinking deeper. How do you tell someone, your best friend, that you can't fully trust the person they've been rooting for all along? The guy who, just days ago, turned into someone else entirely. The guy who's not who they think he is. The guy who's been lying, and you've been too afraid to admit it to anyone.

It's easier this way, right? To keep up the facade and let her hold onto the version of him she's always known. I'm protecting him in her eyes, even if it means burying the truth.

Though, I'm protecting myself, too. Because once I say it out loud, once the truth is out there, I can't take it back. And then what?

"I know," I say, giving her hand a squeeze, trying to force a little sincerity into it. "Thank you. I'm okay, though, really."

Lies.

She doesn't press. She just nods, offering a quiet smile that hits way too close to home. She's already seen through the surface and knows something's off, but she's giving me the space to keep pretending.

I don't know how to make it better. I don't know how to make any of this better. So I do what I always do when things get too real. I push it down and bury it.

"Back to you, though. Tell me what you're envisioning for this wedding."

She knows exactly what I'm doing. Fishing for a distraction, hoping to drown out the heaviness creeping in. Without missing a beat, she starts laying out a detailed plan, making it crystal clear she's been thinking about this for a lot longer than she's let on.

I settle back, letting her enthusiasm wash over me. It's a nice, calming thing to focus on. My beautiful friend's eyes sparkle as she talks about flowers, color schemes, and everything else she's dreamed up for her big day. I can almost see it all, like a little vision coming to life.

"Let me guess," I say. "Red velvet cake?"

"You bet. And you'll be my maid of honor...again?"

Her voice is full of that hopeful light, as if there's any chance in hell I'd say no. This is Juliette we're talking about. My sister from another mister. The one who's been there through every twist and turn and who's earned every bit of happiness coming her way. She's the one who always makes everything feel just a little brighter. So hell yeah, I'm going to be there for her.

She was engaged before, but we both know that wedding wasn't *her* wedding. Her ex-fiancé let his mom take the reins and plan the whole damn thing, like Juliette's dreams didn't even matter. Thank god it never happened.

"Duh! It's going to be beautiful, J. I'm half tempted to drag you wedding dress shopping right now so I don't miss any of it."

She tosses her head back in a laugh. "I promise whenever I go shopping, I'll make sure you're not working so we can video chat."

"Deal," I reply with a wink, feeling the pull of a smile that's been stuck all day finally breaking free.

Then, the sound of heavy footsteps thuds against the porch, the unmistakable sign that Knox is home. Their cat's excitement is immediate, the furry little thing darting off the couch like a bolt of lightning, heading straight for the door.

As soon as Knox walks in, his eyes immediately find Juliette. And the moment they do, the air between them shifts. I can't help but watch the way they exchange smiles, so quiet and knowing, like they've built their own little world around each other. It's the kind of look that only comes when two people are completely wrapped up in each other. The kind of look I used to think would never stop being a part of my life.

And then, the massive man bends down and picks up the cat, cradling it against his chest with the kind of tenderness I didn't know Knox even had in him. He strokes the fur gently, his face softening in a way that catches me off guard. It's a side of him I don't think anyone really gets to see. Most certainly not the Knox everyone else knows.

I roll my eyes at the utter perfection of the scene in front of me, unable to stop the smirk that tugs at the corners of my mouth. "Juliette. You're a lucky bitch. If I didn't love you guys so much, I'd hate you."

She chuckles, shaking her head. She absolutely knows she's guilty of setting the bar too high. She twirls the ring on her finger, clearly still getting used to the feel of it. "I am lucky. Very much so." She pauses for a second, then her eyes light up. "Oh! You'll stay for dinner, right? I think Callan and Lucy are coming, too."

"Of course! I've got nowhere to be."

I've been trying to keep busy, to not dwell on things I can't change, but seeing Callan today? That's a whole other ball game. Last night was...a lot. More than I was prepared for. I was glad to be on the back of his bike, the wind in my face, the world rushing by without any expectations. It was the closest I've come to feeling free in a long time.

Now, with dinner on the horizon and the chance to see him again, there's a part of me that's more than a little anxious. My stomach drops, and my palms start to sweat. The thought of being in the same room as Callan, surrounded by everyone else, knowing he's the only one who has even a hint of the truth about what happened with Dillon... It's enough to make my heart race.

But I'm definitely looking forward to seeing Lucy. I didn't get to catch up with her much last night, and she's such a sweet-heart. She's got this quiet, bubbly energy that somehow makes you feel like everything's going to be okay, even when the world's a little messy. Right now, I think I could really use that feeling.

Right on cue, there's a knock at the door. Knox heads over to answer it, and Lucy's cheerful voice greets him with her usual enthusiasm before she breezes into the kitchen, arms loaded with grocery bags.

"I hope you don't mind, but I brought some ingredients to whip up dessert," Lucy announces. "I had a feeling we'd all end up here tonight."

"You're a saint," Juliette declares, rushing to help Lucy unload the bags.

"Agreed, your desserts are legendary," I add, stepping into the kitchen. "Jules, go sit and relax with your man. I can help Lucy."

She nods, giving me an exaggerated look of relief. "For the best. I'm more of a liability than help in the kitchen."

I can't help but laugh as she shuffles off to the living room, where Knox is still fussing over the cat like he's the one who's had a rough day. Meanwhile, Lucy is already on top of everything with graceful movements, like she's done this a thousand times before. I watch her for a second, appreciating the calm energy she exudes, and then our eyes meet. She flashes me an easy smile.

"What can I do to help?" I ask. I'm trying to sound like I've got my life together, but let's be real, I'm just here to follow directions.

She eyes the ingredients, tying an apron around her waist. Where did she even get that?

"Would you mind measuring out the sugar and flour? Twenty-five grams of sugar and two-forty of the flour," she asks, her voice calm as she sets up her own station.

"Uh...translate to American, please."

She laughs. "Sorry. About two tablespoons of sugar, two cups of flour."

"That I can manage," I say, relieved that I'm not about to need a degree in chemistry. I sift through the drawers for the right measuring cups, finding them and getting everything set up for her. This small task is oddly comforting. Focused, simple.

I'm about to ask what else I can do when I hear the familiar rumble of a motorcycle outside. My stomach does a little flip, the sound instantly bringing Callan to mind. It's strange how just a noise can do that, like he's everywhere and nowhere all at once. I don't know if it's the excitement or just the fact that he's...there, but my pulse quickens and the tension from earlier creeps back in.

"So, Bree. How have you been doing?" Lucy asks, her voice light, but I catch the subtle concern behind it.

"Good," I reply, maybe a little too quickly.

"Good?" She raises an eyebrow. "You sure? Not that I'm trying to pry."

My smile falters for a second, but I quickly mask it. "I'm fine, really. I'm guessing you talked to Callan?"

She nods. "Aye, I could tell he was worried about something, so I asked. He didn't tell me specifics, just that you might like to talk to someone at some point."

Her eyes drop down to my hand where I'm pulling at my shirt sleeve again, then back up to meet my gaze. "You don't have to talk about it," she says gently. "Just know I'm here, if you ever need to."

I give her a small, grateful smile. "Thanks, Lucy. Maybe I'll take you up on that someday."

"Whenever you're ready." She gives my hand a gentle squeeze as the front door creaks open, signaling Callan's arrival. She looks over toward the sound, her lips curling into a smile. "Ah, looks like the party's arrived!"

His voice filters in from the hallway first. Deep, smooth, threaded with that familiar rumble of laughter that always lands low in my stomach. The flutter starts before I can stop it. A quiet little stutter in my chest that shouldn't mean anything.

My heart kicks, bracing for the awkward tension I've been dreading since last night. But then I see him standing there with that easy grin and eyes that look at me like I matter.

And just like that, the knot in my stomach loosens.

Huh.

That's...interesting.

"Hey, what did I miss?" he asks, glancing between Lucy and me with that trademark half smile of his. There's this effortless confidence in the way he stands, like he's completely at home in his own skin, and it makes him seem so damn... steady. And for some reason, that steadiness makes my pulse do a funny little dance.

"Oh, just girl talk," Lucy teases, giving me a knowing look as she lets go of my hand.

I manage to pull off a small smile, trying my best to play it cool, but my pulse? Yeah, that's still racing like it's trying to escape my body. "Lucy was just...prying a little."

Callan's eyes meet mine, and there's a hint of concern in them.

"How are you doing?" he asks.

I shrug. "I'm good. Just helping Lucy with dessert."

He nods, but I can tell he's not entirely convinced. He glances at Lucy, who's busying herself with the measuring cups, and then back at me. "Can we talk for a sec?"

My heart skips a beat, but I nod, following him to the door. Just before I step onto the porch, I catch a glimpse of Juliette, her brow furrowed as she gives me a puzzled look, clearly sensing something is off. I force another smile, hoping she doesn't ask too many questions.

The cool evening air is a welcome relief, and I take a deep breath.

"So, what's up?" I ask, leaning against the railing.

He runs a hand through his hair, looking out at the yard for a moment before turning to face me. "I just wanted to check in, make sure you're all right after last night. I know it was a lot."

I nod, a little too quickly. "Yeah, it was." I pause, trying to find the right words. "I'm okay, though. Really."

"Are you sure? Because if you need anything, I'm here. You know that, right?"

I can't help but smile at that. It's a genuine one this time, because I do know. And it means more than I can say. "I know. Thank you."

He nods, satisfied for now. "All right. Just...don't forget it."

"I won't. Pinky promise."

His presence is more comforting than nerve-wracking now, but I'm still wrestling with the thought of Lucy possibly knowing something's up. It's not that I don't trust her, it's just...

this thing with Dillon is still so fresh. I'm not ready to talk about it yet, not even with someone as sweet and understanding as Lucy.

"We should probably head back inside," I say, nodding toward the door. "Before they start wondering what we're up to out here."

He chuckles, giving me that mischievous look I've come to expect from him. "Aye, you're probably right. Don't want to give them any ideas."

I roll my eyes. "Please. As if."

We head back inside, and I slide back into my spot next to Lucy, who's now stirring something in a large bowl. She looks over at me with a knowing smile but doesn't say anything.

Juliette glances up from where she's sitting with Knox in the living room, a little crease forming between her brows. I catch her eye and offer the smallest smile and a subtle shake of my head that says, *I'm okay. Nothing's wrong.* She holds my gaze for a beat longer, then nods.

Callan slides into the bar stool across from me, that playful glint still dancing in his eyes.

"So," he says, grabbing a spoon from the counter, "what culinary masterpiece will this be?"

"Chocolate cake," I say. "And knowing Lucy, it'll be the best thing you've ever tasted."

"Bold claim. Might need a sample first. For, you know, quality control."

I raise a brow. "You just want the batter."

"I'm offended by the accusation," he says, already reaching. "But also...yes. Obviously."

Lucy slaps his hand away with a wooden spoon. "Back off. You can have a piece after it bakes."

"You wound me, Lou. Denying a man in his time of need."

"You had your time of need outside," she says with a wink, then glances at me. "He good?"

I nod, biting back a smile. "He's fine. Just a little dramatic."

Callan points the spoon at me. "That's slander, and I'll see you in court."

"Good," I shoot back. "I've always wanted to yell *objection* in real life."

Lucy groans. "I'm surrounded by toddlers."

"Correction," Callan says. "Highly attractive, emotionally complex toddlers."

Knox's laughter rings out. "That's not the win you think it is, bud."

We all laugh, and things might not be perfect for me right now, but they're okay. Okay enough for me to breathe a little deeper, and that's something I can work with.

I woke up this morning feeling surprisingly refreshed, which is a minor miracle considering the whirlwind the past few days have been. Now I'm about to head back to the States and go through the whole jet lag thing all over again. Because that's *always* a treat.

The idea of leaving this bubble where everything actually feels okay has anxiety settling back in. I try to get it together, zero in on the task at hand like that'll somehow keep the spiral at bay. *Fold the damn clothes, Bree.* But my hands are trembling, and I keep refolding the same sweater like that'll fix whatever's cracking open inside me. Tears prick at the corners of my eyes, threatening to spill over at any moment.

I blink hard, biting the inside of my cheek as I do a quick once-over of my room at Rose's, making sure I haven't left anything behind.

Juliette's perched on the edge of the bed, watching me with that little frown she gets whenever she feels guilty. "I'm so sorry I can't take you to the airport," she says, her voice soft. "If I had known you were coming, I wouldn't have booked my appointment."

I wave her off with a reassuring smile. "Don't worry about it, Jules. I came here to surprise you, not for you to put your entire life on hold." The last thing I want is for her to feel bad. She's got enough on her plate already, and as for me? Well, I'm just trying to survive this whole mess and get back to normal. Whatever that even is at this point.

I turn back to the suitcase, pulling at the zipper like it's personally offended me. It's not budging. Not. At. All. "Damnit. Sit your skinny ass on top of this for me? I can't get it zipped."

She bursts out laughing and hops off the bed. She makes her way over to the suitcase and perches on top of it like she's some kind of delicate bird. Her thin frame barely even makes a dent.

I roll my eyes. "Come on, put some muscle into it!"

She bounces up and down dramatically, making a show of it. Finally, with one last tug, the zipper gives in, and I manage to wrangle it closed. "There we go," I say, wiping my hands. "Crisis averted."

Juliette slides off the suitcase and, without a word, wraps her arms around me. She presses her cheek against my shoulder, and the weight of her sadness seeps through the hug. "I wish you didn't have to go," she murmurs. "These past few days have been a dream."

I squeeze her back, my throat tightening just a little, because this is harder than I expected. "I'll come back as soon as I can, you can count on it." And I mean it. There's nothing holding me in one place anymore. Well, nothing except Nugget, but he's portable. I'll figure it out. One way or another.

"Ugh, well, Callan should be here to pick you up any minute. My appointment is thirty minutes away, so I better get going." She gives me a sad smile. "Be so careful, okay? Text me at every stop on the way back?"

"You know I will."

She holds my gaze for a moment, then her voice turns teasing, yet still serious. "You're also not off the hook. You never told me what happened with Dillon, and I'm giving you a pass for now, but you owe me the full story at some point."

I wave her off. "Yeah, yeah. Now shoo before you're late."

She rolls her eyes at my dismissive tone but doesn't fight it. She gives me a final hug, then heads out the door, leaving me with that lingering feeling of already missing her before I've even left.

I flop onto the bed, letting out an exaggerated sigh. My brain immediately jumps into overdrive, running through a marathon of thoughts I'm definitely not ready to deal with. I try to push them aside, but they're persistent little buggers. I just need to survive today and keep it together.

I glance around the room like it's going to offer me some kind of wisdom. Spoiler alert—it doesn't.

seven

CALLAN

We've been riding to the airport in silence, but it's buzzing with all the things we're not saying.

I know why, though, and I get it. I do. With every minute that passes, I chew on the inside of my cheek, wanting to ask anyway. Just to make sure she's really okay.

"Excited to get home?"

The words are out before I can stop them, and the second they're hanging in the air, I cringe. *Really, Callan? That's what you go with? You might as well have asked if she's looking forward to a root canal.*

She doesn't snap, though. Just bounces her knee like she's trying to shake something off while picking at her thumbnail. Her eyes are glued to the window. She looks a million miles away.

"Honestly? Not really," she says quietly. "This was a nice break from reality."

I sigh, mentally kicking myself. "Aye, I get that. I'm sure you'll be back soon enough. Just say the word, and I'll find some trouble for us to get into. Intentional trouble, mind you."

She lets out a small laugh, and I swear, it's like someone just took a giant weight off my shoulders. Seeing her all...sad? Yeah, no. It's unsettling. It's like watching a puppy get its tail stepped on. Just wrong on every level.

"Intentional trouble?" she asks, a hint of curiosity in her tone. "Is that a Callan specialty?"

"Only on the weekends."

She raises an eyebrow, a little playfulness creeping in. "I might just take you up on that."

I blink, surprised at how much that catches me off guard. She actually looks like she's considering it.

I clear my throat. "So, uh, where are you staying when you get home?"

I catch the smirk she's trying to hide out of the corner of my eye. "Worried about me?"

"Actually," I admit without hesitation, "I am."

She meets my gaze. "I'll be okay, Callan. I've been staying with my parents for a while. I'm going to start looking at places in the next couple weeks."

I nod slowly, but it's not enough.

"Still," I murmur, "you don't have to play it all cool with me. Doesn't hurt to make sure you're actually *safe*, aye?"

Her shoulders tense, her fingers toying with the seam of her jeans like they're suddenly fascinating. "I know," she says, quieter this time. "But I'll be fine. I've got it figured out."

I want to call her on it. Tell her she's allowed to not be strong for five bloody minutes, but her guard's inching higher.

So I pull back. "All right," I say with a small nod. "Just...if you need anything, don't hesitate to call."

She gives me a small smile, lips curving just right. "I know, Callan."

"Good," I say, keeping my voice casual. "But seriously, don't go getting into trouble without me."

There's a challenge in her eyes. "That's a promise I might hold you to."

We keep the conversation light, but in the back of my mind, I'm counting down the minutes. Every damn second with her has been better than the last, and this ride to the airport feels way too damn short.

I shift the truck into park, kill the engine, and hop out before she can reach for the door. It's not like I need to, but there's this pull, this need to help her down, to hold her hand in mine one more time.

"Thank you, kind sir," she teases.

"Anytime, milady," I reply, giving a mocking bow, but my gaze lingers on her a beat longer than usual.

I take her bag, my hand brushing hers when I pass it to her. I *maybe* did that on purpose, but I'm not about to admit that out loud.

"Well, this is where I leave you, lass."

She nods, but there's disappointment in her expression. Or am I just reading too much into it?

"Callan, I..." she starts, then hesitates, biting her lip. I'm not sure what it is about the way she does it, but it hits me right in the gut. The little movement makes my thoughts scatter.

Her eyes meet mine, and for a second, the world holds its breath. "Thank you. For everything."

I shrug, trying to play it cool, but I probably look like I'm overthinking the hell out of the whole thing. "Wouldn't have it any other way."

Wouldn't have it any other way? What the hell was that? Might as well have flat-out admitted I've got feelings for her. Great. This whole situation is way more complicated than I was prepared for.

So, I do what I always do. I force a smile. "Besides, it's not like I had anything better to do, right?"

Great. Nailed it. That was *definitely* worse.

She raises an eyebrow, and I catch the little flicker in the corner of her mouth, that almost smile, and my heart skips a beat. It's like watching the sun peek through the clouds. I want to see her *really* smile. I know it's not my place to ask for it, but I can't help the thought of being the one to make her smile again, after everything she's been through. If I could do that, it'd be worth it.

"Well," she says softly. "I appreciate it. More than you know."

She leaves me with a small wave, and I watch her walk toward the entrance, her blonde hair catching the light with every step. The air is heavier, almost charged. Then she glances over her shoulder, and our eyes lock.

For a second, everything else...stops.

I force myself to look away. *Don't read too much into it.* She's walking away. It's like any other goodbye. Doesn't matter that it feels different this time or that I don't want to let go. It's only a trip to the airport. That's all. If I make it awkward, she'll feel it. And I'm not about to make this harder than it needs to be.

I clear my throat, pushing those thoughts aside, and throw out the first thing that comes to mind.

"Bye, Sunshine! Don't forget to wear sunscreen!"

She turns around and looks at me like I've completely lost my mind. I mean, c'mon, did she really think she'd get away without me trying to embarrass her or at least get a laugh?

"You're practically glowing. At this rate, you might start attracting seagulls. Just looking out for you."

A blush creeps across her cheeks, and I swear, it's the cutest thing I've ever seen. She sticks her tongue out at me, and I almost lose it right there.

"You're ridiculous," she says, but there's amusement in her voice.

I grin, a rush of pride flooding in that comes from knowing I've gotten under her skin in the best way. She rolls her eyes, mutters something half-hearted, and I eat it up like it's the best thing I've tasted all week.

My grin fades almost as fast as it comes. Because then it hits me.

I'm going to miss her.

That wasn't part of the plan. I don't do *missing* people. I don't sit still long enough to let anyone get close. It's easier that way. No roots, no complications. And yet here I am, standing still like a damn idiot, watching as she rolls that suitcase behind her that I suddenly want to set on fire.

I keep telling myself I'm just looking out for her. That pushing her to open up and trying to keep her safe is about her, not me. But maybe that's bullshit. Maybe I want to save her because some part of me is desperate to believe I should.

And that's the real kicker because when did she become the thing I don't want to walk away from?

BREE

I can't explain how I went from *"hey, thanks for the motorcycle ride"* to texting Callan every day. It started innocently enough—a simple check-in from him the day after I landed to make sure I got home okay.

Then, somehow, it turned into good morning texts. Photos of his day. Late-night calls that stretched until one of us fell asleep with the phone still pressed to our ear.

It's been three months, and now I'm sitting cross-legged on my new couch in my condo. I'm renting in Lexington close to work, and I've toured a few houses. I found one place with original hardwood and a clawfoot tub that practically seduced me on sight. I almost signed right there on the spot for the bath situation alone, but...it didn't feel right. Nothing's whispered home to me yet.

I'm staring at my phone. The screen lights up with his name, and my heart does that stupid flutter thing again.

CALLAN:

Morning, Sunshine. How's the new place treating you?

I can't help the smile that spreads across my face as I type back.

ME:

Still living in Box City. Thinking of declaring myself mayor.

The response is immediate.

CALLAN:

Send me a picture. I need to make sure you haven't buried yourself alive in cardboard.

I laugh and snap a quick selfie, surrounded by the chaos of my half unpacked living room, wild hair piled on top of my head with an exhausted look on my face. I hit send before I can overthink it.

Three dots appear, then disappear, then appear again.

CALLAN:

Christ, woman. You're a disaster. A cute one, though.

The compliment makes my cheeks flush, and I'm glad he can't see me. This has been happening more and more lately— these comments that toe the line between friendly teasing and something else entirely.

My phone buzzes again.

CALLAN:

You know what you need?

ME:

Please don't say more boxes.

CALLAN:

A distraction. Video call?

I glance down at my ratty T-shirt and gym shorts, then at the mess surrounding me. What the hell. It's not like he hasn't seen me looking worse.

"There she is," he says when his face appears on my screen, all tousled hair and a lazy smile. He's sitting in what looks like his office at the distillery. "How's my favorite American this morning?"

I roll my eyes but can't stop grinning. "Exhausted. Still surrounded by boxes, in case you forgot."

Callan leans back in his chair, lacing his fingers behind his head. He's in a black T-shirt, forearms on full display like he doesn't even know they're a weapon. His smile curls slowly, like he's got all the time in the world.

"It suits you."

I groan. "You're relentless."

"Only with you," he says, so casually I almost miss the implication.

Then he winks, and the tension breaks just enough to let me breathe again. Sort of.

I shift on the couch, tucking one leg underneath me. "What are you even doing at work this late?"

"Had some paperwork. Figured I'd get ahead of it." He shrugs, eyeing the screen. "You look good, Bree."

I tuck a strand of hair behind my ear, suddenly self-conscious. "You need your eyes checked."

He doesn't take the bait. Just tilts his head, studying me like I'm a puzzle he likes taking his time with. "My eyes are just fine, lass."

"Callan..." I start, not even sure what I'm going to say.

"I miss you," he cuts in, his voice dropping lower.

My heart stutters. We've been dancing around this for weeks, maybe months. Every late-night call, every text that lingers just a little too long on "goodnight," every time I find myself smiling at my phone like an idiot.

I miss him, too. And not in the "we're just friends" kind of way.

His eyes hold mine through the screen, and I wish more than anything he was here. That I could reach out and touch him, figure out if what I'm feeling is real.

"I miss you, too," I admit, the words slipping out before I can overthink them. "More than I probably should."

His expression softens, and he leans closer to the camera. "There's no 'should' about it, Sunshine. It is what it is."

I bite my lip and glance down, fingers fidgeting with the hem of my shirt. "And what exactly is it, Callan?"

When I glance back up, he's running a hand through his hair, hesitation in his eyes. "It's me, sitting in this office at midnight, calling you instead of going home because hearing your voice has become the best part of my day."

My breath catches. "Callan—"

"I know the timing is shit," he continues. "I know you're still sorting things out."

The walls I've built around my heart since Dillon tremble. "We live on different continents."

"I'm aware," he says with a soft huff of a laugh that doesn't quite reach his eyes. His thumb brushes along the edge of the screen, like he wishes he could reach through it. "And I'm not trying to make anything harder for you, Bree. I'm not asking you for anything. Truly."

I blink, heart thudding. "Then why tell me?"

His gaze holds mine. "Because I'm not a fan of bullshit," he says with a sudden grin, that familiar mischievous glint returning to his eyes. "Speaking of which, are those Power Rangers on your shirt?"

I glance down at my ratty sleep shirt, mortified to realize he's right. It's my ancient, faded Power Rangers tee from college that I only wear when no one's around to judge me.

"Hey! Don't change the subject," I protest, but I'm already laughing, grateful for the shift in energy. "And yes, they are. Pink Ranger was a feminist icon, thank you very much."

"Oh, absolutely," he agrees, nodding with mock serious-ness. "Though I was always partial to the Green Ranger myself. Bad boy with a heart of gold and all that."

"Of course you were." I roll my eyes. "Let me guess, you had the action figure?"

"Had? I still have it somewhere," he admits, not even slightly embarrassed. "Might be worth something someday."

I'm still laughing, but my heart hasn't quite caught up. That moment before the Power Rangers talk, before the teasing, was real. Too real.

And then, just like that, he gave me an out. Let me breathe.

I hug a throw pillow against my chest and watch him talk about his ancient Green Ranger action figure like it's some kind of sacred relic. He's animated, the magnitude of the earlier moment tucked behind his smile.

We've crossed an invisible line neither of us drew on purpose. We didn't plan this. But here we are, and the truth is... I didn't feel lonely tonight. Not once.

IT'S BEEN a few more months. Somehow.

Callan and I still talk every day—little check ins, voice notes, the occasional call when time zones align and one of us can't sleep. But after that night—the *I miss you* night—things eased back into something lighter. No more confessions. No more lines toeing dangerously close to the edge.

Just him, being...Callan. Reliable. Funny. A little too charming for his own good.

And me, pretending the ache I feel when we hang up isn't anything worth naming.

Callan's the one who finally convinced me to tell Juliette everything, though.

It took weeks. I kept telling myself there was no need. That what happened with Dillon was behind me and I could move on without cracking open the whole messy truth.

Except one night, after too many quiet moments and one too-sweet message from Callan that made my throat go tight, I broke. I needed my best friend.

I can still picture Juliette on our weekly video call. She tilted her head and gave me that look of concern that cut right through me.

"What's going on?" she asked.

I tried to play it off. Laughed too loud. Shrugged too hard. But the words came anyway. Once I started, I couldn't stop. I told her everything. The hiding. The fear. The way I'd learned to pretend like I was fine until I couldn't tell the difference anymore.

And the look on her face... It wasn't anger. It was heartbreak.

"Why didn't you tell me, Brianna?" she whispered, tears in her eyes. "All these years. I'm so sorry. I should have seen it. I should have known something was wrong."

That's when I knew I'd really messed up. She only ever called me Brianna when she was mad...or devastated.

I shook my head. "I didn't let you see it. I didn't let anyone see it."

"Still. I'm your best friend. I should have pushed harder,

asked more questions. I thought something was off for a while but..." She held my gaze through the screen, her expression softening into one of pure understanding. "I wish I could have been there for you. But I'm here now, okay?"

We cried. We sat in silence. We laughed a little, too, because she snuck in a dumb joke about how she was going to key his truck if she ever saw him in public, as if that would be possible. I loved her for that.

Beyond that, I don't bring Dillon up much. The only connection I still have to that part of my life is Dillon's mom. Every now and then, I'll shoot her a quick text to check in and see how he's doing. She tells me he's doing okay, that he's working on himself. I hope that's true.

Meanwhile, I'm still learning how to sit with silence without assuming it's the calm before the storm, but I'm doing okay, I think.

I haven't been back to Scotland since Juliette's engagement, and now it's finally time for the wedding. I'm so excited, I could squeal. Stepping off the plane, I take a deep breath, inhaling air that feels lighter and fresher, like the earth itself is waking up from a long winter.

Juliette's already waiting for me at the curb, practically leaping out of the car and running toward me before I've even stepped out of the airport.

"You're here!" Before I can react, she launches herself at me in a bear hug, squeezing the life out of me.

I laugh, my arms wrapping around her instinctively, letting her do her thing. "Please. Like I would ever miss this," I say, grinning as the electric excitement radiates off her.

She pulls back just enough, still gripping my arms, her hazel eyes shining with a mix of nerves and pure joy. "I can't believe it's finally happening. It feels so unreal."

"It's happening, and I'm so happy for you. It's going to be amazing."

There's a rush of happiness being back here with Jules, surrounded by the chaos of her new family. It's a little over-whelming, but in the best way. And as much as I'm thrilled to have her as my escort today, there's still a tiny part of me that wished it had been Callan.

I've been on a few dates over the past few months, all wildly unsuccessful. Take Drew, for example, who couldn't stop complimenting me, but not in the way you'd hope. It was more like, *"You have the most unique nose, but not in a bad way,"* and *"Your eyebrows are amazing,"* followed by the gem, *"Your face is really aesthetically pleasing."* What the hell is that supposed to mean?

Then there was Tony, who decided to take me to the most expensive restaurant in town, setting the bar way too high from the get-go. After the bill came, he casually admitted he didn't have the money to pay for it. And, because it couldn't get much worse, he had the audacity to ask if I could give him money for a ride home. I mean, really? I don't think I've ever fled a date so fast in my life.

That was the last straw. There was no way anyone could hold a candle to the blue-eyed Scotsman who'd been taking up residence in my dreams. Damn Callan and his infuriating charm. His handsome face. His rock-solid body. His sexy motorcycle. Just...*damn.*

Callan MacKenzie snuck into my heart. I've tried to deny it, but once I saw him that way, I couldn't unsee it.

As we drive from the airport, I can't stop my mind from drifting to him. The way his eyes crinkle at the corners when he smiles. The rich timbre of his laugh. The surprisingly gentle way he teases me, always knowing how far to push before pulling back. My stomach flutters with nervous anticipation at the thought of seeing him again. I'm not even sure what's going to happen when I do see him. I only know I want to.

Juliette's voice cuts through my thoughts. "Are you sure you don't want to stay at my house?"

I laugh. "No thank you, ma'am. You and your soon-to-be husband need all the privacy you can get. I hear you like to keep a certain someone up all night."

The instant blush creeping up her face makes me laugh even harder. "Jules, come on. It's me. If I had a man like that, I'd be running him ragged every night and still be ready for round two...or five or six by breakfast."

She looks mortified, and I can't help but grin, thoroughly enjoying myself. Mission accomplished. And honestly, I wasn't lying.

"I take it back," she says. "I'm not sure I'm glad you're here."

"Admit it," I say, "you'd be lost without me."

"You're right," she agrees. "I would be."

BREE

Juliette looks like an absolute dream today. It's not fair for one person to be that gorgeous. I swear, I sobbed. We're talking full-blown ugly cries when she and Knox said their vows. They're the most beautiful couple I've ever seen in my life.

We're all sitting around at the reception, drinks in hand, when Juliette suddenly gets everyone's attention. She stands up, her eyes scanning the crowd as she clears her throat. "So," she says, her voice a little shaky but full of excitement. "We have news to share."

Knox leans into her, looking like the proudest husband in the world, and I'm already about to lose it because, well, how can you not look at them together and just melt? They're *that* couple. They have one of those rare, soul-deep connections that makes you believe in love again.

She takes a deep breath, and for a second, I wonder if she's going to drag this out for a little while longer. But no. She just drops the bombshell. "We're expecting!"

I choke on my drink, sputtering as everyone erupts into

cheers around us. My heart's racing, and all I can do is sit here stunned as shock and absolute joy floods through me. This is happening. Juliette and Knox are going to be parents.

Knox pulls her into a tight hug, holding her like he's never letting go. His eyes are full of amazement and protectiveness, and I just know they're going to be incredible parents. This little one is going to grow up in a home filled with so much love.

I nudge Lucy next to me, still trying to wrap my head around the news that just rocked my world. "Did you know?" I whisper, my voice catching in my throat.

Lucy shakes her head, eyes wide. "No! I'm just as shocked as you are!"

I let out a shaky laugh. "Well, I guess we're going to be aunties soon," I say, my voice wavering between half laughing and half sobbing because it's just all so overwhelming and wonderful at the same time.

She snorts, her eyes a little glassy. "Can you imagine? Little Knox and Juliette babies running around here?"

I grin, swiping at my eyes. "I can't even. They're going to be adorable."

The energy in the room shifts almost instantly, the buzz of excitement growing louder as the news sinks in. The entire atmosphere has been injected with pure happiness. People are already flocking to Juliette and Knox, offering their congratulations and showering them with hugs, love, and the kind of genuine excitement that only comes from knowing someone's dream just became a beautiful reality.

It's amazing, everything about this. But I can't help the tug in my chest, the bittersweet twinge. Maybe it's because I'm standing on the outside looking in, knowing that this kind of love and happiness feels just out of reach for me.

With a deep breath, I shake it off. No point in wallowing in my own head when everyone else is basking in the glow of this incredible moment. So, I step away, quietly slipping off to the side enough to give myself space to collect my thoughts. The last thing I want is to get emotional in front of everyone.

I grab a glass of champagne from a nearby table, taking a slow sip as my eyes drift over to the dance floor. Everything is gorgeous, and as I watch her and Knox, I let the music wash over me, the rhythm filling the gaps where words might fall short. They're surrounded by love, and for now, that's enough. There's nothing but good things in the air tonight.

My mind drifts back to when I saw Callan as I walked down the aisle. Damn, he looked fine as hell standing beside his brother, all tall and confident, like he belonged in the spotlight. Our eyes locked for a split second, and I swear time seemed to stretch and snap back in an instant.

There was something in his gaze, something I couldn't quite put my finger on. Longing, maybe? I couldn't tell, but it hit me in a way that left me breathless. It was like he could see right through me and was just as affected by this strange, magnetic pull between us. For a moment, I couldn't help but wonder what it would be like if things had turned out differently.

I shake myself out of my thoughts and refocus. Today isn't about me. It's Juliette and Knox's day. But even as I try to push it away, I can feel his gaze on me during the ceremony, burning through my skin and making my heart race in a way I couldn't have predicted.

I'm tucked in my quiet corner, nursing my champagne and watching the dance floor chaos unfold. Tonight, I'm content to simply observe from the sidelines until I hear that familiar, smooth voice.

"You look beautiful."

I freeze, the champagne glass in my hand suddenly heavy. That deep, gravelly tone is unmistakable. *Callan.* My heart stutters, and I force myself to take a slow breath before I turn around to face him.

He's even more striking up close, like some dream carved into reality. His kilt fits him perfectly, hugging his muscular frame in all the right ways, while his white shirt stretches across his chest. I can't seem to tear my eyes away.

I clear my throat, forcing my voice to stay steady. "You clean up pretty well," I say, inwardly relieved that my words come out without giving away the butterflies doing somersaults in my stomach.

He raises an eyebrow, a smirk tugging at the corner of his lips. "Pretty well? That's what I get after all this effort?"

"Fine, you look *very* dashing. Don't get too cocky about it."

He steps closer, his voice dropping to a low, teasing murmur. "Too late. I was feeling pretty confident when I noticed you couldn't stop staring."

Oh, shit. So this is happening. The flirty thing. Well, game on.

I scoff, crossing my arms and giving him my best unimpressed look. "Oh, please. I'm just making sure the kilt's authentic."

He chuckles. "Aye, well, there's only one way to find out, isn't there?"

My face instantly heats up, and I'm pretty sure my entire neck is glowing now. Damn it. I shake my head, trying to shove the blush down. Yeah, he's totally winning this round. "Behave yourself! We're at a wedding, for crying out loud."

"With you around? Not a chance."

I roll my eyes, but that damn smile's already pulling at the corner of my lips, giving me away. "Well? Are you going to teach me how to do this dance everyone's throwing themselves into, or what?"

His brows shoot up. He looks totally thrown off, like I just asked him to teach me how to juggle flaming swords. "You... want to dance. With me?"

"Oh, please, Callan. I'm an American woman standing next to a man in a kilt. You're lucky I haven't gone feral yet."

There. Now *I'm* winning.

His deep, hearty laugh fills the air, and I swear, my stomach flips. Like, it *literally* flips. And all I can think about is how badly I want to hear that laugh again. And again. And again.

"Aye," he says, "but you might regret it."

I raise a brow, pretending to give it some thought. "Oh, I doubt that. How bad could it be?"

He smirks, and I can practically see the mischief dancing in those eyes of his. "Well, Sunshine, there's more to it than you think."

I step a little closer, the air between us suddenly charged. "Then show me, Callan. I'm ready for it."

Wait. Hold up. Are we *still* talking about dancing? Because the way his eyes just darkened? Oh, god. Yeah, we might've just crossed into a whole different territory.

He slides his hand into mine, and the heat from his touch shoots straight up my arm, lighting me up in a way I definitely wasn't prepared for. He sets my champagne aside and, with that smirk still in place, says, "All right then, let's see what you've got."

I follow him onto the dance floor. Everyone else is already spinning and stepping to the lively Scottish tune, looking way more graceful than I could ever hope to be. I'm pretty sure my limbs are about as coordinated as a baby deer on ice.

Callan pulls me close, his hand settling on my waist, the other still holding mine like he doesn't plan on letting go anytime soon. And suddenly, the rest of the world falls away. I hear the music, feel his touch, and all I can think about is how this might be the most dangerous game I've ever agreed to play.

"It's called a ceilidh dance," he murmurs, his breath warm against my ear. "Just follow my lead."

Okay, sure. Following his lead sounds simple enough, but then we start moving, and I quickly realize I am *completely* out of my depth. The steps are fast, way quicker than I thought, and way more intricate. Definitely not the slow swaying I'm used to. It's like we're on fast-forward, and I'm trying to catch up. I stumble a couple of times, but every time I do, Callan's arms are right there, supporting me, keeping me from making a complete fool of myself.

"Sorry!" I laugh, the heat rising in my cheeks. But honestly? I'm not that embarrassed. This is *way* too much fun, and Callan's just rolling with it. I've probably trampled his shoes more than a dozen times, but he doesn't seem fazed in the slightest.

He flashes me a grin that lights up his whole face and makes my brain short-circuit. I forget how to breathe for a second, and I force myself to focus. Then he leans in just a little, and his voice drops to that low, smooth tone that has absolutely no business doing what it does to me. My heart races, and I'm pretty sure my panties are packing their bags and making a run for it.

Nice try, body. Keep it together.

"Don't worry about it," he says. "I'm pretty sure my feet can handle it."

We keep moving, and soon enough, I stop worrying about the steps, or let's be real, the absolute mess I'm making of this dance. Instead, I focus on the way his thumb brushes over my knuckles and the sound of his laughter, which is doing absolutely nothing to slow my heart down.

When the song finally ends, I'm breathless from all the dancing and laughing, and I can't help the smile that spreads across my face. It's the kind of smile you can't shake, no matter how much you try to act cool about it.

Callan rests his hands on his hips, trying to look casual, but there's that smirk creeping up on his lips. "Looks like you'll have to start training to keep up with me, lass. I'm starting to think you enjoy stepping on my toes."

"Only because you look so good when you're trying to hold me up," I tease, and that smirk on his face turns into a full-on grin.

He takes my hand again, that confident, easy grip of his sending a jolt through me as he leads me off the dance floor. "Come on, Sunshine. Let's get you something to drink."

"I think I've earned more than just a drink," I say, quirking my brow. "How about a medal for my amazing dance skills?"

He chuckles as he guides me toward the bar. "I'll get you a drink, and we'll talk about that medal later."

With our drinks in hand, we slip away to a quiet spot. I settle into a chair, taking a sip and letting out a contented sigh. The atmosphere is a little more peaceful here, away from all the chatter and clinking glasses. My eyes wander over to where Knox is spinning Juliette around with so much joy that it's contagious. I've missed seeing her smile like this. Pure happiness is written on her face, and it's impossible not to feel a little lighter just being around it.

"It's great to see them like this, aye?" Callan says, his voice quiet, the usual teasing gone.

"It really is," I agree. "Can you believe we're going to be an auntie and uncle?"

Callan's grin stretches wide, his gaze fixed on Knox and Juliette. "Aye, I'm so happy for them. They deserve it."

He takes a slow sip of his drink, but then his eyes drift over to mine, holding my gaze longer than necessary. "How have you been, Bree?"

"I've actually been really good," I finally say. "I've been on a few dates, but my life mostly consists of work and my dog. You already knew that, though."

His smile falters for a moment. It's almost unnoticeable, but I catch it. The brief crack in his easygoing facade. "Dates, huh? Didn't know about that."

I can't help but notice the slight tightening around his eyes and the way his fingers flex around his glass, like he's trying to keep a grip on something. Is he...disappointed?

I want to ask him, but before I can even open my mouth, his resolve softens. It's like the whole thing never happened, and he's back to that easy smile, the one that always disarms me.

"So, dates? Anyone special?"

"Honestly? No. It's been horrific." I dive into the story of my disastrous dates, the ones that made me question if the universe had a secret vendetta against me. I tell it all, from the awkward silences to the terrible pick-up lines. It feels good to joke about it, and when Callan laughs, that familiar comfort eases back into place.

He's shaking his head now, still trying to catch his breath. "Wow, Sunshine. Sounds like you haven't dated a real man yet."

The words land heavy. His piercing gaze locks onto mine. He's not just talking about the dates. He's saying something else entirely. And the *way* he says it, that challenge in his tone, makes my pulse jump.

Oh, great. There it is. That heat building between us, that irresistible pull. We both know I'm not one to shy away from a challenge. So I smirk, leaning in closer until the space between is almost nonexistent. I match the gleam in his eyes with one of my own.

Somewhere in the back of my brain, there's a little voice whispering, *You know how this ends.*

Only, another voice—louder, cheekier, definitely fueled by booze and curiosity—is like, *Okay, but what if it doesn't end badly? What if it's just fun?*

What would it hurt to give in?

"Careful, Callan," I murmur, my voice soft and teasing. "You really shouldn't test me."

I genuinely don't know if I'm leaning closer because I want to or because he's making it impossible to stay away. His pull is magnetic in the most inconvenient way. Either way, I'm all in.

He leans in even closer, his breath a whisper against my ear.

"But where's the fun in that?" he murmurs.

Oh.

Oh no.

His chest brushes against mine, and my heart forgets how to beat like a normal organ. Just like that, any last scrap of restraint I had?

Gone.

Torched.

CALLAN

Every fiber of my being is screaming at me to pick her arse up and haul her to my truck like some damn caveman. It'd be reckless. Wild. And yet...it's all I can think about.

But I don't move. Not a step. I know better than to act on the desire without thinking about the fallout. I know what it'd mean if I pushed, how fast we'd burn through something that's already hanging by a thread. I don't want to be another decision she regrets.

So I stay rooted, even though my hands are twitching at my sides and my heart's thudding like it's trying to knock itself loose from my chest.

I need her to look away, sit back, laugh it off. Hell, shove me if she has to.

She doesn't. She stays.

And fuck me, she's closing the space between us. I swear if she tilts her head an inch more, I'm done for. I don't think I've ever wanted to make a move this badly in my life.

I can't. Not unless she does.

This has to come from her.

Her eyes are locked on mine. "What are you thinking?"

I swallow hard, the dryness in my throat almost painful. "I'm thinking you should probably back away," I say, but the words come out like a growl, a sound I barely recognize as my own. It's rougher than I meant, but hell, it's impossible to hide how much she's messing with me.

Her lips curl into that teasing smile, and damn, it should've been a warning. "Probably," she says, but still doesn't move. Instead, her hand slides up my forearm, slow and deliberate, the touch sending a shock of electricity straight to my groin. "But what if I don't want to?"

My jaw tightens, my pulse thumping so loud in my ears I can hardly hear anything else. Every fiber of my body is begging me to pull her closer, to breathe her in, to feel her body against mine. I resist, and instead grit my teeth, the heat from her hand spreading through me like wildfire.

"Then you're going to make this a whole lot harder for me," I mutter, the words scraping out of my throat like gravel.

Her smile widens, mischievous and knowing. She's aware of *exactly* what she's doing to me. And then, just when I think I might lose it, she leans in a fraction closer, her breath warm against my ear. "Maybe I like making things hard," she murmurs, and hell, I damn near lose it right there.

I don't even have time to fully process what she says before a booming laugh bursts from me. It's ridiculous, helpless. I've completely lost control of the situation. And the sparkle in her eyes? Hell, it's driving me absolutely mad.

It's like fate gave me everything I've ever wanted...and then laughed in my face, making her so damn impossible to reach.

"Kiss me, Callan," she dares. "Before I lose my patience and start kissing you myself."

Well, now she's really done it.

"I was hoping you'd say that."

I don't waste any time. My hand finds her face, my touch gentle, but everything else about me? Far from it. My mouth crashes into hers, desperate and ravenous, like I've been starving for this for far too long. She gasps against me, and that sound...god, it's like a spark to a fuse, sending a rush of heat straight through my veins.

Her lips part, giving me just enough space to dive in. I taste and explore every inch of her with a hunger I don't want to fight.

I lose track of time, place, all of it. The only thing that matters is her. The way her fingers tug at my collar, how she bites down on my lip hard enough to make my blood burn.

I pull back to meet her eyes. She's lost in this, too, her pupils blown wide with desire, and fuck, it drives me crazy. "Careful," I murmur, my voice rough and barely holding on. "I might bite back."

She presses her lips together in this teasing, innocent pout, but there's no hiding the devilry dancing in her eyes. "Is that a promise?"

A low groan rumbles deep in my chest, and hell, every part of me wants to pull her right back to me, to taste that wild, intoxicating energy between us again. Then reality crashes in like a cold bucket of water, and I'm reminded of where we are.

We're smack dab in the middle of my brother's wedding.

I shift my gaze to check where the hell we are. Knox and Juliette are staring at us, jaws hanging open like they've never seen two people kiss before. Lucy's looking like she might pass out, her eyes wide with shock, while Rose is barely holding it together, amusement written all over her face.

Then there's Bree. She follows my gaze, sees the audience we've unintentionally gathered, and what does she do? She laughs. Not just any laugh, but that genuine, carefree kind that makes everything else fade away. Her head tips back, and the sound hits me like fireworks going off in the dead of night. Bright, explosive, and impossible to ignore.

And hell, if I'm not laughing, too. It's contagious, and before I know it, we're both sitting there, grinning like a couple of fools. Her eyes are shining, her smile lighting up the darkness around us, and for a second, I forget everything. She's perfect.

But damn it, as much as I want to pull her into my arms again and kiss her senseless right here, right now, I need to get a grip. This is a wedding. There are guests.

As she wipes away the tears from laughing so hard, there's a shift. There's that look in her eyes again... The one that tells me she's not afraid to bend a few rules if I'm game. If she keeps looking at me like that, I'm going to need to find something to hide the bulge in my kilt.

"Come home with me, lass." The words spill out before I have time to think, but it feels right. So damn right.

Her smile turns wicked. "Took you long enough to ask."

I chuckle, leaning a little closer. "Had to make sure you were actually up for it, Sunshine."

"Well, now that you've finally figured it out..." she trails off, leaning in just a bit closer.

The real question is, can I keep my hands off her long enough to get us out of here?

I don't waste another second. I pull her to a stand, my grip on her hand tighter than it probably should be, but hell if I can help it. I'm already addicted.

As we weave through the crowd, I catch the looks on Knox's and Jules's faces, wide-eyed, probably trying to piece together how the hell this escalated so quickly. But I don't care. I don't care about anything except the woman at my side.

We stop to say our goodbyes, but it's all just noise. A blur of nods and half smiles while my mind stays locked on the heat of her hand in mine and the way she leans into me ever so slightly.

I've known Bree for almost a year now, but every time I look at her, it's like discovering her all over again. The beauty was obvious from the start. Anyone with eyes can see that. What got me above all else was the way she could make me laugh without even trying. The way she carried herself with this impossible mix of lightness and strength, like the world could throw whatever it wanted at her, and she'd still find a way to smile through it.

Right now, all I can think about is how I could love her fiercely, endlessly. Maybe I didn't realize it at first, but I feel it now, burning deeper with every second I spend with her. And hell, if that doesn't terrify me.

But I'm done holding back.

By the time we get to my place, the tension between us is a living, breathing thing. It makes it damn near impossible to think straight. I try to keep my hands to myself, but every time I glance at her, every time her fingers brush against my back in those slow, teasing patterns, I unravel a little bit more.

I fumble with the keys, cursing under my breath when they slip between my fingers. It's pathetic, really, how just being near her turns me into a complete wreck. But then I look over, and she's watching me with that knowing little smirk, like she enjoys seeing me struggle. Like she's perfectly aware of the war raging inside me. It only makes me want her more.

I finally get the damn door open, and the second we step inside, the air shifts. We've crossed into a place where the rules are different and none of them involve keeping our hands to ourselves.

The heat between us roars back to life. I've got her pressed against the wall before I can think better of it, my hands already moving and greedy to memorize every inch of her. Her body fits against mine too perfectly, like she was made for me.

Her lips hover just shy of mine, and that's all it takes. The need crashes into me, messy and overwhelming. All I want is her. Just her.

Her skin's warm under my fingertips, impossibly soft, and when she shivers? Fuck. That tiny reaction nearly unravels me.

I tilt my head, deepen the kiss, swallowing every soft sound she gives me like they're fuel. My hands tangle in her hair, pulling her closer, like if I hold her tight enough, I'll finally quiet the ache that's been clawing at me since the moment we met.

I already know it still won't be enough.

"God, I've wanted this for so long," I murmur against her skin, my lips tracing a path down her neck, each kiss making it harder to hold on to what's left of my restraint.

She angles her head, granting me more access. When a soft moan escapes her lips, it's music to my ears. "Me, too," she breathes, her fingers threading into my hair.

And I do. I need her in a way that borders on desperation, but she deserves more than just urgency, more than the heat threatening to consume us whole. So, with every ounce of control I have left, I pull back just enough to find her gaze. My fingers slip between hers as I tug her gently toward the stairs.

She follows me without hesitation, her fingers laced tightly with mine. As we reach the top, she halts, stopping me. Did I misread this? Am I rushing her?

I turn, searching her face, but there's no uncertainty in her eyes. Just pure, unfiltered desire.

"Race you." She blows a kiss in my direction, and then she's gone, sprinting down the hall before I can even react.

For half a second, I'm rooted to the spot as I watch her take off like she didn't just have me on the verge of completely unraveling.

Then it clicks.

"Oh, you're in for it now, Sunshine," I growl, taking off after her.

She's fast. I'll give her that. But I've got longer legs and a whole lot of motivation. She lets out a breathless laugh as I close the distance, her smile wide, eyes shining with pure, reckless delight.

I catch her just before she crashes into the bathroom. One arm wraps around her waist, and I spin her clean off her feet, hauling her against me. She lets out a breathless yelp that turns into a laugh, and then turns on her heel, looking up at me with flushed cheeks and bright, triumphant eyes.

"I had no idea where I was going," she admits.

I can't help the bark of laughter that rips from my lungs. "You, what?"

"I've never even been in your house before!"

"So your plan was to start a race you couldn't finish?"

Her breathing's uneven now, lips parted as her gaze flickers to my mouth. "Just...keeping you on your toes."

I lean in, my lips ghosting over hers, our breath mingling. "Sunshine, you have no idea what you just started."

Without another word, I sweep her into my arms, cradling her against me as I carry her down the hall. Her arms loop around my neck, fingers playing with the hair at the nape of my neck as I nudge open the door to my bedroom with my foot, not willing to let her go for even a second.

And then we're falling into the room, onto the bed, and into each other, a mess of tangled limbs and breathless laughter. For a moment, neither of us moves, hearts racing, chests rising and falling in sync. Bree's hair is a wild halo around her, her cheeks flushed, her smile nothing short of devastating. She's never looked more beautiful.

I inch closer, slow enough that she can feel every fraction of space between us disappear. Her breath catches, her body tensing ever so slightly. It's barely noticeable, just the faintest shift, but it's enough.

And then I see it.

Fear.

It flickers in the depths of her gaze, raw and unguarded. And it fucking guts me.

Her hand drifts toward mine, slow and cautious, like she's testing the waters, uncertain whether she's ready to take the leap. I stay still, letting her make the decision.

I can almost hear the internal battle that's holding her back. And when her fingers finally brush against mine, a small breath of relief escapes her as her body relaxes, her shoulders releasing the tension that's there.

My voice is a quiet murmur. "I'm right here."

They're more than just words. They're a promise I know she hears. I'm not going anywhere. Not until she knows, deep in her bones, that she's safe with me.

Our eyes lock, and in that instant, I think she sees it, too. The promise, the silent vow I'm offering. That I'll take care of her heart, of her body, of everything she's willing to trust me with.

She breathes me in, her lips brushing tentatively against mine, soft and gentle. Trusting. It's not just a kiss. It's a quiet surrender, like she's letting herself believe good things are still possible.

eleven

BREE

Damn it. I'm being awkward. This was supposed to be *fun*. I thought I could go with the flow and be chill and sexy and all the things women in movies seem to pull off without blinking. Except the truth is... I'm rattled. It's been a while since I've let anyone this close, and now that I'm here, wrapped in him, I'm completely out of my depth.

The last time I felt anything remotely like this was with Dillon. And even that feels like a different lifetime. He's the only one I've ever actually been...intimate with. And now I'm here, half tangled in sheets and unexpected nerves, trying to remember how to be with someone new without letting my past write the script.

My heart is hammering, my breaths a little too shallow. I want to play it cool and act like I've got this, but every time I look at Callan, the knot in my stomach tightens.

And yet, despite all the nervousness bubbling up inside me, Callan's just...being Callan. Calm, cool, and collected with that easygoing confidence of his. He's lying here, still fully clothed, holding me in a way that makes everything around us fade into the background. All I can focus on is the steady rhythm of his breathing, the warmth of his touch, and the way his presence seems to anchor me, making everything else...less important.

"Are you okay?" His voice is low, almost a whisper, like a stone dropping into still water and sending ripples through everything I've been trying to hold together. There's no pressure in it, no urgency. Just quiet concern threaded through every syllable like he genuinely *wants* to know—not because he's supposed to ask, but because he cares.

I look up, and his eyes meet mine with an intensity that burns straight through me. Not heat. Not lust. Just this anchoring light that makes me want to crumble and lean in at the same time. His hand rests lightly on my back, fingers barely touching like he knows I'm fragile as he lets me set the pace. And maybe I am fragile. Maybe I'm one deep breath away from falling apart. The scariest part?

I don't hate the way it feels to have someone there to catch me.

I nod, because the words won't come. They're stuck somewhere between my ribs and my throat, tangled up in all the things I've never let myself say out loud. I want to tell him that I'm scared. That I haven't let anyone this close in a long time. That this moment is so safe, it almost hurts.

And it's him.

This reckless, wild, maddening man with his rough hands and easy smile. The one who rides too fast and lives too loud. The one I always thought was too much. And yet, here he is. Quiet and steady.

Who knew Callan had a soft touch and the patience of a saint?

Right now, I'm borrowing courage from the way he looks at me. From the way his touch tells me I don't have to be anything more than exactly what I am. And for the first time in a long time, that feels like enough.

Which is probably why my mouth blurts, "I'm sorry. This isn't what you signed up for."

My voice wobbles at the end, damn it. I was aiming for breezy. The Bree who cracks jokes and never lets anyone see the full emotional breakdown brewing under the surface. That's our thing. We banter. We toss sarcasm back and forth like a hot potato. Not...this.

I try to backpedal, fast. "I mean, unless what you signed up for was an unhinged woman having a minor emotional crisis in front of your very symmetrical face. In which case, congrats."

His mouth twitches like he's fighting a smile, which only makes my brain spiral harder.

"Seriously, though," I add, softer now. "You didn't ask for this."

As I say it, part of me wonders if maybe he kind of did. Not with words, but in the way he shows up. Every time. No expectations. No pressure. Just...him.

He doesn't hesitate. "Hey, don't apologize. This... Whatever this is, it's not about signing up for anything." His voice is unwavering, like it's a simple fact. The way he says it settles my nerves. All the swirling thoughts in my head slow down, and suddenly, I don't feel so out of place.

"Besides," he adds, with that teasing grin that has his eyes sparkling, "I don't care if you're beside me, above me, or below me. I'm just glad you're here."

My heart skips a beat. Then he shoots me a playful wink, and just like that, the tension melts away.

If there's one thing Callan's good at, it's breaking through all the heavy stuff. I can't help but chuckle, a laugh bubbling up before I have the chance to stop it.

"You're insufferable," I tease.

He doesn't say anything at first, just leans in and presses a gentle kiss to my lips. It's soft, slow, and leaves me breathless. Everything else fades away—my thoughts, the room, the world —and all I can focus on is him, the warmth of his lips, and the way it makes everything else seem so far away. The sound of my contented sigh fills the room, and I swear, I could stay right here, just like this, forever.

Finally, he speaks again, his voice hushed. "I want you to know I don't expect anything, lass. We can go back downstairs and have a drink, I can take you back to Rose's, whatever you want."

I don't need to think about it. The idea of walking away from this doesn't sit right. I don't *want* to go anywhere. Not yet.

"I'd like to stay right here," I say softly.

A tender smile plays on his lips. "Aye, I'd like that, too," he murmurs, his thumb brushing gently across my cheek.

I lower my gaze for a second, trying to gather my thoughts. "You know, I've imagined this moment more times than I care to admit."

His gaze sharpens. "Oh? Do tell, Sunshine. What exactly did you imagine?"

I let out a small, breathless laugh, lifting my eyes to meet his. "Well, it usually involves being a little less clothed," I admit. There's humor in my voice, but I can tell from the way he watches me that he hears more than just the joke.

He hums as he runs his fingers gently through my hair. "That's all right, lass. We can take it slow."

Oh, he's dangerous. Not just in the reckless, bad boy way. That I can handle. This is worse. This is the kind of dangerous where a man is patient and sweet and says all the right things in a voice that could melt the polar ice caps. The kind that makes a girl start picturing things she has no business imagining. Like

Sunday mornings tangled in sheets or lazy afternoons spent stealing kisses just because.

I'm in trouble. Big, stupid, sweet Scottish man trouble.

He leans down, his lips skimming mine for a second time. So gentle but hesitant. The kiss deepens slowly, each brush of his lips igniting something inside me. His hands roam my body, fingers tracing lines of tenderness and heat that sends shivers through me.

He pulls away just enough to trail his lips along my jaw, down my neck, each kiss lingering like a quiet promise. His hand slides to the zipper of my dress and time stops. He pauses, his breath warm against my skin.

"Is this okay?"

I nod, my voice barely a whisper. "Yeah, it's okay."

I shift slightly, sitting up to give him room to slide the straps off my shoulders. The fabric slips down, pooling at my waist, and the sudden brush of cool air against my skin makes me shiver.

He rises, his eyes never leaving mine, and takes my hand to pull me to my feet. The dress slips the rest of the way, puddling on the floor, leaving me in nothing but my lace bra and panties. His gaze doesn't waver, his expression hungry and reverent, making my pulse flutter wildly.

His eyes wander slowly, like he's taking in a masterpiece, and I feel every inch of his stare like a touch.

"You're breathtaking," he murmurs, and the words hit me like a spark. There isn't a single part of me that wants to hide from him.

My fingers find the buttons of his shirt, trembling in a way that betrays me. One by one, I ease them open, revealing smooth, warm skin and muscle that makes my breath hitch in my throat.

My fingers graze over the hard line of his chest. "If I had

known this was hiding underneath, I'd have demanded a private showing sooner."

This still counts as innocent, right? I mean, technically, I'm clothed if you count underwear. And he's just shirtless. In a kilt. Which, god help me, is doing *things* to my insides I wasn't emotionally prepared for.

I've dreamt about a moment like this with him. Quiet little fantasies I'd never say out loud. Only now, it's happening. He's real. This is real. And it's so much better than anything my imagination could've cooked up.

I still don't know how far I want to take this. My breath quickens, my heart pounds like it's not sure whether to race forward or hold back. But here, in this moment, with his hand skimming gently over my hip, his touch asking instead of taking, this feels right. Not rushed. Not dangerous. Just... safe. Like maybe I don't have to decide everything all at once. Like maybe I can let myself want him, one heartbeat at a time.

The sheets are cool against my skin as we fall back onto the bed together. The solid weight of his body presses into mine, heat radiating off him.

I bite back a gasp as his lips trace a path down my body. He moves slowly, pulling the straps of my bra down with such care that I feel it all—the soft glide of the fabric, the cool air hitting my exposed skin, and the sudden rush of goosebumps that follow. The feeling of him, of his mouth on me, is almost too much. Every touch sends a jolt of desire and vulnerability through me that I haven't felt in ages. It's as if he's claiming pieces of me with each kiss, each caress, and I can't decide whether to pull him closer or keep my distance.

When his teeth graze my nipple, a moan escapes my lips, the sensation shooting straight through me. My back arches off the bed, pressing into his touch, wanting more. His tongue swirls around the sensitive bud before he sucks it into his mouth, and I see stars.

My fingers tangle in his hair as he lavishes attention on my breasts. Each flick of his tongue, each gentle scrape of teeth, sends another wave of pleasure crashing over me. I'm breathless, panting, and completely lost in the feeling of him worshipping my body.

When he pulls away to stand beside the bed, the absence of his touch is immediate. But his eyes never leave mine.

His slow smile does nothing to calm the heat between us. "You have no idea how much I want you right now," he says, his voice gravelly, like a whisper of promise and desire. I hear the weight of his words, feel it settle into my bones.

That's when the panic rises. Not from the way he looks at me. God, no. It's everything else. The intensity in his gaze, the rawness in his voice that makes my pulse spike and my breath shallow. I want him. I want this. And yet, there's a chasm between wanting him and being ready for this. My skin hums under his touch, but my mind can't keep up.

I shift on the bed, fingers fumbling with the edge of the blanket as I try to distract myself from the way my body reacts to him. His touch. His words. Everything about him is like a magnet pulling me closer, but my hands, my nerves—they're reaching for anything that can keep me from falling too fast.

Callan doesn't move quickly. Doesn't rush. Instead, he kneels beside the bed, his hands gentle as they find mine. His thumb strokes across my knuckles, and when he looks up at me again, the heat is still in his eyes, but there's also patience.

"Hey," he says, his voice a gentle rumble. "No rush. Not with me."

My skin tingles under his touch. He's giving me every chance to stop him and trusting me to choose whether or not I do.

Callan watches me for a moment, his eyes tracing every little shift in my expression. Then, slowly, he stands. "I want to make you feel good," he says gently, like he's considering his words carefully. "That's all I want. You don't have to do anything you're not comfortable with, but..."

His eyes meet mine, searching with the same intensity, but more tender now. "I have an idea, if you're open to it."

I give a small nod. "Okay."

His mouth curves into the smallest, encouraging smile. Like he knows I'm trying, and that alone matters to him.

"Touch yourself," he says quietly. "Do whatever feels good. I won't do anything unless you ask me to."

Oh.

I didn't expect that.

The way he says it isn't dirty or performative. It's more like a gift. Like he's handing the reins over to me and saying, *Here. You set the pace. You're in control.*

I reach down slowly and slip my fingers beneath the lace of my panties. He watches me with a fierce intensity, his gaze darkening as my fingers graze my most sensitive spot. I'm already wet, my body responding eagerly to Callan's commanding presence.

"That's it, lass. Let me see you," he murmurs.

I let out a soft moan, my hips lifting slightly off the bed as I circle my clit with featherlight touches. It's almost too much, the combination of his stare and my own fingers pushing me toward the edge embarrassingly fast.

He's watching me like he's starving, and I'm the only thing that can satisfy him. Like he wants to devour me whole.

My fingers move faster, circling and stroking, teasing myself higher. The pressure builds with each passing second, and I watch as he palms his cock through his kilt, his jaw tightening with each circle of my fingers. The sight of him touching himself, the raw need etched across his face, the barely restrained hunger in his eyes almost sends me over the edge.

"Christ, you're perfect," he breathes, his voice strained as his hand presses rhythmically over his kilt. The muscles in his forearm flex with each stroke, and I can't tear my eyes away from the hypnotic movement. "Keep going, just like that."

My back arches involuntarily as pleasure builds, coiling tighter with each pass of my fingers. I'm not performing for him. This is too raw, too real for that. Being watched by him this way is intoxicating.

"Callan," I gasp, my free hand clutching at the sheets. "I'm close..."

His palm stills. "Let go, Sunshine. I want to see you come undone for me."

His voice is a velvet command that unravels me completely. I fall apart under his gaze, wave after wave of pleasure washing over me as my body trembles. I can't hold back the cry that escapes my lips, my hips bucking against my hand as the orgasm crashes through me.

As I slowly come back to myself, I become acutely aware of Callan's presence. He moves toward me then, lowering himself to the bed and pulling me into his arms. His lips brush gently against my forehead, my cheeks, and then, finally, my lips.

"That was the most beautiful thing I've ever seen in my life," he murmurs, his accent thicker than I've heard it before.

"Wait, what about—"

My hand reaches for him, but he catches it, bringing my fingers to his lips instead. "Don't worry about me," he interrupts. "That was for you."

I raise an eyebrow. "Very chivalrous of you."

His grin is wicked. "I am Scottish. We invented chivalry, didn't we?"

"Pretty sure that was the French," I mutter.

He gives an exaggerated gasp. "Lies. Slander. You're lucky I like you."

"Like me?" I tease, nudging him with my foot. "After all that? Just like?"

That deep, rumbling laugh escapes him, wrapping around me like a warm blanket. "Fine. I'm utterly ruined for anyone else."

"Better," I whisper, right before his mouth finds mine again, soft and unhurried, like he's not trying to spark a fire but steady the one that's already burning between us.

When I finally press into his chest, flushed and breathless, he wraps me up without hesitation, tucking me under his chin like I'm his favorite thing he's ever held.

twelve

CALLAN

B ree stayed the night, and I'm still trying to wrap my head
around it. Her smooth, bare legs are peeking out from
under the sheets. She's wearing my shirt and nothing else. It's
damn near killing me how she looks so soft and completely at
ease, curled up in the quiet morning light. I should be embarrassed, watching her like a creep. But I can't help myself.

I kept my distance last night, though. I didn't want to freak
her out or mess up whatever this is between us. So, I stayed on
the edge of the bed, practically hanging off it like a damn
acrobat while I let her have her space and find comfort in her
own time. Now it's late morning, and she's still out cold.

Bree. The woman who's usually buzzing around, talking a
mile a minute, always on the go, acting like she's got somewhere
more important to be, snoozing like she hasn't got a single worry
in the world. It's almost as if the universe hit the pause button
on her for once.

Last night definitely didn't go like I thought it would, but
that's not a bad thing. It was vulnerable. Real. And if there's

one thing I know, it's that having her trust me is worth more than any impulsive moment of lust.

Not that I don't want that, too. Hell, I want it more than my next breath.

But watching her and really *seeing* her struggle? It actually fucking wrecked me. Bree, who's always so strong, so ready to face everything with a smile or a joke, struggling in a way I can't even begin to understand... All I wanted was to make it better for her. I would've done anything to take away her hurt, even if it was just for a second. I would've taken on the world if it meant she didn't have to carry that weight anymore.

My whole life, I've been the one who steps outside the lines. Always looking for something to break the monotony, always pushing myself a little further than I probably should. It's like I can't sit still, so I fill the space with distractions. Sometimes, I wonder if I've been doing it just to avoid feeling too much. I always seem to find myself testing my own limits.

Knox was always the protector growing up. The steadfast one who always had his shit together. Lucy was sweetness personified. And then there was me. The wildcard. I was barely three when Dad passed, so I don't remember much about him. What I do remember is Mum and Knox, and the way they struggled to keep it all together.

So, I did my own thing. Always have. It's easier than dealing with the unspoken stuff.

But with Bree? It's different.

The few times I've been with her, I haven't craved the chaos. And that's what really messes with my head. How many other women have I sat with in hotel rooms, watching rom-coms? Zero. None. With her, I did it without even thinking about it.

Just...being near her is enough. Her presence alone gives me a rush but not the usual adrenaline-fueled kind. I care about her. I want to be her safe place. I find myself simply wanting more of *her*. I don't usually do this...emotional stuff. And that's what scares the hell out of me.

The sheets rustle, and I glance over in time to see her eyes fluttering open. Most people would call them blue, but they're not. Not really. They're the shade of blue you see in the sky right before dusk, shifting with every little emotion and every change in her mood. It's like her eyes have lived a thousand lives and held a million secrets.

Damn, that's some sappy shit right there. What is she doing to me?

"Good morning," she murmurs, her voice still wrapped in sleep, but somehow, the sweetest sound I've ever heard. The whole room gets brighter, like the sun's just decided to show up.

"Morning, Sunshine," I say, a little too much affection slipping into my voice. "Sleep well?"

She stretches beside me, and my shirt rides up her thighs in a way that's almost criminal. For a split second, my gaze dips. I mean... I'm only human. I drag my focus back to her face. *Pay attention.*

I did sleep, eventually. After hours of lying there, her soft breaths in the quiet darkness replaying in my mind. Every second of last night is etched into me, like it matters more than anything else ever has.

"Mm, very. Your bed is dangerously comfortable."

I chuckle. "Aye, it's a struggle to leave it most mornings." And right now, that's the truth. There's something about her lying here at ease in my bed that makes everything else seem less important. The world outside could burn down, and I wouldn't care as long as I could stay right here, next to her.

Her blonde hair is a mess across the pillow, strands spilling in every direction, and damn if it doesn't wreck me in the best way. She belongs here. This is exactly where she's meant to be. The thought sneaks up on me, wedges itself somewhere deep, and I have no clue what the hell to do with it.

I should shake it off and make some cocky remark, but instead, I just stare at her like she's the first bit of peace I've seen in a long time.

"Are you hungry?" I finally ask.

"Starving..." She rolls over onto her side to face me. "For food that is."

I can't help myself—I lean in to steal a quick kiss. Just a brush of my mouth against hers, but it's enough to make my pulse stutter and my self-control falter.

I reluctantly pull back and haul myself out of bed, forcing my legs to work as every part of me screams to climb back in.

I've spent the last few hours staring at the ceiling, wide awake, thinking about all the things I want to do to her because the truth is, I'm aching for her. Physically, painfully aching. Have been since the moment she fell asleep, tangled up against me like it was the most natural thing in the world.

"I'm going to grab a quick shower before making breakfast," I say, turning away from her and adjusting my boxers as casually as possible. My body's betraying me in the most obvious way, and the thin fabric isn't hiding a damn thing.

"Take your time," she calls after me, her voice still husky with sleep.

I slip into the bathroom and close the door, leaning against it as I exhale slowly. My cock is painfully hard, throbbing against the cotton of my boxers. The pressure's been building all night, through every innocent touch, every quiet breath beside me.

I turn the shower on, cranking the temperature to cold, hoping it might help. All I can think about is Bree in my bed, wearing my shirt, her scent all over my sheets.

"Fuck," I mutter, stepping under the spray.

The water cascades down my chest, over my stomach, and still, I'm rock hard. I close my eyes, trying to think of anything else, but my mind keeps circling back to her.

I wrap my hand around my length but immediately stop. No. I can't do this. Not with her just on the other side of that door. It feels...wrong, despite how badly I need the release.

I pull my hand away, gripping the shower wall instead, letting the icy water pound against my back. My body's still throbbing, demanding attention, but my mind's made up. I'll suffer through it.

"Gentleman," I mutter sarcastically to myself. This is Bree. She deserves better than me getting off while she's innocently waiting for breakfast in the next room.

I stand there until my breathing steadies and my body calms down enough that I can function. The cold water helps but not enough. This is going to be a long morning.

When I finally step out, I wrap a towel around my waist and stare at my reflection in the steamy mirror. "Get it together, MacKenzie."

I brush my teeth, splash more cold water on my face, and finally work up the courage to open the door.

I find her sitting on my bed, sheets pooled around her waist, scrolling through her phone. My T-shirt hangs loose on her frame, slipping off one shoulder to reveal smooth skin I'm desperate to taste. When she looks up at me, her smile nearly stops my heart.

I turn to grab a change of clothes from the dresser, towel still barely hanging onto my hips. "I'm just gonna get changed real quick."

"Want me to look away?"

I glance over my shoulder with a smirk. "Not necessary. I'm fairly confident in my assets."

She lets out a laugh, shaking her head. "Cocky."

"Only when I've earned it."

I grab a pair of boxers, jeans, and a plain tee, catching the way her eyes settle on me before she quickly looks back at her phone, totally pretending not to sneak a peek. I shake my head with a chuckle and head back into the bathroom, changing quickly and trying not to think too hard about the girl in my bed wearing my shirt and absolutely nothing else underneath it.

Gentleman, remember? Gentleman.

I rake a hand through my hair and step back into the room, fully dressed and trying like hell to look composed. "Feel free to use the shower and help yourself to whatever you need in the bathroom." I gesture toward the en suite, my tone casual, though my mind is already running wild with all the things I could do with her in there. "I'll get the food started. Come down whenever you're ready."

"Yes, sir."

Fuck.

Two little words, and they nearly level me. Her voice is all sugar laced with mischief, and it lands like a sucker punch to every muscle in my body—especially the one currently doing all the thinking. My brain flatlines. Blood rushes south so fast I see stars.

I cock a brow, trying to play it cool, like I'm not seconds away from begging her to say it again. "You calling me sir now?"

She shrugs, all false wide-eyed innocence. That shirt of mine hangs dangerously off one shoulder, revealing smooth skin I could spend the rest of my life kissing. "I'm just following orders. You're the one in charge, right?"

Christ.

My frayed self-control is hanging by a thread, and she's

standing there with the scissors, one finger on the blade, smiling like she knows exactly what she's doing.

I shift, trying to ease the pressure in my jeans, and bite back a groan. "You keep saying things like that, and breakfast's gonna be very delayed."

Her teeth sink into her bottom lip.

"You're going to be the death of me, Sunshine," I mutter, voice rougher than I mean for it to be. "Get that perky arse ready and come downstairs."

I turn before I do anything extremely ungentlemanly, like toss her back in the bed and make her say it again.

Preferably while not wearing anything at all.

"Fine," she calls after me. "But only because I'm feeling generous!"

I make my way downstairs, scanning the kitchen for what I've got to work with. By the time she makes her way down, what started as a simple bacon and eggs situation has somehow morphed into a full-on brunch feast. I might've gotten a little carried away, but whatever. It looks damn good.

When she walks in, she lets out a little gasp. "Oh my gosh, this looks amazing! I figured you'd offer some burnt toast or something."

I clutch my chest dramatically. "You've cut me deep, lass. My culinary skills are a work of art, and here you are, insulting them like that. I might never recover."

She bursts out laughing. "Oh, come on. I'm just giving you a hard time. Seriously, this looks like it belongs in a fancy café, not a kitchen that could probably double as a war zone."

The counter is covered in plates of golden French toast stacked high, dusted with powdered sugar. There's thick-cut bacon, scrambled eggs with chives and cheddar, and fresh berries tossed in a bowl.

"All made in twenty minutes," I say. "Impressed yet?"

She just blinks at me. "Are you secretly auditioning to be someone's husband?"

I grin. "Careful now. You keep this up, and I'll start charging you for brunch. It's gourmet, after all."

"I'll take my chances." She pops a berry into her mouth, eyes fluttering shut when she lets out a moan. And I am not okay.

I grip the edge of the counter.

God help me.

"Well, you've been warned." I step back, giving her a slow, teasing bow. "I'll be accepting payment in the form of compliments...or, if you're feeling generous, maybe something a little more creative."

Her brows lift, amusement dancing in her eyes. "Oh? And what exactly would that be?"

I smirk, letting my gaze sweep over her in a way that makes her cheeks flush. "I don't know, Sunshine. Maybe a whispered thank you in that pretty little voice of yours... Preferably right up against my ear."

She bites her lip, but a smile breaks through anyway, and damn, if that isn't the best payment I could ever ask for.

When I gesture for her to sit, her eyes light up in that way they do when something small makes her genuinely happy, as if me making her breakfast has already become the highlight of her morning.

I load her plate up with all the good stuff because she deserves it. More than that, I *want* to do this for her, even if she doesn't realize how much I enjoy it.

For a while, we eat in easy silence. Then she looks up, something curious in her expression, like a thought is teetering on the edge of her tongue. Instead of speaking, she turns toward the window, her gaze lingering outside.

"I didn't get a good look last night, but you have some

incredible views here," she says, her voice almost reverent as her eyes glance over the landscape.

"Aye, I do."

I catch myself smiling, a little proud, even though I don't really want to admit it. This place is my pride and joy. I've put in blood, sweat, and probably more money than I'd care to count into getting it where it is now. When I first bought it, it was a dump. A far cry from the place I wanted it to be. But the location? The loch just out the back with the hills rolling around me? I couldn't pass it up.

There's peace here, a stillness that feels like it could swallow me whole if I let it. It's not as remote as Knox's place up in the mountains, but it's mine.

The neighbors aren't too far, but they're far enough. I'm surrounded by hills, water, and the kind of tranquility that makes me feel like the world could stop spinning for a moment, and I wouldn't mind one damn bit.

I'm the kind of guy who can thrive on chaos. I'm the one people turn to for a good time, the guy who's always ready to take things to the next level. Hell, even I get a rush from it. Adrenaline's the closest thing to feeling alive that I know.

The thing is, I've learned over the years that I can't be that guy all the time. There's only so much wild I can take before I need to step back and breathe. That's why I chose this place.

It's like a reset button. After the loudness of life, I need the calm to clear my head. To remind myself that I don't always need to be "on."

Maybe that's why Bree's been so good for me. She offers a stillness that lets me recharge. I can just...be. It feels damn good.

I catch myself zoning out, getting lost in the view, the way the light hits the water and paints everything in shades of gold. Then I refocus, pulling myself back to the moment. That's when I see Bree again, still staring out the window, her hair catching the light in a way that makes everything feel like it's a little too perfect.

I can tell she wants to say more but she hesitates. Instead of speaking, she looks back down at her plate, her fork absently pushing food around.

"Is everything okay?" I ask.

Her gaze flickers back to mine, still a little guarded. She gives me a half smile, but it doesn't reach her eyes. "Yes, great, really. I just, uh...wanted to thank you. For last night and this morning. I didn't want to make it awkward because I definitely already did that last night."

I lean back, crossing my arms as I give her a look. "No need to thank me. I promise you, lass, there was nothing awkward about that for me."

Her cheeks flush, a faint pink creeping across her skin, and damn, if that isn't just the most adorable thing.

"Get that smirk off your face, Callan," she warns, her voice full of amusement and mild embarrassment.

"Who, me?" The smirk stays, of course, because I can't help it.

Just as she's about to respond, her phone rings, and I watch her face shift into full-on panic. "Oh my god, it's Rose. I didn't tell her I wasn't going back to her place last night."

I can't resist teasing her. "I'm pretty sure she figured it out. In fact, I think everyone did."

Her hand shoots out and swats me on the arm, and yeah, I definitely deserved that. I rub the spot where she hit me, pretending to be wounded.

She answers the phone, taking it from her ear and muttering under her breath before putting it back up to her face. "Good morning, my favorite Auntie Rose!" she says, though there's a nervous edge in her voice that she doesn't quite manage to hide.

There's a brief pause as she listens to Rose.

"I had...a lovely time, yes," she winces, and I bite my lip to keep from laughing. I already know exactly what's being said on the other end of the line, even though I can't hear a single word of it. The tone, her expressions, the way she's squirming... It all speaks volumes.

"Um, I'm sure Cal will bring me back in a little while?" she says, looking at me like she's not sure what to do. I nod, offering a reassuring smile.

"Okay, yep, no problem. I'll see you a bit later then. Okay, bye!"

She hangs up and leans her head back with a groan, her face practically glowing with embarrassment, and I can't hold it in anymore. A laugh bursts out of me, loud and full of amusement. She's just too adorable, and I'm eating it up.

"Stop it! It's not funny," she protests. "Let's call one of your aunts and give her a play-by-play, see how much you like it!"

I raise an eyebrow. "If I know Rose," I start, "then she probably congratulated you but asked you to spare her the details, considering I'm kind of one of her bosses."

Her eyes narrow, and that's all the confirmation I need. I hit the nail on the head, and she knows it.

"Right?" I tease. "That's probably why she was so diplomatic. She didn't want to hear all of it. Just the highlights."

Her eyes narrow even further, suspicious delight warring on her face. "You're terrible," she mutters, but there's no real heat behind her words.

"Only for you, lass." I flash her my most charming smile. "So, what's your plan? Going to see Juliette today?"

She shakes her head. "No, I don't think so. I'll give her one day of wedded bliss before I go bothering her with my antics."

"Back to Rose's, then?" I ask, though I don't want her to leave just yet. It's a rare thing, having her here, and I'm not ready to give that up.

She offers a subtle nod, taking a sip of her coffee, eyes darting over to me. "Yeah, I guess so. She said she's going to be out most of the day, but she'll be back later in the afternoon."

"It's my lucky day then," I say, resting my elbows on the table. "Unless you're wanting to get back?"

A sly smile spreads across her face. "What did you have in mind?"

"How about a ride? I kinda missed having you on the back of my bike."

I say it casually, but that ride six months ago still haunts me in the best way. Her body pressed close to mine, her laughter in the wind, the rush of adrenaline that came as the world fell away. But I'll never forget the way she looked when we stopped, the bruises on her body that didn't belong there. It stayed with me.

I can't get that moment out of my head.

Now, I want a do-over. I want to give her the ride of her life, where nothing but pure joy fills the space between us. No worries. No past hurts. Just the freedom of the road and her laughter in my ear.

She raises an eyebrow, glancing down at her bare legs with a smirk. "Only one problem there, danger boy. I'm currently pantless and have nothing else to wear."

She's cute. I definitely didn't forget about that.

"Don't worry," I say with a wink. "I might've picked up a few things for you, just in case we ever found ourselves in this situation again."

Curiosity dances in her eyes. "Well, color me intrigued," she says, propping her chin on her hand. "Whatcha got for me?"

thirteen

BREE

Apparently, Callan had a little chat with Juliette, and voilà, everything fits just right. I'm rocking a fitted black leather jacket, tight black jeans, and ankle boots that scream, *Who is this girl?* Not exactly my everyday vibe, but honestly, I'm not mad about it.

I give myself one last once-over, tugging the leather into place, and *damn*. I look good. Callan knew exactly what he was doing.

"Damn, Sunshine," Callan mutters, his voice full of that mischievous spark I've come to expect from him. His eyes roam over me, like he's appreciating a rare, expensive piece of art. "You look like you were made to be on the back of my bike."

I can't help myself. I give a little spin, letting the leather catch the light. "Not gonna lie," I say. "I'm inclined to agree. You might've just created a monster."

His lips curve into that infuriatingly charming smile, and I damn near melt into a puddle right there. But I don't. I'm stronger than that...mostly.

"That so? Sounds like a challenge, lass."

I step closer, letting my gaze linger on him longer than necessary. The way his own jacket stretches across his broad shoulders, clinging just enough to make me wonder what's underneath... It's lethal. The way his jaw shifts as he smiles does things to me that I'm not prepared to handle. He's pure temptation.

I arch an eyebrow, leaning in a touch and letting the teasing lilt in my voice do all the heavy lifting. "You think you're ready for that kind of trouble?"

His grin turns dangerous. When those blue eyes flare with that wild, irresistible spark, it's the kind of look that promises everything I should probably stay the hell away from. It's impossible not to want it when every inch of me is screaming *yes*.

"Oh, I'm more than ready," he says, his voice rough around the edges. "Question is, can you keep up?"

I tilt my head, casual, like this is just another challenge I'm about to dominate. His gaze doesn't move, not even a blink, and the air between us practically crackles. This tension could set fire to the entire block if we're not careful.

Then he moves, reaching for my brand-new helmet with a confidence that screams he's in control of every second. He holds it out, his smirk practically daring me. "Ready to ride, monster?"

I take the helmet from his hands, our fingers brushing in a way that sends a jolt of electricity straight through me. His touch lingers, but just for a second. "Born ready," I say as I slip the helmet on.

He leads me out to his motorcycle, and it really is a thing of beauty. A sleek black beast that looks like it eats lesser bikes for breakfast. The late morning sun hits the polished chrome, making it glint like something straight out of a dream.

Callan swings his leg over with that effortless confidence

that's so *him*. The engine roars to life, deep and satisfying, rumbling through the air like it's alive and daring the world to keep up.

I hesitate for half a second, taking in the man, the bike, the moment. Then, without overthinking it, I climb on behind him. The second I press against him, the heat from his back seeps through the leather, and everything clicks into place. The strength of his presence is undeniable, and it's like my body just *knows* this is where I'm supposed to be. A perfect fit.

My arms naturally lock around his waist, and I can't help but dig my fingers into the worn leather of his jacket. The movement pulls me closer to him, and for just a split second, the muscles under his jacket flex slightly, like he's subconsciously reacting to my touch.

I lean in close, yelling over the roar of the engine. "Where are we going?"

He turns his head enough for his voice to carry over the noise. "My favorite spot!"

Without another word, he guns the throttle, and the bike surges forward like it has a mind of its own. The rush of wind hits me instantly, cool and exhilarating. Everything around us speeds up, the world blurring in the best possible way. It's like the air, the ground, and the whole damn world is moving with us. Alive, and maybe just a little bit reckless.

I smile against his back, the thrill of the ride pulsing through me. Every turn he takes, every shift in speed, sends his muscles flexing under my grip. I hold on tighter, not just for balance, but because there's something magnetic about being this close to him. It makes my pulse race faster than the bike beneath us. It's not just from the ride anymore. It's *him*.

It's different this time. The sun shines down on us, casting everything in that golden light that makes the world seem like it's in slow motion. The landscape blurs past in a sweep of green fields, flashes of wildflowers, and the smooth curve of the road, but none of it really holds my attention like he does.

We roll to a stop, and for a moment, I'm completely disoriented. How long have we been riding? Ten minutes? An hour? Time slips through my fingers, the blur of the scenery and the calming scent of Callan filling the air like some kind of irresistible, distracting cologne.

I can't stop noticing it. I'm torn between wanting to inhale it like it's the world's greatest perfume and trying to ignore the fact that it's making my pulse quicken. Not that I'd ever admit that.

Nope. Definitely not.

I'm doing my best to shut down the mental gymnastics because I really just want to enjoy today.

As I climb off the bike and take in our surroundings, I realize I've been here before. I remember how stunning it was the last time, the air thick with fall's chill, everything draped in the cool shadows of midnight, silvered by the moon. This time, in the daylight, with spring starting to paint the world with color, it's like stepping into a whole new place. A different kind of magic entirely.

The air is crisp, sharp with that earthy scent only spring can bring, the smell of life waking up from its long winter nap. Everything's so still and quiet, but it's the kind that feels alive.

Sunlight spills over everything, filtering through the scattered clouds. It catches the rolling hills, casting shadows that shift as if the land is breathing in time with the wind. And the snow stubbornly clings to the hillsides in patches, like winter's refusing to let go, unwilling to admit defeat.

And then there's the lake. It's like a scene from a postcard. Timeless, untouched, and impossibly calm. The surface sparkles, glinting in the sunlight, so impossibly smooth and clear it feels like stepping into another world.

I take a deep breath, letting the brisk air fill my lungs. "I could sit here forever and never get tired of this view."

Callan dismounts in one smooth, practiced motion, pulling off his helmet with that easy confidence of his. Before I can shift, he's in front of me, his presence like a magnet I can't escape. His hands are strong but careful as he reaches up to remove my helmet, cradling my head like it's the most natural thing in the world.

"You see why I come here often, aye?"

That damn accent of his makes even the simplest words sound like poetry. I could listen to him say the dumbest thing in the world and still get lost in it.

I glance at him, ready to answer, but then I catch sight of how he's standing, tall and broad-shouldered, looking out at the horizon like he owns the whole world. For a second, the view doesn't register. It's just him, standing there, that steals my attention. Watching him is like its own kind of magic, pulling me in, making everything else fade away.

It should be strange, right? This big, leather-clad guy just standing still in the middle of all this nature, like he's part of it, not some intruder just passing through. But with Callan, it's not strange at all. It just...fits.

I reach for his hand, craving that little bit of contact like it's the air I need to breathe.

He looks down, his gaze softening when he sees our fingers tangled together. That small smile tugs at my heart, and when he squeezes my hand, it leaves me breathless.

"You're going home in, what, four days?" he asks.

I wish he hadn't brought it up. That little reminder yanks me out of this perfect, blissed-out bubble I've been living in since I got here. Here, there's no crappy job with a boss who acts like "personal time" is just some fairytale people tell themselves to get through the day. No exhausting drama with drunken exes.

It's just me, my best friend, the kind of scenery that makes your soul lighter...and him.

"Yep," I say, sighing dramatically. "I wanted to stay longer, but apparently *living the dream* isn't a valid excuse for more time off. Who knew?"

He shrugs. "Well, at least you're not dealing with me full-time."

I laugh. "Oh, trust me, I'm definitely gonna miss you. Especially when I'm knee-deep in a pile of...you don't want to know." I make a face like the very thought of it is a crime. "I'll be wishing I was here, getting distracted by your ridiculous charm instead."

He leans in just enough to make my pulse skip. "You know, I was going to fire back with some snarky comment, but...I'll take that as a compliment."

"As you should," I reply. Because as much as I tease, I mean every word.

I need to figure out what I'm doing here, and what I'm doing with *him*.

Over the past year, I've gotten dangerously close to feeling too much for Callan. And it's not just a crush or a passing phase. It's deeper than that.

What I had with Dillon was real. Sure, the end was messy, there's no denying that. Before it all fell apart, it was easy, young love. It was comfortable in a way that felt like it could have gone on forever if life hadn't decided to ruin it.

But with Callan? It's exhilarating in a way I didn't even know I was capable of feeling. He's the kind of person who makes your blood race, who pushes you to take risks you'd normally avoid, who somehow manages to be both infuriating and irresistible all at once.

I can't love him, though. That's not how this works, right? Besides, it doesn't matter. He doesn't seem like the type to settle down, and even if he was, I'm not sure he'd want to settle down with *me*. So what's the point of even thinking about it?

I know myself well enough to realize I can't go too far with this. A little thrill is fine, but too much, and I'll catch feelings. That's what I do. I care too much. I always have. I let myself fall into things until it's more than just fun, more than just a temporary escape.

A kiss never hurt anyone, right?

My mind races in a thousand different directions as Callan's hand lands at the small of my back, pulling me closer. His solid body presses against mine, and the world shrinks down, until it's just us, alone in this charged little space. Every inch of me is acutely aware of the heat radiating off his skin, the strength in the hand at my back.

He leans down, his breath warm against my neck. His voice is a soothing murmur that sends a shiver down my spine. "What was that you were saying about a kiss never hurting anyone?"

Oh god. How much of that did I say out loud? My heart stutters, heat flooding my face as I hope and pray he didn't hear every single word.

I swallow, trying to steady the erratic pounding of my pulse. The world feels like it's tilting, spinning just a little too fast for me to catch up. "I, uh... I didn't mean—"

He cuts me off with a chuckle, his thumb brushing the edge of my jaw. "Don't worry, Sunshine," he says, his voice low and full of that playful confidence. "I'm not going to bite."

He pauses. "Unless you want me to."

And there it is. That wicked gleam in his eyes that does *things* to me, making my heart race and my knees weak. I can't help but laugh, even as my mind scrambles to catch up with my body's reaction. "You're not playing fair."

His smile widens. "Never claimed to be, lass."

There's no point in trying to backtrack now. I do the next best thing and take a deep breath, pulling myself together. "What if I said yes?" The words tumble out before I can stop them. "What if I said I wanted you to?"

His hand slides up from my back to cup my face. The touch is gentle, but there's nothing soft about the look in his eyes.

This is so dangerous. I could blame last night on alcohol and all the wedded bliss surrounding us. But now, I've got no one to blame but myself.

His gaze drops to my lips, and my breath catches in my throat. "Be sure about this, Sunshine," he murmurs. "Because once I start, I don't think I'll want to stop."

My answer comes not in words but in action. I rise onto my tiptoes, closing that last sliver of space between us. Our lips brush, and that whisper of contact is like striking a match to kindling.

His control snaps. His hand slides to the nape of my neck, fingers threading through my hair, tilting my head with just the right amount of force. His teeth catch my bottom lip in a gentle bite that sends a shockwave through every single nerve in my body.

I gasp against his mouth, and he doesn't hesitate. His lips press harder, deepening the kiss with an intensity that matches the heat pooling low in my stomach. It's everything I never knew I needed and more. Explosive. Consuming. His tongue traces the seam of my lips, and when I open for him, he groans, a sound so raw and hungry it vibrates through my entire body. The taste of him is addictive, and I crave more with every passing second. His tongue slides against mine, not demanding but coaxing.

I press closer, my hands fisting in his jacket, desperate for something to hold on to as his kiss turns possessive. His teeth graze my bottom lip again, tugging gently before soothing the sting with his tongue.

His other hand moves down to my waist, fingers digging into my hip. A soft moan escapes me as he pulls me flush against him, the hard planes of his body pressing into mine.

I'm completely lost in him. It's just us and the way his tongue moves against mine, the heat of his body, making me feel like I'm the only thing that matters in this whole world.

We stumble back, crashing against the bike, its cold metal digging into my back. His body molds perfectly against mine, and suddenly I can't tell if we've been kissing for minutes or hours. Or hell, maybe it's been seconds, but none of it matters. The only thing that does is him, and the way he feels so damn good, so *right*.

He pulls away and steps back. I'm left standing in front of him, breathless, my heart hammering like it's trying to make a break for freedom.

I've been wandering around in a layer of emotional fog, and he's the one who's managed to pull me out of it. I could try to convince myself that it's just the adrenaline, the way his lips felt like they were made for mine, or the way he looks at me like I'm not just a random person in his life but, I don't know, *important*.

Deep down, I know better. It's not just the kiss—though *holy hell*, the man kisses like he was put on this earth solely for that purpose. And it's not just the rush, or the way my chest feels like it's about to explode every time he looks at me like I'm his favorite problem to solve.

It's everything. It's the way he texted me good morning for

six months straight, no matter the time zone. The way he remembered that I hate bananas but love banana flavoring. It's how he actually listened when I vented about work and never once made me feel like I was too much. It's how he makes me laugh when I least expect it and somehow always knows when I need a minute of quiet instead of words.

It's the way he makes me feel like I could completely fall apart, and he'd be there, hands out and ready to catch every piece without a second thought.

BREE

"What do you mean he's going into work today? Doesn't he know he's supposed to be out here, whisking you off on a romantic, honeymoon-worthy adventure?" I tease into the phone.

Juliette's laughter bursts through the line. "We're leaving for our honeymoon tomorrow, so he had to go to the distillery to wrap some stuff up," she says. "Besides, now I get to hang out with you all day. Get your butt over here."

"Well, in that case, yes, ma'am. Let me just check with your aunt to see if it's okay to borrow her car for the day." I start heading toward the kitchen.

"She's already good with it," she assures me. "I texted her this morning."

I chuckle. "All right then, I'll be there in a bit!"

I hang up with Juliette, toss a quick goodbye to Rose, and grab the keys from the counter. As I slide on my boots—yes, the ones Callan gave me—I can't help but give them an extra moment of attention. Like, seriously, how did a pair of boots end up making everything more...*real?*

Yesterday was *wonderful*. Callan is like the perfect cocktail of funny, witty, and so easy to be around. Also, ridiculously hot. Even so, it's not just his charm or the way he can make me laugh at the most random times. It's the way he makes the world lighter. He's got an energy I didn't know I needed until he walked in and handed it to me on a silver platter.

When he brought me back to Rose's place, I could practically feel the hesitation hanging in the air. Both of us were trying to figure out how to stretch the moment without actually saying it out loud. He didn't want to say goodbye, and I sure as hell didn't want to let go either. It was like we both knew something, but neither of us was ready to acknowledge it yet.

Now, here I am, pulling up Juliette's gravel driveway. She's sitting on the porch, glowing in a way that only someone about to become a mom can, like the universe itself is shining down on her.

"Hello, precious mama!" I squeal, completely forgetting how to walk for a second and nearly tripping over my own feet as I dash up the porch steps. I throw my arms around her, squeezing her like I might never let go. It still doesn't seem real. My best friend, the one who used to steal my clothes and gossip about the guys we used to *think* were cute, is going to have a baby. A *baby*.

It feels like just yesterday we were two clueless teenagers trying to figure out how to survive high school, and now...now she's about to bring a tiny human into the world. It's surreal in the best way.

"How is my future niece or nephew treating you?" I ask, plopping down on the chair next to her.

She flashes a grin, her hand instinctively resting on her stomach like it's already second nature. "Not too bad. So far, I'm just horribly exhausted. And a little nauseous, but I'm not complaining."

"Ah, the joys of pregnancy. This is amazing, Jules. You and Knox are going to have the most gorgeous baby on the planet. Seriously. I'm so excited for you."

I swallow hard, trying to push the lump in my throat down before it decides to make an appearance. The truth is, I wish I could be here for all of it. The doctor's appointments, the cravings, the late-night chats where she vents about everything. I'm going to miss so much of this just because I'm too far away.

"Thanks," she says quietly. She gives me a slight smile, but then her expression shifts. "So uh, I think we have something to talk about?"

Oh. Yep, that's fair. I pause, and for a split second, it feels like my heart might launch itself straight through my ribs. I give her an exaggerated eye roll, trying to pretend like I'm not internally panicking. "You're talking about me with my tongue down your brother-in-law's throat in the middle of your wedding reception, I assume?"

She leans forward with that glint in her eye, the one that means *you better spill*, and I know I'm not getting out of this. Looks like we're definitely having this conversation now.

"I don't know what to tell you," I begin, dragging a hand through my hair, clearly avoiding eye contact. "The sexual tension between the two of us has been simmering since I was here last time. Like, straight up cooking. I couldn't resist."

She nods like she's been expecting this and raises an eyebrow. "And...?"

I swallow again, stalling. "And nothing," I admit, finally cracking. My shoulders slump a little, the weight of it all suddenly a lot heavier. "I went home with him. Chickened out. Did some...almost third base stuff. You know, the usual."

She's watching me closely now, waiting for the punchline. So I give it to her.

"But there was zero penetration..." I pause for effect, "*from him*," I add quickly, a grin sneaking its way onto my face as I throw her an extra curveball.

She levels me with a flat look, eyes narrowing like she's trying to decide if I'm messing with her or genuinely being this vague. "That's all you're going to tell me? I don't think so. Spill. Like you would ever let me get away with so little detail."

A laugh escapes my lips because, well, she's absolutely right. "Are you sure you've got your hormones in check enough to hear the details? Because between your wedding night and what went down yesterday, they might not be able to handle it."

She settles into her seat, folding her legs up on the chair and getting comfortable for a long, juicy story. She leans back slightly, her eyes practically glowing with anticipation. "Oh, I'm ready."

This is about to get a whole lot more real than I was planning. The words bubble up, threatening to spill over, and if I'm being honest, I can't stop them now even if I wanted to. So, naturally, I do what any semi-sane person would... I bare every last detail, no matter how small, no matter how scorching hot.

The words tumble out in one wild, unfiltered confession. Every heated moment, every unsure thought, and every intense, spontaneous decision is out there. There's no going back or pretending I didn't just spill my soul all over the place.

When I finish, Juliette's jaw is practically on the floor, her eyes wide, her shocked expression full of disbelief. "Holy hell, Bree. How are you feeling about all of that?"

God, I love her. She's not cheering me on like some reckless friend, telling me to "go for it" without a second thought. No, instead, she's genuinely concerned about how I'm processing it all. She's always tuned in to the emotions of everyone around her, and right now, she's all in, focused on me. The way she cares so deeply makes my heart swell, and suddenly, all that chaos I just unleashed doesn't feel so overwhelming.

"Honestly?" I ask.

She nods. "Always."

"I do like him, which is terrifying," I admit. "And I apparently have some intimacy issues. but none of this matters because I leave in a couple days and don't have plans to come back, unless it concerns you."

Juliette tilts her head in the way she always does when she's really listening. She hears what I'm saying and what I'm not. The stuff I'm trying to hide behind, the bravado, and the walls I've built up over the years. She's looking at me like she already knows everything, like she's been reading me the whole time without me even realizing it.

"What, I just opened the verbal floodgates and left you speechless?" I ask, trying to deflect with humor, but there's a little wobble in my voice I can't hide.

She smirks, a small laugh slipping out. "Not speechless. Just...processing."

It's almost like she's seen this kind of mess before, and it doesn't faze her at all. She doesn't rush me, doesn't judge.

Oh, right. She *has* been here before.

I nod, the realization sinking in. "I guess you understand better than anyone, huh?"

Her eyes soften even more, her expression gentle but knowing. "I do. I also learned the hard way that the things that scare us the most are the ones worth fighting for."

She reaches out and takes my hand, giving it a gentle squeeze. "Bree, I've seen you go through the highest of highs and the lowest of lows. I've never seen you light up the way you just did, even while you were panicking."

A lump forms in my throat, and I have to bite my lip to keep the tears from falling. It's like she just reached into my chest, pulled out all the chaos, and made it feel...okay.

"This is probably just infatuation. I mean... You've seen him. You married what might as well be his twin."

She shakes her head. "Infatuation doesn't make you terrified. It doesn't make you question your life plans. What you're feeling? That's real."

I let out a frustrated sigh, half laughing, half groaning. "Well, shit. That sucks. So much for my blissful bubble."

She quirks an eyebrow, and I wave her off, trying to brush it aside. "Let's just keep this to ourselves for now, please? Callan hasn't made any moves that tell me he feels this...strongly. I'm pretty sure he's just having fun."

"It's your life, Bree. I won't interfere. Unless, of course, I deem it necessary."

"Brat," I mutter, sticking my tongue out at her.

She smirks, unphased, and sticks her tongue out right back. "Real mature."

I roll my eyes, but she doesn't let up. "Seriously, though," she continues, her tone shifting slightly, "you couldn't have chosen a better guy. Cal is great."

I let out a breath, a little too long for it to be just a casual exhale. "Yeah, I know," I admit. That's kind of the problem.

Juliette and I are at Rose's for dinner. Knox is picking Juliette up on his way home. The kitchen smells like roasted garlic and fresh bread, and my stomach is already preparing itself for an overload of carbs.

Rose leans forward, practically buzzing with excitement. "Let's talk baby names!"

"Oh, hell yes," I say with a grin. I'm all in. "Girl names or boy names first?"

"Girl names," Rose answers without hesitation. "I'm pretty sure it's going to be a girl."

Juliette leans back in her chair, arms crossed casually, a slight smirk on her lips. She's watching us with the kind of amused patience only she can pull off.

I start mentally sorting through names. "Okay, girl names. What about—"

"I'm not naming her after you," Juliette cuts in, her voice dry but full of that familiar sass.

I laugh, throwing my hands up in surrender. "Come on, Brianna Marie is a classic!"

Rose glances between us. "Well, if I had to pick something *classic,* I'd go for Grace or Ella."

"I like the sound of Ella," Juliette considers. "It's simple but elegant."

"Hmm... What about something with a little more edge? Classic with a bit of flair?"

Rose rolls her eyes. "You two are impossible. This is supposed to be fun, not a debate over whether the baby's name will sound like a rebel or royalty."

Juliette leans forward. "I'm listening."

I give a playful shrug, rolling the idea off my tongue. "What about...Maisie?"

The moment the name leaves my lips, Juliette's eyes light up. "Oh, I love that!"

"Yeah, see? A little edge, a little charm. It works." I smirk, watching her nod. "Maisie MacKenzie. Sounds good, doesn't it?"

"It does," she admits.

"And then her middle name can be Brianna," I say, not even trying to hide the smug grin spreading across my face.

Juliette throws her head back and laughs. "Nice try, but no."

I shrug. "Worth a shot."

Then, my phone buzzes in my hand.

"Oh, is it lover boy?" Rose teases in an overly curious tone, but I'm already glancing down at the screen, my stomach giving a little twist.

"I highly doubt that," I say, but when I see the name, my brain short-circuits for a second. "Oh, uh...it is."

"You going to get back to him?" Juliette asks.

I shake my head, a tug-of-war pulling inside me. "Nah, not right now. We still need to discuss baby boy names. And eat." The last part comes out with a bit more enthusiasm, but I'm starving. It's also easier to focus on food than whatever is going on with Callan right now.

Juliette and Rose dive right back into their baby-name debate, but my attention drifts. It's not that I'm not interested. Hell, I'm completely invested in whatever name they choose for the little one, but my mind keeps wandering back to Callan. I try not to think too much about it. It's just one message, right?

An hour later, Knox swings by to pick up Juliette. I do my best to hold it together as I wave them off, watching their car disappear down the road. They're about to have the best honeymoon, and I'm so freaking happy for them. The pit in my stomach isn't because of them, though. It's because I know I might not see Juliette again for a while.

And the idea of that... Well, it's hard to swallow.

I shake it off, trying to ignore the sudden flutter of nerves in my stomach as I pull my phone out of my pocket. There it is. The message from Callan. My heart does this weird flip. I stare at the screen for a second, not sure of what to expect. Maybe some casual "Hey" or "What's up?"

Instead, I get...

CALLAN:

You. Me. Ghost tour in Edinburgh.

Well, how could I possibly say no to that?

CALLAN

She said yes. We're going on an actual date.

I'm sitting in the driver's seat of my truck, and I'm pretty sure I've been smiling like a damn idiot for the last fifteen minutes. I know I'm usually all about keeping my cool, but right now? Screw it.

It's the middle of the week, but I managed to snag a couple of days off, which I rarely do. My team at the distillery is more than capable of running the show without me for a bit. I'm the one who usually pulls the late nights and early mornings, checking in at the family distillery with Knox, but today's different. Today's for her.

I asked if she wanted to stay in Edinburgh for a couple of nights before she flies out. She's heading back soon, and I figured, why not make the most of the time we've got left? Show her a little more of Scotland, give her something to take with her that's more than just the sight of me looking like a distracted fool every time she walks into a room.

To my surprise, she agreed. No hesitation.

I didn't tell her where we were staying, though. Call it part of the plan to keep the mystery alive. She probably thinks I've already booked some posh hotel with views of the castle or some fancy, crowded spot everyone's always recommending.

I pull into Rose's drive, the tires crunching over the gravel as I shift the truck into park. Before I even get out, the front door swings open and Rose's standing there, already waving me inside with that amused smile of hers. Bree's behind her, slipping on her shoes, ready to head out.

"Hey!" Bree's eyes light up the second she spots me. It's like a damn switch flips. The moment her face lights up like that, all excited and happy to see *me*, my heart does something funny.

"Hey, beautiful." Then I turn to Rose "Aren't you looking lovely on this fine day."

Bree's bright laugh rings out, and just as I'm thinking about how much I love that sound, a sharp smack lands on my arm.

Rose.

"Oh, you," she huffs. "You think flattery is gonna save you for stealing her away from me?"

I chuckle, leaning against the doorframe. "It's always worth a shot."

"Well, you're right," Rose says. "But it's not gonna work. Not on me, anyway." She shoots me a look that says *nice try*, then turns to Bree with open arms. "Come on, get over here and give me a hug. It was so wonderful having you here."

Bree rolls her eyes at me, smirking as she steps past. I shrug, flashing Rose a knowing grin. "You sure? 'Cause I was talking to you, you know."

She snorts. "Uh-huh. Keep dreaming, lover boy."

I grab Bree's bags and head for the truck. After tossing them into the backseat, I glance up in time to catch Bree pulling away from Rose. She spots me, her lips curving into that small, playful smile that always makes me feel like I've just dropped off the edge of a damn cliff.

Before I even realize it, I'm smiling back. It's instinct at this point.

My hand finds the small of her back without a second thought, my fingers brushing against the fabric of her shirt, the warmth of her skin seeping through. It's nothing, just a touch... Except it's not. Not when it's her.

I've always thought adrenaline was my thing, the rush of a hard ride, the snap of a well-timed decision. That was what kept me sharp. But right now, with her this close, those endorphins come from somewhere else entirely.

She glances up at me, her eyes shining with that familiar, almost electric energy that makes it impossible to look away. "Sure am." Then, without missing a beat, she calls over her shoulder, "Bye, Rose!"

I guide her to the truck, and when I open the passenger door, she slides in effortlessly, all graceful and unhurried. Like she's done this a hundred times before. And maybe it's stupid, but I like the way it looks. Her in my truck, tucked into the seat like she was always meant to be there.

I round the front, sliding into the driver's seat, and immediately feel the weight of her gaze.

She breaks the silence first. "How much do I owe you?"

I glance at her as I twist the key in the ignition. "For what, lass?"

She shifts in her seat, the playful confidence from before slipping. "For the hotel, or wherever we're staying?"

"Not a thing, Sunshine." I glance at her from the corner of my eye. "I've got a place in Edinburgh. I do enough business there that it made sense to have somewhere to stay."

Her lips press together like she's turning that over in her head, trying to decide if that answer satisfies whatever question she isn't asking out loud.

"Two bedrooms," I add. "In case you don't want to get snuggly."

Her head tilts, and I swear I can see the moment she decides to roll with it. "And here I thought you'd want to spoon all night."

I chuckle, shifting the truck into gear. "Oh, don't worry. If you ask nicely, I might still let you."

Her laughter bursts out, bright and carefree. I could listen to it forever and forget the rest of the world even exists.

And then there's her scent. Honey and wild roses, winding through every breath I take. It's making it hard to focus on the road and keep myself in check when all I want to do is pull over and—

"That sounds great," she says, breaking into my thoughts. "And I don't think we'll need the second bedroom."

"Music to my ears, love," I mutter without thinking. The moment the words slip out, I wince. Damn it. I didn't mean to come on that strong. I glance at her out of the corner of my eye, half worried I've crossed an invisible line.

She doesn't seem to mind. Her eyes are still shining, and she's got that playful spark lighting them up like she's not bothered at all. If anything, she looks a little more relaxed.

Her phone rings, and I catch the way her expression shifts into a quick grimace before she masks it.

"Everything all right?"

"Probably not," she mutters under her breath, already reaching for the phone. "It's the hospital where I work. I better take this."

"Hi, Lis—" She doesn't even get the full name out before whoever's on the other end barrels over her. Her shoulders tense, and she sits a little straighter, fingers tightening around her phone like she's bracing for impact.

"No, I can't come into work tomorrow. I'm not even in the country," she says, her voice clipped.

I steal another glance at her, and it's like I'm looking at a stranger. Gone is the Bree who teases without missing a beat. In her place is someone wound too tight, her grip on the phone white-knuckled, her jaw set like she's biting back words she'd rather not say. Her eyes darken, focused on a point in the distance, not really seeing anything at all.

"Lisa, my time off has been approved for months. I'll be back in the country on Friday."

The voice on the other end of the line gets louder. I can't make out the words, but I don't need to. Bree's fingers are twitching like she's holding back the urge to launch her phone across the cab.

"No, I can't find a flight that leaves today... You're writing me up? For being on vacation with my *approved* vacation time?"

A pause. Then, flatly, "Okay. Yeah. Bye."

She jams her finger against the phone screen with force and puts it down slowly, her hand still gripping tight.

Her face has gone pale, and her chest rises and falls a little too fast in an attempt to force all that anger down and lock it up before it spills over.

"I'm sorry," she says. "I shouldn't have answered that."

"Don't apologize, lass. I'm just pissed off that someone's made you feel like that."

She lets out a short laugh, but there's nothing cheerful about it. "It's just Lisa. My boss. She's awful. I've been trying to get a transfer, maybe move to another hospital, but nothing's working out. With everything going on this year, switching jobs probably isn't the smartest move."

"Aye, I get that. You could always quit and move to Scotland instead," I suggest, half joking.

Okay, fine. Not joking at all.

She tilts her head, eyes narrowing slightly like she's actually *considering* it. "Scotland, huh? And what would I do here, exactly? Become a whisky connoisseur like yourself?"

A slow grin tugs at my lips. "Well, you could always work on perfecting the accent. It's crucial for blending in."

Her light, easy chuckle drifts through the air and sinks into me, making itself comfortable. The tension in her shoulders starts to loosen. "I think I'd be better off with the whisky part."

"Fair enough. If you ever decide to make the move, I'd be happy to offer my expertise in both areas." I glance over, letting my gaze linger a second longer than necessary before adding, "I'm a generous guy like that."

I throw in a wink just to make sure she knows I'm only *half* kidding.

She shakes her head, her smile easy now. "I'll keep that in mind. Just don't expect me to go full Highland cow with the accent."

A loud bark of laughter bursts out of me. "Bree... I've heard a lot of things in my life, but that? I don't know what that even means, but I'm terrified."

"Have I rendered the infamous Callan MacKenzie speechless?"

"Hardly." I shake my head, still chuckling. "I'm just trying to picture you with a Highland cow accent. Might be a bit too... shaggy for my taste. Pun absolutely intended."

She groans, rolling her eyes, but I catch the smile she's trying to hide. "Oh, please. You know you'd love me even if I sounded like a barnyard animal."

That word again. *Love.* She tosses it out so easily, like it's just another joke, but it hits me square in the chest. Does she even realize she's said it?

"You're something else, Sunshine. I think I'll keep you," I

murmur, keeping my voice light, but there's no mistaking the truth behind the words.

Reaching across the console, I let my hand settle on her thigh. There's a split second where I hesitate and every nerve in my body screams at me to be careful, to not rush this and ruin whatever incredible thing is building between us. Bloody hell, I like this woman. More than I should.

Before doubt can sink its claws in, her fingers slide over mine, curling gently into my palm. I glance her way, and the look she gives me completely undoes me. It's not a big, flashy smile, but just a small curve of her lips. It's her eyes that hit me like a damn wrecking ball. Deep. Endless. Her lashes flutter, and I catch the tiniest hitch in her breath, barely there, but enough to make me forget every reason I was hesitating in the first place.

I'd give anything to keep that look, to keep her, just like this.

A couple hours later we're pulling into the underground car park beneath my building. I bought this flat last fall when business started picking up in Edinburgh. At the time, it was just a practical decision. A place to crash when I needed to stay close to the action. It's turned out to be a lifesaver for these last-minute trips.

I shift the truck into park and hop out, circling around to help Bree with her door. With her bags slung over my shoulder, we head toward the lift, the click of her boots echoing against the concrete.

"This is a nice place," she says, glancing around as we walk. "Is it new?"

"It is. I was one of the first to buy a place here."

As we step into the lift, I shift her bags higher on my shoulder. She watches me with a hint of amusement in her eyes. "Do you always insist on carrying everything, or is this just part of your charm?"

I smirk, pressing the button for my floor. "I'd say it's about 70 percent charm, 30 percent me trying to show off."

Her lips twitch. "Good to know."

The lift dings as it begins its ascent, and for a minute, neither of us speaks. The silence stretches, and the air itself seems charged. Maybe it's the close quarters. Or maybe it's the way we've been dancing around whatever this is all damn day.

Bree shifts, fingers toying with the strap of her purse, but her gaze stays locked on me. "So, do I get the grand tour when we get inside?"

"Depends. You planning to behave, lass?"

She lifts a brow, her expression pure mischief. "Absolutely not."

Christ. She has no idea what she's doing to me.

The doors glide open, and we step into the hallway, the lights above casting a golden glow across the polished floor. The rhythm of our footsteps is the only sound, echoing as we move down the corridor.

I unlock the door and push it open, stepping aside to let her go in first.

"Dang," she breathes, her voice hushed as her eyes roam the sleek, modern space. "This place is gorgeous. And so different from your house."

She's not wrong. The flat is a world apart from my usual style. Open floor plan, dark accents, and arched windows framing a view of Dean Village that makes the whole place look like it's floating above the city. The furnishings are clean, sharp, and sophisticated. It's the kind of place you see in glossy magazines. The opposite of what anyone would picture when they hear my name.

I lean against the doorframe, watching her take it all in. "Thanks, lass. You want your bags in the spare room or mine?"

"Yours," she says without a second thought, already kicking off her shoes as she steps farther into the flat. I can't help the smirk tugging at my lips. She's making herself at home, and damn if it doesn't feel...right.

After stashing her bags in my room, I wander back out to find her sprawled on the white couch in the living room, feet propped on the coffee table. She's got that cheeky grin on her face.

"So, this is how your alter ego lives, huh?"

"Yep," I say with a shrug before dropping into the chair across from her. "The real me prefers pizza boxes and mismatched socks, but, you know, appearances."

"Of course," she laughs, her eyes crinkling at the corners. "Really, though. It's gorgeous."

Her gaze drifts over to the bookshelf that spans an entire wall of the living room, and she raises a brow. "I didn't know you were such an intellectual."

I lean back, stretching my legs out in front of me and making myself comfortable. "Aye, I guess I don't advertise that. Gotta keep the mystery alive, lass. Wouldn't want you to get too cozy."

"Oh, trust me," she says, motioning to the furniture and spotless surfaces. "Cozy isn't exactly the vibe I get here. More like...dangerously pristine."

I chuckle. "Good. Keeps people on their toes."

She tilts her head, narrowing her eyes. "You mean it scares them off."

"Same thing," I shoot back with a wink.

Her laugh softens as she shifts, pulling her legs up onto the couch. "What time are we going on this ghosty tour, then?"

"Not until dark, so we've got time to relax. Thought we could order takeaway before we head out?"

"Sounds great. Mind if I freshen up? You can order whatever. I'm not picky."

"Sure thing," I say, nodding toward the hallway. "Your bags are in my room, first door on the left. The en suite's all yours."

"Thanks," she replies, flashing me another smile before making her way down the hall.

And as she walks away, well... There's no point pretending I don't notice the sway of her hips or the way her jeans hug her just right. It's impossible not to look. Hell, I'd challenge any man alive to resist.

My mind doesn't exactly behave, either. My imagination runs wild with the thought of her soft, smooth thighs locked around my waist. Even better would be tasting her and hearing her moan my name as she comes undone on my tongue.

I run a hand through my hair, letting out a slow breath. She's down the hall, trusting me to be a gentleman, and here I am, letting my imagination get the better of me.

I glance toward the hallway, half expecting to see her standing there, ready to catch me in my not-so-gentlemanly thoughts. Guess that's the price of being this damn attracted to someone. My brain's running at full speed while my body's stuck in slow motion.

sixteen

BREE

Holy hell, this is the nicest bathroom I've ever been in. The walls and floor are covered in dark marble, giving it this ridiculously luxurious vibe, and the floating vanity with its huge, backlit round mirror looks like something straight out of a magazine. Then there's the walk-in, frameless shower that's practically begging me to use it. Honestly, it puts every spa I've ever been in to shame.

By the time I tear myself away from my new favorite place in the flat, the scent of herbs and spices hits my senses. It's enough to make my stomach growl as I follow the aroma down the hall.

"What is that mouthwatering smell?" I call out, rounding the corner into the kitchen.

Callan is standing at the counter, unpacking paper bags stuffed full of takeout containers. He glances over his shoulder, his signature smirk already creeping onto his face. "I hope you like Thai," he says casually. "I grabbed a bit of everything. Didn't know what you'd be in the mood for."

A container of pad thai lands on the counter, followed by a

bowl of green curry that looks like it could put all other curries to shame.

"There's more in the other bag. I just haven't opened it yet."

"More, huh? You're really going all out. Is this your clever way of ensuring I'm too full to leave?"

He shoots me an exasperated look, but I catch the corner of his mouth twitching. I'm not fooled. He's pretending to be annoyed, but I can see right through it.

"I'm just teasing," I add quickly, waving him off before he can say anything. "You're in luck. I love Thai. This is all great."

His shoulders relax slightly. For a guy who wears *unbothered* like a badge of honor, it's kind of sweet that he's so tuned in.

I grab a little bit of everything from the spread, my plate quickly turning into what could only be described as a sampler platter of dreams. The second I take my first bite, it's like my taste buds have been hit with spicy, tangy fireworks. Someone definitely worked a little magic in that kitchen.

I pause, trying not to look like a complete savage as I bring my hand to my lips, fighting the urge to talk with my mouth full.

"Mm, wow," I manage after swallowing. "This might be some of the best Thai I've ever had."

"Hell yeah, it is," he says. "I always order from this place when I'm in Edinburgh." He takes a bite of his own, nodding like it's the same level of life-changing every time. "They've got everything. Sweet, spicy, savory. They know exactly what I need."

"High maintenance, are you?"

"Nah," he says, leaning back in his chair. "I just have standards."

I snort. "Sure, let's call it that."

He chuckles, shaking his head as he digs back into his food, and I can't help but smile. This feels easy, natural, like it's the most normal thing in the world to be sitting here sharing food and teasing each other.

"So, are you always this generous with your takeout orders?" I ask.

He shrugs. "Only when I'm trying to impress someone."

My heart skips a beat, and I immediately tell myself to relax. It's just Callan being Callan. Confident, playful, and probably just saying it to get a reaction. Still, the way he says it, like it's a fact he's not even trying to hide, sends warmth rushing to my cheeks.

I should laugh it off, but my brain has already decided to run a marathon.

"Well...it's working."

"Good." His voice drops an octave. "Because I've got a few more tricks up my sleeve."

And just like that, my pulse kicks into overdrive.

"Damn it, Callan," I mutter, pacing the room as I glance over my shoulder for what feels like the hundredth time. "I'm not going to be able to sleep tonight."

We're supposed to be winding down, but there's no way my brain is shutting off. My nerves are fried from the creepy stories and that eerie history lesson during the tour. Even though it's over, the unsettling vibe lingers. I swear there's a bizarre, heavy pressure behind me, like someone is standing there breathing down my neck. And not in the way I'd prefer.

Callan, of course, grins like he's having the time of his life. "Well, at least you won't be alone. Didn't the guide mention something about nocturnal visitors who like to hang around people who can't sleep? Maybe you'll get lucky."

He pauses for dramatic effect, clearly reveling in the chaos he's causing. Then, just when I think he can't make it worse, he adds with a wink, "Or, you know, we could always leave the light on. I hear ghosts are terrified of lamps."

"Hilarious," I deadpan, though I'm fighting the urge to laugh because his smug delivery is infuriatingly perfect. "Well, you're the one who has to deal with me now."

"You're telling me that outgoing, outrageous, little Miss Sunshine is afraid of ghosts?"

I roll my eyes, but I can't completely hide the nervous laugh that escapes me. "I'm not afraid of ghosts," I say, trying to sound more confident than I feel. "I just...respect them. And tonight, they're definitely earning my respect."

He laughs that deep, teasing chuckle that makes my stomach do flips. "So, you're telling me that if a ghost knocked on the door right now, you wouldn't be like, 'Hey, come on in, I've got snacks!'"

I glare at him, even though my heart is racing in that *ridiculous* way it does when I'm caught somewhere between wanting to slap him and kiss him senseless. "I'd offer them some cookies," I say. "But only if they promise to stop whispering in my ear. And maybe stay on the other side of the room, please."

"You're something else." He smirks. "Have I mentioned that I'd like to keep you around? Because if I haven't, I definitely would."

Great, now I'm internally swooning. *Perfect.*

I force myself to sound unaffected, but inside, I'm a total mess. *Pull it together, Bree.* "Oh, you'd like to keep me around, huh?" I tease, trying to keep my voice light. "And here I thought I was just a temporary distraction."

He doesn't miss a beat. He leans in a fraction closer,

making sure every word hits exactly where he wants them to. His eyes lock onto mine, suddenly serious, and it makes my breath hitch in my throat.

"You're far more than that, Sunshine. I hope you know that by now."

And just like that, I forget how to form a coherent thought. What is it about this man that makes everything happen in slow motion? He's got this way of turning everything into something too real, and now I'm stuck between wanting to melt into it and run for the hills.

I've spent so long keeping everything at arm's length, and here he is, crashing through every wall I've built with nothing but a few words.

"Callan, I..." My words get stuck in my throat, tangled up in everything I'm too scared to say. What can I even say? That I'm falling for him harder than I ever thought possible? That the thought of leaving in a few days is tearing me apart?

The words don't come, not the ones I need, anyway. Not even close. So, I do what I've done more than once around him. I lean in, my lips finding his, hoping that this kiss will do what my voice can't.

His hands grip my hips, pulling me closer, and I can feel every inch of him. His lips are soft but insistent, and when his tongue meets mine, it's slow and careful, like he's making sure I feel it. *Really* feel it. And I do. Every second. Every move. This is everything I can't say, everything I'm terrified of admitting, wrapped up in one small moment of intimacy and the way he holds me.

I could try to make sense of it. I could tell myself it's just chemistry or a distraction, but with his lips on mine, I know that's not true.

I melt into him as the kiss deepens, turning desperate and urgent, like we both know we don't have time to waste. His hands traipse down my back, slipping under my ass. In one smooth motion, he lifts me effortlessly. The sudden closeness, and the strength in his grip, sends a jolt of electricity through me. My pulse spikes, racing to keep up with everything he's making me feel.

My legs wrap instinctively around his waist, my body responding to his every move and every shift. There's no space between us and absolutely no hesitation. Just heat and everything I've been fighting to keep locked up letting loose in the form of a kiss that says everything.

He carries me to his bed, not breaking the kiss for a second. My hands grip his shoulders as he moves, his body pressing against mine in all the right ways.

When we finally reach the edge of the bed, he lays me down gently, almost as if he's afraid I'll break, unsure of how far to push, of what I want and what I need. There's a tenderness in the way he moves, like he's reading me and waiting for my cue. His body covers mine, all heat and muscle, his hard length pressing against my thigh.

My breath hitches, and I fight the sudden, uncomfortable surge of panic bubbling up from my stomach.

I've dreamed about him above me and how it might feel to have him this close. Now that it's real, it's almost overwhelming. His body is warm and hard, pressing me into the bed, and for a brief, terrifying second, it feels like I'm trapped.

Not by him. He's not doing anything wrong, but by the sudden rush of panic clawing up my throat, fast and ruthless.

No, no, no. God damn it, not again.

My mind scrambles, trying to reconcile the fantasy with the reality. I *want* this. I want *him*. Still, my body doesn't trust that I'm safe yet.

Why am I scared?

Because I've only ever been with one person.

Because that person was supposed to protect me, and he didn't.

And now, even though Callan's touch is careful and his eyes are kind, my body still hesitates.

I force myself to take a slow breath, steadying against the storm trying to pull me under. My thoughts are a tangled mess, spinning in a dozen directions. Part of me is trying to pull away, even as the rest of me screams to get closer, to bridge the gap, to reach for that connection I'm craving so much.

"Hey." His voice is rich and calm, cutting through the chaos of my mind like a lifeline. "Take your time."

I nod, trying to swallow down the knot of fear. He's here. He's patient. *He's not going anywhere.* And while the tension in my body doesn't completely melt, that thought, at least, helps keep the panic at bay, if only for a second.

Then, his eyes flicker with sudden light. "I have an idea, if you're up for it?"

He stands, giving me a moment to breathe as I prop myself up on my elbows. My pulse spikes, not because I'm scared, but because I'm intrigued. "You and your ideas... What is it this time?"

Without a word, he heads toward the closet. The rustle of fabric fills the room, and then a few seconds later, he emerges with two neckties in his hand.

"I've always hated these *feckin'* things," he says. "But I think they're about to be useful."

I arch a brow, utterly confused. What in the world is he planning? My mind races, trying to connect the dots, but all I'm getting is a big ol' question mark.

He stretches his arms out in front of him, the ties dangling from his hands. His eyes meet mine, and just like that, the playful glint in his gaze turns a little darker, a little more dangerous.

"Tie me up."

Heat floods through me. He's got to be kidding. Right? The challenge in his voice tells me he's completely serious.

My breath falters. "What?" My brain's still trying to catch up with what the hell he just said.

His response is a slow, knowing curve of his lips that always makes my heart race and my thoughts scatter. It spreads across his face as he waits for me to figure it out. "You heard me," he says, voice smooth as honey, but there's an undeniable edge to it. He gives the ties another shake, that teasing gesture making the air between us thick with tension.

"Tie me up," he repeats. "You're in charge."

In charge? The idea is both terrifying and thrilling. What the hell am I supposed to do with that? The look in his eyes tells me there's no backing down. The ball's in my court.

"You're not serious," I say blankly.

Callan, of course, doesn't flinch. "Oh, I'm dead serious."

The gleam in his eyes, that look of pure certainty, makes it clear that he's all in.

I swallow hard, heart thudding a little too loudly. My hands tremble as I take the ties from him, my fingers brushing against his briefly. The silk is cool and smooth, a sharp contrast to the heat building.

"Okay..." I say, my voice a little shaky. I'm not entirely sure I'm ready for this, but damn it, I think I want to see where it goes.

Callan grins, that devil-may-care smile of his spreading as he pulls his shirt off with a single motion, the fabric gliding over his skin. Every one of his muscles flexes in the golden light as he stretches out on the pillows near the headboard. He's comfortable in his own skin and completely at ease with whatever's about to happen. It's magnetic.

I find myself drawn to the way his body moves. Every inch

of it seems to scream control. Power. But right now, he's laid back, offering all of himself. To me.

He's being so open and trusting with me, and it's affecting me in ways I didn't expect. And, well... *I see what he's doing here.*

With a deep breath, I move to straddle his waist, my knees sinking into the mattress. Callan watches me with those piercing blue eyes that track my every move as I slowly inch closer. My heart pounds so hard I swear he must be able to hear it as I lean forward, gently taking one of his wrists.

The tie slides through my fingers like water, smooth and cool as I thread it around his wrist. My hands are careful, a little unsure at first, but I keep going—once, twice around his wrist and the headboard, the soft rustle of fabric the only sound between us.

His pulse thrums beneath my touch, steady and unbothered, while mine's thundering like it forgot how to behave.

"Not too tight?" I whisper, eyes glancing to his.

Callan watches me like I just handed him every dirty secret I've never said out loud. His pupils are blown wide, gaze dark and molten.

"It's perfect," he murmurs. "Looks like you know what you're doing."

I can't help but smirk a little at that. "Maybe I do."

I lean across him, my breasts brushing against his torso as I stretch to reach his other wrist. His breath hitches, and I feel a surge of confidence knowing I'm affecting him just as much as he's affecting me. I take my time with the second tie, deliberately letting my fingers trail along the inside of his wrist before looping the fabric around it.

I sit back, letting my eyes trail over him. Every inch of his exposed skin pulls my attention, from the rise and fall of his chest to the way his abs tighten as he shifts beneath me.

He's completely at my mercy, and I can't help but appreciate how *delicious* he looks like this. I should probably savor this slowly, but knowing me, I'm about two seconds away from devouring it all.

"Is that okay?" I ask.

His lips curve into a smirk, eyes gleaming with an intensity that makes me physically ache to touch him. "More than okay," he murmurs. "I'm all yours, Sunshine."

His words send a surge of desire mixed with a thrill of power through me. My nerves melt away, replaced by a growing hunger and a desperate need to explore every inch of him.

I trail my fingertips down his smooth skin, tracing the lines of his muscles, relishing the way his breath hitches at my touch. I can't resist leaning down to press a soft kiss just above his heart.

Sitting back, I slowly peel off my top. Callan's eyes darken, his gaze darting hungrily over my body as I unclasp my bra and let it fall away. I shimmy out of my jeans next, kicking them aside until I'm completely bare before him, exposed and vulnerable, yet empowered by his heated stare.

"Fuck, you're gorgeous," he breathes. His arms flex against the restraints, fighting the urge to reach for me.

I move to straddle him again, leaning down just enough to tease his lips with mine. I pull away slightly, letting the space between us stretch out for a breath before I kiss my way along his jaw.

"Is this how you thought this would go?" I whisper against his skin.

He releases a low groan, his breath shaky. "I could have only hoped."

With deliberate slowness, I drag my hands down to the waistband of his jeans. My eyes glance up to meet his heated gaze as I pop the button open. The sound of his zipper lowering fills the charged air between us. He lifts his hips to help as I peel the denim down his thighs, my pulse quickening at the sight of him in only his black boxer briefs, the outline of his erection clearly visible through the fabric.

Tossing his jeans aside, I hook my fingers into the elastic of his underwear and tug them down, freeing his impressive length. It springs up against his taut stomach, and I lick my lips, desire pooling low in my stomach.

"You're killing me, lass," he murmurs, his voice heavy with need. "Christ, the things I want to do to you right now."

I smile, feeling a new surge of boldness as I wrap my fingers around his thick length, giving him a slow stroke from base to tip. He groans, his hips lifting slightly off the bed, seeking more of my touch.

"Patience." I lean down to press a featherlight kiss to the head of his cock. He sucks in a sharp breath, his muscles tensing beneath my hands.

I flick my tongue out, licking a slow circle around the tip before tracing the ridge along the underside of his shaft. I take my time as I lick and tease, drawing out every satisfying moan and gasp. I finally wrap my lips around him, taking him deep as I hollow my cheeks. His groan vibrates through me, sending electricity racing down my spine and pooling between my thighs.

"Fuck, Bree," he pants, straining against the ties. His abs flex and quiver as I work him with my mouth, taking him as deep as I can. The sensation of him heavy on my tongue, the salty tang of his arousal, and the way he throbs between my lips is intoxicating. I'm drunk on the power of reducing this strong, controlled man to a trembling mess with just my mouth.

seventeen

CALLAN

The ties were the best idea I've had in my entire life. I'm watching her confidence grow with every passing second, every small shift, and every glance. She's unlocking a new layer of herself right in front of me, and I can't look away. There's a fire in her eyes, and I've got a front-row seat to the show.

She's swallowing my cock like it's her last meal, and I'm about to shoot my load down her pretty little throat if she doesn't quit.

"Bree," I manage to croak out between gritted teeth. "You're killing me."

She eases back slightly, looking up at me like an angel with her perfect lips wrapped around my cock. I have to shut my eyes. This image alone would be enough to do it for me.

She won't be getting any further direction from me. She needs this control. She's calling the shots, and it's the sexiest thing I've ever witnessed.

She releases me slowly, her eyes sparkling with desire. "We can't have that now, can we?"

She shifts, straddling my hips and teasing me. I want nothing more than to thrust into her tight heat, but I won't move. I need to let her take what she wants.

She leans down, her hair cascading around us like a curtain, and captures my lips in a searing kiss. I can taste myself on her tongue, and it only fuels the fire burning inside me.

"Callan," she breathes, my name a prayer on her lips. "I need you."

Those three little words nearly undo me.

There's no more doubt in her touch, no hesitation in the way she moves with me. She's not asking for permission anymore; she's telling me what she wants, and she's damn sure of it.

"Are you sure?" I whisper, my voice rough with the need to hear her say it one more time, to see it in her eyes.

Even as I ask, I know the answer. She's ready. I'm going to make sure she knows that I'll never rush her, but that she can take whatever she needs from me, whenever she wants.

She responds by reaching for the ties binding my wrists, her fingers deftly working the knots loose. As the restraints fall away, I flex my hands, relishing the freedom. I don't move. Not yet.

I'm waiting for her to tell me, in her own way, that this is the moment. When she looks at me, her lips parted, I know. She's taking control in a way that I've never seen before.

Bree takes my hands in hers, guiding them to her hips as she positions herself over me. The heat of her core hovers tantalizingly close. Anticipation thrums through every nerve in my body.

She's teasing me, dragging out every second as she sinks down onto me, gripping me tight. A guttural moan tears from my throat as I'm consumed by her, my fingers digging into the soft flesh of her hips.

She begins to move in a slow, sensual rhythm that's both torturous and divine. Her hands splay across my chest as she rises and falls, taking me deeper with each downward motion. I'm lost in the sight of her above me, a goddess in her own right.

"Bree," I groan, my voice strained with the effort of holding back. "You feel so fucking perfect."

A smile plays at the corners of her lips. She knows the effect she has on me and the power she wields right now. And god, does she wield it well.

Her pace quickens, hips rolling and circling, driving me closer to the edge with every stroke. The tension coils tighter in my core, the pressure building to an almost unbearable level.

"That's a good fucking girl. Taking my cock like it was made for you."

Her eyes fly open, a raging inferno of need beneath them. This sweet lass has a thing for praise, it seems.

My hands map every curve and dip of her body, committing it all to memory. I want to savor every second of this, every gasp and moan that falls from her lips. She's a vision above me, her skin glistening with a sheen of sweat, her eyes half lidded with pleasure.

"Callan," she pants, her nails digging into my skin. "I'm close."

Those words spur me into action. I sit up, wrapping my arms around her waist and pulling her flush against me. The change in angle draws a sharp cry from her throat, her head falling back in ecstasy.

I bury my face in the crook of her neck, my lips skimming the sensitive skin there. "You've got me so deep, love. Take what you need. Use me."

Her back arches, pushing her perky tits forward. I can't resist leaning down to capture a nipple between my lips, sucking and teasing with my tongue.

She whimpers, her rhythm faltering, and with a breathless cry, she shatters in my arms, clenching around me like a vise. The sensation is almost too much and threatens to pull me over the edge with her.

I hold her tight as she rides out the waves of her release, whispering praises into her skin. "That's it, love. You're so beautiful like this."

She locks eyes with me, pure ecstasy written across her face, and whatever restraint I had left shatters. There's no holding back. Not when she looks at me like that. With one final thrust, I spill myself inside her, my release hitting me like a tidal wave. I bury my face in her neck, muffling my groans against her sweat-slicked skin as the aftershocks course through me. Bree clings to me, her body still trembling, her breath coming in short, sharp gasps.

For a long moment, we stay tangled together in a way that feels too perfect. Her body presses against mine, warm and soft, and I swear, I could stay here forever, just breathing her in.

Then slowly, almost reluctantly, Bree lifts her head from my shoulder. Her eyes find mine, and for a heartbeat, everything goes still. She's stripped bare before me, but it's not just her body. It's her heart. And that takes my breath away.

She's trusting me. Completely. And the importance of that settles with a fierce protective instinct. Her trust is a precious gift, and I vow that I'll *never* betray it.

Her fingers trail lightly over my chest, and I lift a hand, tucking a stray lock of hair behind her ear, my thumb brushing the curve of her jaw.

"You okay?"

She nods, but the look in her eyes says more than words ever could. This isn't about what just happened. It's about us. What we are. What we could be.

I cup her face, letting my forehead rest against hers. "I've got you, Bree," I whisper.

Gently, I shift us, guiding her down until we're lying side by side, limbs tangled in the sheets. Bree moves with me easily, her body fitting perfectly against mine.

After a minute, she props herself up on one elbow, her hair falling in waves around her face. She looks down at me with a shy smile. "Thank you," she murmurs.

I study her, trying to catch a glimpse of the thoughts swirling behind her eyes. "For what, love?"

She hesitates for just a second before answering, her voice barely above a whisper. "For this." She pauses, then adds with a softness that makes my heart ache, "For knowing what I needed, even when I didn't."

And just like that, I'm gone.

That one sentence hits harder than anything. Cracks right through the steel trap I keep bolted around my feelings.

She's right. I *did* know. And it's not because I'm some emotionally intuitive saint. I'm not. Hell, I'm probably the last guy anyone expects to be composed, or patient, or tuned in.

But I've been paying attention. Every single day.

We've been a world apart, in different continents, time zones, and still, she became the one person I couldn't go a day without hearing from. Sometimes it was ten minutes. Sometimes an hour. Sometimes just a text that made me laugh in the middle of a brutal day.

Those calls and texts became the best part of my day. I didn't realize until just now, hearing those words slip from her lips, how much I've come to need them. To need her.

I'm in love with her.

It's not just affection or loyalty or the protective instinct that kicks in when she's hurting. It's all of it. The way she sees the world, and herself—so damn brave, even when she's doubting everything.

It's love, and it's wrecking me.

The thing about me is, I don't just *say* those kinds of words. Not unless I know they won't unravel everything. This is something I don't want to mess up.

So instead of saying everything that's climbing up my throat, I just look at her.

She's not doing anything spectacular. No grand gesture, no big smile. She's just there, being honest, being her. I want to take her face in my hands and tell her she's the best thing that's ever happened to me. That I'd tear apart the damn planet if it meant keeping her safe.

But I don't. Instead, I let my hand brush against her cheek, my thumb tracing the line of her jaw. "You don't have to thank me for that, love," I whisper, my heart pounding. "I'll always give you what you need."

Her lips part slightly, a question hanging in the air, but she doesn't speak. Instead, she watches me with an unreadable expression. Then, after a beat, she leans down, pressing a slow, lingering kiss to the corner of my mouth.

I tilt my head, not wanting to leave it at that. I catch her lips fully, deepening the kiss just enough to make sure she knows that this isn't only about tonight or the way she fits against me like she was always meant to be here.

It's about *her*.

Always has been.

eighteen

BREE

I 've never felt this free. This alive. Hell, at this point, I'm not sure I've ever actually *felt* before. I'd let this man ruin me in every way imaginable. He moves, shifting to the edge of the bed, and the loss is immediate. A whimper slips out before I can stop it, because good god, the ache is unbearable, like something vital has been ripped away.

"Easy, Sunshine." He scoops me up effortlessly, carrying me into the en suite like I weigh nothing. My brain? Nowhere to be found. My body? Fully at his mercy.

He sets me on the counter, his warmth leaving a ghost of itself on my skin, and I can't do anything but watch, helplessly mesmerized as he adjusts the water. Patient. Unhurried. Like he has all the time in the world. If it were me, I'd be throwing the damn thing to full blast and climbing him like a tree, but he waits, completely in control.

Finally, he comes back to me and slides his hands underneath my thighs. My legs, apparently having a mind of their own, wrap around him instantly. I could probably be mad about that if I wasn't so damn distracted by how perfectly he fits against me.

As soon as we step into the shower, there's no doubt that round two is no longer a possibility... It's inevitable. My body knows it. His body knows it. The universe probably knows it, too.

Steam wraps around us, clinging to me, hot and heavy, as I finally find my feet on the cool tile. The water's scalding, but it feels like pure heaven. It pours over us in a steady cascade, trailing between us and over every inch of our skin. I'm trying really hard not to get distracted by the way he looks standing there, water running down his torso and the muscles that never seem to quit, but here I am. Completely distracted. Again.

I may or may not be drooling. This man is *fine*.

I can't help it. My arms curl around his neck, pulling him closer, because I *need* him. I need his lips and his body against mine, right now.

He groans into my mouth, the sound vibrating through me and all the way down to my toes. That low, rough noise just might shatter me in the best way. When I think I might lose control, he pulls back, his hands sliding down my spine with a slow, deliberate touch that's almost too much to handle. They settle on my ass, squeezing gently.

"I brought you in here to take care of you, lass," he mutters. "Not to fuck you up against a wall."

I can't help the grin that pulls at my lips, even though my pulse is thundering in my ears. "I guess I could be cool with either option."

"You're insatiable," he murmurs. Before I can blink, he spins me around.

His hands are sure as they reach for the shampoo, and I swear, I shiver from the mere brush of his fingers through my hair. It's so gentle, so tender, as he massages the shampoo into my scalp.

I should be lost in it. I *am* lost in it, but then a soft ache creeps in behind my ribs. This is so sweet. Too sweet. My heart can't quite keep up, and it physically hurts with the thought that this is fleeting.

I'm leaving. This has an expiration date stamped clean across it. Still, his hands are in my hair, and he's being so careful with me.

I want to tell him not to stop. To keep doing this. Keep looking at me like I mean something. Even if it's only for now. Even if it's only until I pack my bags and get on a plane.

I want it all to last. And I hate myself a little for wanting.

I don't pull away, though. I stay there, letting him rinse my hair, his hands working with such care. He lathers my body with slow, careful hands, and in between each touch, he presses kisses to my shoulders, my neck.

Somehow, amidst the quiet ache, I lose myself in the softness of his kisses.

When the water finally shuts off, the loss of his touch is too sudden, but he wraps a warm towel around me and takes my hand. I follow him into the bedroom, sitting on the edge of the bed, my heart still fluttering as he pulls on a pair of boxer briefs and nothing else.

God. The sight of him, half dressed and ridiculously sexy, does things to me that probably shouldn't be legal. Heat flares low in my stomach, and a pulse races in places it definitely shouldn't. He's completely oblivious. He throws me a casual glance over his shoulder, like he's the most dangerous thing in the room.

"Here, lass." He hands me one of his shirts, and my skin heats up like I've been left in the sun too long. It's a shirt, but the way he gives it to me? It's a *gift*. I'm not giving it back. "Put this on and meet me in the living room."

I'm already halfway melting. There's no point in trying to hide the effect he's having on me. "Yes, sir."

His eyes smolder, but that smirk—oh, that *smirk*—plays across his face like he's got some sort of secret master plan, already two steps ahead and perfectly aware of exactly what he's doing to me.

Without saying another word, he strides out of the room, leaving me hot and bothered.

I slip into his shirt, the fabric swallowing me, and follow him. I'm still trying to catch my breath from this whirlwind of... whatever the hell this is as I step into the main living area, and freeze.

There's Callan, casually prepping tea like it's the most normal thing in the world. The kettle's whistling, steam rising, and he moves with such ease, like we didn't just have the most mind-blowing, earth-shattering sex a few minutes ago.

Is this real life? I have to blink because there's no way this is real. This man, who just completely wrecked me in the best possible way, is now making me tea. What kind of alternate universe have I stepped into?

He turns to face me with a mug in his hand, and time slows as he hands it to me, the heat seeping through the porcelain and into my palms.

I make my way to the couch, my legs a little wobbly, and pull a blanket over my lap as I sink into the cushions. The moment I settle, it hits me how perfect everything feels. Outside, the village and river glimmer beneath the moonlight. It's romantic as hell.

He slides in beside me, his leg brushing against mine under the blanket. The casual closeness makes my heart flutter, like it's double-checking I'm still breathing. Because if this is real, then it's the kind of life I never want to wake up from.

He clears his throat, shifting beside me. "I don't know how to bring this up, but uh..." He hesitates for a beat before continuing, his voice dropping a little. "We didn't use protection."

The seriousness in his gaze would probably be alarming in any other situation, but right now? It's kind of funny. I can't help the laugh that bubbles up. It's sweet, really, that he's worried. This man, who just brought me to the edge of oblivion and back without a second thought, is now concerned about... well, *this*.

I can't help but smile at him, the tension easing a little. "We're okay. I've got us covered. As long as you don't have something I need to worry about...?"

"Christ, no, lass. No, not at all." His voice is filled with pure relief.

"Perfect." I grin over the rim of my mug. "Then we can do that again, and again...and again."

His rich laugh fills the room, and before I can process it, he's pulling me into his side. His arm wraps around me, strong and steady and I rest my head on his shoulder, inhaling the scent of leather and spice that's unmistakably him. Comforting, familiar, and yet always just a little intoxicating.

There's a calm that settles over me as I close my eyes, the rise and fall of his chest beneath my cheek grounding me in a way nothing else ever has. This is happiness. Simple, but real. More real than anything I've felt in a long time.

His presence is everything. The echo of his laugh still rings in my mind, and this closeness between us, how we fit together perfectly, just feels *right*. This is where I'm supposed to be.

I WILL BE FOREVER grateful for the way Callan put me at ease yesterday. I feel like a brand-new woman. One who's been thoroughly fucked. Bent over the edge of the couch, on the kitchen counter, in the shower...and just now, in the truck because I couldn't wait. Honestly, I almost had my way with him right there in the middle of the pub. The way he looks at me like he'd set the whole damn world on fire to keep me warm is enough to make a girl lose all sense of public decency.

No complaints here, though.

However, reality is creeping in like an unwelcome third wheel, and I don't like it. We're not technically a *thing*, and yet, the thought of leaving tomorrow hits like a sucker punch to the ribs. Rude.

It's stupid how much I want to stay. The pull is so strong it feels like my whole body is in on it, like my heart and bones have already made the decision and are just waiting for my brain to catch up. The idea of walking away isn't just sad. It's a betrayal to something I don't even have words for yet.

I'm such an idiot. I did this to myself. This is reckless. It's hard not to feel like I'm standing on the edge of something that could be so much more. I know I should take a step back—if only my brain had a clue what was good for me.

Who am I kidding? I'm not going to do that.

We're lying in bed, and it's as natural as breathing. Like we've been doing this for years and could keep doing it for a million more. His body fits against mine like it was made to be here, our breaths syncing without effort.

And maybe that's why it hits me just how different this is.

With Dillon, I think there were signs long before things went south. His temper would flare over nothing when he drank. Those arguments always ended with me apologizing, even when I wasn't sure what for. It was never bad enough to realize how easily it could spiral into something worse.

With Callan? The guy doesn't have a mean bone in his body. Not a single one. I've never heard him raise his voice, not even when some drunken idiot sloshed half of his beer all over his jacket. He just laughed it off like it was nothing. It's so *different*, so much more peaceful. If Callan were any more patient, he'd qualify for sainthood.

And yet...I'm leaving. We haven't talked about what this is or what happens after I go. Is he waiting for me to say something? Oh, shit. He probably *is*. This sweet, damn near perfect gentleman has been treating me with such care, and instead of questioning why that feels so out of character for him, maybe I should've been asking myself why I haven't been considering more.

Then the doubt fizzles out, and I think... What do I have to lose? What's the worst that could happen if I go all in?

We couldn't be in a more vulnerable position if we tried. Skin against skin, limbs tangled in a warm, sleepy knot. The sheets are a mess around us, his fingers idly tracing lazy circles on my arm.

My chest feels tight. Not in the scary *I'm having a heart attack* way, but more like what happens when you want to say something big. Something that could change everything.

I don't know what I'm waiting for.

"Cal?"

His thumb pauses for a second. "Mm?"

"Can I ask you something?"

"Always."

That word lands heavy. It should be reassuring. It almost is.

"What happens when I leave?"

His arm tightens around me. "What do you want to happen?"

"I don't know..." I whisper.

He shifts beside me, propping himself up on one elbow to look down at me.

"Brianna..."

I freeze. Brianna? My full name? I didn't think he even knew my full name.

He's looking at me with amusement and something more... intense. Then his hand moves to tilt my chin, bringing me face-to-face with him.

"You want me to tell you what I want first?"

It's like he has me hypnotized right now. I couldn't speak if I tried. All I can do is nod.

He chuckles. "Well, there's a beautiful, golden-haired, blue-eyed, American lass who happens to have ruined me for anyone else." He traces a finger down my jawline, eyes crinkling with mischief. "You've certainly gotten your money's worth. I've never seen anyone so...enthusiastic."

Heat floods my cheeks. "Are you actually teasing me about my sexual appetite right now?"

"Absolutely." His grin is downright wicked. "I think my neighbors might have heard you last night."

I swat at his chest, mortified but laughing. "You're terrible! If I recall correctly, you weren't exactly quiet yourself."

"True enough." His laughter rumbles through him, but then his expression shifts, growing more serious. "I wasn't just talking about the sex, lass. Though that's been," he kisses my forehead, "quite remarkable."

My heart stutters. "What were you talking about, then?"

He takes a deep breath. "I was talking about how I feel when I'm with you. And how I'm not ready for that to end just yet."

"What are you saying, Cal?"

"I'm saying..." His thumb traces my lower lip, his gaze never wavering. "What if this doesn't have to end tomorrow?"

"I have to go back. My flight—"

"I know you have to leave." His voice is gentle but insistent. "I'm not asking you to cancel your flight. I'm asking if we could try."

The unspoken question hangs between us. I know what he's asking without him having to spell it out, but part of me needs to hear him say it.

"What exactly are you suggesting?" I whisper, my heart pounding so hard I'm sure he can feel it.

His fingers slide into my hair, cradling the back of my head. "I'm suggesting that maybe we don't have to say goodbye. Not permanently."

I swallow hard. "Long distance is...complicated."

"Most things worth having are," he counters. "Look, I'm not saying it'll be easy, but I'm willing to try if you are."

Of course I'm willing to try. How could I not? I'm in love with the man.

This is terrifying. A leap without a net. Long distance is going to be a bitch. The timing sucks. Logistics will be a nightmare. But he's here right now with his hand in my hair and hope in his voice, and I'd be an idiot to pretend that doesn't mean everything.

Even with how uncertain this is, it might be the easiest yes I've ever said.

I smile. "I'm in."

His brow lifts. "Aye?"

"*Aye.*"

He lets out a laugh that warms me from the inside out. "Thank god. I would *not* be okay if you went back to the States and started seeing someone else."

"Oh. Well, that's...a pretty intense way of telling me you have jealousy issues."

His smirk is pure trouble. "Lass, I have exclusivity issues. Specifically, I need you to be exclusively mine."

I don't waste another second. I grab his face and crash my lips to his, pouring everything into the kiss. Every ounce of fear, longing, and hope I've been too afraid to put into words. I need him to feel it. "Say it again," I murmur against his lips.

"You heard me just fine, love."

"Then say it again," I whisper.

He leans in, his lips brushing my ear. "You're mine," he says, drawing each word out like he's savoring the taste of it. "Want me to write it down? Maybe get it notarized?"

I laugh, pressing my forehead to his. "That's actually a good idea. You should definitely do that."

He grins. "Then let's make it official, over and over again. Now get the fuck over here and get on top of me."

A slow smirk tugs at my lips as warmth spreads through me, anticipation curling low in my stomach. "Yes, sir," I purr, already moving. Already *his*.

nineteen

BREE

I can't believe it's time for me to leave. This *sucks*.

If I'm being brutally honest, I think I started falling for him the moment we met, which was almost a year ago now. I was still knee-deep in my mess with Dillon back then, clinging to a relationship I knew was broken. Pouring myself into fixing what was never meant to be whole again. And now, here I am, standing on the edge of something that could actually be mine if I let it.

Walking away will be like leaving a piece of me behind that I'll never get back.

I need to stop overthinking. I really do. Because right now, he's lying next to me, still asleep, his breath slow, his body warm against mine. These are our last few hours together, and I refuse to waste them stuck in my own head.

He shifts slightly, his fingers brushing mine, and I go still, not wanting to wake him just yet. I want to freeze this exact second where the world feels like it's still mine. To memorize every small detail, like the way his lashes rest against his cheeks, that half smile lingering even in his sleep, the messy hair I tangled with my fingers last night.

The truth is screaming at me. I'm running out of time.

His eyes flutter open, and for a split second, he looks confused, still caught between sleep and waking. Then he catches me staring, and that sleepy, dopey grin spreads across his face.

"What?" he mumbles, his voice rough with sleep, not quite awake but fully aware of me. That awareness makes my heart leap into my throat.

"You drool when you sleep," I tease. It's a lie, of course. He doesn't drool.

His brow furrows as he wipes at his mouth. Then, realization hits and he glares at me, the corners of his mouth twitching as he fights back a smile.

"You're a brat," he grumbles, pulling the blanket over his head.

I laugh and tug it back down. "You're cute when you're grumpy, you know that?"

He can't fully hide his smile. "Stop flirting. I'm mad at you."

How am I supposed to leave this? Leave him?

He's smirking like he's got the world at his feet, while I'm here with my heart pounding, knowing that time is slipping through our fingers. It's too much.

"What's wrong?"

"Nothing," I lie. I shake my head, hoping he won't hear the tremor, but he does.

His gaze sharpens, those piercing eyes narrowing as he reads me like an open book. "You're thinking about it again, aren't you?"

"Maybe." I sit up, pulling the blanket tighter around me,

trying to choke down the knot in my throat. "This whole leaving thing sucks."

"You're not *leaving* leaving," he says, like it's that simple. "You're just...temporarily relocating. We'll see each other again soon. I'll be texting you memes and random thoughts until you can't stand it anymore in the meantime."

I force out a shaky laugh, but it doesn't quite reach my heart. The ache is still there. He's trying to make it better, but the thought of leaving still feels like a mountain I can't climb. "You make it sound so easy."

He pulls me back down, his arms wrapping around me like he's trying to keep me tethered to him. I let him, burying my face in his chest, even though my mind won't stop thinking about the goodbye that's coming, and how much I'm already dreading it.

"It's not," he murmurs, his voice full of that certainty that makes me want to believe him. "We'll figure it out. You'll see."

He sounds so sure, but the knot in my stomach won't loosen.

"And you're right, this does suck," he continues, "but you're here right now, and I can think of a few different ways to hold us both over until next time."

I can't help but laugh, the tension easing as I tilt my head back to look at him. He's incorrigible, and I just happen to love it.

"Oh yeah? You mean something like this?" I tease, taking his index finger between my lips and letting the tip graze my tongue as I pull it deeper into my mouth, watching his eyes darken.

Before I can take it any farther, he flips me onto my back, his hands moving so fast I'm left gasping for air. His body hovers over mine, the heat between us a live wire, crackling with every breath.

"You want to tease me, lass?" he growls. "I'll show you teasing."

I'm all for it. *Yes, please.*

I barely have time to register his wet finger slipping into my already soaked pussy before his teeth graze over my sensitive nipple.

I burn the image into my brain and save it in my personal *lust library* for later reference. This is one I'll definitely want to revisit.

I'm CLUTCHING my purse in the passenger seat of Cal's truck. The closer we get to the airport, the more my heart hurts.

"Don't let them trick you into paying extra for leg room," Callan says, his voice light and teasing. "Just take up yoga and learn to fold yourself like origami."

I steal a glance at him, catching the moment his easy smile falters. It's subtle, but it's enough for me to notice. He's doing what he always does by throwing out jokes and trying to keep things upbeat. His laugh comes quick, but it's strained and not as genuine as usual. Today, the mask isn't working. He's just as scared as I am.

It almost makes me angry because I don't want him to deflect. I need him to stop pretending this is just another ordinary goodbye. I want him to say something real. Part of me wishes he'd tell me not to leave and give me a reason to stay.

But this is who he is, and it's one of the things I love about him. Maybe it's easier for him than it is for me. Maybe he's already made peace with it, while I'm wondering how the hell I'm going to manage walking away.

My heart's screaming to stay, even though logic says I can't.

My mind flashes back to life before him. Dillon's suffocating control, the constant fear gnawing at my insides, the nights spent convincing myself I deserved better but never believing it. And then Callan happened. Everything about him was the antidote to the poison Dillon left behind. He made me feel free. He made me feel...alive again.

Now, I'm being asked to walk away from all of it.

It's a cruel twist of fate, really.

So, no. I can't be angry with him for trying to make light of all this. I get it. This is how he holds it together. I guess I've been retreating into my own head for the same reason. Even as I try to justify it, my chest tightens with the realization that he's the reason I started believing I deserved better. Not just better than Dillon, but better than the life I've been living where I was too scared to take or feel anything too deeply.

Now, as I watch him with his hands tight on the steering wheel, throwing out jokes like it's second nature, I can't help but wonder if he's just as fragile as I am. He's holding it all in behind those words that don't quite reach his eyes. Maybe he's just as scared of what comes next.

"Callan..."

"Yeah?"

I want to tell him that I'm terrified to go back and he's the only thing that's ever felt like home, but the words are stuck in my throat. If I say them out loud, I'm pretty sure it'll only make this harder for both of us. I'm not sure I'm ready for that kind of emotional whiplash.

So instead, I force a smile. It's small, shaky, and probably about as convincing as a toddler pretending to be a dinosaur. I quickly look away, hoping he won't notice the way my heart's on the verge of shattering. "Nothing," I mumble.

Real smooth.

He doesn't let it slide. "No. That's not nothing. You're not going to just leave without saying what's on your mind."

I don't have to look at him to know his eyes are fixed on me. The pressure makes the words spill out before I can stop them. "I'm scared, okay?" I admit, my voice trembling. "Scared of going back. Scared of everything being the same. Of everything falling apart again. And scared of whatever," I gesture vaguely between us, "this is."

There's nothing but the sound of our breaths filling the silence before I continue. "I don't know how to leave and not feel like I'm making the biggest mistake of my life, but I also don't know how to stay. I can't just exist in this...in-between."

He's frozen for a moment, and then his expression shifts into shock. His lips part, but no words come. His eyes flicker between me and the road with emotions flashing too quickly for me to catch.

"I didn't know you felt that way," he finally says. His gaze isn't the usual playful, teasing spark I'm used to. And that uncertainty in his eyes? It makes the hole in my chest feel a hell of a lot bigger. I didn't mean to hurt him, but somehow, I've done exactly that.

"I didn't know how to tell you," I admit. "You seem so...at ease with all of this, and I'm just..." I trail off, the words slipping through my fingers. I close my eyes for a moment, trying to control my breath. "I don't know what to say, Cal. I'm afraid."

The truck suddenly feels too small. I'm too nervous to look him in the eyes, but I catch his hand rubbing over his face out of the corner of my eyes.

"You should've told me." His voice is firm, and the words land with more force than I'm ready for. I want to argue and tell him that I didn't know how, or that I wasn't ready to expose myself like this, but he's right. And it stings.

"I know I should have," I say, determined to keep my voice steady. "But it's not that simple. You're always so unbothered. It's weird to talk about...sad stuff with you."

His grip on the steering wheel flexes, knuckles paling as his lips press into a hard line. A muscle tics in his jaw, his eyes locked straight ahead while frustration radiates off him in waves.

"That hurts, Bree." His voice is quieter now, but there's no mistaking the strain in it. "I just told you it would kill me to see you with anyone else, for Christ's sake, and you don't trust me enough to be *sad* around me?"

The guilt hits me immediately. The last thing I ever wanted was to make him feel like I don't trust him or like he's not enough.

"That's...not what I meant," I manage, but even I can hear how weak it sounds.

"Then what did you mean? Because right now, it sounds a hell of a lot like you're saying I'm not the guy you can turn to when you're hurting."

I messed up, and now I need to fix it. I need him to understand.

"That's not it," I rush to explain. "It's just... You handle everything so effortlessly. I don't want to be the one who drags you down with my mess."

For a second, I think he's going to snap, but when he speaks, his voice is calm. I should know better.

"Bree, you're not a burden. You're never a mess to me. Don't shut me out. Don't think I'm too...*whatever* to care."

He reaches over and his fingers brush mine, and god, I needed that. The second our skin touches, that familiar warmth spreads through me, silencing the chaos in my mind. He tightens his grip on my hand. "I want *all* of you. Good, bad, and everything in between."

I take a shaky breath. "I don't usually let people in like that," I confess. "I kind of just...deal with it myself."

"Not anymore, you don't," he says firmly. "If you're scared, tell me. If you're sad, angry, hell, if you hate my guts, *tell me*."

I don't stand a chance against this man. He's out here saying all the right things, holding my hand like I'm the most precious thing he's ever touched and looking at me like I hung the damn moon.

I should probably say something deep and meaningful to match, but my brain? Useless. All thanks to that ridiculous accent that turns my insides to mush.

"Okay," I whisper.

"Aye?"

"Yes, *aye*." I smirk.

He exhales slowly, his voice dropping lower. "I'm terrified, too, Sunshine. Don't think for a second I'm not. I just wanted to make you smile one more time before I have to watch you walk away."

Oh, come on. That's not fair. How am I supposed to keep it together when he says things like that? I'm seconds away from throwing myself at him and ugly crying into his shirt.

And then, as if he can sense I'm teetering on the edge, he tilts his head, his lips twitching. "So, did we just have our first fight?" he asks. "Is this where we kiss and make up?"

The tension around us splinters, cracking wide enough for something softer to slip through, and I let out a laugh. "Yeah, yeah. I guess so."

CALLAN

The sound of gloves hitting heavy bags, the rhythmic pounding of feet against the canvas, it's all music to my ears. The gym's air is thick with sweat and leather, and it's exactly the kind of atmosphere I need right now. A place to work out the chaos and focus on nothing but the next punch.

Goddamn it. I'm an idiot. She's right. I suck at feelings. I can handle chaos, but emotions? That's the part I've never quite figured out how to fix or finesse, and now I'm sitting here with the echo of her footsteps fading into the airport, and this fucking ache behind my ribs that won't let up.

Because she's gone. I know it's just for now but still. I let her walk away without being the guy she needed me to be.

It's not just that I miss her already. It's that I wanted her to know she could lean on me. That I'd show up. That I'd stand in the damn storm if it meant shielding her for even one second. But I didn't say that.

Instead, I gave her half of what she deserved. Played it cool when everything in me wanted to grab her hand and tell her she's not alone anymore.

I want to be better for her because this isn't just some passing fling for me. This is her. Bree. And she's got this way of laughing and looking at me like I might actually be worth something.

I drag in a breath that scarcely fills my lungs. Still tight. Still heavy. Letting her go without telling her how much she matters? That's a mistake I can feel down to my damn bones.

I need to drown out these thoughts.

Adrenaline's the answer. That rush, that raw energy that pushes everything else out of my mind. I just need to chase it. I need to move and get out of my head before it consumes me completely.

Drew, the owner of the gym and an old friend who's seen me at both my best and worst, spots me the second I walk in, a shit-eating grin already plastered on his face. "Long time, no see, killer." He tosses me a pair of gloves from the shelf.

I catch them without missing a beat, slipping them on and letting my fingers curl into the padding. "Yeah, I've been busy trying not to make an arse of myself," I mutter, already moving toward the bag. I don't need to say much more. My body remembers the rhythm, and I'm itching to get into it.

He just raises an eyebrow, clearly entertained by my tone. "You know the drill, man. Don't half arse it. The bag isn't gonna hit back."

I roll my neck, giving it a few cracks for good measure. "You know, Drew, I *really* wish it would. Might make this a bit more interesting."

Without waiting for his response, I step in and slam my first punch into the bag, but it's not nearly enough. My fists begin to move faster, harder. A jab, a right hook, then another as the bag swings back, only for me to meet it again with relentless force. Every punch I land feels like I'm trying to destroy the uncertainty, the anger, the helplessness crawling under my skin.

"Keep your guard up!" Drew's voice cuts through the air, but it's background noise, barely registering. "You're here to control the fight!"

Control. Right. That's what I'm after. I'm losing it in every other part of my life, but this I can control. My fists pound the bag harder, faster, as if each hit might erase the image of her walking away from me.

Sweat pours down my face, stinging my eyes, but I wipe it away without a second thought. Each strike reverberates through me, and the faster I hit, the louder my heart pounds. The bag isn't the enemy. She's not the enemy. But god, I'm battling something much bigger than I can handle.

Drew steps closer. "Focus. You're not gonna solve anything by swinging at thin air. Quit letting your mind wander."

I grunt in acknowledgment as I launch into another series of punches. The burn in my muscles and the rush of exertion are almost enough to make me forget. For a second, I'm only aware of the bag, the force of my strikes, and the primal rhythm of my breath.

Adrenaline surges. The temporary escape. My thoughts clear and the world narrows down to nothing but the power of my fists and the sharp sting of each punch. It's almost enough to make me believe I've got control.

But the fear's still there, creeping in from the edges. This isn't fixing anything.

"Cheer up, you sour puss."

I shoot Lucy my best death glare, but it crumbles quickly. She has this way of cracking through my defenses, and damn it, it's impossible to stay mad at her.

"Oh no, not the death stare," she teases. "Should I start drafting my will?"

"You're lucky you're my sister," I grumble.

"And you're lucky I'm this charming," she quips, launching a plastic spoon in my direction.

I dodge it with a laugh. "Charmingly annoying, maybe."

Her smile slowly fades as she starts unpacking the take-away. "Seriously, though. I hate seeing you so mopey. It's not like you."

I swipe a hand over my face. It's been a week since Bree went back home. A week of restless nights and days spent staring at my phone, willing it to ring. This isn't the first time she's left. She's always had a life to return to, far away from mine.

But this time, she left after I'd held her and memorized the way her body fit against mine. After I'd tasted her lips and breathed in her moans. After I'd loved her in every way that mattered.

She took a piece of me with her, and for the first time, I'm not sure how to be myself without her here. This is new to me, and the emptiness gnaws at me. I hate it.

I grab a couple of beers from the fridge and set them on the table. Lucy showed up with dinner, and the least I can do is act like I'm happy she's here. Which, to be fair, I am. She's my sister, and she's always had my back, but it doesn't take a genius to know I'm not exactly the best company right now.

She raises an eyebrow at the beers. "What, no wine? You really know how to spoil a girl."

I pop the caps off and slide one over to her. "You're lucky you got anything. Showing up unannounced has its risks."

She laughs, pulling out plates and setting them down with exaggerated care. "You'd miss me if I didn't."

I won't argue with that.

We're barely settled at the table when she clears her throat, the kind of sound that screams *I've got something to say.* I take a long sip of my beer, stalling as the cold liquid slides down my throat.

Her eyes are locked on me, though. Full of curiosity and the right amount of concern.

"Okay..." she says slowly, weighing her words carefully. "You want to talk about this? Or should I keep pretending you're fine?"

I set my beer down with a thud and run a hand through my hair, trying to pull my thoughts together. "Pretty sure you just ruined the pretending option," I mutter.

"Good," she says. "Because you're terrible at it."

I drag a hand down my face, taking a deep breath. "You want the truth?"

Her eyes practically sparkle as she leans forward. "I already know the truth," she says smugly. "I just want to hear you say it."

I take a beat, trying to swallow the lump in my throat. "It's about Bree."

She claps her hands together. "I knew it!" she exclaims. "I've been waiting for you to figure it out for months."

I can't help but laugh, a small sense of relief creeping in. "You're such a pain," I mutter, shaking my head.

"I'm just trying to help," she says. "Now, come on. Spill the details. What happened?"

I lean back, and the knot in my chest loosens with each word. I tell her everything.

Bree and I talk every day, even if it's just for a few minutes on the phone in between texts. The time difference and her work schedule are tough, but we make it work. I do my best to keep things light, cracking jokes and staying upbeat, even when every call leaves me wanting more.

She doesn't need to hear about how much I hate the silence when we hang up, or how every goodbye twists in my gut. How I catch myself reaching for her in the middle of the night only to find the bed empty. How I've developed a completely irrational hatred for time zones.

So I do what I can. Swallow the ache. Focus on being the guy who makes her laugh instead of the one who misses her so much it's pathetic. I hold onto the hope that, at some point, this whole long-distance thing won't feel like I'm slowly bleeding out.

I can still hear her voice in my head from our call earlier.

"Hey, love," I said. "How's everything?"

Bree's voice came through the phone strained, even if she was trying to mask it. "Oh, you know, same old. Busy, but fine." Her words were clipped, too rushed, like she was trying to sound normal, but I could hear it. The exhaustion. The cracks in the armor.

I stayed quiet for a moment, knowing she wouldn't open up unless I pushed a little. "You sure?"

A soft laugh came through the line. "I'm fine, Callan. Really."

I knew she wasn't fine. I could feel it through the silence, the way she hesitated a little too long before responding. "You don't have to lie to me, Bree. What's really going on?"

There was a long pause. I could hear her breathing—slow, heavy, like she was trying to keep it together. Then, finally, she spoke, her voice the softest whisper. "It's just...a lot, you know? I miss you."

I knew she was struggling but hearing it out loud tore me apart.

"I miss you more," I said, my voice thick with emotion. "You don't have to hide that from me, you know."

Her voice wavered again, and I knew she was holding back tears. "I know, Callan. I just... I don't want to be that person."

"You're not that person, Bree," I said fiercely.

She fell silent, and I could almost feel the weight of the moment between us. I wanted so badly to reach through the phone, to hold her, to make everything better.

"I'll be okay," she finally said.

She's not okay. And no matter how much I tell myself I'm doing enough, I know I'm not. Not even close.

"I think...I should go visit her."

"Well, of course you should," Lucy replies. "It's a two-way street, aye? She came to you. Now it's your turn to haul your broody arse over there."

I snort. "More like a twelve-hour flight across an entire ocean, but sure, we'll call it a street. Nice, easy commute."

I can joke about skipping the country, but the truth is, I'd do it in a heartbeat just to see her.

BREE

It's been one of those days where the clock seems to run faster than I can keep up with. From the moment I walked through the hospital doors, it's been a blur of urgent beeping monitors, frantic calls, and an endless parade of patients. It's been three weeks since I got back from Scotland, but it feels like a lifetime ago. The excitement of that whirlwind trip is long gone, replaced by the constant pressure of being back in this chaotic routine.

My feet are killing me, and each step is a reminder of how much ground I've covered with no time to rest. We're under-staffed again, which means everything is just that much harder. My body is on autopilot, running on fumes, and my head is pounding.

I slide into the breakroom, completely exhausted as I lay my head down on the table. Just one second. It's all I need to try to catch my breath before the mayhem drags me back in.

My phone buzzes. I groan, realizing I haven't checked it in hours. *Shit.*

There are two messages from Mom, asking if I'm coming to

dinner. I'm not, and honestly, I can't muster the energy to explain why. There's one from Juliette, a sweet check-in because she always knows when I'm overwhelmed. But it's the one from Cal that does me in.

CALLAN:

Hey, I know today's been rough, so I just wanted to remind you that you're literally one of the coolest people I know. If life were a pizza, you'd be the extra cheese. No one can resist you, and you make everything better.

I stare at it for a moment, a lump rising in my throat. It's such a Cal thing to say. Sweet and goofy. It's just what I need, but it's also the thing that's about to break me.

I miss him something fierce. Three weeks have passed since I came home, and it feels like both forever and the blink of an eye. Time's become a blur of endless twelve-hour shifts, snatched meals between patients, and crashing into bed only to wake up and do it all again. My thoughtful neighbor has been looking after Nugget during the day, saving me from losing my mind completely.

No matter how full my days are, I can't escape the ache. I catch myself wishing for just one moment to breathe, just enough time to hear his voice. The way I keep expecting him to walk through the door like he's just running late is ridiculous. Like he's not thousands of miles away, living his life on the other side of an ocean. That empty space where he belongs just keeps stretching, growing bigger, and I don't know how to fill it.

It's getting late in Scotland, but he always insists I call whenever I get a chance. *"Doesn't matter what time, Sunshine. Just call me,"* he'd told me the other night, like he already knew I'd try to argue.

I stare at his name on the screen, my thumb hovering over the call button. I'm a second away from hitting it. Before I can, a text from the charge nurse pops up, dragging me back into reality.

BOSS LADY:

We need you in Room 12.

I let out a sigh, locking my phone and shoving it back into my pocket. Figures. There's never a quiet moment around here, and today's no exception.

As I turn to leave, my partner in crime, Zoey, strolls in. She's always a burst of energy, even while the rest of us are running on empty. "Where are you off to? I was planning on dragging you into some gossip," she teases, flopping into the chair I just vacated.

"I've been summoned," I reply with an exaggerated roll of my eyes. "God forbid I get five minutes of peace."

She huffs, tossing her braid over her shoulder. "Shoot. Fine, I guess I'll see you when we head out."

"Yep, see you later." I give her a quick wave before heading out the door. My steps are quick, but my mind isn't. All I can think about is how much I need to hear his voice tonight.

Two more hours. Just one hundred and twenty minutes, and then I'm off for a few days. *I've got this.*

A panicked voice shouts my name from down the hall. "Bree, hurry up!"

My heart skips, adrenaline surging as I spring into action and break into a jog. The squeak of my sneakers echoes against the tile floor, almost jarring in the otherwise quiet hall. I race toward the room, the harsh glare of the fluorescent lights above making everything too bright and way too intense. I don't hesitate. There's always someone who needs me, and I've never been the one to stop.

Inside the room, chaos reigns. Voices clash, orders being thrown out over the sound of monitors screaming their warnings. I step in, moving like I've done a thousand times before, hands already working with precision. Every motion is instinct, my training taking over and pushing everything else out of the way.

There's no time to acknowledge the discomfort in my legs or the throbbing headache that's been lingering for hours. I focus with steady hands, despite the rush of everything around me. I clamp down on the exhaustion creeping in and the thoughts trying to pull me under. I breathe in even breaths. One task, one movement, one heartbeat at a time.

Minutes stretch into what might be an eternity. Then slowly, it starts to settle. The frantic energy in the room dissipates, leaving behind an almost oppressive silence.

I lean back against the wall, the aftermath of it all crashing over me in one heavy breath. For a moment, my pulse is the only thing I hear. The edges of my vision blur for a second, but I fight it off.

I step into the hallway, the world moving on around me as though nothing's changed. Nurses bustle past, patients shout out requests, the familiar hum of the hospital continues its rhythm. For some reason, I'm...out of sync. My feet get heavier with each step, like I'm walking through molasses. My heart hammers, too fast, too loud, and my hands shake so much that I have to force them into fists to stabilize myself.

Dizziness creeps in.

The world tilts.

My knees give way beneath me. My body slams to the floor, hard and sudden, pain exploding up my spine. Muffled voices call my name, but it sounds as if I'm underwater.

My body is untethered, disconnected, like I'm floating outside of it. The exhaustion I've been pushing down for days finally demands its due, but there's nothing left inside of me to fight it.

MY ENTIRE BODY feels like it's been steamrolled, reversed on, and then run over again for good measure. Every muscle hurts, and even blinking feels like too much effort.

I squint up at the too-bright fluorescent lights, which only intensify the throbbing behind my eyes. My brain is struggling to process where the hell I am. Stiff sheets, incessant beeping, an awful sterile smell...

Wait. Am I in a hospital bed?

"Jesus Christ, Bree. You scared the absolute shit out of me."

I wince, my neck protesting as I turn to find Zoey sitting beside me. Her eyes are wide, her face an expression of panic and fury, like she's torn between hugging and strangling me.

Oh yeah, that's right. I passed out in the middle of the damn hallway. Just dropped like a rock.

"Sorry," I mumble. "I'll try not to inconvenience you next time."

She snorts, though the concern still lingers in the way her brows furrow. "You can't even quit the sarcasm when you're half dead."

I manage a weak smile. "What can I say? It's my best quality."

Her chuckle fades almost as quickly as it comes, and she shifts, her tone more serious now. "Bree, you're dehydrated and exhausted. You *know* better."

She's right. I *do* know better. I'm a nurse for god's sake. How the hell am I supposed to help other people if I can't even take care of myself?

"I'm fine." The words don't sound convincing to me. Hell, they sound exactly like the lie that they are.

"Yeah, sure. That's why you collapsed during your shift,"

she shoots back. "You're running yourself into the ground, Bree. It's not fine. *You're* not fine."

I close my eyes for a second. "I know. I've picked up too many extra hours."

What I won't tell her, what I won't tell anyone, is that I've been purposely keeping myself busy to prevent my mind from spiraling. Because when I'm still, when I have time to think, all I do think about is him.

Zoey's sigh is softer this time. "You'll be good to go home here in a bit, but I'll drive you," she says. "You have no business getting behind the wheel today."

I don't argue. I'm too tired to fight her on this. "Okay, fair enough. Wouldn't want to add *terrible driver* to my list of faults."

She rolls her eyes but snorts a laugh. "Sarcasm and self-deprecation. Your two favorite coping mechanisms."

I smirk, but the moment is short-lived as a realization smacks me in the face. I never got back to Callan. Or my mom.

"Shit, Zoey. Where's my phone?" I move quickly to sit up straighter, which is a mistake because the room sways.

"Oh, here." She pulls my phone out of her pocket. "Don't worry, I called Mama Bear and told her you were a little woozy. Figured you didn't want her storming up here."

"Callan...?" I ask. Zoey knows all about him. She has since the beginning. There was no hiding how obsessed I've been, not from her.

She gives me a sad smile. "I did try to call him from your phone, but it went straight to voicemail. I sent him a text instead. I hope that's okay. I only saw, like, one or two of your dirty messages in the process."

My jaw drops. "Zoey!"

She shrugs, completely unbothered. "What? It's not my fault you two have the texting habits of horny teenagers."

I groan, snatching my phone from her hand. "Please tell me you didn't open anything you shouldn't have."

"Define *shouldn't have*." She grins, and I resist the urge to throw my pillow at her.

I know she's just teasing, but the thought still makes my stomach flip. I really hope she didn't go scrolling back too far. Let's just say there was a phase when Callan and I were swapping some...*very* risqué photos. Knowing Zoey, if she had seen anything, she'd absolutely let me know all about it. Probably with detailed commentary on his impressive...package.

I unlock the phone, trying to act casual but my heart sinks a little when I see there aren't any new messages from him. Not too surprising, I guess. It is the middle of the night over there.

"Well, thank you." I reply, truly grateful. Zoey may drive me crazy sometimes, but she's the kind of friend everyone needs. Especially when you're lying in a hospital bed trying not to feel like a complete failure.

"Of course." She waves it off. Then her eyes light up with the kind of excitement that only comes from a juicy story. "Now, let me tell you what I heard about Lila and Dr. Rhodes..."

I can't help but laugh, settling back into the pillows as she launches into full gossip mode. My body might feel like it's been hit by a truck, but at least my spirit will get a boost.

twenty-two

BREE

Z oey dropped me off an hour ago, and I was *so* close to drifting off into blissful sleep. I showered, slipped into my comfiest pajamas, and collapsed onto the couch with Nugget. My body is beyond exhausted, but apparently, my brain missed the memo. I'm wide awake.

Just as I start to sink into the glorious embrace of the couch, there's a knock at the door.

Ugh.

Nugget's ears perk up, and he's already glaring at the door as if the boogeyman himself is standing on the other side. I give him a soft chuckle, rubbing behind his ears. "Chill out, boy. Let's see who it is first before we go into protector mode."

He huffs in response, still glaring at the door. He reluctantly starts to calm down. I sigh, already bracing for whatever awful interruption is about to happen and slowly creep toward the door. You know, just in case it *is* the boogeyman or, god forbid, a door-to-door salesman.

I crack the door open and freeze.

What the—

There's no way. No freakin' way.

Callan.

My brain takes a second to process it, but even then, I can't seem to figure out if this is real or if my tired eyes are playing tricks on me.

"Callan?" I whisper, almost afraid to say his name out loud in case I've somehow slipped into a weird dream state. Is this really happening?

But then there's the unmistakable pressure of his fingers on my skin. His thumbs glide gently across my cheeks. He cups my face in his hands like he's afraid he might lose me if he blinks. His eyes sweep over me, scanning, searching, making sure I'm not broken in any way. I'm *so* close to losing it because he's looking at me like *he* might fall apart if I'm not okay.

His voice cracks, words tumbling out in a rush, as if he's been holding his breath this whole time. "My god, I was so worried. I didn't get the message until I was stepping off the plane."

And that's it. The second those words escape his lips, the sobs I've been holding back for three long weeks come crashing to the surface. I've kept them locked up tight and buried under layers of distraction since the moment I came home. Every single day without him was like walking around with a piece of myself missing.

I clutch the front of his shirt, my hands trembling as the fabric absorbs the tears I've been too afraid to let fall until now. "I missed you...so...much," I manage, my voice breaking with each ragged hiccup.

His strong arms are around me in an instant, pulling me close as he kicks the door shut behind him. "Come on, lass," he murmurs. He presses a tender kiss to the top of my head, and in that moment, everything that's been spinning out of control finally starts to settle.

"You need to sit," he says softly, his hand guiding me but not forcefully.

He's not wrong. My legs have turned into jelly, and the condo's small enough that the living room's only a few feet away. He lowers me onto the couch, and then, without hesitation, pulls me onto his lap. Normally, I'd have something sarcastic to say about being treated like a baby, but right now, I don't have it in me. I don't want to fight it.

Being cradled in his arms with the strong beat of his heart under my cheek... It's like finally breathing after being underwater for too long. It's everything I've been missing.

"What are you even doing here?" I finally ask, still in complete disbelief.

"Surprise?"

I smirk, leaning in to press my lips against his neck. "Surprise, indeed."

Nugget, who's been silently observing us like some furry little judge, lets out a quiet whine from his spot on the floor. My heart sinks a bit at the sound. "Oh, shoot! Poor Nuggie's probably so confused." I extend my hand, gesturing for him to come over. "Come here, sweet boy."

Nugget trots over, tail wagging, and rests his head on the edge of the couch. Callan's body tenses beneath me, stiffening like a board.

"Are you okay?"

He clears his throat a little too quickly. "Um, yeah. Totally fine."

He doesn't look fine. His eyes are locked on Nugget like the dog might decide to rip his face off. Cal's hands are practically frozen, his fingers twitching, bracing for an attack that doesn't come. It's not the reaction I expected. Nugget, with his big, wide eyes and floppy ears, is about as harmless as a marshmallow, but it's clear Callan's bothered.

"Are you...afraid of dogs?"

His gaze snaps back to me, eyes wide for a split second before he exhales a long, drawn-out breath. "Aye. That's one way to put it."

I don't want to laugh because I can tell this is no joke, but...

"You're telling me that big, bad, fearless Callan MacKenzie is scared of precious fluff balls?"

He winces, clearly not thrilled with where this conversation is heading. And that's when it hits me. I try to hold it in, but a laugh bursts free before I can stop it. "I'm sorry, oh my gosh, I'm so sorry." I gasp between giggles. "It's not funny, I swear. I promise Nugget won't harm a hair on your head. But Cal... Dogs? Of all the things, it's *dogs*."

"I was attacked by one when I was little," he admits. "Vicious thing."

Well, now I feel like an asshole.

"What kind of dog was it? Not a German shepherd, I hope."

He shakes his head quickly, his gaze flickering toward the floor. "It was a...uh...chihuahua," he confesses.

And that's when I lose it completely. "A chihuahua?" I gasp, barely able to get the words out between fits of laughter. "I didn't realize ankle biters could leave such emotional scars."

His face flushes bright red. "Aye, laugh it up. Those wee devils are more ferocious than you'd think. All teeth and attitude."

I try to compose myself, wiping tears from my eyes. "I'm sorry, I really am. It's just... I never expected you to fear a dog that only just reaches your knees."

"That's because they're sneaky," he argues. "You don't know what it's like to face off with one of those wee bastards. They come at you from all directions, all teeth and no fear. It's like a battle of wills."

I raise a brow, still laughing but trying to hold onto some semblance of seriousness. "A battle of wills, huh? And who won in the end, Callan? The chihuahua?"

"Aye," he mutters. "The chihuahua won. And don't you forget it."

I can't help but soften, my grin fading as I meet his eyes. "Well, Nugget's a sweetheart, I promise. How about we introduce you two properly? You're the two most important men in my life."

A slow smirk creeps onto his face as he eyes Nugget with a suspicious glance. "The two most important men, huh? Should I be jealous?"

I laugh, shaking my head. "Only if you're worried about him stealing your side of the bed. He's a cuddler."

Callan leans in closer, his voice dropping into a teasing murmur. "Don't worry, lass. I don't plan on sharing your attention."

"You're trying to distract me," I scold. "Just hold your hand out and let him sniff you."

Nugget stares up at us with his head tilted to the side. His big brown eyes are wide, trying to understand every word we're saying.

Callan stretches out a reluctant hand, fingers stiff like he's facing down a coiled viper instead of a wagging tail. I try not to laugh, but it's hard when he's so...serious.

The tension in his shoulders tells me this is no joke to him, though. I can see he's fighting more than just embarrassment. Nugget, oblivious to Callan's obvious apprehension, sniffs his outstretched hand with enthusiasm. His tail wags harder, and with no warning, he plants a big, wet lick right on Callan's knuckles.

I bite my lip, watching as Callan freezes. His eyes widen in shock, quickly morphing into disgust.

"What was that?"

"He likes you."

He glances from me to Nugget, his brow furrowing in confusion. "That's how he shows it? By slobbering on me?"

I scratch Nugget behind his ears. "It's a compliment, trust me."

Callan sighs, shaking his head, but I notice the faintest curve of a smile tugging at his lips. "This beast and I have very different ideas when it comes to compliments."

"Do you, though?"

He holds my gaze for a beat, then glances back at Nugget, the corner of his mouth quirking up a little more. "I suppose you're right. Maybe I can learn something from him after all."

It doesn't catch me off guard in the slightest when Callan leans over and, with a mischievous glint in his eyes, licks my cheek. I burst into laughter, wiping my face with the back of my hand. "Exactly what I thought."

His smirk deepens, clearly pleased with his impromptu display of affection. "I'm just following Nugget's lead. Thought I'd give it a shot."

I shake my head, still chuckling as I lean back against him. "You're lucky I'm too exhausted to give you a hard time about that."

twenty-three

BREE

W e've fallen into a comfortable silence. I'm tucked into his arms, my body finally surrendering to the comfort and safety he offers. It's the kind of peace I've been yearning for.

"I'm so glad you're here," I whisper.

His lips brush against my temple in a gentle kiss. "Can we talk about the fact that you've been working yourself to death?"

My stomach tightens, and I quickly shake my head. "Can we...not?"

I mean it. I really don't want to talk about it. The truth is, I'm not sure I can without falling apart. I've been drowning in work, pushing myself to the brink just to avoid confronting how much I've missed him. What if I scare him off?

His usually carefree expression shifts, turning serious. He looks down at me, his hand gently rubbing my arm. "Bree... What's going on?"

His genuine concern melts away the last of my reservations. "I missed you. Terribly. Picking up some extra shifts was a good distraction. Well...until it wasn't." I wince.

His arms tighten around me, pulling me closer, and I revel in the rise and fall of his chest as he exhales a deep sigh. "I missed you, too. More than you know." His voice is low, thick with guilt and longing. "But you can't keep doing this to yourself. It's not healthy."

I nod against him, my voice barely a whisper. "I know." I pause, fighting the lump in my throat. "But every time I stop moving, stop working, I think about how far away you are, and I was afraid..." My voice cracks, betraying me in the worst way. I just stopped crying, damn it. And now, the tears are threatening to spill again.

He pulls back, lifting my chin to meet his gaze. "Afraid of what, Sunshine?"

My heart stutters, and I take a shaky breath. "That the distance is too much, and that it might not be worth it for you."

A flicker of hurt flashes crosses his face, and guilt claws at me. I want to take it back. I need to take it back.

"Have I ever, even once, given you the impression that this isn't worth it?" he asks, his voice strained. "That we aren't worth it?"

I shake my head. "No, you haven't. It's just...my own insecurities getting the best of me."

His thumbs swipe away the tears that have slipped past my control. "Listen to me, Bree," he says, his voice unwavering. "You are worth everything to me. The distance, the long nights, the missed calls...all of it. I crossed a fucking ocean for you, and I'd do it a million times more."

There's a lump in my throat the size of an iceberg. I'm pretty sure if I open my mouth again, it'll just be a chorus of ugly sobs. Instead of replying with some profound, heartfelt declaration of my own, all that comes out is, "I'm sorry."

"Please don't apologize," he says. "It just breaks my heart to know you've been struggling like this on your own...again." His head inclines slightly, his gaze locking with mine, searching for the reassurance he needs. "You can trust me, aye? I don't say things I don't mean," he continues. "And I meant it when I said we'd figure this out together."

I nod as his words work their magic. He's peeling away the layers of fear I've been suffocating under, and for a moment, I can breathe again. But even though his words soothe the ache that's been gnawing at me for weeks, it doesn't change the fact that I'm living two separate lives.

There's the one without him, where I work, exist, and force myself to get through the days. Where I'm just passing through, waiting for something to give. And then there's the life I have when we're together, the one that feels more like me than anything else. It's everything, but it's fleeting.

"Hey," he says, pulling me from my thoughts. "I'm here. Even if you think I'm too good to be true."

I blink, completely thrown off. "What?"

He shrugs, his grin turning playful. "You've got that look, like you're waiting for the other shoe to drop. I promise, I'm real. You want me to prove it?"

I raise a brow, a smile tugging at the corner of my lips. "How exactly would you do that?"

He leans in closer, his breath warm against my skin, and my whole body shivers with awareness. His lips hover a breath away from mine.

"Could an imaginary boyfriend do this?"

He presses a gentle kiss to the tip of my nose, his lips lingering just long enough to make my heart skip a beat.

I open my mouth to speak, but before I can, he tilts his head, his lips brushing my cheek in a way that sends sparks across my skin. When his mouth moves to the corner of mine, the whole world narrows to this single, suspended moment. He's so close but not close enough.

"Or this?" he murmurs.

And then, without another word, his lips finally meet mine.

The kiss starts slow, the unbearable longing burning through every inch of my body. His lips move against mine with a hunger that matches my own, and it's impossible to hold back. My hands tangle in his hair, tugging him closer, every inch of me craving him. My body presses against his as if it's the only place I've ever known, and the only place I ever want to be.

I needed this. Weeks of distance and emptiness fade into nothing and every second apart is wiped away, replaced by his heat and the raw urgency of our bodies colliding together. His lips are soft, but the kiss is anything but gentle. It's desperate, frantic, like neither of us can get close enough, and I'm lost in it. Lost in *him*.

When we finally pull apart, our foreheads meet, both of us gasping for breath. It's still not enough.

"Real enough for you?" His voice is a deep rasp, but the tenderness underneath it makes my heart clench.

I laugh, breathless, my fingers brushing over his jawline as I nod my head slowly. "Yes," I whisper. "You're very, very real."

"I'm not going anywhere," he replies. "Not as long as you'll have me."

I pull him into another kiss. There are no words to express how much I've missed him, so instead, I let my lips do the talking. When he responds, pulling me deeper, every ounce of that need is met.

When we break apart again, his fingers glide over my cheek, tucking a loose strand of hair behind my ear. "I'm pretty sure I just kissed you into a puddle. Admit it. I'm unforgettable."

"A puddle? Humble much?" I raise a brow, fighting a laugh.

"Let's not get carried away. You're more like...mildly memorable."

His jaw drops in offense. "Mildly memorable? I'm wounded. I crossed an ocean and faced your beast of a dog to get to you."

"You're lucky I like you," I tease.

"Lass, I just kissed you like it was my life's mission, and all I get is a *like*?"

"Well..." I drag the word out, tapping my chin like I'm deep in thought. "I suppose you could've done a better job."

Before I can say anything else, he lunges at me, tackling me onto the couch with a playful growl that sends a rush of excitement through my veins. "Take it back!"

I burst into laughter, my chest heaving as I try to catch my breath. "Okay, okay! I take it back, you ridiculous man!"

I can see the satisfaction in his eyes as he hovers above me, still holding me down. "Better. I knew you'd come to your senses."

I shake my head, my giggles slowing. "You're impossible."

"And you're stuck with me," he says softly, his voice turning serious as he rolls us onto our sides, wrapping his arms around me with a sense of finality that makes my heart swell. "Forever, if I have my way."

Yeah. Me, too.

twenty-four

CALLAN

Bree's curled up against me on the couch, her head tucked under my chin where she belongs. She's out like a light, breathing slow and even. My arm's completely numb under her, and I swear my neck's going to start a protest any second now, but I don't dare move. I'm not even thinking about it. No way I'm disturbing this.

Her fingers are tangled in my shirt, like she's trying to anchor herself to me. It's cute, even if it is painful. My arm's about to fall off, and my neck feels like I've been holding it at an awkward angle for the last hour because, oh wait, I have. I couldn't care less, though. I'd stay like this for days if it meant she'd stay here with me, looking all peaceful and...well, sleepier than I've ever seen her.

When I walked in earlier and caught the way her shoulders sagged and the dark circles under her eyes, it hit me hard. Her light had dimmed, and I wanted to punch something. But even with her exhaustion taking over, she's still the most beautiful thing I've ever seen.

My thoughts keep pulling me back to that conversation, to the way her voice cracked when she let those fears slip out. It cuts deeper than I want to admit, the fact that she's been fighting this battle alone while I've been a world away. The space between us feels like an endless stretch of desert, wide and impossible to cross, and I don't have a damn clue how to fix it.

I meant it when I said she's everything to me. I'd burn down every barrier, climb over every wall, do whatever the hell it takes to make this right. She deserves that, and I'm gonna make sure she knows it.

A strand of her hair falls across her face, and I can't help myself. I gently brush it away, being as careful as I can not to wake her. She stirs a little, nuzzles closer, and damn if that doesn't hit me right in the chest.

"I love you," I whisper, even though I know she can't hear me. "I'm going to fix this. I promise."

She lets out a contented sigh, and her fingers tighten around my shirt, making my heart squeeze in discomfort. I've never felt this way about anyone. It's not just the fact that she's beautiful or funny or that she drives me wild in ways I never thought possible. It's more than that. I've never imagined myself feeling like this for anyone. Hell, I always thought I was the type of guy who'd be fine with casual. I even convinced myself that the whole "one person forever" thing was a bit of a fairy tale. I was so wrong.

I need to figure out how to make this work. I could visit more, but I'd have to have a word with Knox about that. Maybe I could find work here in the States, but that would mean stepping away from the family business. Not exactly an easy choice.

As I'm tangled up in my thoughts, she shifts against me and her eyes flutter open. She blinks a couple of times before focusing on my face, and the soft, sleepy look in her eyes makes everything inside me settle.

A slow, lazy smile spreads across her lips, and I realize I've been staring at her like an idiot. And for some reason, that makes me feel like the luckiest idiot alive.

"Hey," she murmurs. "How long was I out?"

I press a kiss to her forehead, letting my lips linger for just a moment longer than usual. "A couple hours. How are you feeling?"

She blinks up at me. "Better."

Before I can respond, her stomach growls loudly, and I can't help but quirk a brow at her. "Let's get you fed. You're going to need your strength for what I have planned for you."

Her cheeks flush that perfect shade of pink, but there's a spark in her eyes as her grin turns downright troublesome. "Oh, really? And what exactly do you have planned, Mr. MacKenzie?"

I stand, pulling her up with me, our bodies brushing as I keep her close. "First, dinner. Then..." I lower my voice, trailing slow kisses down the curve of her neck, savoring the way she shudders against me. "I'm going to show you just how much I've missed you. Every. Single. Inch."

She lets out a gasp, and it's all I can do not to carry her off right then and there. "Well, when you put it that way..."

I chuckle, forcing myself to take a step back. "Food first, love. Can't have you passing out on me later."

Her smirk widens as she leans in, her fingers trailing down my chest and leaving a line of heat in their wake. Her lips brush my ear, and her voice drops to a teasing whisper. "You're right. Can't get too distracted."

Distracted? I'm one kiss away from losing all sense of reason. *This woman.* She'll be the death of me, and I'll go willingly, smiling the whole way. I'll even throw in a "thank you" as I trip into oblivion.

twenty-five

BREE

We're sitting at my ridiculously small kitchen table, eating the breakfast Callan made before I even rolled out of bed. And by "eating," I mean I'm nibbling while watching him fidget like a caffeinated squirrel. His knee's bouncing, and his fingers are tapping out a whole symphony on his ceramic mug.

"You're awfully restless," I say, biting back a laugh as his drumming picks up speed.

He freezes and gives me one of those sheepish, knowing looks. "Sorry. I don't sit still very well."

I raise an eyebrow, fighting to keep my tone serious. "What, is my tiny condo too boring for you already? Does the absence of a medieval castle and rolling hills throw you off?"

His eyes go wide, like I actually think he's offended by my humble abode. "No, lass. It's not you or the place." He gestures vaguely around, his Scottish accent coming through a little stronger. "It's me. I need to do something, even if it's just pacing."

"I'm kidding, Cal. We can go out and do something today, though."

"We don't need to go anywhere just for me," he says as he leans back in his chair. "It's been less than twenty-four hours since you passed out at work. I'm perfectly happy staying here. Especially after the workout I gave you last night."

My cheeks instantly flush, and I narrow my eyes at the smug grin spreading across his ridiculously handsome face. Workout is an understatement.

I clear my throat, trying to regain my composure. "Well, I'm fine now. Better than fine, actually." I meet his gaze, my lips curving into a slow, deliberate smile. "And I'm not opposed to another...workout."

His eyes darken, that signature smirk tugging at his mouth as he leans forward, his voice dropping to a teasing rumble. "Is that so, Sunshine? I figured you might need more recovery time."

I lift my chin, meeting his intense stare with as much confidence as I can muster. "I'm tougher than I look, MacKenzie."

"That right? Guess I'll have to test your limits then."

"Guess you will," I say, my voice steady despite the way my heart is pounding. Two can play this game, but with Callan, I'm starting to think winning might mean losing, and I'm not mad about it.

Just as he reaches for me, a loud knock at the door shatters the moment, making us both jump.

"Bree? Are you there? It's Zoey. I brought soup!"

I groan, dropping my head to the table in defeat. "Of course she did."

He chuckles, leaning back and running a hand through his hair. "Your friend has impeccable timing. Can't wait to meet her."

"Bree?" Zoey's voice calls again, more insistent this time.

I sigh, dragging myself up from the chair. I crack the door open before Zoey barrels inside, a giant container in her hands and concern radiating off her.

"Hey, Zo. You didn't have to do this, but I do appreciate it."

"Of course I did," she says, already making a beeline for the kitchen. "You fainted at work yesterday for Christ's sake. It's the least I could—"

She cuts off mid-sentence, stopping dead in her tracks as her eyes land on Callan. He's at the sink, sleeves rolled up, hands soapy as he washes the dishes like some kind of domestic god.

For a moment, the only sound is the faint clinking of plates against the sink. Then Zoey whips her head toward me, her eyebrows practically hitting her hairline. "Uh, Bree? Who's the dishwasher?"

Callan looks up, and of course, he hits her with *that* smile. The one that's practically designed to make people forget how to function. I roll my eyes so hard I'm surprised they don't get stuck.

"You must be Bree's wonderful friend, Zoey," he says smoothly, stepping forward and pulling her into a hug like they're old pals.

He's laying it on thick, but the look on Zoey's face is absolutely priceless. I'm pretty sure she's seconds away from fanning herself.

"Shut the fuck up," she blurts, eyes darting between us. "*This* is Callan? You literally fainted yesterday, and now he's here, looking like...that?"

Callan laughs, the sound rich and velvety as he leans back against the counter. "I was already on my way for a surprise visit when I heard the news. Thought I'd better stick around and make sure she doesn't pull another stunt like that."

"Well, aren't you just Prince Charming?" Zoey quips,

turning to me with a wicked grin. "Bree, you've been holding out on me. He's even hotter in person."

"Hush, don't feed his ego."

Callan smirks, thoroughly enjoying himself. "I assure you, Bree keeps me humble."

Zoey snorts, plopping the container of soup down on the counter. "Uh huh. I bet she does." Her eyes sparkle with playfulness as she glances between the two of us, clearly storing ammunition for later.

He clears his throat, the corners of his mouth twitching in amusement. "Actually, I was just about to take Bree out for some fresh air. Doctor's orders and all that."

"I'll get out of your hair. Here I was, thinking Bree was sitting here all alone, but I see I have nothing to worry about."

I huff out a laugh. "Yeah, yeah. Thank you, though, for bringing this by," I say, nodding toward the soup container.

She waves me off like it's nothing. "Of course. Text me later?"

"You bet," I reply as I walk her to the door. Once I've shut it behind her, I turn around to find Callan leaning against the counter, arms crossed.

"I can see why you two are friends."

I roll my eyes, crossing my arms as I lean back against the door. "Oh, really? And what's that supposed to mean?"

He shrugs. "Just that she's every bit as feisty as you are. Makes perfect sense."

I smirk, pushing off the door and closing the distance between us. "Feisty, huh? Is that your polite way of saying *handful*?"

He tilts his head, pretending to consider it. "Maybe. But I'm not complaining."

I arch an eyebrow just inches away from him. "You think you can handle all this 'feistiness'?"

His hands slide to my hips, firm as he pulls me closer. "I think I've been handling it just fine, Sunshine."

I laugh softly, my fingers trailing up to rest against the beat of his heart. "Kiss me, *Prince Charming*. And then I need to go get ready for whatever it is we're doing today."

"As you wish, my lady," he replies, his tone dripping with mock chivalry. When he leans down, there's nothing mocking about the kiss that follows.

His lips claim mine as his grip turns possessive on my hips, anchoring me against him like he has no intention of letting go. The kiss is slow, his tongue teasing mine in a way that's almost maddening. He's taking his time, savoring every second and every reaction.

I let out a quiet sigh against his lips, my fingers curling into the fabric of his shirt to keep myself grounded, even as he tilts his head to deepen the kiss. My thoughts blur into a single, all-consuming focus—*him*.

God, I missed the way he kisses me like I'm the only thing that matters, like he's trying to memorize every detail, every sigh, every shiver. His lips move against mine with a deliberate intensity, all hunger and tenderness that makes my knees weak. Each brush of his lips, every subtle shift, sends a wave of heat coursing through me, melting away the time and distance that kept us apart.

When we finally break apart, I'm breathless, my lips tingling, my thoughts completely scrambled. Callan's dark eyes lock onto mine, smoldering with a desire that makes it hard to focus on anything except the idea of dragging him back to bed and letting the rest of the day disappear.

He takes a step back with restraint that's as frustrating as it is endearing. "Go on, get ready," he says. "As much as I'd love to keep you here all day, I think some fresh air will do us both good."

I give a reluctant nod, even as my body protests the distance between us. "Give me fifteen minutes."

WE'VE BEEN WANDERING through the local farmer's market for a while now, and Callan's enthusiasm is borderline contagious. He's like a kid let loose in a candy store, stopping at every stall with wide-eyed curiosity. His excitement doesn't discriminate. He's just as enthralled by jars of local honey as he is by handmade candles.

He's carrying a bag stuffed to capacity with a loaf of sourdough, a jar of strawberry preserves, and, inexplicably, a knitted hat he insisted I needed. Even though it's May, and I'm currently sweating in the afternoon sun.

He halts abruptly at a booth overflowing with jars of spices, his face lighting up like he's just discovered treasure. Grabbing one, he twists the lid and sniffs dramatically. "This one smells like trouble," he declares, holding it out to me.

I take the jar from him, laughing as I read the label. "Cajun seasoning? Yeah, I can definitely see you causing a kitchen fire with this."

He tosses the jar into his already overflowing bag. "Or creating a culinary masterpiece. You'll thank me later."

I shake my head, biting back a smile as I watch him move on to the next stall, where he immediately strikes up an animated conversation with the vendor about beeswax candles. Life with Callan, I realize, is going to be anything but boring.

After a few more stops and a bag that's probably pushing its limits, he looks at me sheepishly. "I think I've got more than I can carry. You ready to head back?"

"Yep," I say, nudging his arm. "Let's go unpack all your

goodies. Though I'm starting to think we'll need a second kitchen just to store your spice collection."

He chuckles, adjusting the bag on his shoulder as we start walking. "All part of the plan to keep you well-fed, Sunshine. My grandmother would be so impressed with me right now."

"Mission accomplished," I tease. "Though I should probably call my parents when we get back. I kind of bailed on dinner last night."

He raises an eyebrow, a sly grin creeping across his face. "And what's your excuse going to be? Sorry, Mom and Dad, I fainted, and my ridiculously handsome Scottish boyfriend showed up and distracted me?"

"Something like that. Minus the 'ridiculously handsome' part."

"Please tell me I get to meet them."

I blink at him. "You're excited about meeting the parents? Who *are* you?"

"They're the people who made you who you are," he says simply, like it's the most obvious thing in the world. "Why wouldn't I want to meet them?"

Well, hell. That was awfully fucking sweet.

I loop my arm through his. "Well, my dad's a bit of a jokester, so prepare yourself for some *questionable* humor."

"Questionable, how?" he asks, glancing down at me with a look of amusement and curiosity.

"You'll see," I say. "Oh, and my mom? She'll absolutely ask you a million questions. So maybe think of your top three proudest accomplishments in life because she's going to want to know them all."

He chuckles, completely unfazed. "I've already survived you, Sunshine. I've got this."

twenty-six

BREE

"You ready?" Callan asks, his voice even and calm. As in, everything I'm not right now.

I blow out a long breath. "As I'll ever be."

We're about to head to my parents' house for dinner, and I'm a bundle of nerves. I surrender my keys to Callan and slide into the passenger seat of my sedan. He climbs in with an ease that's almost unsettling, his confidence radiating as he pulls out of the driveway. Meanwhile, my palms are practically glued to my thighs from sweat.

What really gets me, though, is his grin. It's *huge*. A full-blown, dimple-showing, can't-wait-for-this kind of smile. He's actually looking forward to this, and frankly, it's weirding me out.

"You're humming," I blurt.

He shoots me a quick, amused glance, his hand tapping lightly on my thigh in time with the rhythm of his tune. "Am I? Didn't notice."

"Well, you are," I say, narrowing my eyes at him. "And you're...happy. Like suspiciously happy."

209

He laughs, his thumb brushing a lazy circle on my leg before returning to the beat. "You make it sound like a crime to be in a good mood."

"No, it's just... You're about to meet my parents, Callan. My dad's a bit protective. Shouldn't you be at least a little nervous?"

He just shrugs. "Bree, I'm Scottish. You think I can't charm my way past an intimidating father? I've got whisky, a firm handshake, and an accent that practically does the work for me. What more could the man want? Besides, I've got the best reason to win him over. You."

I've never had to do the whole *boyfriend meets the parents* routine as an adult, and it feels like I'm walking into a pressure cooker. For him, though? This is just another chapter in his ongoing adventure, and he's handling it with the same effortless confidence he brings to everything.

He reaches over, his calloused hand wrapping around mine, giving it a gentle, reassuring squeeze. "Hey, it's going to be fine."

"They might grill you like a steak," I warn. I'm only half joking.

He lets out a lighthearted chuckle, and it immediately makes me feel better. "Sunshine, I've faced far worse."

"Mmhmm. You've never seen my dad during football season."

"Ah, American football. That's the one where they don't really use their feet and stop every five seconds to have a chat, right?"

I let out a laugh and smack his arm lightly. "I *know* you're screwing with me. Not that you're wrong."

The knot of nerves in my stomach loosens. It's stupid, really, but this easy banter, this back-and-forth that feels so natural, is exactly what I need. With him, I'm never nervous for long.

He glances at me again, this time his expression more serious. "Seriously, though. You're all I see. That's all that matters."

My heart does a little flip at his words, and more of the tension leaves my shoulders. "You're the best," I say, squeezing his hand.

As we pull up to my parents' house, though, the nerves start to creep back in. My mom's flowerbeds are in full bloom, vibrant and alive with color, but right now, they're more intimidating than welcoming.

Callan's smile hasn't left his face, and when he turns to me, it's like he's about to embark on a grand adventure, not walk into a potentially terrifying situation.

"Ready?" he asks.

I glance at the house, then back at him, my hand hovering over the door handle. "I guess," I mutter, though it comes out more as a question than an answer.

He leans over, brushing a quick kiss to my temple. "Don't worry, Sunshine. I've got this."

"Famous last words."

As we reach the front door, I steal one last glance at him. He's still completely at ease, his posture relaxed, his expression confident. Before I can reach for the doorknob, the door swings open to reveal my mom with a warm smile on her face as she takes us in. "Bree! Callan! Come in, come in."

The moment feels surreal, like I'm watching it happen from somewhere above myself. I step over the threshold and Callan releases my hand, immediately extending his to my mom with that disarming charm of his. It makes me both proud and a little bit nervous.

"Mrs. Smith, it's a pleasure to finally meet you," he says, his accent thick and smooth as he hands her the bouquet of flowers he bought at the farmer's market. "Thank you so much for having me."

Mom beams at him, clearly charmed already. "Oh, please call me Shannon."

The comforting scent of pot roast wafts from the kitchen, mingling with the familiar scent of Mom's favorite candles. It's cozy and homey, but it makes my stomach flip. It's soothing and anxiety-inducing all at once.

"Honey, they're here!" Mom calls out, her voice filled with excitement, and I hear my dad's heavy footsteps approaching from the living room.

He appears in the entryway with his *protective dad* stance. His eyes land on Callan, and I can practically feel the evaluation happening.

"Well, well," he says, his tone just shy of a challenge. "So you're the young man we've been hearing so much about."

Callan stands tall, looking every bit the part of someone who's used to being sized up. "Aye, sir. I hope so at least," he says, extending his hand.

Dad takes it, giving it a solid shake. "Strong grip," he comments, a hint of approval in his voice. "Tom, by the way."

"Callan MacKenzie, sir. Great to meet you."

I stand off to the side with Mom, watching the exchange like I'm in the middle of a carefully orchestrated negotiation. Dad's eyes narrow slightly, assessing him in that way I know too well. Then, as if he's found a way to push just a little further, he asks, "Play any sports, Callan?"

Yep, here we go.

"Used to play rugby," Callan replies casually, not missing a beat. "Still watch a fair bit."

Dad's face lights up. "Rugby? Always thought that was just football for people who didn't mind dying young."

Callan lets out a hearty laugh, his deep voice rumbling in the most endearing way. "Aye, something like that. You watch?"

To my complete shock, Dad nods back. "Watched a match once when I was stationed overseas. Took me half the game to figure out the rules, but damn if it wasn't entertaining."

And just like that, it's like a switch flips. Suddenly, they're sitting side by side on the couch, gesturing wildly at the screen as Dad pulls up a rugby highlight reel to stream. They're laughing, trading jokes about brutal tackles, and comparing notes like old pals.

I stand frozen in the doorway, completely forgotten as I watch the scene unfold. My mouth opens, but no words come out. I blink at my mom, who's standing beside me, equally stunned.

"What just happened?" I whisper, almost in disbelief.

Mom looks all too pleased. "Don't question it, honey. Come on, I could use some help finishing up in the kitchen."

I shake my head, still processing how quickly they've hit it off. I follow her, but I can't resist stealing a few glances over my shoulder at Callan and Dad. It's like they've known each other for years, not mere minutes.

"So," Mom says, handing me a bowl of salad to toss, "he seems lovely."

I laugh softly, still a little amazed. "Yeah, he really is. I didn't expect Dad to warm up to him so fast, though."

She chuckles, glancing at the roast in the oven as she adjusts the heat. "Your father is a sucker for anyone who can talk sports."

"Yeah, I've noticed."

Mom turns to me with an eyebrow arched in that way she always does when she's about to ask something personal. "Well, tell me," she continues, wiping her hands on a dish towel, "how's it going? Him being here?"

I pause, heat creeping across my face. "It's only been a day, but I'm really glad he came."

"He's smitten with you, you know."

I crinkle my nose, trying to play it off. "Smitten, huh?"

She swats my arm with the dish towel. "He's only turned around to look at you seven times in the few minutes we've been in here."

I peek over my shoulder, and sure enough, Callan is sneaking a glance at me, his reassuring smile instantly making my heart skip a beat.

I turn back around, rolling my eyes, a little embarrassed but smiling all the same.

"Mmhmm," Mom mumbles. "That's what I thought."

I focus on setting the table, because if I stop moving, I might actually have to process the fact that this is happening. My parents, my boyfriend, and me, all sitting down for a perfectly normal, not-at-all nerve-wracking family dinner.

Mom calls the guys in, and the kitchen fills with the usual clatter of plates and silverware. I look up just in time to see Callan stroll in like he's lived here his whole life.

The audacity.

By the time we settle, with Callan and me on one side and my parents on the other, I realize the tightness in my chest has loosened. Either I'm finally relaxing, or I'm moments away from a stress-induced blackout. Fingers crossed for the first one.

Dad is still firing off questions, and Callan, the absolute menace, handles each one with that allure of his. No hesitation, no flustered stammering. Just smooth, confident answers like he was born for this exact interrogation.

"This smells delicious, Shannon," Callan praises as he fills his plate. "I hope Bree has the recipe. She's been trying to perfect her pot roast for a while now, I hear."

I shoot him a look, but he just winks at me, completely unfazed.

"Oh, of course!" Mom says, beaming, clearly delighted by the compliment.

Ah. I see what he's doing.

He's got this all down to a fine art, making sure everything goes smoothly and making everyone comfortable. What I love most is how easy it all is. None of it feels forced. This is just who Callan is.

As we dig in, Callan, ever the charismatic storyteller, dives into tales of his travels, his eyes lighting up as he describes the wild, untamed beauty of the Scottish Highlands. Mom leans on the table, hanging onto his every word. Dad, usually a tough nut to crack, nods along, his serious expression giving way to something that looks a lot like respect.

He's impressing the hell out of my parents right now, but last night? Well, he had me pinned to the mattress, whispering absolute filth in that same accent while proving, in explicit detail, that his talents extend well beyond storytelling. He's got that rare skill that turns even the most proper, put together woman—which I am *not*, but still—into an absolute wreck, all because he knows exactly what he's doing and exactly how to do it.

I clear my throat and force my attention back to my plate, trying not to squirm in my seat. *Dinner with my parents is not the time for this*, I scold myself.

But with the way Callan is handling this... I can't help but imagine all the ways he could put that confidence to better use later. Preferably with fewer clothes and significantly less talking.

"So, Callan," Dad says, pulling me out of my sex-hazed thought. He pauses to take a bite, his eyes shifting from his plate to my boyfriend. "What exactly do you do for work?"

Pride flickers across Callan's face, his posture straightening. "My brother and I run the family distillery. Fourth generation to do so."

Dad nods, his curiosity piqued. "That sounds impressive. What's it like, running a family business?"

Callan's smile is subtle but genuine. He's comfortable here, talking about something that clearly means the world to him. "It's a lot of hard work, but it's rewarding. There's history in every bottle we make, a piece of our family in every step of the process."

I watch as Callan talks about the distillery, answering Dad's questions with ease, his passion for the work shining through. I'm content to just sit back, to let him share as much as he wants. I want my parents to get to know him.

Throughout the entire meal, though, Callan has kept his hand firmly on mine. It's a small gesture, but the way he holds it, the constant reassurance of his touch, makes me feel like I'm the center of his world while conversation swirls around us.

I can't help but notice the way he's eating with his left hand, his grip on the fork a little clumsier than usual, like using it feels unnatural, but letting go of my hand is simply not an option. It's both ridiculously sweet and mildly amusing, watching this otherwise capable man fumble through dinner just to keep me close. The effort is unnecessary, but the sentiment? Absolutely heart melting.

I catch a glimpse of Mom from the corner of my eye, her gaze fixed on Callan as he laughs at something my dad says. She's watching him closely, and I see any hesitation start to fade. I know she's been worried about me opening up to someone again, especially someone so far away. She was cautious when I first told her about Callan, unsure of the distance and the time zones and the uncertainty of it all.

There's a shift from guarded concern to something closer to

admiration. She knows how much he's been there for me these past months, how every day he's been a constant in my life, even from miles away. How he listens, how he makes the effort, and how he makes me laugh.

As Callan shares a story, her smile widens in a way that tells me she's letting herself see him as someone worthy of her trust.

I can't help but breathe a little easier.

twenty-seven

CALLAN

The scent of roast and cinnamon still lingers in the living room as the conversation shifts from casual to...serious. Bree stands up to head to the restroom, and it's the perfect opening.

Shannon clears her throat, and it grabs my attention immediately. There's no escaping this.

She leans forward, her eyes locking with mine, and just like that, the mom vibe is turned up to full volume. The playful tone from dinner disappears. "So, Callan," she starts. "What are your intentions with our daughter?"

I settle back into the couch, Shannon and Tom looking at me like I'm on trial. I've got no lawyer. There's no manual for this.

"I love her," I say, the words simple but true, and lock eyes with Shannon first, then Tom. "She's the most incredible woman I've ever met. My intention is to make her happy, to support her, and to build a life together if that's what she wants."

Shannon doesn't blink as she watches me, her gaze sharp,

like she's reading between the lines of every word I say. Tom breaks the silence a second later. "Nice to hear but life together isn't just words. It's action, sacrifices. Are you ready for that?"

His words hit me like a ton of bricks, and for a second, the pressure of their expectations presses down on me. The silence stretches out, and I can almost hear the weight of it, like it's got a voice of its own. I give a slow nod, meeting his eyes and letting him see that I'm not just hearing him, I'm *getting* it.

"Aye, I know it's not easy," I say, because of course it's not. Nothing worth a damn ever is. "So you know, I haven't told her I love her yet. Not because I don't mean it but because I want to be sure she's ready to hear it. I don't want to throw it at her like a net and hope she stays. She deserves better than that."

A flash of something I wouldn't quite call approval crosses Tom's face before he quickly masks it with that *dad* expression again. Shannon looks at us, her eyes flickering between her husband and me, assessing, making sure we're on the same page.

"We just want to make sure she's safe," Shannon says, her voice softer now but no less serious. "That she is loved. We've seen her hurt, Callan. And as parents...it destroyed us, watching her go through that."

"I understand why you'd be worried," I say, my tone genuine. "Bree's been through more than anyone should, and I can see how it's affected you both. I've seen the way she's been before, and I'll be damned if I let that happen again."

Bree thought this would be hard for me, that it would rattle me. She couldn't have been more wrong. It's an honor. Sitting here with her parents and telling them how much I love her and want her in my life. After everything with her piece-of-shit ex, getting the chance to show them just how different I am from him? That's the least I can do.

"She's safe with me," I tell them, my voice unwavering. "Always."

The words hang in the air, and for a moment, it feels like time slows down. The look in Tom's eyes softens a touch. Shannon nods, her expression still protective, but maybe just a little more willing to trust me.

Bree steps back into the living room, a hesitant question on her lips. "Everything okay?"

I glance up at her, giving her a reassuring smile that's more for her than anyone else. "More than okay," I say with a wink. "I hope?"

Shannon and Tom chuckle at that. "Yes," Shannon agrees, nodding with a warm smile. "All good."

Relief hits me like a wave, and I don't waste a second. I pull Bree in closer, my arm slipping around her shoulders as she nestles against my side. Her body relaxes immediately, the tension I didn't even know was there melting away in an instant.

Yep. Nailed it. This whole *meet the parents* thing? Piece of cake.

twenty-eight

BREE

W e're heading back to my place now, and I can finally let out the sigh that's been waiting to escape for hours. I let my mind wander a bit, and of course it lands on how good Callan looks with one hand steady on the wheel, the other resting low on my thigh. It's impossible not to get a little lost in the way he sits there, like everything around us could fall apart, and he'd still have it all figured out.

"Thank you."

He glances at me, brows furrowing, his focus shifting just enough for me to see the confusion flicker in his eyes. "For what?"

"For being so perfectly you and getting my parents to adore you."

The corner of his mouth lifts into that signature smirk. "Well, I can't take all the credit. I had a pretty great motivation."

It still catches me off guard when he's sweet like this. I expect sarcasm, some sharp remark, but then he surprises me with *that*.

"Or," he says, "your parents might just have really low standards."

I burst into laughter. Now *that* is what I was expecting.

I shake my head, trying to suppress my smile. "I knew you couldn't resist."

His chuckle fills the car as his fingers give my thigh a gentle squeeze. "Come on, you love it."

Damn it, I do. I can't deny that. His quick wit and the way he keeps me on my toes, it's one of the things that got to me from the start. It's *him*, and it's perfect in its own maddening way.

We pull up to my condo, and I feel...better. Maybe it's the relief of surviving dinner with my parents, or maybe it's the fact that, somehow, he managed to charm his way into their good graces in record time. Or maybe it's the way he looks ridiculously sexy in that confident way of his.

He shifts the car into park and turns to me, those blue eyes glinting in the low light, full of mischief and just enough arrogance to make my pulse do something very irresponsible.

"So," he drawls, tilting his head slightly. "Are you going to invite me up for a nightcap?"

I raise a brow. "A nightcap? Who says that anymore? Besides, I'm pretty sure you've got nowhere else to be," I tease.

His laugh sinks in and leaves a smoldering heat in its wake.

"Fair enough," he murmurs as he cuts the engine. His eyes never leave mine.

Before I even realize I'm moving, I lean in, drawn to him like I don't have a choice in the matter. His hand is there in an instant, fingertips grazing my cheek in the softest, laziest way, like he has all the time in the world to touch me. And maybe he does.

I swallow, forcing myself to break the silence, to break

whatever spell he's cast. "Come on," I say softly, almost too softly, as I open the door and step out into the cool night.

When we reach my door, his hand drifts over the small of my back, just the lightest brush of his fingers, sending a shiver straight down my spine.

I fumble with the keys, suddenly all thumbs because I don't know how to focus when he's standing so close. Judging by the way his breath skims the back of my neck, he knows exactly what he's doing.

Finally, the lock clicks, and I push the door open, stepping inside. I turn to him, offering a small, knowing smile.

"So," I say, leaning against the doorframe, "still want that nightcap?"

He takes a step forward, his gaze never leaving mine, a slow smirk tugging at the corners of his lips. "If that nightcap is in the form of you naked and spread wide open for me, yes."

My breath catches at the sheer confidence in his tone. His strong, sure hands find my waist, pulling me in without hesitation. Before I can come up with a witty response, his lips crash into mine.

I melt. My back meets the wall, and any thought of teasing him disappears the second his hands tighten on my hips. His scent, so familiar and intoxicating, fills my lungs, wrapping around me as his body presses flush against mine. His fingers dig in like he's already staking his claim, and when his tongue brushes against mine, full of intent, I feel it *everywhere*.

The world outside blurs. My pulse pounds in my ears, my body arching into him on instinct and craving more. Judging by the way he deepens the kiss, his hands sliding lower, his grip turning a little rougher, he knows exactly what he's doing to me.

He breaks away, tracing his lips down my neck. My eyes

flutter closed, my fingers tangling in his hair. I need more of him. More of *everything*.

"God, I've wanted to do that all night," Callan breathes, his voice filled with a hunger that matches my own.

I pull at his shirt. "Bedroom. Now."

He grins, that wicked, unrestrained smirk that makes my pulse spike, and lifts me effortlessly. I wrap my legs around his waist as he carries me down the hall, his lips never leaving mine.

We stumble into the bedroom, the door slamming shut behind us. Clothes hit the floor in a hurry, discarded without a second thought. It's impossible to care about anything except the way he makes me feel like I'm alive, electrified, and entirely his.

His body is enough to make anyone weak in the knees, but it's the way he looks at me with desire and tenderness that's truly devastating in the best way. He lays me down gently on the bed, his hands warm against my skin as he moves with purpose. His lips graze my neck, trailing a path to my chest. His expert hands cup my breasts, rolling my nipples between his fingers. His tongue dances between them, teasing and flicking.

His touch sets my skin ablaze, every nerve ending humming with need. Callan takes his time, savoring every inch of my body like he's committing it to memory. His lips trace down to my stomach, his tongue dipping into my navel before continuing lower.

A gasp escapes me as his fingers slip between my thighs, finding me already slick. "Callan," I breathe, his name a plea on my lips.

He glances up at me through his lashes, his eyes dark with lust. "I love hearing you say my name like that," he murmurs.

Without warning, he dips his head, his tongue sliding through my folds. My back arches off the bed, fingers fisting in the sheets as waves of pleasure roll through me. He explores me with a singular focus, alternating between broad strokes of his tongue and more targeted attention on my most sensitive spot. My thighs tremble, toes curling, as he builds me higher and higher.

"Don't stop," I gasp, my fingers threading through his hair, holding him exactly where I need him.

He groans against me, the vibrations sending sparks shooting up my spine. His fingers join his mouth, slipping inside me with practiced ease, pressing just right.

I'm lost to the sensation and the overwhelming pleasure that threatens to consume me entirely. Every flick of his tongue, every thrust of his fingers, brings me closer to that edge.

"Please," I whimper. "Don't stop."

My pleas only spur him on, his movements becoming more deliberate. His tongue swirls around my clit with an intensity that makes my vision blur at the edges. His fingers pump in and out, finding that perfect rhythm that has me seeing stars.

I'm lost in a haze of euphoria, my world narrowed down to the points where his skin meets mine. The way his stubble scrapes deliciously against my inner thighs. The heat of his breath ghosting over my sensitive skin.

My body tenses, every muscle pulled taut. And then, with one final curl of his fingers, one last flick of his tongue, I come undone. Waves of ecstasy crash over me, my cries echoing off the walls as I reach my climax.

Callan works me through it, his movements slowing but not ceasing, drawing out my pleasure until I'm weary and spent.

I've barely come down from the high when he looks up at me, his blue eyes resembling a storm, wild and untamed. "Still not enough."

Lucky for him, I'm nowhere near done with him, either.

He climbs onto the bed beside me, his hands finding their

way across my body with a teasing precision, his fingers dancing along every spot that makes me twitch and squirm. A soft laugh slips out as I try to pull away, but he's relentless.

"Please," I whisper, knowing exactly what's coming next.

He smirks, moving his hand between us as he fists his hard length, guiding it to my entrance. With one smooth thrust, he fills me completely.

Our bodies find a rhythm like they've always known each other, every stroke showering me in ecstasy.

"Christ, Bree. You're incredible," he groans. "The way you taste, how tight you are. So fucking perfect."

He swells inside me, his pace quickening as he chases his release. His thrusts become more demanding, more urgent, and the anticipation inside me tightens, ready to snap.

"Come for me, love," he murmurs.

His words push me over the edge, and I'm consumed by the most intense orgasm of my life. His gaze locks onto mine as he gives a final thrust, his body shuddering, muscles tensing. The warmth of his release spreads through me like a slow-burning fire. It's primal, raw, and incredible. Like nothing I've ever experienced before.

His movements still, but he doesn't pull away, instead resting his forehead against mine. For a moment, there's nothing but the sound of our ragged breaths mingling in the space between us.

Slowly, he rolls to his back, pulling me with him as my head rests in the crook of his neck. He presses a tender kiss to my forehead, his strong arms holding me tight. I feel safe. Cherished.

"That was..." I trail off, searching for the right words, but none seem to do it justice.

"Mind-blowing? Earth-shattering? Life-changing?"

I laugh softly. "That's one way to put it."

He leans in, his lips brushing a tender kiss against my forehead, then my cheek, before finally claiming my lips in a slow, almost languid kiss. It's a perfect balance after the heated frenzy.

"You know," he murmurs, lips still hovering a whisper away from mine, "I think I might need another nightcap."

Before I can even think, my teeth sink into the curve of his bottom lip. "Maybe you should ask nicely."

A growl rumbles from his chest, his eyes darkening with that familiar hunger. "Please," he begs. "May I have another?"

I drag my fingers down the firm lines of his torso, savoring the heat of his skin beneath my touch, letting the tension hang between us for just a moment longer. "Well, since you asked so nicely..."

The shift happens so quickly, I barely have time to register it before I'm straddling him, his hands gripping my waist with a possessive urgency. My breath catches as I lean down, capturing his lips in a kiss that burns with the promise of *more*. He's already hard again beneath me, and I lift myself just enough to sink down onto him slowly, relishing the delicious stretch as he fills me inch by glorious inch.

He throws his head back against the pillows, a low groan escaping as arousal ripples through him. His face is a study in tortured pleasure with his eyes squeezed shut, jaw clenched, lips parted in a silent plea for more.

His eyes flutter open and find mine. "Fucking hell, Bree. You're so beautiful like this."

The rhythm builds naturally, our bodies moving in sync. There's no rush this time. I revel in every long stroke as he watches me with an intensity that has me close to the edge once again.

His skin is hot under my palms as I brace my hands on his

chest, picking up speed, guided by the firm grip of his fingers on my hips.

"That's it, love. Take what you need."

I whimper in response, too lost to form words. He sits up suddenly, wrapping an arm around my waist to pull me flush against him. The heat of his body radiates into mine, every inch of him solid and unyielding. The new angle has me gasping, clinging to his shoulders as he thrusts up into me.

"Look at me," he commands softly.

I focus on him. The sound of his voice is enough to unravel me, but then one of his hands skates up my back to tangle in my hair. He softly yanks my head back to expose my throat. He latches on, sucking and nipping in a way that sends bolts of electricity straight to my core, and I shatter completely.

I'm still trembling when Callan's rhythm falters, his breaths growing ragged against my neck. I pull back to watch his face, mesmerized by the play of emotions across his features. His brow furrows, eyes squeezing shut as a low groan escapes his lips. His muscles tense, a light sheen of sweat glistening on his skin. I feel him pulse inside me, his hips jerking upward in short, sharp thrusts.

And then his eyes snap open, those blue depths eclipsed by his blown pupils. For a heartbeat, I forget how to breathe. This man is devastatingly beautiful in a way that isn't fair to the rest of humanity, or to me, specifically, because I'm the one who has to act like I haven't just been struck by lightning.

twenty-nine

BREE

The week vanishes in a blur, leaving me with our last morning together before Callan heads back home.

There's a sadness in his eyes he isn't trying to hide, and it makes me want to drop everything and jump into his arms right this second.

I reach across the table, my hand finding his like it was made for this exact purpose. His fingers weave through mine, and I grip them like they're the only anchor in a very unsteady world. "I'll try to visit soon," I whisper, mostly to convince myself.

His thumb sweeps over my knuckles, a touch that feels like a promise, even though it carries the weight of goodbye.

"I'll hold you to that, lass," he says, his voice thick with that accent I can never resist.

Soon can't come fast enough, which is wild, because for weeks I've been pretending I don't know what this is. The truth is sitting heavy on my tongue, waiting for its moment. I'm in love with him.

The second that realization clicks into place, I start spiraling through all the *how the hell do I say this without ruining everything* scenarios.

Option one: just blurt it out. *"I'm in love with you. Do you love me back?"* Simple. Direct. And...painfully awkward. It would be like ripping off a bandage, but holy hell, that's gonna sting.

Option two: soften the blow, make it less of a thing. Casually drop it into conversation like it's no big deal. *"Oh, by the way, I'm in love with you. But it's fine, right? Totally normal, no pressure!"*

Option three: ask to go home with him. Like, really plead. Maybe throw in a dramatic, *"I can't live without you,"* for full effect.

Before I can say any of it, my phone buzzes against the wooden table. It's just a text, but when I glance at the screen, everything shifts.

Dillon.

My stomach lurches. My pulse stutters, then kicks up in a way I *really* don't like. For a moment, I just stare, frozen in a split second of denial, as if ignoring it might erase the fact that he's reaching out at all.

"What's wrong?" Callan's voice pulls me back, his brow furrowed as his worried gaze locks onto mine.

I hesitate, my mind scrambling for options. Play it off? Wave it away? Anything to avoid this conversation. But even as the thought crosses my mind, I know I can't. Not with Callan leaving today.

"It's..." My voice falters, my heart screaming at me to rip the bandage off already. "It's Dillon," I say, wincing as I meet his eyes.

His shoulders go rigid, the easy posture he wore just moments ago vanishing in an instant. The crease between his brows deepens, and there's a sharp edge to his voice when he finally speaks, low and controlled, but crackling with restrained fury.

"What does he want?"

I swallow hard and glance down at the screen. "He's asking if we can talk."

His gaze snaps to mine so fast it roots me to the spot. "And do you want to?"

My fingers fidget along the edge of my phone, searching for something solid in a moment that feels anything but. "I don't know," I admit, my voice small. It's a confession, one that lands gently but echoes between us like a crack of thunder.

His grip on my hand tightens. "You don't owe him anything," he says. "Not after everything he did."

"Maybe not," I reply softly. "I do think I owe it to myself to hear him out, though."

The air between us is fragile, stretched thin by words we haven't said. His eyes flicker with something raw, a battle waging just beneath the surface. Between his instinct to protect me and the trust he's trying to give. He exhales slowly, his shoulders loosening by a fraction, but the tension in his jaw remains, a telltale sign of the fight he's not really winning.

"If that's what you want," he says quieter, but no less firm. His gaze holds mine, unshakable. "But you're not doing it alone."

A bittersweet smile tugs at my lips. I love him for saying it, but I know I can't let him follow through. I love the way he just steps in with no hesitation, like shielding me from the world is second nature to him. It's in the solid focus of his eyes, how they stay fixed on me as if to memorize every shift in my expression, and in the way his hand remains firmly around mine, like holding on tightly enough could block out everything else.

And yet, this isn't a battle he can fight for me.

"I know you're worried," I say, my voice firm. "But I don't think this is something you should be there for. I'll make sure I meet him somewhere public, like for coffee or something."

His lips part like he wants to argue, but he catches himself, the words dying before they make it out. Instead, he leans back slightly, his thumb still brushing gently over my knuckles. "I don't like it," he admits. "But I'll respect it."

"Thank you," I whisper, giving his hand a squeeze. "I'll be okay. I don't want to spend our last day thinking about...him."

His gaze softens, the sharp edges of his worry easing enough to let a breath of warmth slip through. He exhales slowly, nodding. "Aye. Last day, no distractions." He tries for a smile, but it's tinged with that sadness we've been dancing around all morning.

Determined to shift the mood, I flash him a teasing grin. "You know, I've been thinking that maybe I should start a list of all the things I need to do before you leave. Top of the list? Learn how to survive without your amazing cooking."

His brow arches. "You'll manage," he quips. "Though you'll miss me before you miss the cooking."

I scoff, giving him an exaggerated once-over. "Debatable."

That smile of his spreads across his face, the kind that starts in his eyes and takes its time reaching his lips. He's looking at me like I've just said something profound instead of making a bad joke about his cooking.

"What?" I ask, suddenly self-conscious.

"You know," he says, his voice dropping to that intimate register that makes my spine tingle, "I can't wait for you to visit again. Having you wake up in *my* bed. The way the light hits the hills at dawn—it'll be the first thing you see every morning."

"And at night," he continues, "you'll fall asleep to the sound of the wind through the trees, wrapped up in my arms, knowing you're exactly where you're meant to be."

Is he *trying* to make me cry? Because mission accomplished. Here I was, trying to make a joke about food, but now I'm blinking furiously, trying to keep my emotions from spilling all over the place. I can't even be mad about it. I know goodbye is lurking just around the corner.

I sniff, tilting my head back. No tears. No crying over his disgustingly sweet, perfect, life-ruining words.

Then he squeezes my hand, and damn it, a tear escapes.

I groan. "You're making it real hard to argue with you, you know that?"

"Good," he murmurs, pressing a kiss to my knuckles. "Because I don't plan on giving you a single reason to change your mind."

I'm so over airports. They're soulless with nothing but bright lights and endless rows of uncomfortable chairs that are designed to drain the life out of you. Normally, it's the sadness that gets me. Goodbyes in general are never easy. I'm not the one leaving. I'm the one being left behind. I didn't realize how much harder that would be.

Every step Callan takes toward those automatic doors feels like someone wringing the air out of my lungs. I thought I'd be okay. I told myself I could handle this, but just imagining the moment he disappears has me crumbling.

We kept the goodbye short. It's not forever after all. It's not really goodbye. I'll be with him before I know it... I just don't know *when* that will be. I told myself I wouldn't cry, that I'd hold it together so he wouldn't see me falling apart.

When he steps through the doors, my composure falls apart. The tears spill over before I can stop them, my lip trembling as I bite down hard, blinking furiously in a useless attempt to keep it together. My hands swipe at my cheeks, but it's a losing battle. Let those bitches fall.

He turns back, his eyes catching mine through the glass, and he notices. Before I can process it, he's striding back. By the time he reaches me, I'm a full-on mess. The sight of him rushing to me makes the tears flow even harder.

"Hey," he murmurs, his hands gently cradling my face, his thumbs brushing away the tears as if they can fix the heartbreak. "None of this. You know I can't leave unless I know you're okay."

And then, just like that, his teasing grin breaks through, the one that always makes my heart trip over itself. "And also, I owe you an 'I told you so.' I *knew* you'd miss me bad."

A laugh bubbles out of me, shaky and choked with tears, but it's there. I swat at his arm, shaking my head. "You're insufferable, truly."

He chuckles, leaning closer so his forehead rests lightly against mine. "Aye, but you like me anyway. Besides, you'll be on your way to me soon. You'll get sick of me again in no time."

I laugh. "Oh, I doubt that. You're too good at being an annoying, lovable pain in my ass."

His arms come around me fast, tight and fierce. "I'll make sure to send you the world's most obnoxious selfies every day," he promises. "Just so you don't forget how lucky you are."

As we pull apart, I try to steady myself, plastering on a smile even though it wobbles at the edges. "I'll be counting down the days."

He winks at me with that signature mix of mischief and charm that should honestly come with a hazard warning. The warmth in my chest spreads like wildfire. How is this man simultaneously sweet and hot as hell? He looks at me like that, and suddenly my heart's doing the Macarena, my brain drifting to thoughts like *I could leave tomorrow...*

Then, as if he knows exactly what he's doing to me, he leans in and presses a soft, lingering kiss to my lips. It's the kind of kiss that says everything he hasn't. *I miss you already. You're mine.*

"All right, Sunshine," he murmurs, pulling back to meet my eyes. "Here's the deal. You get in that car and drive off. I'm not stepping foot inside until you're out of sight."

He knows how much this goodbye is shredding me, yet somehow, here he is, making me feel like the center of his universe.

"Okay." I finally nod.

His eyes sparkle, that familiar glint of wickedness lighting them up. "Go before I start thinking about how much I'm going to miss you and ruin my manly reputation."

I can't help but laugh. His ridiculousness is the only thing that keeps me from completely losing it. "You're impossible," I say, backing away slowly and trying to keep it together, even though my feet seem to get heavier with every step.

He responds with a lazy salute, the corners of his mouth curling into that smile that always gets to me. As I climb into the car, he doesn't move. He just watches me.

I shift into gear and pull away from the curb, but I can't stop myself from glancing in the rearview mirror one last time.

There he is. Standing still. Watching me go. His smile is there, but it's laced with the same weight I'm carrying. That sadness, that ache, that longing to not be apart, to not say goodbye.

I push it down, telling myself it's just for a little while. Eventually, everything will fall into place. Even if the space beside me is too quiet and empty now.

I blink rapidly, but the tears are already back, welling up and blurring my vision. I'm supposed to be strong, supposed to drive away with my heart intact, but it's impossible. He's *still* standing there.

I take a breath, shaky and uneven. Then another. As I press my foot to the gas, every part of me is screaming to turn around.

CALLAN

The door clicks shut behind me, and the rich scent of oak barrels and whisky hits. The distillery is my second home. A sanctuary in the chaos.

Well, *usually*.

It's been a week, and that goodbye still lingers like a bruise I can't stop pressing. Every time I try to focus, I see Bree's blue eyes staring back at me, hear her laugh, feel her hair slipping through my fingers as if still holding onto her.

Today's the real kicker, though.

She's meeting up with her ex.

I tell myself it's fine. That I trust her. That it's just a conversation, not some grand reunion. My brain doesn't give a damn about logic. It just loops the same torturous reel—her sitting across from him, tilting her head the way she does when she's really listening.

I try to focus and bury myself in the usual grind, but it's useless. No matter what I do, I keep seeing them together. I can't decide who I'm pissed at more. Her ex for being the absolute piece of shit he is, or myself for letting this eat at me like

237

I'm the one who lived it. I wish I were there to knock that bastard into next week.

That son of a bitch didn't just break her heart. He broke *her*. Left bruises, got inside her head and made her question herself. That kind of damage doesn't just fade with time. It lingers and turns into scars that don't show, except...I see them.

And that kills me.

Here I am, sitting useless in this office, pretending I'm not miles away. I can't protect her or stop him from doing it all over again. It's a fucking nightmare.

I want to believe she's strong enough to handle it. Hell, I *know* she is. That still doesn't deter the thoughts of her standing in front of him, hearing his voice, letting him exist in her space again. Every time I think about it, a steel band tightens around my ribs, squeezing the air right out of me.

I shake my head, trying to clear the fog building up in my brain. There's no point in sitting around, letting this mess of thoughts consume me. I grab the tablet from my desk and head to the shipping area where I can lose myself in the routine.

Crates line the walls with labels that offer nothing but numbers and destinations. No opinions or feelings, just business. I catalog shipments, check quantities, and confirm addresses. The work asks nothing of me. It's a mindless process I can disappear into.

I get to work, and after a while, I don't know how long it's been. Minutes? Hours? Time gets lost somewhere between shifting crates and scribbling notes, between moving and *not thinking*.

I'm shoving another crate into place as the sound of heavy footsteps drags me back to reality.

"You look like hell, brother," Knox says, stepping beside me.

I run a hand through my hair, fully aware I probably look as wrecked as I feel. "Thanks for the compliment."

Knox doesn't flinch. "Juliette told me about Bree and the ex. Have you heard from her?"

I shake my head, pulling my phone from my pocket to check the time. "No, it's still early there. She's not meeting with him for a few hours yet."

He shifts, propping himself against a stack of crates, arms crossed. He gives me a look that tells me he knows exactly what's going on in my head, even if I don't say a thing. "You're worried."

"Of course I'm worried," I snap. I drag in a breath, trying to get a grip. "Sorry. I just...hate this whole damn situation."

He nods. "Aye, you don't need to apologize. I don't love the idea of this either, and Juliette is sick over it. You'll let me know when you hear from her?"

"Of course," I reply. And then the guilt hits me.

I'm an asshole. My sister-in-law is pregnant, and I haven't asked Knox how *she's* doing.

"How's Juliette been feeling?"

A grin spreads across my brother's face—the same one that only ever makes an appearance when he talks about Juliette. "She's still having some bad days, but she's handling it like a champ. You want some good news?"

I lift a brow. "If it's not about my future niece or nephew, I'm not interested."

He chuckles, but there's a smugness to it. "We had another scan yesterday. The babies are perfect."

My head jerks up. "Babies? As in...more than one?"

"Twins," he says, grinning like he's just hit the jackpot. Because holy shit, he has.

I let out a low whistle, scrubbing a hand down my face. "Damn. No wonder Jules has been sick as hell."

Knox lets out a hearty laugh. "Aye. You think I'd be scared but...nah. It's incredible."

I clap him on the shoulder, genuinely happy for them, even with all the crap swirling in my own mind. "Congratulations, brother. Uncle Callan at your service. I'll be corrupting your wee ones with bad words and sneaking them sweets before dinner."

"I wouldn't expect anything less."

I take a deep breath, shaking off the cloud hovering over me. "I might have an early lunch and take the bike out for a bit."

What I'm not telling him is that I need to get the hell out of here. I need to get my blood pumping and break the constant loop of worry and jealousy that's gnawing at me. The sound of the engine roaring beneath me and the wind in my face is the kind of clarity I'm after.

I'm not trying to run from anything or anyone but being trapped in my own head feels a hell of a lot like suffocating.

Knox quirks a brow, the silent question clear as day. *Is that really a good idea?* He doesn't have to say it. He thinks I'm looking for trouble, that I'm just itching to stir something up.

Maybe he's right. Maybe he's not. Either way, I'm not in the mood to justify it. I give him a quick nod and keep it short.

"It'll be fine." The words slip out easy enough, but inside? Inside, there's a storm brewing.

"Just don't do anything stupid."

"Wouldn't dream of it."

As I turn to leave, his voice calls out behind me.

"And, hey... I'm here if you need to talk. Anytime."

I pause at the door, not turning around. I nod again, just once, the weight of those words landing more than I want to admit.

thirty-one

BREE

The coffee shop is quieter than I expected. I'm here a bit early, not because I'm eager, but because sitting at home with my nerves twisting me into knots wasn't an option.

The door swings open, and my body reacts before my mind catches up. Every muscle goes tight, my heart picks up its pace, and my stomach plummets. Dillon steps inside, his eyes scanning the room.

It's been over six months since we've been face-to-face, and yet, the sight of him still tears me up.

I straighten in my chair, my fingers gripping my mug harder than I should. This is it. The moment I've been both avoiding and waiting for.

Dillon's eyes lock onto mine, and a slow smile spreads across his face. He saunters over with the same self-assured swagger that used to make me weak in the knees, and when he slides into the chair across from me, that familiar cologne hits my senses. It's that same scent that once made my heart race but now only turns my stomach.

"Bree," he says, no trace of the slur I'd become so accustomed to. "You're looking good."

For a moment, I'm caught off guard. He also looks...good. Not in a *holy shit, take me back* kind of way, but in a healthy, content way. His eyes are clear. His skin isn't that blotchy shade it used to turn after a binge, and there's color in his face now, not that grayish hue I used to lie to myself about. His clothes are clean, not slept in. His hands don't shake when he lifts his coffee. It's exactly how I used to hope he'd look when we were together. Back when I thought I could fix everything and believed I was the one who could make him happy.

I force myself to meet his gaze, steadying my breath. "Thank you. You look well, too."

He leans back in his chair, eyes studying me as if nothing's changed, as if he still has the right to look at me like that.

"I've missed you, you know," he says, his voice dropping just enough to make it sound sincere. "It's been...different without you around."

Once upon a time, that line might have made me believe we could just slide back into the way things used to be. But I'm not that girl anymore.

I take a deep breath in an attempt to anchor myself. "Dillon, I need to say some things. And I need you to listen."

His eyebrows raise slightly, a flicker of surprise before he nods. "All right, I'm listening."

I clasp my hands together on the table, willing them not to shake. "What you did to me..." My voice cracks slightly, but I push through. "It wasn't okay. The way you treated me, the things you said, the way you...hurt me. It was abuse, Dillon."

Now that the words are out, I almost regret saying them. I'm surprised when he winces, his jaw tightening, his shoulders slumping as if the weight of everything we went through is suddenly crashing down on him. It's the first real sign of emotion I've seen from him in years.

"That's uh..." He clears his throat, his voice quieter. "That's why I wanted to talk to you. I've been going through a treatment program... Been sober for a few months now." He pauses. "I know I fucked up, in more ways than one. I'm so sorry, Bree. Truly."

The sincerity in his words catches me by surprise. It's a tone I haven't heard from him in a long time, maybe *ever*. I'm not sure how to respond.

"I appreciate that," I say carefully, my voice steadier than I feel. "Still...an apology doesn't erase what happened."

He nods, his gaze dropping to the floor. "I know. I don't expect it to. I just...needed you to know that I get it now. What I did was unforgivable."

The words hang in the air between us, and a part of me aches at the honesty in them. I want to stay guarded, but something about the way he says it breaks through my walls. Maybe it's the way he's finally owning up to it, the way he's not trying to make excuses.

A lump forms in my throat, but I swallow it down. This isn't how I thought this conversation would go. I'd prepared myself for anger and denial, not this quiet admission of guilt. It's almost worse because now I'm not sure how to react.

"Why now? Why reach out after all this time?"

He exhales slowly. "Part of my recovery is making amends," he says quietly. "But more than that, I needed to face what I'd done. To you, to us."

A tremor runs through me, memories flooding back. The shouting matches, the shattering glass. It's hard to separate the past from the present, especially when it feels like it happened just yesterday.

An image of Callan flashes in my mind, all kindness and

mischief. He's the one who keeps me going, the light in the dark. I've moved on. I hold onto that as I draw in a breath.

"I hear you," I say. "But I'm a different person now, too. I've found a peace I didn't think I'd get." I pause, meeting his eyes. For a split second, I almost let the old affection slip in. "I'm in a good place now. In a relationship with someone who...treats me the way I deserve."

The words are strange, almost like a relief. Saying it out loud makes it real.

"I've worked hard to get where I am," I continue. "And I just want to keep moving forward."

He doesn't say anything right away. His eyes flicker with regret, or maybe understanding. Whatever it is, it's clear that he's hearing me. It's enough. The space between us feels a little less heavy and a little more like closure.

I'm ready to let it all go.

Dillon nods slowly, the movement stiff like it's taking everything in him. "I understand. And I'm...glad you've found someone who treats you right." His voice wavers, and he swallows hard. "You deserve that, Bree. You always did."

I'm finally catching a glimpse of the man I used to know. The one I trusted before everything fell apart. I'm grateful that I'm seeing it now.

I offer him a small, genuine smile, feeling lighter than I have in a long time. "Thank you. I really hope you find peace, too, Dillon. I do." It's true. I want that for him.

He nods again, a sad smile pulling at the corners of his mouth. "I'm working on it. One day at a time, you know?"

Before I can say anything else, my phone rings. I'm almost relieved for the distraction, but then I see the name on the screen, and an uneasy sensation coils in my stomach. Lucy. We text constantly, but she's never actually called me before. That's...weird.

"Um, sorry," I say, already reaching for my phone. "Do you mind if I grab this? I don't want to be rude, but..." I trail off, not sure how to explain the flutter of nerves in my stomach, the way my pulse picks up.

He shakes his head. "Not at all."

I stare at Lucy's name flashing on my screen. Lucy's a texter. She sends me strings of emojis, funny memes about coffee, and pictures of customers' dogs that visit her café. She never calls.

I slide my finger across the screen, a thousand possibilities racing through my mind. The way my heart is pounding, you'd think I was answering a call from the president, not my friend.

"Hello?"

The silence on the other end is louder than words.

And that's when I know... Something's wrong.

thirty-two

CALLAN

The hum of the distillery fades into the background as I step outside, shrugging on my leather jacket. The air is cool and thick with the scent of damp earth, but at least the sky's clear for once, after what felt like a week of Mother Nature's personal water torture.

The engine roars to life, a deep, satisfying growl that settles my restless bones. It's not just a machine—it's the closest thing I've got to therapy. That sound, that vibration under me, has a way of drowning out all the noise.

I ease out of the lot slowly, but the moment I hit the edge of town, the open road stretches out ahead of me, and it's like the world gives me an invitation I can't say no to. The tires bite into the wet asphalt, and I can't help myself. I twist the throttle and the bike surges forward.

The hills rise in the distance, cloaked in mist. The river to my left is a whole mood, raging and foaming from the rain, determined to make a statement. I get it. I've been there.

Every bend in the road dares me to push faster, lean harder.

It's raw energy, untamed, like it doesn't give a damn about anything except right here, right now.

The wind cuts through me, but in the best way. It's the kind of cold that slaps you awake, clears out the fog, and makes every nerve fire on all cylinders. This is exactly what I needed.

I lose track of time until the first mist of rain starts to fall. *Really?* I tilt my head back just in time to catch a raindrop square on my visor. So much for clear skies.

The road ahead winds tighter, snaking through trees. The river's roar grows louder, matching the thrum of the engine beneath me. The rain picks up, slicking the asphalt, but I don't slow down. I twist the throttle more, lean harder into the curve, and feel that rush that sharpens everything, dials it all into razor focus. The bike's not just below me, it's *with* me. Out here, we're invincible.

At least, that's what I think...until I see a flash of tawny fur darting out of the brush.

"Fuck!"

Time slows in that split second, the deer standing motionless in the middle of the road, its wide eyes locked on mine. My heart lurches into my throat as instinct takes over. Brake, swerve, don't wipe out, but my mind's already screaming *too late.*

I yank the handlebars as the tires lose their grip on the gravel. The bike jerks beneath me, throwing me off balance. There's no saving it now. No miracle recovery. Just the sickening realization that I'm going down, and there's nothing I can do to stop it.

The world spins in a violent kaleidoscope of gray skies and green trees. My body becomes weightless, disconnected from the bike I was one with just moments ago. The handlebars wrench free from my grip as I'm catapulted through the air, a helpless trajectory that seems to last forever.

For a heartbeat, I register the glint of the guardrail as I sail over it, the silver flash like a final farewell to solid ground. Then it's nothing but open air, the rush of water growing louder and louder.

There's this perfect, terrible moment of suspension where I think, *this is going to hurt.*

Then gravity remembers I exist.

Wind howls past my helmet as I claw uselessly at nothing. Below, the river waits, swollen and angry. I hit the water with the force of a sledgehammer, the impact knocking every molecule of air from my lungs.

Christ, it's cold. Like thousands of needles stabbing every inch of my skin. The current immediately seizes me, tumbling me like I'm nothing more than a pebble.

The river roars its victory as it drags me under.

thirty-three

BREE

"Bree—"

Lucy's voice crackles through the line in a distraught, breathless rush of words I can barely understand. There's one, though, that hits me like a lightning strike.

Accident.

The world tilts. My heart slams against my ribs, and my lungs refuse to pull in enough air. A cold, trembling wave of panic rises.

I press the phone closer to my ear, as if anything could make this less terrifying. My words come out in broken pieces, shaky gasps strung together. "Is he okay?"

The silence on the other end is its own answer. When Lucy finally speaks, her voice is frayed, barely holding it together. "We... We haven't found him yet."

My knuckles burn from gripping the phone so hard. Everything else is drowned out by the rising anxiety threading through me. My voice trembles as I ask, "What do you mean you haven't found him?"

I don't care if I'm causing a scene. I don't care who's staring.

249

None of that matters. My worst nightmare is unraveling right in front of me, and I'm powerless to stop it. Thousands of miles away, and I can't do a damn thing. It's suffocating. I'm suffocating.

Lucy's words spill into my ear in a frantic, disjointed stream of information that doesn't make sense. "His bike was found on the side of the road near the river, but Callan... He's not there. They think he might have..."

She trails off, her words cracking like brittle glass. The silence that follows feels louder than anything. She doesn't finish the sentence, but she doesn't have to.

The images flood my mind anyway. Callan's face, pale and strained, the water crashing over him and dragging him under. His arms fighting against the current, his breath too shallow, the river swallowing him whole. I feel the overpowering, desperate need for air in my own lungs.

I slam my eyes shut, squeezing them tight. Maybe if I shut everything out, it'll stop. But the thoughts come faster, each one worse than the last. Every possible worst-case scenario plays out so quickly I can't outrun the terror.

Panic sinks its claws deep, settling in my bones. My voice cracks, ragged and shaky, as I choke out, "No, no, no... This isn't happening. It can't be."

But it *is*.

"I'm coming," I say, forcing the words through a throat that feels too tight. My voice steadies just enough, but inside, I'm falling apart. "I'll be on the next flight out."

I don't wait for Lucy's response. I can't. My finger slams down on the end call button, and I set the phone down, my hand shaking so violently I nearly drop it. It takes me a second to realize I'm holding my breath. The room is closing in around me, the walls pressing in tighter with every agonizing second of silence.

Across the table, Dillon's eyes are locked on me, his face morphing into a mask of alarm. I'm already coming apart at the seams, the panic swelling up inside me too big to contain.

"I have to go."

Dillon pushes back his chair, his voice edged with worry. "What's going on?"

I can't find the words to explain as I shove my phone into my bag. "I just... I have to go."

Before he can say anything else, I'm already on the move, brushing past him with my heart racing like it's about to burst out of my chest. I fling the door open and step outside, gulping in the air like I've just come up for breath after a deep dive.

Callan.

He's all I can think about. Getting to him. Seeing him. Holding him.

"He's fine," I whisper under my breath, the words looping in my head like a desperate prayer. *He has to be fine.*

Except doubt is merciless. What if he's not okay? What if...

No. I can't go there. I won't let myself.

I fumble with my phone, hands trembling so badly I can barely see the screen through the blur of unshed tears. I need to book a flight.

My fingers move on autopilot, swiping and searching for the fastest route. Everything is too slow and too complicated. There are too many steps between me and him.

"Bree!" Dillon's voice catches up to me, and then his hand is on my arm, turning me toward him. "What happened? Talk to me."

I blink at him, trying to focus. His face swims in my vision, and I realize tears are streaming down my cheeks. When did I start crying?

"It's Callan," I manage, the name catching in my throat.

"Callan," he repeats slowly, testing the name like he's searching his memory for it, like maybe he *should* know.

And that's when it hits me.

He has no idea who Callan is. Of course he wouldn't know.

"Is he..." He stops, exhales, and starts again. "Something happened to him?"

"Yes." My voice cracks on the single syllable. "There's been an accident. He..." I can't finish the sentence. Reality is closing in, and I can't breathe through it.

Dillon's face softens with concern, his hand still on my arm. "Who is he to you?"

How do I explain Callan? He's laughter on rainy mornings and whispered promises under starlight. He's the feeling of coming home when I never knew I was lost.

"He's..."

Dillon studies my face, understanding dawning in his eyes. "You're in love with him."

It's not a question. The tears on my face are answer enough.

"I need to get to Scotland." My voice sounds distant now, like it belongs to someone else. Someone stronger, someone who isn't falling apart at the seams.

He steps back, running a hand through his hair. "Scotland?"

"Yes, Scotland." My voice breaks. The distance between us feels insurmountable right now, stretching across oceans and continents like a physical wound.

I turn my attention back to my phone, but my fingers won't stop quivering long enough to do anything. The screen blurs through my tears, and I can't seem to focus long enough to find any available flights. What if I'm too late? What if the last time I saw him was truly the last?

"Let me help," Dillon says, his voice calm in a way mine

can't be right now. He gently takes the phone from my trembling hands. "Edinburgh, right?"

I look up at his face. It's filled with concern, not judgment. Not the hurt or betrayal I might have expected.

I nod, unable to form words. My throat feels raw, as if I've been screaming. Maybe I have been, inside my head.

"I'll book you the next flight out," he says, already tapping at my phone screen. "And I'll drive you to the airport."

The kindness in his offer pierces through my panic. *This* is the version of Dillon I used to know. The sober one, at least. The one who once stayed up all night with me, rubbing circles into my back while I cried over things that felt like the end of the world.

The realization is bittersweet. For all the ways we broke, for all the ways we had to step back from each other, I can see he's found his way back to himself.

And that means more than I can put into words.

"Thank you," I whisper, the words seeming inadequate.

My mind races ahead to Callan and the way his eyes crinkle at the corners when he laughs, the stubborn cowlick in his hair that never stays put. The thought that I might never see those details again makes me physically ill.

"There's a flight in three hours," Dillon says, his voice breaking through my spiraling thoughts. "If we leave now, you'll make it."

His words are meant to be reassuring, but all I can think is... What if I'm already too late?

thirty-four
CALLAN

My boots fill with water. The helmet that saved my skull fills as well, threatening to drown me. Instinct kicks in, and I claw at the strap with numb fingers. I manage to wrench the buckle free. The helmet peels away, and I break the surface with a desperate gasp that's half water, half air.

The current is merciless, battering me against rocks that materialize out of nowhere in the churning foam. Every impact is a new explosion of pain. I catch a flash of the shore, the middle of the surging river, and the sky. All whirl past in a dizzying blur.

"Swim, you idiot," I growl to myself, fighting against the weight of my waterlogged jacket.

My arms are leaden as I try to cut through the water, but the river's too angry. Every time I think I'm making progress toward the bank, the current yanks me back into its grip. My lungs burn. My muscles scream. The cold seeps into my bones, making every movement more sluggish.

As I fight against the current, half drowning and fully regretting every decision that led me here, my brain chooses this moment to remind me that I am *not* built for this. I am not some rugged survivalist. I am not the kind of man who wrestles nature into submission.

And yet, here I am.

A massive branch rushes past, missing my head by inches. That would've been it. Game over.

I'm not ready to die, damn it.

I kick harder, arms windmilling against the current. For one glorious moment I make headway, until my shoulder slams into a submerged boulder. The impact spins me sideways, and before I can recover, I'm sucked into a swirling pocket between rocks.

The water closes over my head again, a roaring silence that drowns out everything but my own heartbeat in my ears. Down here, the river has a different voice. A muffled, hollow roar that vibrates through my bones.

My lungs scream for oxygen, every cell in my body demanding what I can't give them. I fight the instinct to inhale, knowing it'll mean death. Instead, I focus on the pale glow of sunlight filtered through water and claw my way toward it. With one final surge of desperate strength, I break the surface and grab tree roots that hang like gnarled fingers from the eroded bank. The twisted, mud-slick lifelines are salvation in my hands. I cling to them, gasping and choking up river water that burns its way back out of my lungs.

For several moments, I hang there, every muscle trembling with chilled exhaustion. The roots creak ominously, threatening to give way under my waterlogged weight. I need to pull myself up, but my arms feel disconnected from my brain's commands.

"Move," I rasp to myself. "Fucking *move*."

Agonizing pain radiates through my side where something

has surely been broken, or worse. Each breath is a losing battle, but I refuse to stop.

I test one of the thicker roots, wrapping my fingers around its rough surface. It holds. Gritting my teeth against the pain in my shoulder, I haul myself up an inch, then another. I try to find my footing but *fuck*. A searing, burning pain tears through my thigh, hot enough to steal my breath. My teeth grind against the scream scraping at my throat, and I force myself to push past it. It's not like I have any other choice.

Every motion sends jolts of pain ricocheting through my skull. Blood drips into my eyes, turning the world into a blur of red. I take the chance to wipe at it with a shaking hand, only to realize it's already coated in the stuff. It's everywhere, running down my face, soaking into my clothes, smearing with the dirt I'm dragging myself through.

Inch by agonizing inch, I claw at the ground, digging my fingers into the wet earth until, finally, my body collapses onto the bank.

The gash in my side throbs in time with my heartbeat, blood pouring freely now. I press my hand to it, but my fingers are too weak to stop the flow.

My eyes grow heavy, the edges of my vision blurring into darkness. The pain dulls, replaced by an eerie stillness. I know I should fight it, but the weight dragging me under is too strong.

And yet, through the haze, one thought cuts through with startling clarity.

Bree is going to be pissed if I die.

She'd be furious that I got myself into this mess, that I didn't fight harder, that I even *considered* leaving her like this. And that's almost more terrifying than bleeding out in the dirt.

The sky above me tilts and swirls, clouds merging into strange patterns. Funny how the mind works when it's shutting down. Colors seem too bright and sounds are too distant. They slip farther away, like I'm watching the world from the wrong end of a tunnel.

Bree's face flashes in my mind, furious and terrified, but beautiful.

The thought barely forms before the tunnel stretches impossibly far, the last sliver of light flickering...

And then, nothing.

thirty-five

BREE

The wheels of the plane hit the ground with a jolt that rattles my teeth and sends a fresh surge of panic through my body. I grip the armrests until my knuckles ache, willing the plane to hurry and let me off.

The godforsaken Wi-Fi didn't work the entire flight, leaving me stranded with nothing but my own frantic thoughts. No updates. No news. No lifeline to the outside world. Just endless hours of silence, my mind spinning through every horrifying possibility.

As soon as the seatbelt light blinks off, I'm up, practically shoving my way down the aisle. I don't care about the annoyed mutters from the people I pass. My heart feels like it's about to explode, pounding so hard it's all I can hear.

The moment I'm through the airport, my eyes scan the crowd. And then I see Juliette, standing stiffly by the arrival gate. Her face is pale, her shoulders tense. She doesn't wave. She doesn't smile.

The knot in my chest tightens as I approach.

"Did they find him?"

She shakes her head, slow and reluctant, her eyes heavy with worry. "Not yet," she says quietly. "But they're searching. Knox is out there, and they've got people—"

"I need to go," I cut her off, my words tumbling out in a rush. My breath is coming too fast, too shallow, but I don't care. "Where's the hospital? Or the river? Anywhere he might be."

Juliette reaches out, her hands firm and unmoving as they grip my arms. It's the only thing keeping me from bolting. "We'll go. You need to breathe first, okay? Just breathe."

I want to scream at her to let go, to stop telling me what to do when I'm drowning. How am I supposed to breathe when the panic's wrapped around me like a vise, squeezing tighter with every second that passes?

Instead, I nod. I swallow back the fear climbing my throat, forcing it down even though it threatens to choke me.

She pulls me into a quick hug, her warmth anchoring me. I don't hug her back. I can't seem to make the right movements, but I let her hold me for just a moment.

"Come on," she says softly. "Let's get you there."

Her hand brushes my arm, and I barely register it. Every step I take is mechanical, like I'm not even in control of my own body anymore. I can't shake the image of Callan in my head. Alone. Cold. Hurt. Or worse.

The drive is a blur of rain-slicked roads, the world outside melting into a haze that matches the mess inside my brain. I try to focus, but my thoughts bounce around too much. Juliette's voice drifts through the fog, but it doesn't reach me. Her words are muffled, meant to fill the silence between us, but it's all I can do to hold myself together long enough to even hear her.

By the time we pull up to the makeshift command center near the river, my hands are already trembling. The scene before me is straight out of a nightmare.

Flashing lights from rescue vehicles cut through the rain,

illuminating the muddy banks. Volunteers move like shadows in the downpour, their faces hollow with exhaustion, their movements automatic, as if they've done this too many times before.

I don't wait for the car to stop before I'm out, my body reacting before my brain can catch up. My boots hit the mud, and my eyes scan the crowd. I look for anything that will tell me he's here. That he's alive. That this suffocating, bone-deep fear gnawing at me isn't the new air I'm forced to breathe.

None of the faces are his.

A burly man steps into my line of sight, his fluorescent rescue jacket glaring under the floodlights.

"Are you family?" His accent is so thick I can barely make the words out.

I open my mouth, but no sound comes. I can't even find the oxygen to answer him, let alone form the words.

Juliette steps forward, her small frame somehow commanding as she positions herself between me and the rescuer.

"We're family," she says with quiet authority, her voice steadier than I could manage. "Both of us."

The rescuer's eyes dart between us. Water drips from the brim of his safety helmet as he nods, seeming to make a decision.

"We've recovered some gear downstream," he says, his tone neutral. "A helmet. But no sign of him."

No sign of him.

Juliette's hand slips into mine, anchoring me to the present when every part of me wants to dissolve into worry.

I can't breathe. My mind wants to deny it, to scream that there's been a mistake, but the fear I've been holding at bay claws its way to the surface.

"I need to see," I manage to croak out. "The helmet. I need to see it."

He hesitates, like he's searching for some way to avoid what I'm asking. His brow furrows. "Miss, I don't think—"

"Please," I cut him off. The plea is stronger this time, fueled by something far deeper than fear. "I need to know if it's his."

He nods reluctantly, his eyes shadowed with pity. My breath catches with a sharp, painful hitch, because pity means loss. It means regret. It means *too late*.

I do want to follow him, but I also don't. My feet are rooted in the mud, my body screaming to stay right here. But Juliette squeezes my hand, and somehow, I move.

We're led into a canvas tent, and then I see it.

The helmet is battered and scarred with deep scrapes that speak of violence and impact, worn beyond recognition. The sight of it sends an icy chill through my veins, freezing me in place.

The smallest detail catches my eye, almost too insignificant to matter. A sticker on the side. A little heart, faded from the wear and tear, but still unmistakable. It's the one I gave him. The stupid, quirky little heart sticker I insisted he put on as a joke.

It's his.

My legs give out. I hear the sound of someone's knees hitting the ground, and it takes me a moment to realize they're mine. The world narrows to that one small, faded heart sticker.

The rescuer rambles about the search parameters, about how they're expanding the area, about how the river's current is strong but people have survived worse. His words wash over me like they're in another language entirely.

"We're not giving up," the rescue worker says, his voice clearer now. "If he's out there, we'll find him."

. . .

I WANT TO SCREAM, to rage, to tear apart everything standing between me and the man I love. I want to rip the universe in half for daring to place that single, fragile word between me and my hope.

If.

Juliette crouches beside me, draping her arm around my shoulders. She's trembling, too, but her voice remains peaceful.

"Listen to me," she says, forcing me to look at her. "This doesn't mean anything yet. It just means his helmet came off. That's all we know for certain."

Her words are logical, but logic has no place here.

The seconds crawl, dragging me through a haze of helplessness. My mind spins, tripping over worst-case scenarios, getting stuck in the places I don't want it to go. I should move. I should do something. But there's really nothing I *can* do.

And so, I wait.

I clutch my damp jacket tighter around me, but it does nothing to stop the cold burrowing deep beneath my skin. This isn't a chill that comes from the rain. It's an ache that settles in my bones, carved from fear and refusal to let go.

"Do you want to sit down for a minute?" Juliette asks.

I don't answer right away. My body feels like it's made of stone. Even the thought of sitting down seems impossible.

I shake my head, the movement sharp and quick, as if I can physically shake off the suffocating sense of helplessness. "No."

A distant shout breaks through the tense air, and my heart leaps. I spin around, my pulse hammering in my ears, desperate to see him. *Please, let it be him.*

As my eyes scan the crowd, my hope shrinks to nothing. It's just another rescue worker calling out to someone, his voice swallowed by the chaos.

"Bree," Juliette says softly, her hand resting lightly on my arm. "Maybe we should—"

"No," I cut her off, my voice rough and raw. I don't even recognize it as my own. "I'm not leaving. I can't."

I don't know what I'd be running to, or what I'd be running from, but I know this much... I'm not leaving.

She nods. "Then I'll stay with you."

I should be out there. I should be running through the mud, calling his name, doing *something*. But they have professionals. They have teams. They know what they're doing. They have the tools, the training, the experience. All I have is this overwhelming sense of helplessness.

If I found him, what would I even do? What if I find him hurt? Broken? What if... What if I find him *gone*?

I wouldn't survive it. I don't know how to keep living in a world where he's not in it. He's *everything*.

I can't think about that. I can't.

Except the thought keeps creeping in no matter how hard I try to push it away. It hovers at the edges of my mind, threatening to consume me.

Still, I stand here wishing I could do more while times stretches on, cruel and endless. The ache in my chest grows with every passing second, deepening the wound, making it harder to breathe. Every second is a reminder of how much I can't control and how small I feel.

All I can do is wait.

thirty-six
BREE

Time stopped meaning anything the moment I got here. The world outside this riverbank doesn't exist.

The tent flaps rustle with every gust of wind, brittle canvas snapping like it's as strung out as I am. The river murmurs just beyond, its current a cruel contrast to the havoc inside me. Search crews come and go. Flashlights glow in the distance. Somewhere out there, they're still looking for him.

I think I've been awake for nearly forty-eight hours. Maybe more. Maybe less. Does it even matter? Sleep is something that exists for people who aren't running on fumes and sheer desperation. My body begs for rest, every muscle aching, every nerve frayed, but my brain won't allow it. It keeps me upright, keeps me pacing, keeps me stuck in this awful in-between where the only thing keeping me conscious is the terror that if I close my eyes, even for a second, I'll wake up to the worst.

It's sometime in the middle of the night, that much I'm sure of. Everything else is a blur. The rain has stopped, but the weight in the air hasn't lifted. If anything, it's heavier now, and the world has gone eerily still. No cars. No voices. Not even the whisper of wind through the trees. It's like everything is holding its breath. Just like me.

The only sound left is the insistent pounding of my heart in my ears. Proof that I'm still here, still standing. But even that feels uncertain, like it could stop at any moment.

I can feel myself slipping, my grip on reality unraveling thread by thread.

The eerie silence is claimed by the static crackle of a rescuer's nearby radio. My head snaps toward the sound, my pulse surging, breath locking in my throat. For a second, everything is suspended.

Then through the noise, a voice breaks through.

"We've got him. We found him."

The radio crackles again, and the voice delivers the only words that matter.

"He's alive. He's hurt, but he's alive."

A choked sound rips from my throat, somewhere between a sob and a gasp. My knees threaten to buckle, and my vision swims.

He's alive.

Alive.

The one word washes away the terror that's been clinging to me. My vision blurs, the world tilting sideways as relief crashes over me in waves so powerful I can barely stay standing. I press my hand to my mouth, trying to contain the sob threatening to break free.

I want to laugh. I want to cry. This nightmare is about to end.

Then, just as quickly as it arrived, hope is ripped from me. Reality sets in, and my stomach drops.

He's *hurt*.

What does hurt mean? How bad is it? What kind of shape is he in? The image of him broken, bleeding, and unconscious begins to form at the edges of my mind, pulling me back into the worst version of this reality I've been trying so desperately to escape.

"Where?" I manage to gasp, grabbing the closest rescuer's sleeve. "Where is he?"

"I'm not sure, ma'am, but the helicopter's on its way to airlift him out."

Helicopter. They're getting him out of there. That's good, right? That should be enough to settle my racing heart. And yet my pulse is still distraught, the nervousness still alive and jumping its way up my throat.

I have to get to the hospital. I need to see him, hold his hand, and make sure he knows he's not alone.

But the thought of what I might find once I see him... It's unbearable.

How am I supposed to handle it? How will I stay strong for him if I see him like that? How can I be his strength when all I want to do is crumble?

I can't be weak.

Then, in the distance, there's a flash of light and the unmistakable silhouette of the helicopter. They're getting him out.

Juliette appears at my side. "Knox just called. He's with him. They're taking him to Highland Memorial," she says, already pulling her car keys from her pocket. "Let's go."

I nod, unable to speak through the knot in my throat. My body feels weightless, like I might float away if not for Juliette's steady hand on my elbow guiding me back to the car.

The first rays of dawn are just beginning to streak across the sky, painting everything in a surreal golden light. It feels wrong, somehow, that the world can look so beautiful when every nerve in my body is frayed, ready to snap.

"He'll be okay," Juliette says, her eyes fixed on the road ahead. "Callan's strong."

I want to believe her. I need to believe her. But the fear that's been my constant companion for the past two days isn't so easily dismissed.

The rest of the drive is a blur. My fingers dig into my thighs, my knee bouncing restlessly. I don't realize I'm holding my breath until the sight of the hospital looms ahead.

Juliette pulls into the emergency lot, but I'm already moving, my hand grasping the door handle before the tires have even fully stopped. My pulse hammers in my ears, drowning out everything else.

I have to get to him.

The moment my feet hit the pavement, I'm running. The automatic doors slide open, and the sterile bite of disinfectant floods my senses. The smell hits hard, twisting my stomach and turning my anxiety into something almost tangible. The emergency room is alive with nurses darting past in scrubs, monitors beeping in a dissonant rhythm, phones ringing, voices murmuring, all of which blend into a chaotic buzz.

I push forward, gripping the edge of the reception desk. "I'm looking for—"

"Bree!"

I turn at the sound of my name, a jolt of anticipation racing through me, only for my pulse to stutter in a whole new rhythm when I see Knox.

He's striding toward me with long, purposeful steps, but his face is pale and drawn, his eyes rimmed red.

"Where is he? Is he okay? What happened?"

Knox's jaw clenches, his lips pressing together. "He's in surgery right now." His voice is strained. Tired. "They're working on him."

My stomach twists. "Surgery? How bad is it?"

He hesitates. Why is he hesitating?

"Knox," I whisper, my voice uneven. "Tell me."

He exhales sharply, like the words physically pain him. "It was bad, Bree. The river took him farther than we thought. By the time they got to him..." He shakes his head, jaw tightening. "Hypothermia. Blood loss. Internal injuries. Broken ribs. His leg is pretty messed up, too. They don't know the full extent yet."

My legs start to give out, and I'm vaguely aware of Knox's hands propping me up, pulling me back from the edge.

"He's going to be okay, right? He has to be okay."

"They're doing everything they can," he says. "He's tough, Bree. If anyone can pull through this, it's him."

I nod mechanically, my head moving in agreement, but inside, the storm is raging. I can't breathe. I can't think.

Knox's hand is the only thing keeping me upright. Without it, I'm sure I would crumble to the floor.

"I need to see him," I manage to whisper, the words almost inaudible. My throat is tight, but the anxiety in my mind screams louder than I can voice it.

He shakes his head. "He's in surgery, Bree. It could be hours... We just have to wait."

Wait. The word is a prison sentence. I want to demand he take me to him, but the strength in my legs falters, and I'm rooted in place. My hands tremble at my sides, and I want to move, but all I can do is stand here, *waiting.*

Knox shifts his focus, releasing my arm to approach Juliette. There's an edge of concern in his voice as he guides her to a chair. "You need to sit, Jules. You're exhausted. This isn't good for you."

Guilt snakes through me. How did I not think of her before now? Juliette, who has been by my side through all of this, who is *pregnant* and running on just as much exhaustion and fear as the rest of us.

I scrub a hand over my face. "Shit. Jules, I'm so sorry. I wasn't thinking."

She just shakes her head, already sinking into the chair Knox guided her to. "I'm fine," she says, her voice as reassuring despite her exhaustion.

"You need to go home," I try again, because even though I don't want her to leave, even though I selfishly need her here, I can't ignore what's best for her. "Get some rest. Take care of yourself. The babies—"

"This is where I need to be," she interrupts, her gaze locking onto mine.

I nod, swallowing hard. "Okay."

She offers a small smile, tired but sure. "Okay. Any word from your parents or Lucy?" she asks, turning her attention back to Knox.

"Aye, they'll be here soon," he replies, his voice rougher than usual. "Lucy's driving Mum and Dad."

I sink into a chair next to Juliette, my legs finally giving out. "Can you tell me exactly what happened? How did they find him?"

Knox runs a hand through his hair, his fingers tugging at the strands in frustration. His eyes are distant and unfocused, as if he's still on the riverbank watching everything unfold.

"They found him on the bank a few miles from where he went in. He was unconscious but breathing. They think he managed to grab onto something before he passed out."

His voice falters, and for a second, the room is so quiet I can hear my own shallow breaths. "If he hadn't..." He doesn't finish the thought. He doesn't need to. We all know what would have happened.

If he hadn't grabbed onto whatever it was, we'd be planning a funeral instead of sitting in a hospital waiting room.

I lean forward, elbows on my knees, head in my hands as I try to focus my breathing.

"He's alive," I whisper, more to myself than anyone else. "He's alive."

The waiting room fills and empties around us. Nurses come and go. The sun climbs higher in the sky outside the windows. And still, we wait.

The rest of the family arrives, their faces etched with the same worry that consumes me, and yet it feels like I'm watching them through a thick fog.

Juliette doesn't let go of me, her hand a constant touch on my arm, holding me together. Knox, on the other hand, paces near the doorway. I can almost feel the tension radiating off him, like if he moves enough, the clock will speed up.

But the clock keeps ticking its relentless rhythm, reminding me of how little control we have. Every tick is like my own heartbeat, each one a test of my will.

And then, finally, the door opens and a nurse steps through.

"Family of Callan MacKenzie?"

In an instant, we're all on our feet, a collective surge of energy and urgency.

"He's out of surgery," she says, and the room seems to exhale all at once, a rush of relief, of hope flickering back to life. "He's stable for now, but his injuries are severe. He's being moved to the ICU. The doctor will be out shortly to explain more."

Lucy grabs my arm, the pressure in her grip desperate and shaky. Whether it's from hope or dread, I can't tell. I want to tell her everything will be fine, but I can't find the words.

"Can we see him?" Callan's mom, Sam, asks.

The nurse nods, her face remaining neutral. "You'll need to wait until he's settled in the ICU, but after that, yes. Only two visitors at a time, though," she adds. "The doctor will let you know."

"Thank you," Knox says quietly. He's holding it together, but I can see the effort it's taking.

We sink back into our seats. Lucy is crying, her mom's arm wrapped around her shoulders, offering what little comfort she can. Knox resumes his pacing, each step a reflection of the unease he's carrying, while Callan's stepdad, Paul, stares blankly at the floor, his face set in a mask of shock.

I lean into Juliette. I don't know how I'd manage without her. "He's going to be okay," she murmurs, but I catch the subtle tremor in her voice.

Finally, the doctor steps into the room. He introduces himself, but the name doesn't stick. It's just background noise, insignificant compared to the information we're about to hear.

"Mr. MacKenzie's condition is critical but stable," he begins, his tone calm and clinical. "He sustained significant injuries, including several broken ribs, one of which caused a punctured lung. He has a severe concussion, and there was internal bleeding that we've managed to control. His right leg was also badly fractured and required surgical intervention."

Each injury feels like a blow, each word a sharp jab that knocks the breath from my lungs. My stomach churns, and I fight the urge to collapse.

He's hurt. He's broken.

The doctor's gaze softens slightly, but his words don't waver. "The next few days are going to be critical. We'll be monitoring him closely for complications, especially with the head injury and his lung. He's sedated and on a ventilator to help him breathe. The ventilator is temporary."

I swear the ground falls away beneath me as I dig my nails into my palms to keep upright.

"Can we see him now?" someone asks, but the voice seems

so distant, like it's coming from a far-off place. I don't even know who spoke.

The doctor nods, but there's hesitation in his eyes. "He's unconscious, and he won't look like himself. I want to prepare you for that. There's swelling, bruising, and he's hooked up to multiple monitors. It can be difficult to see a loved one in that condition."

Difficult doesn't even begin to cover it. There's a knot forming in my stomach, but I don't care about the bruising, the swelling, or the monitors. I need to see him. I need to see with my own eyes that he's alive, that he's here, and that he's still *him.*

Knox's hand on my shoulder startles me. "You should go first, with Mum," he says softly. "He'd want to see you."

I glance around the room, taking in the weary, worried faces of his family. My eyes land on Lucy and Paul, who offer quiet, encouraging nods.

"Are you sure?"

There's no hesitation, no argument. Just understanding. "Of course," Paul says. "You go with Sam."

A nurse leads us down the hallway, the sterile smell of antiseptic filling my lungs with each step. My heart pounds, each beat echoing in my ears, a rhythm of anticipation and dread.

We stop outside one of the rooms with the door slightly ajar. I take a breath, trying to force my body into some semblance of calm. The nurse turns to face us, her expression unreadable. Her eyes soften when they meet mine.

"It might be shocking at first."

I nod, my throat tight. My body is on edge, a coil of tension threatening to snap with the next breath. I steel myself for what I know is coming.

The nurse pushes the door open, and as soon as it swings back, Sam gasps beside me. The sight hits me like a physical blow, the force of it stealing the air from my lungs. Callan, my strong, vibrant Callan, lies utterly still. His body is unrecognizable beneath the bruises and swelling, a shadow of the man I know. The stark white hospital sheets contrast painfully with the vividness of his injuries, the raw colors that seem to scream of tragedy and instability.

Tubes and wires snake around him, connecting him to the monitors, their rhythmic pulses both a comfort and a curse. The melodic beeps are reminders that he's alive, that his heart is still beating, but the ventilator humming in the background is unnatural, too mechanical, too foreign.

I reach for the doorframe, gripping it so tightly my fingers burn. I use it as an anchor to keep myself standing. I've seen this scene before. Monitors, tubing, machines doing the work a body can't. It's part of my world. It's my job. I've stood at bedsides like this more times than I can count.

But this is Callan.

His chest rises and falls with the help, and it's not the man I remember. Not the man whose smile could light up a room. Not the man who laughed with me, who held me, who made me feel safe.

This man, lying in front of me, feels so far away. So *breakable.*

"Callan," I whisper, his name falling from my lips like a fragile prayer. My voice cracks, but it's all I can manage. Just a breath of sound that trembles in the sterile air.

I've been holding it together, trying so hard to be strong for him, for myself, for the possibility that everything will somehow turn out okay. Now, standing here, looking at him so small, so broken in that hospital bed, a sob rises in my throat.

I try to hold it back, to force it down, but it breaks free anyway, spilling from me in broken, desperate gasps. The ground splinters beneath me, my knees buckle, I'm falling. I slide to the floor, clutching the doorframe.

Sam steps past me, her movements careful and deliberate. She approaches the bed, her face drawn, and I watch her reach for his hand, her fingers trembling as she closes the distance. Her silent strength makes this harder. All I can do is sit here, paralyzed.

I should be by his side. I should be the one holding his hand, offering the reassurance that he'll come back to me.

I squeeze my eyes shut, my breath ragged and uneven, as I try to wrestle the grief and the fear back into submission. I need to get a grip. I need to be strong for him. He needs me. It doesn't matter if every part of me is breaking.

Sam's eyes meet mine, but she doesn't say anything at first. Then she steps towards me, her hand reaching out. "Oh, Bree," she says. "Come here, sweetheart."

It shouldn't be her responsibility to comfort me right now. This is her son, her child, lying there fighting for his life. Yet somehow, Sam is the one being strong, holding it together when I'm barely keeping my composure.

I take a shaky breath, forcing my legs to move, and with a trembling hand, I take Sam's outstretched one. Her grip is firm, and she doesn't let go until she's sure I'm steady enough to stand on my own before she steps back, giving me the space I need.

Up close, it's even worse. The sight of him, bruised and battered, is more than I can bear. His face is a map of cuts and contusions, a tragedy in itself. The slow rise and fall of his chest is *wrong*, controlled. It's not him breathing. It's the ventilator, and it feels like a cruel impersonation of what *should* be.

"I'll give you a few minutes," Sam says. "I'll go see who would like to come in next."

Her strength amazes me. This is her boy, and yet she's the one standing tall when the rest of us are falling apart.

I nod, swallowing hard against the lump in my throat, and slowly move closer to him. My hand hovers over his, my fingers trembling as I fight the paranoia that I might hurt him, like he could shatter under my touch. After what feels like an eternity, I gently rest my fingers against his hand, careful to avoid the IV lines and the tubes. His skin is cool under my touch.

I close my eyes for just a second, allowing the tears to fall, even though I told myself I wouldn't cry. "You're so stubborn, you know that?" I whisper. A weak laugh escapes me, despite everything. "So you'd better fight, Callan. You don't get to give up. Not now, not ever."

The ventilator hums in response, its rhythm too artificial. My grip tightens around his hand, desperate for some kind of sign to prove that he's still here, still fighting. Anything.

I take a seat beside him, pressing my forehead to the edge of the bed. "I need you to come back to me."

I lift my head slowly, my eyes searching his face for any sign of recognition, any indication that he hears me. That he knows I'm here. There's nothing.

God, what I wouldn't give to lose myself in those devastating blue eyes that somehow tear me down and build me back up, all in the same breath. To hear that strong rumble of his laugh that digs under my skin and settles in my bones. To feel the heat of that stupidly perfect grin that cracks through every hard day.

The ache isn't just in my chest. It's *everywhere*, like something fundamental inside me has been scraped out. I swear I can still feel him, but it's like I'm pressing my palm against glass, watching him from the other side, knowing that no matter how hard I push, I can't reach him.

It's the most suffocating feeling I've ever known.

thirty-seven

CALLAN

The world is a mess of noise, and none of it is helpful. Voices drift in and out, machines beep, but I can't understand a damn thing they're trying to say. Somewhere in the haze, I catch snippets of conversation, but it's all muffled, like I'm underwater.

"...doing well without the ventilator..."

The words are clear enough to pierce through the fog, but the rest is lost.

A soft hand presses against mine.

Okay. That's nice.

I try to squeeze it, to let whoever it is know that, yeah, I'm still in here, but my body has apparently filed for early retirement. Nothing moves. I don't even twitch.

Fantastic.

Maybe I died.

I give opening my eyes an honest effort, but they won't budge, either. Fine. I focus on what I can sense. The warmth of that hand, the sure beep of what I'm guessing is a heart monitor, and the smell of something faint but familiar—perfume.

Bree's.

The realization has little time to settle before fiery pain tears through me. My chest, head, leg, hell, even my *hair* hurts. It's enough to drag me kicking and screaming back into consciousness whether I'm ready or not.

I force my eyes open, and the light hits hard. My vision is a wreck. Everything's too bright and unfocused. I blink rapidly, trying to make sense of the shapes swimming in front of me.

I'm definitely in a hospital. Bree's asleep, or, well...half asleep. She's slumped in a chair beside the bed, her body half draped over me, like she's trying to be close even in sleep.

What the actual fuck happened? I was on my bike by the river, and then...damn it. The deer.

I try to speak, but my throat feels like sandpaper. Nothing comes out. My breath is shallow, but I manage to squeeze her hand enough to remind myself that she's here.

I try to talk again, this time forcing the words out in a strained whisper. "Bree..."

It's enough to stir her. Her head jerks up, eyes wide and blinking. Relief floods her face, but there's doubt in her eyes, too, like she's afraid this might be some cruel trick.

"Callan?" Her voice cracks, and she leans forward, gripping my hand as if she's afraid I'll disappear if she lets go. She's shaking, and I can't tell if it's from worry, relief, or the tears she's trying to force away. "Oh my god, you're awake."

I start to speak again, but the effort backfires, my breath catching painfully. Bree's expression tightens.

"Shh, don't try to talk," she whispers, her fingers brushing featherlight over my cheek. Her voice trembles. "I'm going to let the nurse know you're awake."

I don't want a nurse. I want *her.*

I want to tell her everything. Apologies, regrets, promises. I'd recite poetry if I thought it would make that haunted look in her eyes go away. But the words clog my throat, useless and stuck in the wreckage of my body.

Her hand shakes as she reaches for the call button. Her golden hair is a tangled mess, and the dark circles under her eyes make me wonder just how long she's been sitting there, watching over me.

How long have *I* been here?

A nurse enters, her energy a sharp contrast to the fragile nervousness radiating from Bree. "Mr. MacKenzie, good to see you awake. How are you feeling?"

My words come out as little more than a rough, hoarse rasp. "Like...I've been hit by a truck."

The nurse gives a sympathetic smile. "Close enough. A deer and a motorcycle aren't the best of friends." She checks the machines around me, pressing buttons on one with practiced ease.

Bree doesn't laugh. She doesn't even crack a smile as her grip on my hand tightens.

I try again, testing my voice. "What...happened?"

"You took quite the beating. Hypothermia, a nasty gash on your side, a concussion, and a fractured leg. Honestly, you're lucky."

Lucky.

Bree makes a choked sound, something between a scoff and a sob, and I shift my gaze to her. Her eyes are red-rimmed, exhausted, and full of...longing? Anger? Absolute certainty that she's going to kill me as soon as I'm well enough to run?

Probably all three.

"I'll page the doctor. He'll want to examine you now that you're awake."

Bree gives a quick nod as the nurse leaves the room. I try to sit up, but the pain spikes immediately. A groan slips out before I can stop it, full of frustration. My ribs feel like they're being crushed, the pressure unbearable with each shallow breath I try to take.

"Easy," Bree murmurs. She doesn't push, doesn't rush. Just waits, letting me find my rhythm as I struggle through the pain at my own pace.

I manage to settle back down, my body shuddering with the effort, my breath coming in jagged bursts. Finally, I meet her gaze.

"You scared the shit out of me," she says, the words raw and unfiltered. "Don't you *dare* do that ever again."

A weak chuckle escapes me, even though it sends a spike of pain straight through my chest. I wince. "Guess I can't make any promises," I rasp, a smirk tugging at the corner of my mouth despite everything.

She rolls her eyes, though I catch the way she's trying to hold back a smile. "You're impossible." There's no real anger in her voice.

"What the fuck happened to me?"

She takes a deep breath, her eyes never leaving mine. "You hit that deer head-on before you went into the river. More specifically, you broke three ribs, punctured your left lung, fractured your right femur, and got yourself a nasty concussion to top it all off. Oh, and stitches. Everywhere."

As she talks, her fingers are already at work—checking the IV line, adjusting the blanket like it's second nature, her movements calm, practiced, and efficient. She glances at the monitor beside me, then lightly presses two fingers to my wrist, counting silently.

I should probably be more concerned about the punctured lung and the whole near-death experience, but instead, all I can think is... *Bree in nurse mode is the sexiest thing I've ever seen.*

I manage a weak, lopsided grin. "So, you saying I look good, or...?"

Her eyes narrow. "I'm saying you're lucky you're already in a hospital, because when you're better, I might just put you back in one."

Yep. Definitely hot.

Her face shifts. That fierce spark falters, and her voice cracks on the next words. "You've been out for four days, Callan."

Four days? Christ. Seriously? I try to wrap my head around it, but my brain feels like it's trudging through molasses.

"The doctors... They weren't sure when you'd wake up..."

I give her hand a weak squeeze. "Hey," I rasp, doing my best to sound tough, "takes more than a deer to keep a MacKenzie down."

She's not laughing. Not even close. She shakes her head like she's trying to rattle loose everything she's held in. "You don't get it. I was terrified." Her voice rises with unrestrained emotion. "I sat here and watched doctors come and go. I listened to your mom cry in the hallway. I counted the seconds between beeps on your monitor because it was the only proof I had that you were still alive."

She bites her lip hard enough to leave a mark, her hands trembling now. "Everyone's been in and out, trying to be strong. But I couldn't leave. Not once. Because what if something happened when I wasn't here?"

Silence coils thick between us. I swallow hard, but it burns all the way down. Everything hurts. My lungs, my ribs, my throat. Hell, even my damn eyelashes feel bruised. She's looking down at me, eyes brimming, and I hate that I put that look there. That I was the reason she had to be so goddamn strong.

I shift my hand toward hers. It's a clumsy movement, my fingers fumbling against the blanket, but I find her wrist and curl the tips of my fingers around it. Just enough to keep her from drifting away with all that pain she's carrying.

"I love you," I say, pausing to breathe through the tightness in my chest. "I fucking love you, Brianna. And I know that doesn't fix what I put you through, but it's the truth."

She stares at me.

Her eyes are wide and wet and shining with affection I don't deserve, but fuck, I want it. I want her to believe me. To feel every word I just rasped out.

I'm bracing for silence. Or anger. Or maybe nothing in return at all, because after what I've put her through, I'm not sure I've earned anything.

Then she cracks.

Her face crumples like she's been holding it together with tape and twine. The second she breaks, something inside me does the same. Tears spill down her cheeks, and she covers her mouth with her hand like she's trying to hold back a sob. It breaks free anyway.

"You..." Her voice wobbles. "You're such a goddamn idiot."

I blink. Okay. Not what I expected, but not the worst, either.

When her forehead drops to our joined hands, I swear my ribs might snap with the way my heart's beating.

"You scared the hell out of me, Callan. I thought I was going to lose you before I ever got the chance to tell you that I love you, too."

Did I hear that right? Or did the meds fry my brain?

She looks up at me, her eyes swimming, but fierce in the way only Bree can be when she's dead set on cutting straight through me. "You think I sat in this hospital because I felt obligated? I couldn't leave because every part of me is tied to you. Because I love you, and it hurts. It hurts so damn much, but I'd *still* choose it."

I try to speak, but all I can do is look at her, memorize her, like I'll never get another chance.

Her hands move to my face, thumbs brushing my cheeks. "If you ever pull something like this again, I swear to god I will kill you myself. You don't get to leave me, Callan. Not before I've had the chance to love you the way I want to. You hear me?"

And just like that, everything stills. The haze, the pain, the guilt—it all lifts for one aching, beautiful second.

Maybe it took breaking every part of myself to finally understand that I'm tired. Not in my bones. In my soul. Maybe I've spent my whole life running toward danger because I didn't think anything was worth settling down for.

But Bree's here. Angry. Crying. Shaking with all the feelings I've spent years pretending I didn't need.

She presses her forehead to mine as she whispers, "You owe me forever after this."

I do. God, I do.

I wish I could say more. Wish I could make promises, wrap her up in every word I've never been brave enough to say. But my eyes are already closing, the pull of sleep relentless.

This time, I carry her voice with me into the dark. When I open my eyes again, I'll fight to become the man who doesn't just survive.

I'll become the man who stays.

For her.

thirty-eight

CALLAN

"Christ. What the hell were they feeding you in there?"

My stepdad and Knox are practically dragging me inside the house, and it's going as well as you'd expect. I can barely stand on my own, my ribs screaming in protest with every movement, and the crutches? Yeah, they're more like weapons of mass destruction than any kind of help at this point. I've spent the last few days wheeling around the hospital like a champion, but that doesn't exactly prepare you for trying to make it through your front door when you're a complete invalid.

Every step is like I'm climbing Everest, even as Knox's hands balance me, but it's awkward. He's not exactly the nurturing type, especially when it comes to someone as stubborn as me.

"Just a little farther," my stepdad says, his voice strained from trying to hold me up.

"I'm not sure I'm going to make it up these stairs," I mutter, half laughing, half grimacing. At this point, I don't really have much of a choice.

Knox snorts. "You survived a river and multiple surgeries, but a staircase is where you draw the line?"

I glare at him, or at least I try.

Bree is standing in the doorway, her face a mask of pure horror as she watches the scene unfold. I can see the worry in her eyes, the way her hands flutter near her mouth like she's physically trying to hold back her apprehension.

Knox shoots a glance at her over his shoulder, his grip tightening on my arm as I stumble. "It's fine," he calls out, though it sounds about as convincing as a bad joke. "We've got this."

"Do you?"

I try to throw some humor into the mix, even though every breath feels like I'm inhaling fire. "Don't worry," I wheeze, "just a three-man job to get me ten feet." My attempt at a smile probably looks more like the start of a painful coughing fit.

Her eyes dart between Knox and me, her face pale. "This is ridiculous. You shouldn't even be walking. Why didn't you guys call me sooner?"

"Didn't want you to see this circus act," I mutter, immediately regretting it as another sharp stab of pain shoots through my ribs.

"You're going to hurt yourself more," she snaps.

"I'm fine," I grit out. I can see the worry etched on her face, and I hate that I'm the cause of it. "Just...need to get to the couch."

Knox and my stepdad exchange a look over my head, and I can practically feel their shared exasperation.

"All right, tough guy," Knox says. "Let's get you settled before you keel over and undo all the doctors' hard work."

With agonizing slowness, we shuffle our way to the living room, each step a battle of wills between me and my body.

Finally, I collapse onto the couch with a painful grunt. The relief hits almost immediately, but it's not the sweet, satisfying kind. It's more like a temporary truce. My ribs protest the sudden shift, sending jolts of pain through my entire body, but at least I'm not on my feet anymore.

"Well," I gasp, letting my head fall back against the cushions, "that only took three grown adults and a minor miracle. Next time, let's just rent a crane."

Knox snorts again, dropping into the armchair across from me, looking far too comfortable for someone who just helped drag me across the room like a sack of potatoes. "Noted. I'll call the heavy machinery guys for backup."

Bree, hovering nearby with her arms crossed, lets out an exasperated laugh. "If you're well enough to joke, you're well enough to listen to me. You're staying put now."

I flash her a weak grin. "Stay put? Sunshine, you're looking at the king of mobility right here."

She rolls her eyes, but it's softer now. She steps closer and grabs a throw pillow, tucking it behind my back with a tenderness that almost makes my chest ache. "King of mobility, huh? More like king of stubbornness."

"Guilty," I admit, sinking into the couch with a sigh. For the first time all day, I can breathe. Painfully, but still.

"You know," Knox chimes in, "I think I preferred you unconscious. At least then you weren't talking back."

I shoot him a glare, but it's weak at best. "Careful, brother. I might be down, but I'm not out."

Bree groans, her fingers brushing my hair back from my forehead with a gentleness that makes everything else a little less painful. "You need to rest. No more heroics for today."

I catch her hand, bringing it to my lips and pressing a kiss to her palm. "Yes, ma'am."

Knox clears his throat and stands up. "Well, now that you're settled, I should head out. Got some work to catch up on at the distillery."

"Aye, I'm out of here, too. Gotta report back to your mother," my stepdad adds, clapping me gently on the shoulder before heading for the door.

"Thanks for the help, guys."

As they leave, Bree settles on the edge of the couch beside me, her hand resting gently on my arm. "Do you need anything? Water?"

I shift, wincing as my ribs protest the movement. "A time machine to go back and avoid that damn deer would be nice," I mutter while trying, and failing, to get comfortable.

She huffs a quiet laugh, though her eyes are still shadowed with concern. "Sorry, fresh out of time machines. Anything else?"

I glance at her, catching the way her fingers tighten just slightly on my arm. "I guess I could settle for my personal nurse instead."

She shifts closer, moving with care before she leans back against the couch. "Don't push your luck," she murmurs, but I hear the smile in her voice.

I close my eyes, letting out a slow breath. I try to find some peace in the discomfort. The pain is still there, a persistent throb that presses at the edges of my mind, threatening to swallow me whole if I let it.

"You know," I say, "I never thought I'd be so happy to see this old couch."

Her hand moves to my hair, her fingers gently combing through the strands. "I never thought I'd be so happy to see you on it," she replies quietly.

I crack one eye open, looking down at her. There's still a shadow of worry in her eyes.

"I want to kiss you," I mumble.

Her lips twitch into a smile. "Then kiss me."

I let out a frustrated sigh, glaring at my own body like the traitor it is. "Would love to," I mutter, "but I can't *fecking* move. Pretty sure even my eyelashes are broken."

"Don't worry, tough guy," she says, leaning in. "I've got you covered this time."

Her lips brush mine. It's quick but perfect. I barely have time to savor it before the pain meds start pulling me under.

thirty-nine

BREE

The medication's kicking in, and I watch as his body finally begins to relax, his breath slowing, the tightness in his face softening. For a moment, I stay there, watching him as if the mere act of breathing is something precious. It's hard to focus with the way my heart races, that echoing fear clinging to my ribs.

I pull my hand from his hair, fingers lingering for a beat. I should be happy, right? Instead, everything inside me is wound into a knot so tight that I can't untangle it, no matter how much I try to breathe through it.

I stand on shaky legs and move toward the kitchen. Just when I think I might be able to pull myself together and breathe properly, *it* hits.

The air around me thickens as the walls press in. My throat tightens and I break out in a cold sweat. My heart thunders in my chest, frantic and uneven. I reach for the counter, my fingers gripping the edge, hoping for some stability. It doesn't help.

I can't breathe.

More hysteria surges up my spine. I press my fingers to my mouth to hold back the sobs that threaten to break free. He needs me, and I can't let myself crumble now. Not when he's finally starting to heal, and definitely not when he's still so fragile.

I'll be okay. I have to be.

My hand shakes as I reach for my phone, eyes scanning the list of names. I need someone to pull me back and tell me it's all going to be okay. But as I scroll, I realize the truth. I can't call any of them. Not one. They'd worry. They'd rush over, and then Callan would know. I can't let that happen.

I push the phone away, and I stagger toward the sink. I splash myself with cold water, but it doesn't help. I grab the dish towel, rubbing my face as if I can scrub away the emotion that floods me. Slowly, the tension in my chest subsides enough for me to take a deeper breath.

The panic fades, but in its place, doubt settles in. What if I'm not strong enough for this? What if I can't do it? What if I'm not what he needs? The last time someone depended on me, it ended in disaster.

No. Callan is different. This is different. He'll be fine, and we'll be fine.

I close my eyes and draw in another unstable breath, letting the cool granite of the counter press into my palms. The chill is starting to help. Then I hear Callan's steady breathing, and any traces of panic disappear.

I slide back onto the couch, my eyes flickering toward him. I'm hit with that familiar urge to reach out, to touch him, to feel the warmth of his skin beneath my fingertips, just because I can. I stop myself before I can move, hesitation freezing my hand midair. I don't want to disturb him. Not when he finally looks so peaceful. He needs to rest.

Instead, I settle in, pulling my knees to my chest, my gaze

fixed on him. I try to breathe with him, to sync up with the slow, consistent beat of his heart. My eyes linger, tracing the curve of his jaw, the lines of his face softened in sleep.

It's not perfect. Nothing ever is. But as I sit there, watching him, I realize it's a hell of a lot better than it was just a few days ago. And for now, maybe that's enough.

A PAINED GROAN drags me from my fog of sleep. I blink my eyes open, and the darkness of the room wraps around me, thick and heavy. My thoughts feel slow, and I rub at my eyes, hoping to shake off the remnants of sleep still clinging to me.

Callan. My heart skips painfully as I turn my head. There he is, lying so still, his eyes squeezed shut, his face twisted in discomfort. His breathing is shallow, quick, and I can see the tension in every inch of his body, muscles rigid under the blanket.

Oh god, what time is it? The question barrels through, but the answer doesn't matter as much as the look on his face. He's hurting. I can see it clear as day, his brow tight, jaw clenched.

I didn't mean to fall asleep. I'd only closed my eyes for a minute. Just long enough to blink away the ache behind them. Now it's obvious...

It's been longer than a minute. And he's definitely past due for his meds.

I gently shake his arm. "Cal?"

His eyes flutter open, but the clouded look in them sends a jolt of guilt through me. I hate it. I hate seeing him like this.

"It hurts," he murmurs, his voice a raw rasp.

"I know, I know," I whisper back, my heart sinking. I scramble for the lamp switch with the hand not resting on his arm. The soft light flickers on, casting shadows across his pale face, a thin sheen of sweat clinging to his forehead. "I'm so sorry," I murmur, almost to myself, as I finally spot the meds and move to get them. "I'll get your meds, okay? Just hang on."

Reluctantly, I let go of his arm, the loss of that contact leaving a hollow throb in its place. I turn quickly and head for the kitchen before I do something reckless like reach for him again.

My hands are shaking, the glass of water too fragile in my grasp as I fill it. The pill bottle rattles in my hands, and I have to take a deep breath to balance myself.

This... All of this just keeps bringing me back to those days with Dillon when everything was so fragile and unsure. If I didn't move quick enough, if I didn't do *everything* right, things would break, and I wouldn't be able to hold the pieces together.

I shove the memories down, locking them away before they can sink their claws in. This isn't the same. I know that, even if my body doesn't seem to get the message. The fear still clings, threading through my veins, pressing into my ribs like it's trying to carve itself into me.

My hands tremble as I press the pills into Callan's palm and hand him the glass. "Here."

I force myself to meet his eyes, but it's a mistake. He's looking at me like he sees straight through the wall I'm trying to build.

"I'm so sorry, Callan."

He takes the pills easily despite the pain still visible in his eyes. He swallows them down, and then quirks a brow, his voice softer than I expect. "Nothing to be sorry for, lass."

"I should have been on top of it." The words slip out before I can stop them, thick with self-doubt. "You ended up in pain because I—"

"Bree...no." Callan shifts slightly. "I should have had the

meds beside me and an alarm set to take them. That's not your responsibility."

I shake my head, the knot in my throat tightening with every word. "I promised I'd look after you. I should have been more prepared. I should have—"

"Hey," he interrupts again, his voice gentle. Callan's touch is warm as his fingers brush against my arm. "Come here."

I move, settling next to him, my body instinctively leaning into his as his hand finds mine.

He studies me for a long moment, his blue eyes searching mine with an intensity that makes me feel both seen and understood.

"Bree, love, what's going on?"

I bite my lip, unwilling to meet his gaze. "It's nothing. I'm just worried about you."

"Aye, and I appreciate that. But it seems like there's something else."

I let out a slow breath. "I just... I want to do this right."

"And you are," he says, his thumb gently tracing circles on my hand. "Look at you, jumping into action the moment you realized I needed help. That's more than enough."

"You're not failing," he adds quietly, his thumb continuing its soothing rhythm. "I'm lucky to have you."

His words ease the ache of guilt just a little. It feels good to hear him say it, especially when I can't seem to hold myself together. I glance up at him, meeting his gaze this time.

"Do you know that it felt like my heart was ripped from my chest when Lucy said they couldn't find you?" My voice catches, and I fight the tremor in it. "I couldn't breathe, I couldn't think." I force myself to keep going, to say it out loud, because I need him to hear this. "I'm not saying this to make you feel bad, I just... I need you to understand."

He nods, and right now, his eyes aren't just looking at me.

They're holding me. Their usual bright blue hue has darkened, replaced by something stormy, like the sky before a downpour.

"You mean *everything* to me. I know you're silly, adventurous, spontaneous...and I love that about you. I do. But god, Callan, if I had to go through this again, I don't know if I'd survive it."

There's fear in his eyes. This is coming out all wrong. I don't even know what I'm trying to say at this point.

"You walked away with broken bones this time, but for a while I was terrified that I'd lost you...forever."

What I don't say is that loving him this past week has been like standing on the edge of a cliff. Every smile, every touch, every stolen moment where he made me feel alive has been followed by the constant ache that tightens around my chest, knowing that one wrong step, one leap too far, and I could fall.

If he ever slipped away, I'd be left standing at the edge of a life I built around him, staring into the emptiness left behind. I'd have to figure out how to breathe without him.

His expression twists with regret, his voice rough. "Christ... Bree. I'm so fucking sorry."

I give him a sad smile. "We're both sorry, and I'm not sure there's anything to be sorry for. I just need you to be careful. I need you breathing and alive, Callan."

He leans forward, and there's no mistaking the small gasp of pain that escapes him as his body protests the movement. The need to get closer to me outweighs the discomfort. His rough, calloused hands cup my cheeks with a tenderness that makes my breath hitch. The contact sparks across my skin, sending a rush of warmth straight through me.

His gaze locks onto mine, unwavering, intense, like nothing else exists but the two of us. His eyes are full of promise, an unspoken vow that might shatter me if I let it.

"Anything for you," he whispers.

CALLAN

I'm a moron. I've spent my whole damn life living for the rush, chasing every thrill without a second thought. Not once did I stop to think the one thing that matters more than all of it is *her*.

This incredible woman who's willing to tear apart her world just to be with me. I can't keep being so...impulsive. Not when she's counting on me. Not when I'm the one who's promised to show up, to protect her, to make sure she has a future.

I never should've been on the road that day.

I didn't think about how much she needs me. How much *I* need her.

And now? I hate myself for it. For the selfishness. For the fact that she's sitting here, worried about whether I'll make it home in one piece. She deserves better than a man who makes her wonder if he's going to walk out that door and never come back. She deserves better than me.

"I'll do better. I can change."

She leans into my touch, her warmth the salvation I don't

deserve. "I'm not asking you to do that," she says softly. "I'm just asking you to be safer. You wouldn't be you if you weren't somewhat impulsive and a little insane." She smirks, but I can see the concern lingering behind it.

I don't have any witty comebacks for her right now. This is too real. The thought of losing her because of my own damn ego is unbearable. Humor's not going to fix this, not this time.

Her smirk fades the moment my thumb brushes over her cheek. "I mean it. I'll do better. I can't lose you. Especially not because I couldn't slow down long enough to see what I have right in front of me."

Her eyes soften, but there's a shadow of fear lingering in the depths of her gaze. *I* put that there.

Her hand settles over the steady thud of my heart. "I'm not going anywhere."

I nod, my throat tight, the lump there threatening to choke me. "You have my word. No more taking stupid risks just to feel alive. You make me feel alive. Just you, Sunshine."

For a long moment, she studies me, trying to figure out if I mean it. And then, slowly, she nods, the faintest smile curving the corners of her lips. "Good. Because you and me? We've got a lot of life to live together. And I'm not letting you off the hook that easily."

I exhale a breath I didn't realize I was holding. "I'm not going anywhere, either," I whisper into her hair. "Not now, not ever."

They're not just words. They're a promise I intend to keep, no matter what it takes. For her, for us, for the future I almost threw away without a second thought. It's not just about slowing down anymore. It's about fully understanding what's at stake. And I won't make that mistake again.

I'm sitting with Mum, letting Bree get some much-needed sleep in an actual bed instead of on the couch. It's strange, not having Bree hovering nearby. She's been running herself ragged. I practically had to beg her to take a break. It's like she doesn't know how to stop.

Mum sits across from me, her hands folded neatly in her lap, her usual lively chatter replaced by a heavy silence. It's not like her. Normally, she's full of stories, questions, or a gentle scolding. Today, there's none of that. Just this quiet, palpable tension hanging between us.

I've been home for a few days now, and every day, without fail, Mum shows up with the same determined smile. But I know her too well. There's a tightness around her eyes, a stiffness in her movements. All little cracks in the facade she doesn't think I notice.

I shift in my seat, the ache in my ribs a sharp reminder that I'm still a long way from my normal self. The pain is manageable, but the awkwardness in the air isn't.

I finally catch her gaze. "You okay?"

"Aye, I am now." Her voice is calm, but the look she gives me could peel paint off a wall. "Do you know how hard it is not to slap you upside the head? It's like trying to hold back a sneeze in a room full of pepper. Near bloody impossible."

I wince, scratching the back of my neck. "That bad, huh?"

"Worse," she says, leaning forward. "You're lucky I've got some self-control or you'd be nursing another concussion on top of everything else."

"You are not allowed to die before me, child," she continues, her voice cutting through the air like a whip. "I didn't go through childbirth for you to turn around and waste it on some reckless nonsense."

I snort, shaking my head. "Nice to know it's about your hard work."

"Damn right it is," she shoots back, but her smile softens enough to show the affection hiding beneath the scolding. "Now stop being an idiot and stay alive, aye? And get that girl to marry you. I like her more than I like you right now."

"Mum!"

She waves her hand dismissively. "I'm serious."

I know she is.

"I hear you, but I'm not sure Bree would have me at the moment. I've been a proper arsehole."

"You've always had a good heart, Callan. Sometimes it just takes the right person to help you see it. I see the way you look at her. It's the same way your father used to look at me."

The mention of Dad catches me off guard. We don't talk about him much. "Yeah?"

She nods, a wistful smile gracing her lips. "Aye. Like you've found your home. Your heart."

Well, damn. What do you even say to that? *Thanks for the soul-crushing sentiment, Mum?* Or maybe, *excuse me while I go rethink my entire life?*

I swallow hard. "I have," I admit. "Don't worry. I'm making it right."

She reaches across the coffee table and pats my hand. "That's the MacKenzie curse, love. You're all stubborn fools until you find the right person to knock some sense into you."

I can't help but chuckle, even though it makes me hurt. "Is that what happened with you and Dad?"

Her eyes twinkle with affection, and for a second, I see the spark of the woman she used to be. "Oh, aye. Your father was the biggest fool of them all. Took me years to straighten him out."

"And here I thought it was love at first sight," I tease.

"Love, yes. Sense, though? That took a wee bit longer."

I should talk to her about Dad more often. He died when Knox, Lucy, and I were so young. Most of what I know about him is secondhand. But sitting here, watching the way her face lights up when she talks about him, I'm catching a glimpse of the man I never got to know.

"Did he ever get it together?"

"Oh, eventually. He made plenty of mistakes, but he loved us fiercely. That man would have moved mountains for his family."

There's a pause, but it's not uncomfortable. Finally, she speaks again, her voice quieter.

"You're like him in that way, you know."

I shift, wincing as the pain lances through me. "Aye, well, let's hope I make fewer mistakes along the way."

Her hand lands on mine. "It's what you do after that counts. And you, my boy, are doing just fine."

The knot of guilt that's been tied tight falls away a little, the weight lifting just enough to breathe easier. "Thanks, Mum."

Her lips curl into a knowing smile, the kind she's perfected over the years. "Now, stop feeling sorry for yourself and focus on getting better. You'll be back to your foolhardy self in no time."

I chuckle, the sound strained but genuine. "Wouldn't want to disappoint."

"Good lad." She squeezes my hand and rises, smoothing her skirt as she does.

The room goes quiet again, but it's...nice. For the first time in days, I don't feel like I'm one wrong move away from an aggressive lecture. Progress.

BREE

I slept for hours this afternoon, and I thought I'd be refreshed but...nope.

I'm pacing the bedroom, gripping the phone tight. My parents' voices drift through the speaker, warm and familiar, laced with concern.

Mom's voice comes first. "How's he doing, sweetheart?"

"He's... He's okay," I say, forcing the words out, but they wobble at the edges. I clear my throat, trying to smooth them over.

There's a pause before Dad speaks, his usual gruffness softened in a way that makes me want to cry. "And what about you, kid? You holding up?"

His words hit harder than I expect. Because the truth is, I don't know. I don't know how I'm holding up. I don't even know if I *am* holding up.

"I'm fine."

The silence stretches on the other end of the line. They're not convinced.

"You sure about that?" Mom asks.

I close my eyes as I pinch the bridge of my nose, trying to stave off the pressure that's building. "It's just...a lot—watching him go through this. I'll be okay."

Only, I'm not really managing at all. I'm still waking up with my heart pounding, still battling panic attacks that hit for reasons I don't understand. Callan's here. He's alive. The worst is supposed to be over. So why doesn't it feel that way? Why doesn't it feel *okay*?

"Bree," Mom's voice is softer now, more knowing, "it's okay not to be okay. You've been through hell. You don't have to carry it all on your own."

I flinch. "I'm not."

It's a lie, and my voice is a little too clipped.

"Sweetheart," Dad cuts in. "We're here. Just say the word."

"Thanks," I whisper, my voice cracking, but I swallow it down. "I just... I need to focus on him right now. He needs me."

"And you need to take care of yourself, too," Mom insists.

They're right, of course. I *know* they're right. But the thought of putting myself first seems impossible. The pressure begins to mount like it always does when I try to breathe through the spiral that's already curling around my ribs, ready to pull me down again.

I shake it off, forcing a breath in, and grasp for something to pull myself out of my own head. "Hey, how's Nugget doing? Tell my sweet boy I miss him, and I'm coming to get him soon."

Mom's soft laugh drifts through the line, and I can almost picture her rolling her eyes. "He's fine, Bree. Spoiled rotten. You'd think he owned the place the way he struts around."

Dad chuckles in the background. "He's taken to sleeping on my chair. Won't budge, no matter how many times I tell him to get down. It's like he knows he's untouchable because he's your dog."

The image of Nugget, cozy and stubborn in his new throne, brings a small smile to my face. A fleeting moment of normalcy. "That sounds about right. He's probably plotting to take over the entire house by now."

"He already has," Dad grumbles.

"Well, at least someone's living their best life."

There's a pause, an undeniable silence that enters the conversation.

Finally, Mom clears her throat. "Honey, we've been thinking. Why don't we come visit while you're there? We could bring Nugget, spend some time with you and Callan..."

The unexpected offer hits me hard. The comfort of having them here would be a welcome distraction, a break from the constant pressure of trying to keep it together. And yet, I hesitate. A small knot forms in my stomach as I try to figure out how to say this without making it worse.

"I just...don't want to be a hassle."

"You're not a hassle," Dad chimes in. "You're our daughter. And besides, Nugget misses you. If I don't get him to you soon, he's gonna stage a rebellion."

The thought of my parents in Scotland, navigating the narrow, winding roads and trying to decipher the thick Scottish accents almost makes me laugh. It's a picture I never thought I'd visualize, but it's comforting to think about them here, fumbling through the unfamiliar in their own way. It tugs at a part of me I didn't realize was homesick. "Okay. You've convinced me. Get Nugget here before he starts a full-blown mutiny."

"Good, good," Dad says with a note of satisfaction in his voice that makes me smile. "I'll let him know he's got the green light."

I laugh, a genuine one this time, the tension in my shoulders releasing a fraction. "Love you both. I'll text you later about dates, okay?"

"We'll be ready," Mom promises. "Love you, sweetheart."

"Love you, kid," Dad echoes.

When we hang up, I linger by the window, my arms wrapped around myself as I watch the twilight settle over the hills, deep purples and blues stretching across the horizon. I *love* it here. I really do. The plan was always to be here. I just wish I hadn't crash-landed into it.

I'm about to head downstairs when a thunderous crash echoes through the house. My heart slams against my ribs, a bolt of adrenaline hitting so hard and fast it leaves me lightheaded.

Callan.

I launch myself toward the stairs, taking them two at a time, my socked feet nearly slipping on the hardwood as I round the corner, my breath caught in my throat.

I skid into the living room, my pulse hammering, my brain still primed for catastrophe. And then I spot him.

Callan is in the kitchen, upright but moving slowly, his back to me as he fumbles with the coffee maker. There's a shattered mug at his feet, a mess of ceramic shards across the floor.

He's okay.

He hears me before I can make it to him, turning his head to look over his shoulder with that familiar half smirk playing at the corner of his mouth. "I'm okay," he says quickly, holding up his hands when he sees my face. "Just butterfingers."

I let out a tense breath as I brace myself against the counter. "God, Callan, you scared the hell out of me." There's no hiding the nerves I'm still trying to keep at bay.

He straightens up, his shoulders stiffening as he sets the coffee maker back in place. His eyes drift to the broken mug on the floor. "I'm so sorry, lass," he mutters. "Guess I've still got some kinks to work out."

I take a step closer, my concern creeping in despite his attempt at humor. "Maybe you should sit down."

"I'm fine, Sunshine. Just a bit of a slip up," he says, rubbing his forehead and wincing slightly, though he doesn't let the pain show for long. "Coffee seems to be harder to handle than I thought."

I roll my eyes. "You're lucky I didn't think you fell or something," I joke, kneeling down to clean up the mess, my hands moving almost automatically as I start to gather the broken pieces. "I was ready to call an ambulance for you."

He huffs a laugh, leaning against the counter. "As much as I love the drama, I think we'll skip that part today."

I chuckle, shaking my head as I carefully sweep up the debris. "Good, because I don't think my heart could take another hospital visit right now."

But as I reach for another shard, my hands falter, hovering over the mess, and suddenly, I'm not here. I'm back at my old house with Dillon, kneeling on cold tile, my fingers trembling as I pick up the pieces of a different mug.

Dillon had thrown it, and it had exploded against the cabinets. I cleaned it up, silent and careful, my stomach knotted so tightly I could barely breathe.

I blink, and the memory fades as quickly as it came.

Callan reaches out, his fingers brushing my shoulder with an unexpected tenderness. "I'm really sorry. I didn't mean to give you a scare."

I swallow hard and stand up, dumping the broken pieces into the trash. "It's okay," I say, forcing a small smile. "I'm just... a little on edge still, I guess."

His eyes soften as he takes me in, and I see the concern

etched in the fine lines around his mouth. Without saying a word, he holds out his arms, motioning me toward him with a gentle tilt of his head.

"Come here," he whispers.

I hesitate for a moment, caught between my instinct to stay strong and the overwhelming desire to collapse into him.

He wiggles his fingers, a small gesture that breaks through my resistance. "Just for a minute, Sunshine. Let me hold you."

The slightly irrational part of my brain is screaming about how I should keep it together and don't need to be coddled like some fragile little thing. At the same time, there's the other part that's been running on fumes and is desperate for a moment of normalcy with him.

I cross the kitchen in a few careful steps and let myself lean into him, careful not to put too much pressure on his still-healing body. He pulls me against him, his heartbeat strong and alive beneath my cheek. His arms encircle me completely, one hand cradling the back of my head while the other traces slow circles on my back.

His hands settle on my waist as he pulls back slightly, a playful gleam in his eyes. One moment they're soft and inviting, the next piercing and mischievous. "You're tense, love. If you need to work out that tension, I'm happy to volunteer. Though, I can't promise I won't break anything else."

I roll my eyes, doing my best to suppress the smile tugging at my lips. "You're unbelievable."

Although, I'm not entirely upset by his suggestion. As much as I tell myself I shouldn't, at least not while he's still healing, I miss his touch. I miss *him*.

That grin of his spreads across his face, lighting up his whole expression and making it impossible to be annoyed. It's so unapologetically him, and it's both infuriating and irresistible. As I look at him, a familiar squeeze wraps around my ribs, a quiet ache that doesn't ease no matter how close he is.

"Hey." His voice dips lower. "You don't have to hold back with me, you know."

The sincerity in his eyes makes my heart flip. "I know," I say, my fingers brushing the fabric of his shirt. "I just...don't want to hurt you."

His playful edge melts into something more intimate. There's an obvious understanding in the way his eyes hold mine, his thumb brushing idly against my hip in a way that sends sparks across my skin. "You won't."

Then the spark returns, the corners of his mouth quirking up in a way that makes my stomach flutter. "But just so you know," he adds, leaning in slightly, his breath warm against my cheek, "a little less hesitation and a little more kissing wouldn't be the worst thing."

I take a deep breath, the closeness of him stealing the air from my lungs. My hands rest against his chest, his solid heat beneath my fingertips sending tingles up my arms. When our lips meet, the world tilts, a shiver coursing down my spine as the kiss deepens. Our movements are unhurried but charged, our tongues teasing, exploring, learning each other all over again. It feels like coming home.

His hands slide along my waist, his fingers curling against the fabric of my shirt. When he pulls me closer, the possessiveness in his touch is matched only by its gentleness. It's a contradiction that leaves me breathless. His arm wraps around my back, anchoring me to him as his lips trail to my jawline, the softness of each kiss sending goosebumps cascading over my skin.

The desire radiating off him is a perfect reflection of the fire burning inside me. It's as if every moment of stress, every worry of the past few weeks, melts away.

"God, I've missed this."

His voice is rough, almost broken, as he whispers against my neck. My throat tightens. My heart feels like it's about to burst, but words are useless right now.

His lips brush over my skin, trailing lower, leaving a path of heat in their wake. When he reaches my collarbone, his lips linger, and my knees threaten to give out. There's nothing but the feeling of his mouth on me and the way he presses into me like I'm the only thing holding him up.

His grip turns possessive, but his touch is still careful, like he's balancing on the edge of restraint.

For the first time in what feels like forever, I'm not thinking about anything but us and how we're *supposed* to be.

My fingers slip into his hair. I tug gently, just enough to bring his mouth back to mine. "I've missed you, too," I breathe against his lips.

And then he smiles. God, *that smile.*

It's affection and heat crashing together. Like he's starving yet savoring this at the same time.

But then Callan winces, his body tensing against mine. I freeze, my heart skipping a beat as I pull back, worry rushing in to replace the bliss from just seconds ago.

"Are you okay?" I ask quickly, my hands moving to his shoulders as I search his face. "Did I hurt you?"

He shakes his head, a half smile tugging at his lips. "Nah, just a little twinge. It's nothing."

I take him in. There's pain in his eyes that he's trying to mask. I take a small step back. "We should slow down."

His hand moves quickly to mine, pulling me gently back toward him. His thumb brushes over my knuckles in slow, soothing circles. "You're not making anything worse," he murmurs. "I promise, it's just a little soreness. Nothing I can't handle."

I raise an eyebrow, still not entirely convinced. "You need to sit anyway. Come on," I say, slipping my hand under his arm to help guide him to the couch. He goes willingly, though I don't miss the slight wince he tries to hide as he lowers himself down.

"Fine." He sinks into the couch, his broad shoulders filling the space as if it was made just for him. His legs spread, one arm draped over the back of the cushions, the other resting on his thigh. God help me, I can't look away.

"I won't argue," he continues. "But just so you know, my face is fine. In case you wanted to sit on it later."

"Callan!"

He grins. "You love me."

"Maybe," I say, pretending to consider it as I sit beside him. "Or maybe I just keep you around for your charming accent."

His deep chuckle rumbles through the room, and before I can react, his arm snakes around my shoulders, pulling me firmly against his side. His heat seeps into me, and I can't help but melt a little. "I'll take it, lass," he says. "Whatever keeps you by my side."

I lean my head against his shoulder, breathing in his familiar scent. "Hey," I say softly, my fingers absently trailing up his forearm. "I was just talking to my parents. Guess what."

He leans down, brushing a featherlight kiss against my temple. "Mm, what?"

"My parents are coming to visit soon, and they're bringing Nugget."

Callan's whole face lights up at the mention of Nugget, the discomfort I remember from their first meeting nowhere to be found. "The wee terror himself! I can't wait to see how he takes to Scotland. Think he'll remember me?"

"Are you kidding? He probably dreams about you," I tease.

"You're the only one who lets him get away with stealing food off the table."

"Ah, he's just got good taste," he says with a wink. "So, your parents, too?

I nod, warmth blooming in my chest at the thought of them being here. "Yeah, I'm so excited for them to be here. Oh, shoot." I pause, the realization hitting me. "I should've asked first. Is it okay if they stay with us?"

He turns his eyes to mine, and the affection in his gaze pulls me in completely. "Bree, of course they can stay here. You don't need to ask."

Relief washes over me, and I press my mouth to his. My lips linger until I feel the hitch of his breath. Then I tilt just enough, letting my tongue trace the seam of his lips until his mouth parts for me.

When I finally pull back, his eyes are still closed like he's chasing the ghost of it.

"Thank you," I whisper.

He groans. "You keep doing that, and I'm gonna end up fucking you right here. Or...well. You might be fucking me, since I can't really move"

I let out a laugh. "Behave yourself, *sir*."

He leans back against the couch with a theatrical groan, throwing his head back like he's been mortally wounded. "You're killing me here, lass. One minute, I'm trying to be a gentleman, and the next, you've got me all worked up." He presses a hand to his chest, shooting me an exaggerated look of despair. "I might need some pain meds for this."

I roll my eyes and laugh, but the sound dies off when I notice the way he shifts, like even sitting upright costs him.

His hand moves to his ribs, lingering there a second too long. It's not part of the act.

I ease down beside him. "Hey," I say, quieter now. "Jokes are fine. But let's get you through this first, okay?"

He doesn't answer, just nods once, his gaze dropping as if the pain's finally catching up to him.

I sit there for a moment, watching this man who jokes through broken ribs and pretends nothing hurts.

But it does. I can see it, even when he tries to hide it.

And the truth is... I'm not fine, either. Not while he's like this.

BREE

The doorbell chimes, and my stomach flips. I drag in a breath, pressing my palms against my jeans in a useless attempt to calm myself. It's surreal. Three weeks ago, I was pacing hospital hallways, drowning in fear. Now, I'm pacing the living room, nerves rattling for an entirely different reason. My parents are here.

I glance over at Callan, and the sight of him soothes some of the chaos swirling inside me. He's upright, moving carefully, but there's adoration in his eyes as he watches me like I'm the most fascinating thing in the room. It's a far cry from those long nights in the hospital when every shift of his body made my heart stop.

Some parts of me feel like I'm still walking on unsteady ground, but I'm getting there. I think.

"You gonna answer that, or are we just letting them stand out there till they assume we've fled the country?"

I narrow my eyes at him. "I'm *preparing* myself."

With another deep breath, I swing the door open. My parents are standing on my doorstep, flesh and blood, not just voices on a phone screen. Nugget is wiggling in front of them, all floppy tongue and boundless excitement.

"Surprise!" Mom's voice is bright with excitement, and before I can react, she's crushing me in a tight hug. "Oh, sweetheart, it's so good to see you."

It's hard to breathe, but not because I'm trapped in her embrace. More like...because my heart can't quite keep up. They're here. They're really here.

"I've missed you guys so much," I whisper.

Dad joins the hug, sandwiching me between them. "We've missed you, too, kiddo."

I pull back, blinking away the unexpected tears, only to laugh when Nugget starts demanding attention. I kneel down, wrapping my arms around him as he leaps into my lap, licking my face like he's been deprived of love for centuries. "Oh, I missed you so much, buddy," I mutter, laughing through the wet assault.

Nugget's ears perk up as his eyes land on Callan, his head tilting to the side. And I get it, Callan looks different with his face still bearing the memory of his accident, his leg in a cast as he leans on his crutch.

Mom's the first to notice and hurries toward him, hands reaching out in concern. "Oh, Callan." She pulls him into a gentle hug. "Bless your heart. You've done a number to yourself."

Callan chuckles softly as he hugs her back. "Aye, I've had better days. I'm on the mend, though, thanks to your daughter here."

Dad steps forward then, giving Callan a firm handshake. "Good to see you up and about, son. You gave us all quite a scare."

"Believe me, I had myself worried, too," he admits with a wry smile. "But I'm tougher than I look."

Nugget, ever the little investigator, sniffs at Callan's cast. His tail gives a cautious wag, like he's not entirely sure what to make of it.

"It's okay, buddy," I say gently, kneeling beside him. "It's still Callan."

As if my words flip a switch, Nugget's tail transforms into a blur of motion, and he jumps up, placing his tiny paws on Callan's good leg. Callan flinches, a quick, instinctive movement that I don't miss. He's not entirely comfortable with Nugget's sudden approach. But then he bends carefully, ignoring the obvious protest from his ribs, and scratches him behind the ears. "There's my wee partner in crime. Did you miss me, lad?"

Nugget answers with an enthusiastic round of licks, his whole body practically vibrating with excitement.

"Guess he did miss you," I chuckle.

"Hard to stay away from a face like this." Callan grins, looking up at me with that familiar twinkle in his eye.

Mom watches the scene unfold, her smile soft and a little wistful. "It's good to see you both doing well."

I meet her gaze, matching her smile. "Thanks, Mom. I'll take your bags up to the guest room. You guys sit and relax."

"I'll take them up with you," Dad says, already reaching for one of the suitcases.

"I can manage, Dad."

He raises an eyebrow, giving me *the look*. The one that says arguing is pointless. "Humor your old man, will you?"

I relent, rolling my eyes but smiling as I grab one bag while he hoists the other. The stairs creak softly beneath us as we climb. Behind us, Mom fusses over Callan.

At the top of the stairs, Dad stops, his voice dropping low. "So, how are you really doing, Bree?"

The question catches me off guard, and I pause with my

hand on the guest room doorknob. "I'm...okay," I say slowly. "It's been tough, but we're getting there. Callan's getting there."

He nods, but his sharp eyes search my face. "And the panic attacks?" he asks. "Your mom mentioned you were still having them."

I sigh, nudging the door open with my shoulder and setting the suitcase down by the bed. "Not as often, but...yeah. I'm working on it."

He stands in the doorway, silent for a moment before quietly asking, "Does Callan know?"

"Uh...no," I admit. "I didn't want to put anything else on his plate. He's got enough to worry about."

I glance up, expecting a nod or some sort of easy agreement, but instead, he sees right through my bullshit. He always has.

His face carries a quiet kind of exhaustion that comes from years of holding his own family together. It's not disappoint-ment, never that. But it's a reminder that he knows I've been carrying more than I'm letting on.

And he's right.

I've gotten good at hiding it.

The tight chest, the numb fingers, the dizzying swirl of thoughts that make my lungs forget how to work. I know exactly how to fake uniform breaths and crack a joke before the spiral starts. I know how to bite down on the edge of a panic attack until it feels like I've swallowed glass, all so no one notices. And when I can't fake it well enough, I retreat to the kitchen or pretend there's laundry that needs to be done so I can be alone for a bit.

I swallow hard, looking away as my throat tightens. "I'm fine, Dad."

He steps farther into the room, setting his suitcase down beside mine. "You don't have to do that, you know."

"Do what?"

"Say you're fine when you're not."

I open my mouth to argue, but there's no point. The silence stretches between us until I finally sit down on the edge of the bed, pressing the heels of my hands against my eyes. "It's just... a lot," I admit quietly, my tone wavering despite my best effort to keep it steady.

Dad sits beside me, close but not too close, giving me space to speak if I want to. "You don't have to do it all by yourself." His voice is calm and encouraging. The same voice that reassured me through scraped knees and broken hearts. "That's what we're here for. What *he's* here for."

I shift uncomfortably, my gaze dropping to my feet as if the worn carpet can somehow shield me from the weight in my chest. Letting anyone see my flaws, especially Dad, feels like admitting failure. It's easier to plaster on a smile, to shove the anxiety so far down that it fades into the background.

"I don't want to burden anyone."

His hand rests on my shoulder. "You're not a burden, sweetheart," he says gently. "I know you've been looking out for Callan, but you need to take care of yourself, too."

The sincerity in his words cracks me open, and I feel the telltale sting of tears. I blink them away quickly, swallowing hard against the lump rising in my throat. Breaking down in front of him is like letting the dam burst, and I'm not sure I'll be able to rebuild it.

"I'm trying," I whisper, my voice holding steady. "I just... don't know how to do it right."

His hand tightens on my shoulder. "There's no 'right way,' kiddo. You're already doing it, one step at a time. You just have to let people help you along the way."

I didn't realize how badly I needed to hear those words, how much I'd been holding my breath without even knowing it.

"Now," he says. "Let's see if we can find some lunch before Nugget gets too impatient."

The mention of the dog pulls a small laugh from me.

After lunch, jetlag finally catches up with my parents, and they retreat upstairs. I've been watching Callan flick through TV channels for an hour now.

"You're abusing the remote power," I huff.

He eyes me without moving, lips twitching. "I've narrowed it down to *Sharknado* or a documentary about mushroom foraging."

"Wow. I'm wet."

He smirks. "Same."

I laugh, tucking my legs under me and stealing the remote. "Give me that."

I settle against him, head resting on his shoulder as I scroll. "So...no to fungal education. What about a classic rom-com? Something with a dance montage and a public declaration of love?"

He groans. "Fine. On one condition—there has to be at least one scene where someone dramatically runs through an airport."

"I'll allow it."

He kisses the top of my head. "You're lucky I'm whipped."

I won't argue that.

As I'm scrolling through more options, all I can think about is how much I want to close the small space between us and kiss him. Just one kiss. Or a dozen. But then I'd forget how to think straight, and I'm barely hanging on as it is.

Before I can spiral into more thoughts about what his kiss might taste like, the sound of footsteps from upstairs interrupts me.

I glance toward the staircase just as my parents come back down, looking refreshed after their nap.

"Feel better?" I ask.

"Much," Mom replies, sinking into the armchair with a sigh of relief. "Though I'm still not quite sure what time it is."

Dad chuckles softly, easing into the seat next to her. "I think my body's still somewhere over the Atlantic."

Callan grins. "Well, we've got just the thing to wake you up. How about a wee dram of whisky?"

Dad's eyes light up at the suggestion, his mood instantly lifting. "Now you're speaking my language, son."

forty-three

CALLAN

The Smiths have been here nearly a week, and I swear, Bree *looks* lighter. For the first time in a while, she's laughing more, sleeping better, and not jumping at every unexpected noise. It's a hell of a thing to witness.

Right now, she's off having a girls' day with her mum, mine, Juliette, and Lucy. Which, based on the energy they left with, either involves shopping or drinking. Possibly both.

Tom, on the other hand, was more than happy to hang back, which works out perfectly because there's something I need to talk to him about.

I clear my throat, trying to figure out the best way to say it. Subtlety has never really been my strong suit. Tom glances over, one brow lifting in that all-knowing *dad* way.

"Something on your mind?"

Aye. Just his daughter.

I take a deep breath, my heart pounding a little faster. "I need to talk to you about Bree."

His focus is now entirely on me. "Go on."

This is it. The moment I've been stewing over for weeks, planning every word, every breath, just to get it right.

"Tom...I love your daughter more than anything in this world. She's the light of my life, my best friend." I pause, gathering my courage. "I'd like to ask her if she'd be interested in moving here, but I didn't want to do that without you knowing."

Tom doesn't say anything right away. I can practically hear the gears turning in his head, weighing me against some invisible scale only fathers seem to possess to decide if I'm worthy of what I'm asking.

The silence stretches out, the seconds ticking by slower than they should, until it feels like the entire room is holding its breath, waiting for him to speak. Just when I start wondering if I should say something to reassure him that I'm not a complete idiot, he nods.

It's a very slow dip of his chin, but a nod nonetheless, followed by the faintest hint of a smile. "I know you love her. That much is obvious."

His expression turns serious. "Just promise me one thing," he says. "Take care of her, no matter what. And don't let her hide from you. I already know she'll move if you ask."

The relief that floods through me is immediate, but I hear what he's saying. *Don't let her hide from you.* That's not just a blessing... It's a plea. A father's quiet confession that he's watched his daughter carry more than she should, that he knows how easily she slips behind her own walls. This love, this life I want with her, won't just be built on the easy moments. It'll be defined by the hard ones, too.

Bree's stronger than she gives herself credit for, but I've seen the cracks she tries to smooth over. The way she tucks her pain behind tight smiles, the way she pulls away when life presses too hard. I recognize it because I've been there myself.

And I know that's when she needs someone to see her. Not just the version she carefully curates for the world, but *her*.

That's what I'm promising. Not just to love her, but to *see* her. Even when she tries to disappear. Especially then.

I look Tom square in the eye, my voice firm, the promise I'm about to make more important than anything I've ever said. "I promise you, Tom. I'll take care of her. You have my word."

He nods, a look of approval settling on his face. He reaches out to shake my hand, his grip solid. "That's what I wanted to hear, son. You've got a good head on your shoulders."

"Thank you, sir. That means more to me than you know." The words don't quite do it justice, but I mean every bit of it. Bree's not just my world. She's everything.

We sit in silence for a moment, but it's not awkward. I let the calm settle into my bones, even as the adrenaline creeps in, buzzing just under the surface.

He lets out a low chuckle. "Don't keep her waiting too long. That girl of mine is stubborn as hell, but when she knows what she wants, she doesn't mess around."

Don't I know it. The woman is a force of nature, which, honestly, makes me wonder why she's chosen me of all people. But I'm not about to question my luck.

WE'RE ALL at Knox and Juliette's place this evening. It's the only house in the group big enough to handle this many personalities without someone stepping on toes or losing their cool. The smell of Mum's cooking has been taunting us for the last hour, rich and savory, the kind that makes your stomach rumble even when you're not hungry. The buzz of laughter and chatter fills the space, loud enough to rival a pub on a Saturday night, and it's a welcome kind of noise.

Bree is perched on the arm of a couch with Lucy, her head tilted in that way that shows she's really listening. Then she glances my way, catches me looking, and gives me one of those smiles that hits you like a punch to the gut and leaves you feeling grateful for it.

Damn, this woman. That smile could ruin me if I let it.

Shannon, Rose, and Mum are in the kitchen, chatting and laughing, the sound spilling out between sips of wine. I'm half convinced they're plotting something. Knox, Paul, and Tom are huddled around the dining table, their conversation a wild mix of gestures and animated arguments. Most likely it's about rugby, football, or maybe whisky this time. Whatever it is, it's loud.

Juliette stands beside me, arms crossed, a soft smile playing on her lips as she watches the chaos unfold, but there's a calmness in the way she observes it all.

"This is nice, isn't it?"

I nod, taking in the scene. "It is. Feels like everyone's where they belong tonight." There's a peace in the air that feels earned, like we've all found the balance we were looking for.

She glances at me with a knowing look. "Even you?"

I don't answer right away, my gaze drifting across the room to Bree. She's laughing at something Lucy said, her eyes crinkling at the corners. My heart stutters just looking at her. I know Juliette notices the way my attention locks on Bree without even thinking.

"Aye," I finally say. "Especially me."

It's true, every word of it. With Bree in the room, with all of this life and love, everything has finally clicked into place.

Juliette lets out a soft laugh, nudging me with her elbow. "You're a goner, Callan."

"Don't I know it," I reply, shaking my head. But even as the words leave my mouth, I can't tear my eyes away from Bree.

Shannon's startled yelp interrupts us from the kitchen, followed by Mum's unmistakable bark of laughter.

"What on earth?" Juliette mutters, her brow furrowing as she turns toward the commotion.

I push off and follow her on crutches, moving as quickly as I can with my leg still giving me grief. The sound of Rose's laughter grows louder, and as we step into the kitchen, we find Shannon standing there, holding a bottle of wine that's spilled all over the counter, her face flushed with embarrassment. Rose is doubled over, practically wheezing with laughter, and Mum? Well, Mum is unfazed, calmly dabbing at a splash of red wine on the granite like this is just another Tuesday.

"Careful now," Mum says. "That's not a whisky you can mop up with a biscuit."

Shannon narrows her eyes, her cheeks flushed a bright shade of red. "I'd like to see you manage three glasses and a corkscrew while dodging elbows!"

Mum, ever unruffled, straightens her back with that air of superiority only she can pull off, then smirks. "And yet I've done it, lass, and in heels no less."

Juliette bites her lip to suppress a laugh as Shannon points an accusatory finger at her. "Don't you dare laugh."

"I'm not," Juliette says. "I'm just...observing."

The moment is too perfect, and it only makes Shannon even more flustered. She turns her glare back to Mum, who's still busy wiping down the counter with the same calm efficiency, completely unbothered by the wine that has now made a small mess.

I can't resist chiming in. "Sounds like you've uncovered a hidden talent there, Shannon. Competitive wine juggling, maybe?"

Rose finally straightens up from her laughter-induced

slump, wiping her eyes. "Oh, she'd be brilliant at it, until the final round."

Juliette elbows me lightly. "You're not helping."

I grin. "Wasn't trying to."

Arms wrap around my waist from behind. "What has my mom done now?"

I glance over at Mum, still casually dealing with the aftermath of Shannon's mishap, and can't help but smirk. "Turn away, lass. You'll be embarrassed by your mum's blatant disregard and disrespect for good wine."

Bree chuckles softly. "You're brave, mocking her while she's armed with broken glass."

I meet her eyes over my shoulder. "Bravery," I say, straight-faced, "is exactly what makes me the ideal son-in-law."

Shannon groans dramatically, tossing the last bits of glass into the trash. "God help us all. A smart-mouthed Scotsman with terrible opinions about wine."

Bree tightens her arms around me, her laughter vibrating against my back. "And I wouldn't change a thing."

"Even if I do mock your mum's...destruction habits?"

"Especially then," she says, her voice light and teasing. Just the way I like it.

forty-four

BREE

A few days later, I stand in the driveway, wrapped in Mom's arms, inhaling the familiar scent of her perfume like it's some kind of emotional life raft.

It's hard to see my parents go.

"Take care of yourself, sweetheart," she murmurs, pulling back to tuck a stray strand of hair behind my ear.

I clear my throat, willing my voice to stay strong. "I will." *Probably. Maybe. No promises.*

Dad steps in next, pulling me into one of his classic bear hugs that makes me feel like a kid again, safe and untouchable. I grip the back of his jacket, pressing my face into his shoulder for half a second longer than I probably should.

"You know we're just a call away, right?" His voice is gruff. "Anytime you need us."

"I know." I blink back the sting in my eyes. "Thanks, Dad."

As they climb into their rental car, Nugget barks from the porch, his tail wagging furiously, completely oblivious to the fact that we're saying goodbye. Callan stands beside him, leaning lightly on his crutch, his crooked grin soft but genuine as he waves them off.

The second their car pulls away, something inside me slips.

I stand there, watching until their taillights disappear while the silence of the countryside settles back in around me. It's like my foundation cracks.

Panic hits like a rogue wave with no warning or mercy. One second I'm standing there, rooted to the earth, and the next, everything feels off. The world blurs, the edges of reality falling away. The pressure builds in my chest, suffocating, until I can't tell if it's the air that's harder to breathe or the gravity of my own thoughts.

Callan's calling my name, but his voice sounds like it's coming from a million miles away, distant and muffled. "Bree? Hey, what's wrong?"

I open my mouth to speak, but the words are trapped.

I'm so tired of this. So tired of pretending it's not there, of hiding it from him, from everyone.

The world careens, and I brace myself against the railing, my knuckles white with effort. I try to slow my breathing, but my body's forgotten how to do that, too. Every inhale is shallow and jagged.

"Bree," Callan's voice is closer now but still filled with worry. His hand grips my shoulder, his warmth bleeding into me.

I close my eyes, squeezing them tight. I need to hold it together, but all I want to do is fall apart.

"Bree, love, look at me." His voice cuts through, and I force my eyes open. His concerned gaze meets mine, and for a second, I get lost in the depth of it. His usual spark of mischief is dimmed, replaced by worry.

"That's it. Just breathe with me, okay?" His voice is an anchor in the chaos. He takes a long, exaggerated breath, encouraging me to follow along. I try to match his rhythm, but my lungs are too tight. Each inhale is like trying to draw air through a straw.

His hand shifts from my shoulder to my back. He rubs gentle circles against my skin in comforting, slow movements that somehow makes the storm inside me a little less fierce.

"You're doing great, love. Just keep breathing."

I focus on the warmth of his touch, the rise and fall of his breaths. Slowly, painfully, the grip on my lungs releases. The world stops spinning, and I become aware of the gentle breeze on my skin, the chirping of birds in the distance.

"I'm sorry," I whisper, my voice shaky. "I didn't mean to—"

He shakes his head, his hands gently guiding me into his arms, holding me close like he's trying to pull the anxiousness from my chest with just his touch. "You've got nothing to be sorry for, Bree. Nothing."

I lean into his solid frame. It's grounding. So grounding that, for a moment, I forget about the suffocating panic that's still lingering just beneath the surface.

"Can you tell me what happened?"

"I don't know exactly," I admit. "It's been happening on and off for a while now. Ever since..." I trail off, the unspoken weight of the accident hanging between us. I swallow, then continue. "Sometimes it just hits me out of nowhere. I can't breathe, can't think straight. Everything feels like it's too much, too overwhelming."

His arms tighten around me, pulling me closer, his chin resting on top of my head.

"Why didn't you tell me?" His voice is quiet, almost like a whisper.

I pull back slightly, meeting his eyes. "I didn't want to worry you. You've been dealing with so much already. And I thought... I thought I could handle it."

I watch as a flicker of hurt crosses his face. His gaze drops, and I see his shoulders sag. That's when I realize I've unintentionally chipped away at the trust between us again.

"Bree..." He says my name softly, almost like a plea. "We're in this together. The good, the bad, and everything in between. Let me be there for you like you've been here for me."

I nod, my throat tight, the lump growing as I swallow the rush of emotions threatening to spill out. "I know. I just...didn't want to be too much."

His eyes widen, and for a moment, he's still. He cups my face in his hands, his touch impossibly gentle, like I might break if he holds me any tighter. "Stop right there. You could *never* be too much. Never."

The sincerity in his voice makes my eyes sting with more unshed tears. "I'm sorry," I whisper again, this time not for the panic attack, but for the distance I've put between us.

"No more apologies," he says softly, his thumb gently wiping away the tear that escapes down my cheek. The warmth of his touch sends a tremor through me, and I let out a shaky breath. "Let's focus on how we can tackle this together, aye?"

I nod, a small but real wave of relief washing over me.

"Have you thought about talking to someone? A professional, I mean."

I bite my lip, considering his question. "I've thought about it."

He doesn't say anything at first, just watches me with that unwavering gaze of his, the one that makes me feel like I'm the only thing in the world that matters.

"There's no shame in needing help, love. And if anyone gives you grief about it, they'll have me to answer to."

A small laugh bubbles up, surprising me. Leave it to Callan to make me smile, even when everything feels so heavy.

IT's BEEN a couple days since I let the walls fall down around me and he didn't run.

The house smells like garlic and butter, and Callan's half hobbling around the kitchen on his crutches, determined to make dinner like he's not one wrong move away from toppling headfirst into the oven.

"You know," I call out from the couch, eyeing him warily, "I could help."

He shoots me a look over his shoulder. "You offering out of kindness or because you think I'm gonna burn the place down?"

"A little of both."

He smirks, flipping what looks to be a crab cake in the pan one-handed. "Sit down. I've got it handled."

I settle deeper into the cushions, letting the domestic soundscape wrap around me. It feels...ridiculously nice.

"I was looking at flights earlier," I say after a beat. "I need to head back at some point. I've still got my job, and my plants are probably dead."

Callan goes still for a second, like he's deciding what to say. He doesn't turn around, just stirs whatever's in the pan a little more aggressively than necessary.

Finally, he spins to look at me. "What if you...don't go back."

I blink. "What?"

He limps over with a smirk, like he's not about to ruin me with a single sentence. Dropping onto the couch beside me, he says, "Stay. Move in with me."

"Are you serious?"

"I'm serious. Stay."

My heart stutters, then races ahead like it's desperate to reach a finish line I can't even see. The room suddenly feels too warm, too small, too everything.

"Callan..."

His impossibly warm eyes hold mine. I take in his messy hair and ridiculous grin. His heart's wide open.

"I know it's fast," he says, his Scottish accent thickening with emotion. "And I know you've got a life back there. But these past few weeks with you here..." His voice catches, and he reaches for my hand, his calloused fingers wrapping around mine. "I don't want to go back to a life without you in it."

I search his face for any hint of doubt, any shadow of uncertainty, but all I see is hope.

The practical part of my brain immediately starts listing all the reasons this is crazy. My job. My condo. My family. My entire life is in the States. I'd be leaving everything familiar behind, trading it for rain-soaked hills and a future that's completely unwritten.

And yet, there's the other voice, the one that's been growing louder since I first arrived. The one that whispers how the air tastes different here. How the colors seem brighter, how time moves in a way that actually makes sense. How I've never felt more like myself than when I'm with him.

"My job..." I start, but even as I say it, I know it's just a placeholder for my fear.

Callan's thumb traces circles on my palm. "There are jobs here."

"There's tons of paperwork. I'll still need to go back and forth a few times—"

"Hey," he cuts me off. "I'm sure Juliette can help you with all of that since she just did it. And what about helping Rose out for a bit? While you figure out your next steps?"

I glance over at him, eyebrows shooting up. "What are you thinking?"

He shrugs, all casual, but there's a glint of something thoughtful in his eyes. "We've been talking about expanding the distillery's marketing, especially in the States. Rose is juggling too much on her own, and you know the market there better than anyone. It wouldn't have to be forever."

I blink, caught completely off guard by the suggestion. "Are you serious? I mean...wouldn't that be a bit, I don't know, nepotistic?"

Callan chuckles, the sound low and easy as he shakes his head. "Lass, it's a family business. Everything we do is a wee bit nepotistic."

I bite my lip, turning the idea over in my mind. "I don't know, Callan. What if it doesn't work out? Also...I hate whisky."

That earns a laugh, his eyes crinkling at the corners in a way that makes it impossible not to smile back. "Aye, but that's not a problem, Sunshine. You don't need to like whisky to market it. In fact," he says, leaning forward, "it might even be an advantage. You can approach it from an outsider's perspective. See what'll convince all the other whisky-haters to give it a try."

I narrow my eyes at him, but I can't help the small laugh that escapes. "You're ridiculous."

"And yet you're still listening."

I've spent so long defining myself by nursing, by the years of training, the grueling shifts, the controlled chaos of hospital life. It's who I am. The idea of stepping outside of that makes me nervous, but at the same time, I've been wondering if it's time to try something new.

The words slip out before I can stop them. "But what if I'm not good at it?"

He just watches me. "Then you learn. Same way you learned to be a nurse. Same way I learned to run a distillery."

"What if it causes problems between us? Mixing business and pleasure and all that?"

He shakes his head, his expression serious now. "We're stronger than that, lass. And it's not like you'd be working under me."

"You really think I could do it?"

"I know you could," he says without hesitation, his hand finding mine and giving it a gentle squeeze. "You're brilliant."

The idea of switching careers entirely is overwhelming, but the trust in his eyes makes me feel like maybe I can.

"I'll think about it. But I want you to think on it, too. Talk to Knox and Rose. See what they say, okay?"

Callan dips his chin in a small nod, his lips curving into a faint smile. "I can do that."

"You're really sure? About all of this?"

He edges closer, his hand coming up to cradle my cheek. "Bree," he says, voice rich and rough in that signature rasp, "I've never been more sure of anything. Not in my whole damn life."

His eyes search mine with unmistakable clarity. "I love you. Not just while you're here patching me up. Not just because you make the house feel like home. I love you, and I want more."

My breath hitches, but he keeps going.

"I love the way you take care of everyone else without even thinking twice. The way you fight to hold yourself together, even when you're breaking a little. I love that you call me on my bullshit. I love that you came all this way, and you stayed. Even when it got hard."

His voice is threaded with unflinching tenderness as he continues. "You make me want to be better. Not just for you. For me."

Oh god. This is happening. And now I'm crying.

"Okay," I whisper, my voice shaky but sure. I clear my throat and try to hide the tremble with a smirk. "But don't get cocky. I still plan on roasting your accent daily."

He laughs and tips his head back. "Wouldn't have it any other way."

And then, so quietly it nearly gets lost in the beat of his heart against mine, I say, "I'll do it."

"I'll move in," I say again, firmer now.

Callan doesn't speak. He just wraps me up in his arms like he's afraid I'll change my mind, like he needs to feel it to believe it.

"Sunshine," he murmurs against my hair, a smile in his voice, "you've just signed yourself up for a lifetime of soggy chips and sideways rain. No takebacks."

CALLAN

Months have passed since the accident. Months of physical therapy, patience—not my strong suit—and Bree somehow managing to keep me from climbing the damn walls while I was stuck on crutches. But today's the day. No more crutches, no more aching ribs. Everything is healed, and I'm as close to normal as I'm ever going to get.

But the truth is, Bree's the one who's really changed.

She's been going to therapy every week, like clockwork. She still tries to downplay it sometimes, like it's just a thing she's doing, no big deal. I see her, though. I see the way her breathing evens out faster now, the way she lets herself feel things instead of bottling them up.

I'm in awe of her. Not just for doing the work, but for choosing to. For sticking it out, even on the hard days.

She still gets overwhelmed and has moments where I can see her brain spinning a mile a minute. But she talks to me now. She lets me hold her when she needs to fall apart and doesn't apologize for it after.

I remember the girl who tried to keep everything stitched

tight, who said, "I'm fine," with a smile that didn't quite reach her eyes.

This Bree? She's fucking brave, and I don't tell her that nearly enough, mostly because she gets all squirmy when I do. But I think about it all the time. How lucky I am that she chose to stay. That she keeps choosing it.

And now, today's the day I get back on my bike. No big deal. Just, you know, confronting some trauma.

Totally fine. No pressure.

And seeing Bree in that leather jacket and boots I got her doesn't hurt. Goddamn, she's the sexiest thing I've ever laid eyes on. It definitely makes it all worth it. And that's not even getting into the plans I've got for her on that bike later.

I take a deep breath, forcing myself to calm down as I hear her footsteps coming down the stairs.

"Ready to hit the road, handsome?" Her voice rings out with the kind of excitement that never fails to make me smile.

She stands there, all confidence and curves, wrapped up in a leather jacket that fits so well it should be illegal. My pulse goes completely rogue.

"Bloody hell, woman." My voice comes out rough.

I close the distance without a second thought, hands finding her waist, fingers curling in to feel the heat of her beneath the leather. "You look lethal, love."

My mouth crashes into hers before she can respond, all heat and urgency, a kiss that's been waiting for far too long. She tastes like trouble and home all at once, and I'm completely lost to it. My tongue sweeps along her bottom lip, coaxing out a soft sound that shoots straight through me, setting every nerve on fire.

When I finally pull back, mostly because oxygen is a necessary evil, she's staring up at me, her lips parted, her breath uneven.

"You ready?" I ask, still unwilling to let her go.

Her fingers skim along the edge of my jacket before fisting the fabric, holding me close. "I think so?"

I press one last lingering kiss to her mouth, my lips brushing against hers as I whisper, "Do you trust me?"

Her gaze softens, and she smiles, but there's that hint of curiosity in her eyes. "Always. But can I ask why we're doing this so late at night?"

"You'll see."

The garage light flickers as we step inside, casting long shadows across the floor. Bree stops short. Her gaze locks onto the bike. I can see the storm behind her eyes, the war between past and present, the tightrope walk between fear and trust.

I take a slow step closer to her. "I know it's hard, but we've got this. And I swear, I'll be careful." I reach for her hand, squeezing gently. "I've got precious cargo, after all."

Her fingers twitch in mine. She doesn't pull away, but she doesn't move, either.

I wait.

Her lips part like she wants to speak, but it's her eyes that do so as they search mine, asking the question she hasn't voiced. *Can I do this? Can I trust this again?*

I lift her hand to my chest, right over my heartbeat. "You're safe with me. Always."

The tightness in her shoulders eases. Her breath comes slower. Then, finally, her eyes lift to mine.

"I love you," she whispers.

"I love you more."

Bree swallows hard, her eyes flickering back to the motorcycle. Her fingers tighten around mine.

"I thought I'd be ready," she whispers, "but seeing it again..."

I brush my thumb across her cheek. "Look at me, not the bike."

She does, those gorgeous eyes meeting mine.

"I'm right here," I tell her. "Whole and healed. And I promise you, I'll stay that way."

She takes a deep breath, straightening her shoulders. I can see her working through it, that beautiful mind of hers battling with her heart.

"You'll drive slow?" she asks, her voice stronger now.

"Grandma slow."

A laugh breaks free from her lips. It's the kind that makes you forget everything else, like the world's suddenly right, just because she's laughing.

"Okay, then. Let's do this."

I climb on first. There's a moment where my muscles tense with the memory of impact, but I push through it. This bike isn't my enemy. It never was.

"Come on, love," I call over my shoulder, holding out my hand.

Bree hesitates for a heartbeat before her fingers slide against mine. Then she's climbing on behind me, her body pressed against my back, arms wrapping around my waist.

With a deep breath, I fire up the engine and ease us onto the road, letting the wind whip past, her grip tightening around me in a way that makes me feel ten feet tall.

And then, I see a glimpse of her smile in the mirror. She doesn't ask where we're going because she doesn't have to. The way she squeezes me tells me everything.

She's figured it out.

It's not long before I pull up to the lookout point, killing the engine and tapping the kickstand down before sliding off my helmet. I glance back at her. "Remember this place?"

She takes off her own helmet, her hair a wild mess from the

wind, and I can see that far-off look in her eyes as she stares out at the sprawling landscape below.

She's stunning.

"How could I not," she says softly. "I think I fell in love with you here that night."

I'm taken aback, my heart catching in a sudden skip. The way I remember that night, the first time we were here, she was a mess. Sad. Scared. And I just wanted to fix it, to make her feel safe. Never did I imagine I'd be the one leaving a mark that deep.

"Really?"

"Really." A slow smile spreads across her face. "You brought me to this beautiful place, and you were so concerned for me. Someone you hardly knew. I knew in that moment that I could never settle for anyone who wasn't...just like you. Confident, caring, sexier than hell."

I let out a quiet laugh, but it catches in my chest, right where pride knots disbelief and awe.

She looks around, taking in the view, resting her chin on my shoulder. "It's just as beautiful as I remember. More so, really."

It's dark and still around us, the world holding its breath. The only sounds are the whisper of the night and the rapid thrum of my heartbeat, loud enough that I'm sure she can hear it, too.

"That's because you're looking at it, love," I say, turning to face her fully. "Everything's more beautiful with you in it."

She rolls her eyes, but the blush spreading across her cheeks gives her away. "Smooth talker."

"Only stating facts."

I take her hand, leading her to the edge where the guardrail meets the cliff. "I wanted to bring you here again to make new memories. Better ones."

Bree leans into me. "I like that idea."

BREE

I can't stop staring at Callan, all broad shoulders and that strong jawline I could trace with my eyes for hours. Can't stop staring at the view we're not even close to leaving.

We haven't moved from this spot, and I don't think I want to. It's too perfect here, too *right*.

"I can't believe you're really mine," I whisper as he pulls back to look at me. His eyes search mine, like he's trying to make sure I'm really here, really *his*. Then he traces a finger across my cheekbone, the touch gentle but sending a spark straight to my heart. His hand comes to cup my face, pulling me in for another tender kiss, and every inch of my body tingles with anticipation as he slowly pulls away.

"All yours. Can I let you in on a little fantasy of mine?" His voice drops lower, all velvet temptation.

"Hm, sure. I bet you I have an idea of where this is going, though."

He chuckles, a deep rumble that vibrates in my own chest. "I doubt it, love. This one's been brewing for a while."

I raise an eyebrow, intrigued. "Oh? Do tell."

He leans in close, his breath warm against my ear, his voice just a whisper. "You naked on the back of my bike, hot and ready for me."

My breath catches in my throat, and I don't know whether to laugh or kiss him senseless. A blush creeps up my neck, coloring my cheeks as I try to maintain composure. The heat in his eyes only makes it worse—no, *better*. It's a fire I absolutely want to throw myself into.

"Well, you certainly know how to make a girl feel special." I lean in closer, letting my lips brush against his ear as I whisper, "What are you waiting for?"

His eyes darken with lust at my words, and before I can catch my breath, his muscular arm wraps possessively around my waist. He pulls me flush against him, and I feel the weight of his need as he grinds his hips into mine in a slow, deliberate movement that sends a jolt of desire through me.

"You don't need to tell me twice," he growls before he claims my mouth in a kiss that is pure hunger. I respond instinctively, my hands tangling in his hair, the taste of him intoxicating.

There's a thrill of danger and excitement at the thought of being caught out here, exposed under the open sky. There's also something about the rawness of it, the urgency, that makes everything else fade away. I let him peel off my clothes, piece by piece, until I stand before him, completely exposed, the night air teasing my skin.

He lifts me onto the bike, spreading my legs. "Fuck, how did I get this lucky?" he groans, palming his hard length straining against the denim of his jeans.

My heart races as I meet his gaze, his broad frame outlined by the moonlight, the leather of his jacket catching in the glow. He radiates confidence, strength, and a quiet power that makes me feel both safe and charged all at once.

"Are you ready for this?"

"God, yes," I breathe. "Please."

A cool breeze brushes against my skin, making my nipples tighten. He undoes his belt, unbuttons his jeans, and pulls out his hard cock, stroking its length as his eyes roam over my body.

I'm dying to touch. Taste. *Feel.* I'm getting wetter by the second and can barely stop myself from dripping onto the leather seat.

He inches closer, teasing my entrance but holding back. "Later, Sunshine," he whispers into my ear, "I'll worship every inch of you like you deserve. But for now, we're going to be rough and fast. You'll be screaming by the time we're done."

He always keeps me guessing. One minute he's making jokes, and the next he's talking dirty as hell. I love it. I *crave* it. And I know just the right thing to say to make sure I get exactly what I need from him.

"Are you just going to talk about it, or are you going to take me on your bike right here, *sir?*" My hand traces a slow path down my stomach, stopping just short of where I'm soaked between my thighs. His eyes darken as he watches my fingertips graze the tip of his cock.

He snaps, slamming into me with a ferocity that sends shockwaves through my body. His grip on my hips is possessive, pushing me against the hard metal frame of the bike. The world around us blurs as our movements become frenzied, punctuated by ragged breaths and the sound of leather against metal.

His voice is raw and rough as he mutters his praise into my ear. "Fuck, you feel so good. So tight. So *mine.*"

His words ignite a fire deep in me. I clench around him, eager for more, as he begins to thrust harder and faster. The heat of his skin against mine is intoxicating. His desire-darkened eyes, his lips parted slightly... God, he's beautiful.

With each thrust, he nips at my neck and shoulders,

marking his territory with teeth and tongue. It's almost painful how good it feels. Just when I think I can't take anymore, he leans down, taking my breast into his mouth. His tongue swirls around my sensitive peak, teasing and flicking. I arch my back, pressing closer to his hungry mouth. His stubble against my sensitive skin, the heat of his mouth, of him stretching me, is overwhelming.

I throw my head back. "Oh, god," I moan, my fingers tangling in his hair to hold him against me.

He releases my nipple, looking up at me with eyes full of yearning. "You like that, don't you?"

"Yes," I gasp. "Don't stop."

I'm trembling, so close to the edge. "Please," I whimper, not even sure what I'm begging for. He seems to know exactly what I need, though. His fingers find my clit, rubbing tight circles as he pounds into me.

"Look at me," he commands. I force my eyes open to meet his intense gaze. The moonlight casts shadows across his chiseled features, highlighting the sharp line of his jaw clenched in concentration. Sweat glistens on his brow as he maintains his punishing rhythm.

I'm close, so close. My muscles tense as the pressure builds. He must sense it because he increases the pace of his fingers on my clit, circling faster. "Come for me, love. Let me feel you."

His words send me careening over the edge. I clench around him as ecstasy washes through me. I cry out his name, my nails digging into his shoulders as my body shudders.

He groans, his movements becoming erratic as he chases his own release. With a few final, deep thrusts, he buries himself inside me. I feel his pulsing length as he comes, his face contorting in ecstasy. He collapses against me, both of us panting and slick with sweat.

For a moment, we stay like that, our bodies intertwined,

hearts racing in tandem. The chilled night air caresses our heated skin as I run my fingers through his hair, savoring the weight of him against me, the scent of leather and something so uniquely Callan.

"That was way fucking hotter than I ever could have imagined," he mutters between kisses.

He eases out gently before helping me down and gathering my clothes. "I'd apologize for not having anything to clean you up with but..." He slides his fingers through the slickness between my thighs, reminding me of the mess we made. "I'm not sorry. The thought of you riding home, dripping... Fuck, love. You wanna go again?"

I laugh, snatching my underwear from his hand. "Get me home before someone calls the cops," I tease. "And then? Yes. I want to go again. And again...and again."

He helps me step into my jeans as I scramble to find my boots. "Hey, where are my socks?"

"Hell if I know. Leave them for the wildcats," he chuckles. "I need to get you home. *Now*."

"Wildcats? You're telling me there are wildcats out here and you just had me with my whole ass out?"

I can't believe I'm even asking this.

"Come on, lass. You think I'd let a scary critter get you?" He winks. "But yes, there are wildcats."

My eyes go wide. "You're lucky you're sweet...and hot. Now get me out of here."

He laughs, swinging his leg over the bike, patting the seat behind him. Infuriating, but I can't stop the smile that crests my lips. Life with this man will never be dull or predictable, but I wouldn't have it any other way.

CALLAN

nother infamous MacKenzie gathering. Knox and
Juliette's place is once again a whirlwind of chaos, but
it's the best kind. Their twins, barely a month old, are both
wailing in unison. Juliette is rocking one while Bree tries to
soothe the other.

"Do they always do this at once?" I ask Knox.

He glances over with an amused expression that doesn't
quite mask his exhaustion. "Aye. One cries, and the other is
quick to follow."

I can't help but chuckle. "It's like they've got their own wee
communication system," I muse, eyeing the red-faced twins. "A
MacKenzie conspiracy already in the making."

Knox, the once unflappable distillery heir, now looks like
he's been run through the wringer. His hair is disheveled, and
there are dark circles under his eyes, but there's a contentment
in his gaze that I haven't seen before.

Just then, Juliette manages to quiet her bundle. I think
that's Keira? Honestly, I've lost track at this point. The sudden
absence of one cry seems to startle the other into silence. The

room falls into a blessed hush, broken only by Bree's whispered, *"Thank you, Jesus."*

Bree tiptoes over to me, and with a smile that could melt steel, she carefully transfers...Maisie, I think, into my arms. "Here, Uncle Cal," she says, the warmth in her voice almost as comforting as the tiny, squirming bundle now nestled in my arms. "Your turn."

I cradle Maisie, the weight of her little body sending a rush of affection flooding through me. Her eyelids flutter, but she stays asleep, and for a moment, the world outside our little bubble seems to pause.

Bree stands back, watching me. "You're a natural."

"Don't jinx me." I glance down at Maisie's tiny face, marveling at how fragile and perfect she is. "But, yeah, I think I've got this. For now."

Bree chuckles and takes a seat beside me on the couch, her gaze soft as she leans her head on my shoulder. "You're doing great. And Juliette? She's amazing."

I glance over at Juliette, who's still rocking Keira to sleep. There's a peaceful smile on her face that speaks volumes. It's the kind of smile that says, despite the exhaustion, she's found something worth every sleepless night.

The room is still, almost eerily quiet, save for the soft ticking of the clock and the occasional sigh from one of the babies. The chaos pauses for a brief moment, and we all breathe in the calm before the next wave hits.

"Do you have any idea how incredibly attractive you are right now?" Bree whispers.

I raise a brow, a smirk lifting at the corner of my mouth. "Oh? Is this your way of saying you want one of these wee bundles for yourself?"

She laughs. "Hold your horses, MacKenzie. I'm just saying it's...endearing. I'm appreciating the view."

"Endearing, hm? I'll have you know, I'm always endearing. It's part of my charm."

She rolls her eyes, but there's nothing but love in her gaze. "And modest, too, I see."

"Modesty's overrated," I quip, adjusting Maisie as her tiny fingers curl around mine.

"You know," she says, casually brushing her fingers along Maisie's tiny, socked foot, "if we ever get *married*..." She says it like it's just a thought, a hypothetical tossed into the breeze, but her voice dips a little at the word, like she's testing it out on her tongue.

I arch a brow, not missing a beat. "If, huh?"

She shrugs, feigning nonchalance while her cheeks turn pink. "Well, *if*. Then *maybe* we can talk about babies."

I let out a hushed laugh, careful not to wake the sleeping bundle in my arms. "Ah, so this is a long con. Lure me in with your charm, trick me into marrying you, and then boom. Next thing I know, we've got three toddlers climbing the curtains and drawing on the walls."

She grins wickedly. "Exactly. It's all part of the master plan. You've fallen right into my trap."

I hum thoughtfully, shifting on the couch so Maisie can snuggle deeper into the crook of my arm. "Guess I'll just have to be on my guard. Keep my wits about me."

She's completely unaware that the ring is burning a hole in my pocket as we speak.

I've carried it for weeks now. Tucked it in my pocket every time we've had a quiet night or a sunset walk, thinking maybe it was the one. The moment never feels quite enough—not because she isn't, but because I'm terrified I won't get it right.

Maybe there is no perfect way of doing it. Maybe there's just this, her laughter, my nerves, our messy, beautiful life already unfolding in front of us.

I look at her, hair falling into her face, laughter still lingering in her eyes, and I know there's nothing I want more than to spend the rest of my life getting teased by her.

Then, out of nowhere, the chaos level in the room spikes as Mum bursts through the door, her arms weighed down with bags, her cheeks flushed from the brisk Highland air. "I've brought reinforcements!" she announces, all excitement.

The calm is obliterated. Maisie lets out a soft grunt in my arms, her face scrunching up as she gears up for a full-on meltdown. Over by the window, Keira doesn't waste any time. She's right there with her, turning the air into a symphony of piercing wails.

"Oh, for heaven's sake," Mum mutters. "I'm so sorry."

"Here, let me take her," Bree offers. I gratefully pass Maisie over, watching Bree as she expertly cradles the baby and begins to sway gently. She gives me a reassuring smile as she rocks Maisie back and forth. "See? Like riding a bike."

I raise an eyebrow. "Is it? Because last time I checked, bikes don't scream at you when you mess up."

She laughs, shaking her head. "Not exactly the same, no."

I study her, that familiar heat spreading through my body like a fire on a cold day. I've spent a lot of time picturing our life together, imagining quiet mornings, lazy nights, the dog that listens half as well as we'd like. Seeing her now, holding our niece like she was born for this, unfazed by the chaos of screaming kids, clattering dishes, and at least one questionable crash from the other room, I realize something.

This is it.

Bree cradling our niece, whispering calm words I can not only hear but can *feel*.

Yeah. This. Right here.

This is what I've been chasing, and I'd do it all over again just to land in this moment.

"Bree," I say, my voice suddenly hoarse.

She looks up, still swaying with Maisie in her arms. "Hmm?"

I don't stand. I don't get down on one knee. I don't make a show of it because we don't need one.

"Marry me."

I pull the box from my pocket, opening it to reveal a round diamond flanked by two deep blue sapphires, the exact shade of her eyes. It's bright and impossible not to look at. Just like her.

"You serious?" she whispers, blinking like she's not sure if she heard right.

I nod. "With you? Always."

She just stares for a second, then lets out a breathy laugh that fills the whole room. She looks down at the ring, then back at me. Her eyes are glassy, that expression she wears so effortlessly filled with not only a playfulness I can't get enough of, but devotion. Adoration. *Enchantment.*

"I love you."

I grin. "Is that a yes?"

She leans over, careful not to squish Maisie between us, and whispers against my lips, "Yes."

And just like that, in a room that smells vaguely of baby wipes and roasted carrots, I slide the ring on her finger.

She said yes. And even with the racket of the MacKenzies in the background, it's the only thing I hear.

acknowledgments

I'm not sure how we got here, but somehow, that's a wrap on book two!

My first thank you will always go to you, my dear readers. I'm still in awe that I get to share my stories with you. It's so damn cool. **Thank you** a million times over for being here and sticking with me.

My next thank you goes to my husband, who continues to be my biggest support and understands when I have my face buried in my laptop for days on end. Your patience and willingness to fetch snacks without complaint are deeply appreciated. And to my kids, who tolerate my chaos—thank you for letting me chase these stories while still keeping life beautifully messy.

I'm endlessly grateful to my incredible editor, Sara, who somehow takes my rambling drafts and turns them into something that actually makes sense. You caught the plot holes and the cringey decisions my characters made, and for that, I owe you big time.

To all of the incredible artists who brought this story and these characters to life—I will *never* stop being amazed at your talent. Seriously. I love you.

To Emily, who once again made it so that I didn't have to lose my entire mind over social media content. You are the absolute freakin' best.

Three people in particular deserve a medal for keeping me (relatively) sane—my mom, Lynda, my sister, Taylor, and my bff, Ashlee. A simple thank you will never be enough, but since you get all the book details first, let's go ahead and call it even.

Above all, thank you for letting me tell these stories. You keep me writing and wildly in love with this little world I get to create. Here's to more happily ever afters.

about the author

Alexandra Ayres is a Canadian author living in Kentucky, where she writes steamy, emotionally rich romances about bold women discovering themselves and the love they deserve. She lives with her husband, two kids, and a mischievous Siamese cat. When she's not writing, she's either planning her next travel adventure or sipping on iced coffee, always chasing inspiration one love story at a time.

Website: AlexandraAyres.com

- instagram.com/authoralexayres
- facebook.com/authoralexayres
- tiktok.com/@authoralexayres
- amazon.com/author/alexandraayres
- goodreads.com/alexandraayres